P9-CCA-859

Welcome to West Berlin

To Sassy
with love and affection

Welcome to West Berlin

A Novel

Herbert M. Lobl

Copyright © 2002 by Herbert M. Lobl.

Library of Congress Number: 2002090364
ISBN :   Hardcover   1-4010-4700-9
              Softcover   1-4010-4699-1

All rights reserved. No part of this book may be reproduced or transmitted in
any form or by any means, electronic or mechanical, including photocopying,
recording, or by any information storage and retrieval system, without permission
in writing from the copyright owner.

This is a work of fiction. All characters and incidents are
entirely imaginary, and any resemblance to actual events, or to
persons living or dead, is coincidental.

This book was printed in the United States of America.

To order additional copies of this book, contact:
Xlibris Corporation
1-888-795-4274
www.Xlibris.com
Orders@Xlibris.com
14447

For Dorie

Do people ever reflect, one wonders, that the best way to protect against the penetration of one's secrets by others is to have the minimum of secrets to conceal?

George F. Kennan

APRIL 22, 1955

Day 1 Friday

It had been a cold winter, and a harsh wind from the Polish plains blew across the Oder River and whistled through the narrow streets of Frankfurt/Oder, as it had since the city's founding in the thirteenth century. The night was clear, and as Hans Weber glanced out his kitchen window, he saw the moonlight reflected on the metallic surface of the slow-moving river. He looked at the kitchen clock, with its brass pendulum and Roman numerals. It was almost 4 a.m. He went back to the bedroom and touched his wife's shoulder. She woke instantly.

"I think we should leave, Anna."

"What time is it?"

"Four o'clock."

Without another word, she rose and quickly began to put on the clothes she had laid out on the armchair the night before. Then she went over to the crib and picked up Manfred, their two-year-old son, who was sleeping soundly, clutching his teddy bear. Manfred continued to sleep as Anna gently slipped him into a parka and buttoned him up. Weber meanwhile closed a small suit-case—made of reinforced cardboard—which contained the few clothes they had packed to take along.

"Make sure the gas is turned off," Anna whispered, pulling on her coat. Weber nodded and went back into the kitchen to check on the old stove.

"It's off," he reassured her.

Anna lingered for a moment in the narrow hallway, taking a last look at their possessions in the darkened rooms. Weber opened the apartment door and whispered, "Hurry. We can't miss that train." Weber turned out the light in the hall, and with Anna carrying the baby and he the suitcase, they stepped out onto the third-floor landing. He double-locked the door, put the keys in his pocket and gave Anna, who was tense, a smile and a pat on the cheek. They quietly descended the three flights of wooden stairs. The heavy front door of the building creaked as Weber opened it, but luckily Herr Metzger, the building superintendent, did not peer out of his one-room lodging. Weber had prepared an excuse, in case Herr Metzger were to challenge their early departure, but he was fearful that Metzger, a suspicious and avid police informer, would not be taken in by his tale.

With Anna holding the baby close to her for warmth, they walked quickly along Karl Marx Strasse, which paralleled the river, and then turned to the right on Heilbronner Strasse, toward the railroad station. They avoided a more direct route in order to circumvent the police station, located at the side of the Town Hall. The streets were deserted, and the streetlights, as usual, only dimly flickering in order to conserve electricity. The new Five-Year Plan, it had been announced, would double the German Democratic Republic's electrical output, and the mayor had promised that soon Frankfurt/Oder, like Paris, would be known as the City of Light. At present, the brighter lights shone on the eastern bank of the Oder, where Polish refugees had been resettled after the war when the German inhabitants had been expelled and Frankfurt/Oder's former suburb had become the new Polish city of Slubice.

"Let's wait here a few minutes," Weber said. "The police may be patrolling the waiting room." Anna was shivering but said nothing. The baby was still sound asleep in her arms. Although the railroad station had been rebuilt, the houses on both sides of the underpass were still in ruins. Almost all of Frankfurt/Oder's city center had been destroyed by artillery shelling and uncontrolled fires that had preceded the Red Army's final assault in April of 1945. Rebuilding had only begun in 1951 and was proceeding at a very slow pace, since most of the German Democratic Republic's limited building funds were reserved for so-called "prestige projects," like the Stalin Allee in East Berlin. Taking shelter from the strong gusts of wind, the Webers stood under a clump of trees in a ruined courtyard next to the underpass. A passing truck woke the baby, who started to cry; Anna rocked him back to sleep.

"I think we can go now," Weber said. He picked up the suitcase and they headed up the small incline to the station. Weber pulled open its cast-iron door, and they entered to find the waiting room deserted, the only light supplied by a single naked bulb hanging from the ceiling by two twisted wires. The train to Berlin stood on Track 1. Near the head of the train a conductor was chatting with the engineer, who was leaning out from the side window of the sooty steam locomotive. The Webers climbed aboard a third-class carriage in the middle of the train. The twenty-odd rows of wooden benches were empty except for three men, bundled in rough overcoats and dozing against the window frames, each with a tin lunch box on his lap. The Webers settled on one of the back benches with the baby between them.

A whistle blew; there was a hiss of steam, and the train departed jerkily but exactly on time. Weber looked over at Anna, and she weakly returned his encouraging smile. The train was the day's first local, stopping at every station between Frankfurt/Oder and Berlin. Most of its passengers were workers heading for early shifts in factories along the way or in the Berlin outskirts.

It was still completely dark outside as the train reached Finsterwalde, approximately halfway to Berlin. If challenged during the first part of the trip, the Webers had decided to say that they were going to visit Anna's cousin, who lived in Finsterwalde. That was the story they had told their neighbors, and Weber had left the cousin's address with the principal of the school where he taught, in case he was needed during next week's school vacation. He had used some accumulated overtime to leave one day early.

Weber had bought two sets of train tickets, purchased separately in the last two days from different tellers at the station: one set was from Frankfurt/Oder to Finsterwalde, the other from Frankfurt/Oder all the way to Berlin. This was an added expense, of course, but Weber thought it provided extra security. For the third time he turned to Anna and asked whether she had notified her cousin to confirm their alibi. "Yes, Hans, don't worry," she said, leaning her head back against the bench's worn leather headrest and closing her eyes.

The carriage was filling up with many more workers as the train approached Berlin. It was still dark outside, but now more lights were visible in the houses they passed. The trip was uneventful. The conductor showed not the slightest interest as he collected tickets, but after Finsterwalde, Weber became increasingly nervous. Their more credible alibi was gone.

The Webers had carefully rehearsed what they would say if asked why they were going to Berlin. Going to the capital, after all, was not in and of itself an offense. True, one had to have a reason to go there. Hans would say that he was going to the Education Ministry in search of a new job. That was why he had taken an extra day and left Frankfurt/Oder on Friday instead of on the weekend when school vacation started. He had in fact applied to the Ministry some time ago, but had never received a reply. Still, he worried that their stories would not conform if they were questioned individually. Anna was readily frightened and did not prevaricate easily.

They might be asked that if he was job-hunting, why bring along his wife and baby on an early morning train? They would explain that the trip was also intended as a family outing. Anna had never been to Berlin. They would do some sightseeing: Stalin Allee, the Soviet Military Cemetery in Pankow, and so on. They could account for the suitcase by saying they would be stopping for a visit in Finsterwalde on their return. It was all a bit thin, Weber fretted, but it was the best they could concoct.

The train was full as it reached the Berlin outskirts. All the seats were taken, much pushing and crowding having filled the benches to capacity. As more passengers boarded, some sat down in the aisles with their metal lunch boxes or paper bags with wurst and rolls on their laps. A few zealous Party members read *Neues Deutschland*, the Socialist Unity Party's (or SED's) organ, but most passengers, tired and inured to incessant propaganda, merely tried to catch a few minutes of rest.

Berlin-Friedrichstrasse was the last stop. The train emptied quickly, its passengers mingling with those from another train that had just pulled in on the adjoining track. Weber and Anna were swept along with the crowd, but both stiffened as they approached the controller, who sat collecting tickets from arriving passengers at the head of the stairs leading to the various exits. They had agreed that if any question arose, Weber would do all the talking.

The controller took their tickets without a glance or a word, and they descended the broad staircase to the large waiting room. Anna settled on one of the benches, giving Manfred his bottle, while Weber, putting down the suitcase, sat down next to her and as unobtrusively as possible took off his right shoe. He pretended to massage his foot, while at the same time extracting a piece of paper from his sock. The paper contained instructions from an adventurous old classmate who was known by a small circle of friends to have crossed into West Berlin a number of times. Obtaining this information a week earlier had galvanized Weber into action. Anna had been apprehensive, but he had finally persuaded her that this was their best chance to escape to West Berlin.

They were to take the S-Bahn into West Berlin, but with only a single accessible crossover point, one had to be careful to take the right train in the correct direction. Weber stood up and walked around the large waiting room to get his bearings.

According to the instructions, a police checkpoint could be avoided if one entered the S-Bahn platform through a corridor intended for exiting passengers. The trick was to wait for the exit doors to open and then, hugging the wall, move against the tide of passengers swarming toward the street. This subterfuge was of course well known to the Vopos, but they rarely interfered, except when on the lookout for a scientist or other person whose escape would be prejudicial to the GDR's regime. Sometimes would-be refugees would also be stopped when a Vopo felt bored or particularly sadistic.

As instructed, Weber climbed up one set of stairs and down another toward the S-Bahn corridor, which was underneath the regional train tracks. At that time of the morning S-Bahn trains arrived every four or five minutes. He made two trial runs along the wall to the S-Bahn platform; no one stopped him. The second time there were three persons behind him, who were startled when he turned back.

He returned to the waiting room and told Anna that the coast was clear. Picking up the suitcase with one hand and gripping his wife's arm firmly with the other, Weber hustled Anna, carrying little Manfred, up and down the various stairs toward the S-Bahn corridor. The baby began to cry in the jostling crowd, but his cries, as well as the pounding of his parents' hearts, went unheard amidst the general din.

An S-Bahn train that had just emptied stood at the platform, its yellow metal doors open. The Webers scurried to the rear of the car and crouched down to minimize the likelihood of being spotted from the outside. Friedrichstrasse was the last stop in East Berlin, and all unauthorized passenger traffic beyond this point was prohibited by East German border regulations. S-Bahn stations, bearing the white serpentine letter "S" on a circular green background, dotted both East and West Berlin, the tracks crisscrossing the city in utter disregard of its postwar divisions. The GDR authorities were forced to tolerate what they recognized was an escape hatch because East Berlin badly needed the transportation facilities that the S-Bahn provided.

The doors of the carriage slammed shut, but the train did not move out for another agonizing few minutes. In addition to the Webers there was another young couple sitting anxiously at the other end of the car. At that moment, they were all convinced that the doors would again swing open and the Vopos would enter to haul them off to jail. But instead, the train slowly started to move into the tunnel and shortly thereafter pulled into the small Lehrter Stadtbahnhof station in West Berlin. Hans and Anna clutched each other's hands; they had escaped to freedom.

The Webers had been told to remain on the train until they reached Bahnhof Zoo in the center of West Berlin. They stared excitedly out the window as the train wound its way above ground, around the edges of the Tiergarten with the blackened hulk of the Reichstag—the pre-Hitler Parliament building—clearly visible. Brightly colored advertisements for consumer products in the stations along the way were in sharp contrast to the ubiquitous red banners with exhortative Party slogans, which provided the only spot of color in the East. Entering fellow passengers—West Berlin early risers going to their jobs—did not seem to realize, nor did they seem to care, that a few more souls among them had just made a dangerous getaway.

The Webers left the train at the Bahnhof Zoo station and entered the West Berlin Police Büro, located right on the platform. It was a narrow room, constructed of glass partitions, containing a rough wooden table with a bright desk lamp, a telephone, and a few chairs. A large map of West Berlin covered the back wall. They waited in line behind their two companions, whom they assumed were also escapees, and overheard as the elderly policeman on duty gave them instructions on how to get to the Marienfelde Reception Camp and handed them a small map. Then it was their turn. The policeman was friendly, not officious but somewhat bored by his tedious routine. He smiled at the baby and gave Weber the same information and map.

Weber studied the map for a moment and then apologetically asked, "Would you be good enough, *Herr Wachtmeister*, to tell me once again how to get to Marienfelde?" The policeman patiently repeated his instructions. He also reassured Anna that the baby would be taken care of in the Marienfelde nursery. He then gave them 5 DM to buy subway tickets and a cup of coffee, and with a broad though mechanical smile said, "Don't worry. There is no longer any reason for you to be nervous or afraid. Nothing bad can happen to you here. Welcome to West Berlin!"

*   *   *

Brian "Bud" Cole, Lt. Colonel USAF, was finishing his breakfast. The PX cafeteria was full of American personnel, both military and civilian, though the distinction between the two was not evident since military intelligence personnel often wore civilian clothes. Cole, a career Air Force officer recently assigned to Berlin, was still uncomfortable with the blurring of that distinction. He sat alone, in uniform, at a table for two in the corner of the large dining area.

Cole was content. The eggs had not been overcooked—the German kitchen help did not always understand the meaning of "lightly over"—the bacon was dry and crisp, the hash browns smooth and plentiful. He pushed the brown plastic tray aside and took a quick look at the inside pages of *The Stars and Stripes,* the Berlin Command's weekly newspaper. At times one could learn more about what was really going on at Berlin Command from *The Stars and Stripes* than from the pompous weekly briefings by General Swenson. But today there was nothing of interest. "Just a bunch of crap," Cole muttered to himself as he neatly folded the paper over three times. He looked at his watch—it was ten minutes to eight. He gulped down the rest of his coffee, put on his cap at a smart angle, and stood. He was tall with sandy hair, watchful dark eyes, and pleasant but undistinguished features. He had a football player's shoulders and stride. He nodded to people at a few of the tables as he made his way out past the PX store reserved for U.S. personnel, which sold cigarettes, liquor, and other American necessities—that is, unattainable luxuries for the average Berliner.

The PX was located on Clayallee in a small one-story structure directly across from the complex of buildings that housed Berlin

Command, the American Military Headquarters. It had been the site of Luftwaffe headquarters during World War II and was one of the few locations undamaged by the massive Allied air raids. Some cynical Berliners were convinced that the rival air forces had reached a gentlemen's agreement during the war to spare their respective command posts.

Cole crossed Clayallee, showed his ID to the soldier inside the fortified guard post, and crisply returned his salute. He walked to the left wing of the U-shaped central building and climbed the three flights—two steps at a time—to the steel-door entrance to the 575th Air Supply Squadron, the Air Force unit under his command. The office space had been carved out of a previously unoccupied attic storage area. There were no windows—only skylights—and the low ceilings and intruding roof corners further diminished the limited amount of room. Since his arrival in Berlin four months earlier, Cole had tried to procure more spacious and "respectable" quarters, but his efforts had so far been to no avail. Army and Navy Intelligence had gotten to Berlin first and taken all of the desirable space.

The night-duty clerk responded to Cole's coded ring and opened the door.

"Morning, Colonel."

"Good morning, Sergeant. Anything new?"

"No sir. Quiet night. Just three calls from agents returning from the field."

"Good. Is Herter in?"

"Yes, sir."

Cole walked to his office, automatically ducking to avoid a protruding beam that cut across the middle of the hall. He hung his cap on a hook behind the door, glanced at his desk, and then entered the neighboring office. Carlton Herter, a tall and distinguished-looking man in his fifties, with thick glasses under bushy eyebrows, sat behind his desk abstracting a document.

"Morning, Herter. Are you ready for me?"

"Morning, Colonel," Herter replied in his reedy voice. "Let

me have another few minutes, please. I want to finish reading an interesting report that came in late last night."

"Sure thing," Cole replied and returned to his own office, smiling. Good old Herter, he thought. Night and day, he lives and breathes his intelligence reports. Don't know what we'd do without him.

In fact, the 575th would indeed have been incapacitated without Herter, its only true intelligence professional. A member of the OSS during World War II, Herter had smoothly adapted to the fact that America's principal enemy was now not Germany but the Soviet Union, and without skipping a beat he continued to wage war in the intelligence field. This he did only partly out of a sense of patriotism. Primarily, he had become addicted to the shadowy world of ciphers, codes, and espionage. A man of some private means, he was not dependent, as were the outfit's other civilian employees, on his government pay. Moreover, his material demands were modest. A bachelor, he lived for his work with an almost monklike obsession, regretting that his colleagues lacked his total devotion.

Ten minutes later he entered Cole's office. "Here is the morning list, Colonel," he said, placing a single sheet of paper, stamped "Top Secret" meticulously at the top and bottom, on Cole's desk. Listed in order of priority were the intelligence targets in the GDR that the 575th was assigned to cover.

"Any changes?" Cole asked.

"None since we added the bridge in Frankfurt/Oder yesterday."

"No other changes?"

"No. The rest are our usual airfields, anti-aircraft facilities, ammo dumps, oil storage tanks . . ."

"Yes, yes, I know. Let's check our coverage."

Herter, in charge of the 575th covert intelligence-gathering program, pulled some sheets, partitioned into three columns, from his blue cardboard folder. They contained in the left-hand column the cover names of the unit's twelve "handlers"; next to their names in the central column were the code names of agents sent into the field; in the wider right-hand column were listed the dates of the agents' departure, their expected return, and the targets assigned. The names of the handlers were written in ink; all the other information was in pencil for easy erasure and update.

"Here's some information on the bridge in Frankfurt/Oder which Wiesbaden has made a new priority," Herter explained.

"Why is that?"

"I believe Wiesbaden is updating its information on first-day targets." The USAF's European Headquarters was located in Wiesbaden, West Germany, and the 575th Air Supply Squadron—on paper a quartermaster supply outfit—was the Berlin intelligence-gathering outpost for Wiesbaden's 2050th Air Support Wing.

"The bridge," Herter continued, "is one of the few crossing points over the River Oder and therefore it has been upgraded as one of the targets to be destroyed within the first twelve hours of hostilities. It's reportedly protected by anti-aircraft batteries manned by Soviet, not East German, gunners. There is a limit, you know, to the trust placed by the Red Army in its East German 'brothers.'" Herter smiled, then went on. "There's also an unsubstantiated report that a new radar tracking system is being added to the bridge's air defenses. This could be a harbinger, Wiesbaden believes, of a more general upgrading of air defenses in the GDR."

"I suppose that means we're in for an added workload," Cole remarked.

"Yes, indeed. We'll just have to increase our efficiency," Herter replied. "We should start at Marienfelde. Let's make sure that Pritzer concentrates on his work and doesn't let any refugee with important information slip through his fingers." Helmut Pritzer was the USAF "screener" at Marienfelde.

Cole smiled. "I admit that Pritzer is a bit of a hothead," he said. "He does speak good German, though." He paused and then added, "Moreover, I would have thought that he'd calm down, now that he's a married man."

"Quite the contrary, Colonel. That young German wife of his keeps him hopping." That image made them both laugh.

The two men reviewed the missions of the various agents in the field to make sure that the assignments matched with Wiesbaden's priority list. This was a daily exercise during which Herter watched with approval Cole's rapidly increasing grasp of, in Herter's words, "the nuts and bolts of our noble profession."

For Cole was a newcomer to the intelligence game. He was a pilot who had distinguished himself during the war with more than thirty daylight bombing missions over Germany. The Air Force had recently come to the conclusion that no one could be better at identifying enemy targets than pilots with wartime bombing experience. To put that novel idea to the test, a small number of veteran pilots, including Cole, had been put through an intensive six-month intelligence training program and then assigned to various commands in the intelligence field.

Cole had arrived in Berlin with some misgivings. He had been assured by his superiors that this was the road to rapid promotion, and as the Brigadier General at the Pentagon in charge of the program had told him, "This will be very broadening, Colonel. After all, it's only for a short tour of duty—eighteen months to two years—and wait and see, you'll end up a better pilot for having had the experience."

Cole was unconvinced, but determined to give the assignment his best shot. He had a career officer's suspicion of civilian employees and would have preferred a greater presence of military personnel in his unit. However, the Air Force did not have sufficient personnel with language capabilities and intelligence experience to meet its requirements. Moreover, the military's rotating tours of duty were disruptive for an organization that needed continuity—an element that only civilians could provide. And of course Carlton Herter was different; he was a "real pro," and Cole treated him as he would a fellow officer. Still, Cole longed for his aircraft, where there were no civilian crew members.

*　　*　　*

After the war, the city of Berlin, like Germany as a whole, had been divided into four parts by the victorious Allies. As the wartime alliance faltered, the city's American, British, and French Sectors coalesced into West Berlin, while East Berlin—the Russian Sector, which covered much of the city's center—was sealed off from the West and touted, despite Western protestations, as the capital of the GDR, the German Democratic Republic, as the Soviet puppet state was called. West Berlin itself was an island located deep in the heart of the GDR—a hostage to frequent Russian pressure and harassment. The successful Berlin Airlift, which during 1948 and 1949 dramatically supplied West Berlin with round-the-clock all-weather air support, demonstrated the West's commitment to the enclave's survival. Then, turning a geographic vulnerability into a propaganda advantage, West Berlin began its renaissance as a showcase of democracy and of the material well-being to which West Germans were beginning to accede. Both of the latter were totally lacking in the GDR.

Increasingly, East Germans, drawn to the advantages available in the West, began to flee their homeland. All the refugees were processed through the Marienfelde Reception Camp, which consisted of two dozen barracks on a large open field in the southeastern part of Berlin's American Sector. Almost all of them had fled via East Berlin, for the border between West Berlin and the GDR was blocked by barbed wire, controlled by watchtowers, and patrolled with attack dogs.

Helmut Pritzer had been in a foul mood as he drove to the Marienfelde camp early that misty morning. He'd had a bitter row the night before with his attractive young East German wife, Jutta, about what he had called her scandalous behavior at a party earlier that evening. There was no doubt that Jutta had once again made him look foolish. She had shamelessly played up to a newly arrived lieutenant, smiling up at him with her lips just barely parted. Pritzer knew her repertoire, having been on its receiving end just two years earlier, and could testify to its efficacy. When they arrived home from the party, he had berated her, but she'd slammed the bedroom door and locked him out. Pritzer had spent the night on the living-room couch.

Irate and confused thoughts of his predicament were uppermost in Pritzer's mind as he arrived at the Marienfelde gate. The guard asked to see his pass.

"Are you blind?" Pritzer exploded. "Can't you see the pass on the windshield?" The guard saluted, and Pritzer swung into his assigned parking spot.

He entered the spacious waiting room, where the latest batch of refugees were assembled on rows of wooden chairs, and walked over to the receptionist's desk. She quickly handed him three mimeographed sheets with—for security reasons—only the refugees' first names, listed in order of their arrival, as well as their age, sex, marital status, occupation, and last GDR address. He placed the papers in his briefcase.

Then he went to the far corner of the waiting room, where coffee and hard rolls with small pats of butter were being served by two white-aproned, sour-faced women who were parsimonious in their distribution since they were allowed to take home leftovers at the close of day. Pritzer went to the head of the coffee line, shouldering a young man aside, and helped himself to a roll, three pats of butter, and a cup of coffee. He then headed down a corridor, unlocking and opening the second door on the left.

His office was square and small. There was a desk with two chairs on either side. Pritzer always sat with his back to the window, facing the entrance door, while the refugee being interrogated would sit across from him, with his back to the door. A third chair was placed against a side wall for the unusual case in which two refugees were questioned at the same time. A shelf under the window ledge held some books, including an interrogation manual and an English–German dictionary. A large map of East Germany was taped to the side wall.

Pritzer opened his briefcase, took out a sealed envelope made

available by Herter at the beginning of each workday, and tore it
open. It contained some loose-leaf fact sheets—marked "Secret" in
large black letters at the top and bottom—which indicated the
military targets of current interest to the USAF. Newly added items
were underlined, and Pritzer noted the addition of the bridge in
Frankfurt/Oder.

He glanced at the list of waiting refugees. "The usual gar-
bage," he muttered. An elderly couple from Leipzig—no use seeing them. An electrical engineer from East Berlin—he might have
some technical information if he had worked in some defense-
related activity. That was a long shot, and Pritzer was in no mood
for long shots. A widow in her forties from Finsterwalde, where the
Soviet Air Force had a major installation—he would have to see
her. A couple with a baby from Frankfurt/Oder—they might have
some information on the bridge. He dialed the waiting-room receptionist and asked her to send in the widow and the young
couple.

The widow was very nervous, trembling at this first contact
with a Western official. East German propaganda painted lurid
pictures of the fate that would befall refugees—women sent to
brothels in South America and the like. At times Pritzer derived
pleasure from inspiring such fears in women. He looked at the
widow and imagined that she must have been good-looking when
young. He asked her about Soviet units stationed in Finsterwalde.
She had no idea, she replied; the Soviets stayed in their barracks
and hardly ever came into town. Yes, she knew where the airfield
was but had never been near it. "The whole area is a *Sperrgebiet*, a
restricted area," she said. "There are barriers all around. No one
can get within a kilometer of the base."

Yes, she knew what an anti-aircraft battery looked like. She
had seen many of them in Finsterwalde during the war. No, she
had not seen any since then. No, she didn't know any Soviet military. No, she didn't know anyone who worked for the Soviets. She
was silent, waiting for the next question, her hands joined together
in her lap. She had stopped trembling.

A waste of time, Pritzer concluded. "Thank you," he said abruptly. "That is all. You can go."

"Go where?" she asked, surprised.

"Back to the waiting room," he said gruffly.

As she closed the door behind her, Pritzer thought back, as he often did, to the day two years ago when Jutta had entered this very room and changed his life. She had appeared in the Marienfelde processing line—a lithe figure with long blonde hair and an alluring smile. He had immediately been smitten and soon proposed marriage. To his amazement and delight, Jutta had accepted. He'd had such rosy hopes of happiness then, and today here he still sat, interviewing refugees. In frustration, he pounded the desk with his fist.

A knock at the door provided an answering echo, and Weber entered, followed by Anna holding the baby. Pritzer picked up the phone, dialed the receptionist, and shouted that she knew very well that he never wanted to see couples together, certainly not with a baby. "If you can't remember that," he growled, "we'll have to find someone else who can." The receptionist came running in and ushered Anna back to the waiting room, closing the door behind them.

Pritzer had not as yet said a word to the Webers. Now, alone with Weber, he motioned for him to sit down. "So, Herr Hans, you are from Frankfurt/Oder?" he asked.

"Yes."

"When did you leave?"

"Very early this morning."

"Did anyone see you leave?"

"What do you mean?"

"Any of your neighbors, or anyone else you know?"

"I don't think so. We left at 4 a.m."

"Did the police stop and question you?"

"No."

Pritzer looked down at his sheet and saw that Weber was a teacher. "I assume your school will be aware today of your having left," Pritzer said.

"Yes, but I took today off with my accumulated overtime, and there is school vacation next week."

"I see. Where did you live in Frankfurt/Oder?"

"On Fischerstrasse, next to the river."

Pritzer's ears pricked up. "Could you see the bridge, the main bridge across the Oder?"

Weber smiled. "Of course," he said. "It's right in front of your nose when you look out our kitchen window."

There was no point in continuing the preliminary screening. Weber was acquainted with a priority target. Pritzer pulled out a small light-blue form from the desk drawer and wrote Weber's identifying number on it.

"We're going to take you to one of our offices to ask you some questions," Pritzer informed him.

"What about?"

"Mainly about the bridge."

"What about my wife and child?"

"They'll stay here at the camp."

"I don't want to leave my wife and child, sir," Weber protested. "We've just been through a very difficult few hours. You must have seen how upset my wife is. Let me answer your questions here. I really don't want to be separated from them."

Pritzer showed his annoyance. It was not his habit to negotiate with refugees. "Your wife and baby will be quite safe here, Herr Hans," he said in a peremptory tone. "You have no reason to be concerned."

"How long will this take?" Weber asked hesitatingly.

"Just a little while," Pritzer answered, standing up. "The sooner you leave, the sooner you'll be back." He handed Weber the blue slip of paper and told him to give it to the receptionist.

Weber had scarcely any time to reassure Anna before a smiling and knowing social worker took her in hand, patted little Manfred, who was still clutching his teddy bear, and led them firmly toward a barrack where families were quartered. At the same time Weber was escorted to a station wagon in the parking lot. The car already held two male passengers. No one spoke; any one of them could be an East German spy, Weber reflected. An hour or so later, after a woman had been added to the group, a stooped, middle-aged German driver climbed behind the steering wheel. Without a word he started the car and set out across town for the American Interrogation Center.

*   *   *

The road from Marienfelde traversed the wasteland of bomb-shattered Berlin, the scale of devastation having been so immense that even after ten years of rebuilding, large sections of the city still stood in ruins, with the jagged shells of buildings reaching reproachfully to the sky. The car drove through Steglitz, once a bustling shopping district, where the surviving clock tower of the brick municipal building now surveyed the desolation of surrounding debris and piles of stones in the empty lots at its base.

In contrast, the residential district of Dahlem, an enclave of villas and parks, did not appear to have suffered as extensively, since the destroyed one-family dwellings had been more easily repaired. Also, the abundance of trees provided a screen for war damage not available in the built-up urban areas.

The interrogation center used by the U.S. military intelligence services was located in a villa in Dahlem on the corner of Clayallee and Im Dol, a small side street just a few hundred yards down from the American Headquarters complex. That refugees were questioned there was well known, with no attempt being made to disguise the purpose of the installation.

The driver accompanied Weber and his fellow passengers into the front entrance hall. He handed four sealed green folders to Brigitte Halder, the elegant, dark-haired German receptionist.

"Please take a seat in the waiting room," she told the refugees in a pleasant voice, indicating the villa's former living room, now filled with a dozen metal folding chairs and a table on which were scattered a number of outdated newspapers and magazines.

Brigitte's black labrador, Graf, was curled up on the floor beside her desk. She had been granted permission to bring the dog to the center—for protection, she had said, whereas it was really for his company. She quickly and efficiently checked the green folders to determine where to direct the new arrivals. She then placed a few calls to inform the various interrogators that they had "clients" waiting downstairs.

"Herr Hans," she announced in a loud voice ten minutes later. "Come with me, please." Weber followed her up the narrow, winding stairs. She knocked at the door of Room 4, entered, and with a smile handed Weber's folder to Norman Liebman, who was sitting at his desk inside.

Liebman was a short, balding man with gentle gray eyes and horn-rimmed glasses. He greeted Weber in perfect German, with the hint of a Saxon accent, and asked him to sit down. He glanced at the folder and saw Pritzer's scribble directing him to focus on the Frankfurt/Oder bridge. Turning to a file drawer behind him, Liebman took out and quickly glanced at the summary information Herter made available on all priority targets.

"I understand you lived near the river," Liebman said.

"That's right."

"Did you have a good view of the bridge?"

"Yes. I already told that to the man in Marienfelde."

Liebman understood that Weber was nervous and probably a bit disoriented. He continued his questioning calmly and with consideration. "So I understand. I'll try not to repeat too many questions, Herr Hans. Tell me, how far away was your house . . ."

"We lived in an apartment."

"How far was your apartment from the bridge?"

"About 200 meters."

"What floor was your apartment on?"

"The third floor."

"I see." Liebman paused, then inquired, "Do you have anything special to report?"

"What do you mean?" Weber asked uneasily.

"Did you notice any recent changes on the bridge or near the bridge?"

Weber became apprehensive. Why, he wondered, was he being asked all these questions? Should he be talking about these matters to this German or American or whoever he was? Years of Communist propaganda about warmongering Western spies caused him to be cautious.

Liebman recognized the hesitation; he was quite used to this reaction. Refugees either bragged and exaggerated the information they could provide—which was useless—or like Weber, the more thoughtful and decent ones became suspicious and reserved. These could be useful if they were handled with dexterity.

"Are the anti-aircraft batteries still there?" Liebman asked.

"Anti-aircraft batteries?"

"Yes," he said matter-of-factly, referring to Herter's summary. "The two batteries, one on either side of the bridge on the East bank, manned by Soviets from the 136th Air Defense Battalion."

Weber seemed impressed by Liebman's detailed knowledge. "Yes, they're still there," he admitted sheepishly. "But I don't know what unit the Russian soldiers belong to."

"When did you see them last?"

"Yesterday evening as I was pulling down the kitchen shades."

Now Liebman faced the difficult decision he always dreaded. He felt no qualms about "overt" interrogation of refugees to obtain useful information on the GDR. These people had reached the safety of West Berlin, and it seemed but a fair exchange for them to divulge whatever might be helpful to the Free World. (Liebman did not think highly of that designation for the West, but he was stuck with the jargon of the times.)

What made him uncomfortable were the "covert" operations pursuant to which his unit regularly persuaded refugees to return to the East on spying missions. Yet he could not avoid the obligation to refer refugees with knowledge of a listed USAF target to the 575th covert operations section. Failure to do so would invite dismissal, and any laxity in this regard might be viewed as possible disloyalty.

"You left early this morning?" Liebman asked.

"Yes."

"Does anyone know you've left?"

"Yes and no," Weber answered a bit testily. "Excuse me, sir, but I have already answered these questions at Marienfelde. I have told you all I know about the bridge. You seem to know more about it than I do anyway. My wife and baby are waiting for me at Marienfelde. I know she must be getting very nervous. Can I please go back to them now?"

"I just have a few more questions, Herr Hans. We'll try to finish our conversation as soon as possible." Liebman then asked about Weber's family background, inquired if any colleagues at work or personal acquaintances were opponents of the GDR regime, and probed whether by chance Weber had any contacts with any military or government officials. Weber was on his guard in his responses and offered nothing of value.

"Thank you, Herr Hans," Liebman finally said. "Please go back to the waiting room for a few minutes."

Liebman added some notes to Weber's folder and then dialed the nearby "safe house" from which covert operations were initially dispatched. He thought of Weber's wife and baby as he mechanically placed the call. "I have a body for you," Liebman said wearily, "with priority target information."

* * *

The safe house was a small two-storied villa on Meisenstrasse, a side street off Clayallee with cobblestone sidewalks. Wooden crossbeams, painted a light brown, framed its concrete walls. On the ground floor, only a small grilled window next to the front door faced the street. The lack of any other apertures in front was deemed a security advantage. There was no front lawn, only a pebbled courtyard surrounded by a high hedge; a single evergreen stood near the street lamp.

It was a place primarily devoted to first contacts with potential "returnees." Once recruited, agents returning from missions would generally be met, debriefed, and given new assignments in a variety of public, anonymous locations throughout the city. Nonetheless, the attempt to keep the villa clandestine was a hopeless endeavor. In Berlin's charged atmosphere it did not take long for neighbors watching the daily parade of refugees to comprehend the situation. Consequently, the designation "safe house" was a misnomer.

Three interrogation rooms were located on the ground floor; an upstairs office contained a safe with target information and some agent reports. There was also a small apartment on the second floor that was used sparingly for emergencies, such as for housing "blown" agents before they were evacuated from Berlin.

Weber was driven to the house by a circuitous route in the back of a car that had curtains drawn over the back and rear side windows and a wooden panel between the front and back seats to block any outside view. The car's back doors locked automatically, which caused Weber's anxiety level to rise. Had he fallen into the hands of the Stasi, the East German secret police? No, of course not; these were Americans. There was no need to panic. He was in West Berlin. What about Anna and little Manfred? It had been hours since he'd left Marienfelde. Liebman had promised to get a reassuring message to them. Would he do so? Anna would be anxious. He wasn't feeling particularly confident himself.

Eugene Zandt, a small man whose thick glasses gave him a froglike appearance, sat hunched behind the same type of light wooden desk that Weber had already seen at Marienfelde and the Clayallee Interrogation Center. In the GDR, the official desks were made of gray metal; the Americans, Weber noted, seemed to prefer wood. The driver who had brought Weber to the house handed Zandt the green folder, which Liebman had annotated in his small meticulous handwriting. He motioned to Weber to be seated while he briefly looked at the folder's contents. "Frankfurt/Oder" was underlined in red. Liebman had written "Lived near bridge." That's all Zandt wanted to know.

"So you lived near the bridge?" he inquired.

"Yes," Weber answered.

"How far from the bridge?"

"About 200 meters. Look, sir," Weber said impatiently, "this is the third time today I'm being asked these questions. I have a wife and baby waiting for me at Marienfelde. They must be very worried by now. I want to go back to them. Now."

"Very shortly," Zandt said curtly. "Just a few more questions. Does anyone in Frankfurt/Oder know that you have fled the GDR?"

"No, but what does that matter? They'll all know soon enough that we've left."

"Why is that?" Zandt asked, raising his eyebrows above his thick glasses.

Weber laughed. "Because we're going to write and tell them," he said.

"You haven't done that yet, have you?" Zandt asked with concern.

"No," Weber remarked ruefully, "we haven't had much time to write postcards since we arrived."

Zandt now switched gears. First he had to determine whether the subject was bright enough to carry out a mission. Weber as a teacher would clearly qualify, he surmised. He pushed a piece of paper and pencil across the desk. "Can you," he asked, "draw me a picture of the bridge as you see it from your window?"

Weber protested that he was not a draftsman, but urged on, he drew a passable sketch and handed it back.

"Isn't there something missing?" Zandt asked.

"No, I don't think so."

"Something at the end of the bridge?"

Weber looked blankly at Zandt.

"What about the anti-aircraft batteries?"

Weber flushed. "I thought you were only asking me to draw the bridge," he said.

Zandt, impassive, asked him to sketch the guns. Weber hesitated; this seemed to be spying. Taking a deep breath, he drew two match-box guns on the bridge's far side.

Zandt looked at the sketch and said nothing, then pushed back his chair and stood up. He walked over to Weber, asked if he wanted coffee, and offered him a cigarette. Weber accepted both. Zandt called down to the housekeeper and told her to bring up two cups of coffee. He then began to pace nervously around the small room. Weber turned this way and that so as not to lose sight of him.

"What do you plan to do in the West, Herr Hans?" Zandt asked suddenly.

"I am a teacher and once worked in a post office. I am a good worker—in fact, I love to work, but no matter how hard you try, you can't earn enough in the GDR to make a decent living for your family. That is unless you are an SED Party member, which I am not." Weber looked at Zandt to be certain that he had registered this disclaimer. "I'm not interested in politics," he continued. "Anyway, I finally realized that there was no future for us back there and decided to look for a new and better life in the West. Do you think I'll be able to find a job?"

Zandt continued his pacing. "I'm sure you will," he said. Then he added, as if it were an afterthought, "The American forces in Germany, you know, are always on the lookout for teachers." The housekeeper brought in the coffee on a small tray. The two men helped themselves.

"I am a German elementary school teacher. I don't see what use I could be to Americans."

"I think we could find a job for you."

Weber was immediately on his guard. An offer from an official source meant that something was inevitably expected in return. "Why would you do that?" he asked.

"Because we always need reliable and talented employees, and I'm sure you would be a good one."

"Is that the only reason?"

"Well," Zandt chuckled, "perhaps there is also a small favor you could do for us."

Weber relaxed. He had sized up the position correctly. "What could I possibly do for you?"

Zandt came over to Weber and, leaning toward him, spoke in a confidential whisper: "How about going back to Frankfurt/Oder and taking one more quick look at those anti-aircraft batteries?"

Weber was stunned. It took him a moment to gather his thoughts. When he responded, it was with passion. "Are you out of your mind? We just arrived in West Berlin a few hours ago. We have left all our possessions behind. We risked jail sentences to get here and now that we're lucky enough to have made it, you want me to go back. That's crazy!"

"No one knows you've gone," Zandt insisted. "It's just an hour's train trip, a quick look at the bridge, at one or two things we want you to check out that you can see from your apartment window, and you'll be back. Then we'll fly you and your family out of Berlin and help you find a job. It's the chance of a lifetime. What do you say?"

"I say absolutely not." Weber felt abused by the man, for whom he had suddenly taken an intense dislike. "Thank you for the offer, but I am not going to tempt fate. My family and I are safe in West Berlin, and nothing on earth could persuade me to return to the GDR. Now, please, I have answered all your questions; I want to go back to Marienfelde and be with my family."

Zandt looked at Weber's angry face and concluded that it would be useless to try to budge him. Perhaps, he reflected, he had popped the question too quickly, without sufficient preparatory build-up. Can't win them all, he said to himself. He took the protesting Weber to an adjoining room and told him to wait.

Then Zandt lumbered upstairs to where Major Zachary Muldane, the 575th Squadron's Executive Officer, was conducting his weekly review of the safe house's records and accounts. At Muldane's request, Zandt reluctantly gave him a report on his discussion with Weber.

"So you've screwed up again, Zandt, have you?" Muldane asked with a frown. "Couldn't even get him to take an hour's train ride back?"

There was little love lost between the disciplined career officer and his ungainly, unimaginative civilian subordinate. After being hit in the leg by shrapnel during a daylight bombing raid over Schweinfurt, Muldane had been transferred to the Intelligence Service, where he had become quite adept in the application of interrogation techniques to German prisoners of war. He had put his wartime experience to good use these last two years in reshaping the 575th Air Supply Squadron along stricter military lines.

As usual, Zandt suffered the abuse in silence. He had seen officers come and go, and he was confident that he would outlast Muldane too, as long as he gave him no reason to place a negative report in his personnel file.

"I did the best I could, Major."

"Did you offer him the usual goodies?"

"I started to . . ."

"And?"

"He wasn't interested."

Muldane consulted the briefing folder on the bridge in Frankfurt/Oder and then called Carlton Herter on a secure "scrambled" telephone line.

"Herter?" he asked. "Major Muldane here. We have a live body from Frankfurt/Oder at Meisenstrasse. Do you have anyone else in the field assigned to that bridge?"

"Give me a moment, Major, and let me take a look." There was a short pause while Herter consulted his files. "No, Major," Herter replied, "no one has been given that target as yet. After all, the bridge was a very recent request by Wiesbaden."

"Thank you, Herter," Muldane said, hanging up the telephone. Then, turning to Zandt, he stated, "There is no one else looking at that bridge. We've got to make this turkey go back."

"I've done all I could, Major," Zandt protested. "I tell you he won't go. It's not worth the effort."

"You're hopeless," Muldane snapped. "I'll have a go at him."

He walked down the stairs slowly—his leg wound had left him with a slight limp—reading the Frankfurt/Oder bridge file. Wearing civilian clothes while on covert duty, he introduced himself to Weber as Mr. Jones and politely, in passable German, asked him to come back into the interrogation room.

Weber was upset. "Mr. Jones, I do not understand," he said with agitation. "I have been away from my wife and baby for over six hours. My wife—she is very fragile. She will by now certainly be frantic. I am very worried about her. I have answered the same questions over and over again. Now, please, I want to go back to Marienfelde."

Muldane was mellifluous in his response. "I understand perfectly, Herr Hans. I apologize for all this inconvenience. I will send my driver to Marienfelde immediately to bring your wife and baby back to the villa here. All right?"

Weber quietly nodded.

"Have you had any lunch?" Muldane asked. Weber shook his head. "I'm sorry. We've really given you a very bad time today, haven't we? I'll get us both something to eat." Muldane stepped outside for a moment to talk to his driver and the housekeeper, leaving Weber alone, both surprised and somewhat mollified.

"While we're waiting for our food and your family," Muldane said when he came back into the room, "let me explain what must appear to you as our rather strange behavior." He moved his chair away from the desk and closer to Weber's.

"You may have wondered why we seem so interested in you. Haven't you, Herr Hans?"

"Yes," Weber answered warily.

"Well, speaking confidentially—I wouldn't want you to repeat this—right now we very much need some specific information on the Frankfurt/Oder bridge. And then you walk in this morning, and the information we want is right under your nose in your apartment. Quite a coincidence, wouldn't you say?"

"I am not going back," Weber said vehemently. "I have already told the other man that nothing can make me . . ."

"No one will even try, Herr Hans. Don't forget we're Americans, not Russians. We respect every person's right to free choice. That's what our confrontation with the Soviets is all about, isn't it? Individual human rights."

"I suppose so," Weber answered hesitantly, looking at Muldane with some puzzlement. In a strange way he reminded Weber of a self-confident major in the Red Army who had come to his school in Frankfurt/Oder and addressed his pupils, vaunting the merits of cooperation between their two fraternal Socialist countries. There was also an unmistakable hint of intimidation in Muldane's soft approach.

The housekeeper brought in sandwiches and beer. "While we're waiting," Muldane said, biting into a hard roll liberally stuffed with ham and cheese, "let me tell you a little more about what we're interested in." He drew a rough sketch of the type of radar installations they were looking for and handed it to Weber. "These would generally be within a few meters of the anti-aircraft batteries," he said. "They're hard to hide if you can see the guns . . . you can see the anti-aircraft guns from your window, right?"

Weber nodded.

"Then you'd be able to see this type of radar. No problem at all. You don't remember seeing anything like this, do you?"

"No, Mr. Jones. But frankly, I wasn't paying too much attention to the guns. They've been there so long . . ."

"That's just the point, Herr Hans. One more look, when you know what you're looking for . . ."

"I have already told you. I am not going back."

"And I've already told you that no one will force you to go back. No harm in our talking, though, is there? Have another beer." Weber did.

Muldane kept chipping away. "Just a question of a few hours," he emphasized. "All we would want you to do is take a quick look for the radar installations I showed you; you'd be back the same day and have some D Marks in your pocket; some more money would be very helpful for you and your family now, wouldn't it?"

"We can sure use a little money, that's true," Weber admitted, "but getting some is not worth the risk. Sorry, Mr. Jones."

"There is practically no risk," Muldane insisted. "A short train trip to your apartment, a look out the window, and you're back with perhaps a thousand D Marks in your pocket."

The mention of a thousand D Marks caught Weber's attention. He began to reflect that he was jobless and practically penniless. If, with little risk, he could make some money and get American help in the West, well, it was at least worth considering.

"If I were to accept . . ." Weber said haltingly, quickly adding, "I don't think I will, but if I were to go, how much would you pay me?"

The fish had bitten, and now Muldane just had to slowly reel him in. "I think your little trip would be worth DM 2500 to us."

Weber swallowed hard; converted into Ostmarks, that sum would equal four months of his teacher's pay. "The other man mentioned you might help me find a job," Weber said.

Muldane was annoyed that Zandt had gone that far, but since he had . . . "We can also see about that," he replied smoothly. "Think it over. As I said before, this is your decision. But if you decide to go, you should leave tomorrow morning. The sooner the better; by that I mean the safer it would be."

The door opened, and Anna, holding Manfred and appearing bewildered, came into the room. She saw Weber and, letting out a little cry, rushed into his arms. Muldane smiled benignly at the tearful family reunion. He told the couple they could spend the night in the apartment upstairs and assured them that the housekeeper was well known for the tasty dinners she prepared.

Taking his leave, Muldane said he would come by at eight o'clock the next morning. He wished Weber and Anna a happy first night of freedom. They retired early, after having been served a nourishing meal. The dramatic events of the day had left them exhausted and disoriented. Lying awake before daybreak next morning, with an armed guard downstairs, Weber had the uneasy impression of being held in a golden cage.

*   *   *

A few streets behind the American Military Headquarters on Clayallee was an imposing structure with white sandstone walls and a red tiled roof. A portico supported by four massive columns, each embossed with baskets of flowers, fruits, and vegetables, loomed above its main entrance portals. The building, called Harnack Haus, had large ground-floor halls and rooms, which were now used by senior American personnel for the same type of receptions that the Luftwaffe Command had hosted there a decade earlier. The basement bar was staffed by black enlisted servicemen as bartenders and German girls as waitresses. It was a popular—indeed the only— after-work meeting place for American officers and senior grade civilian employees.

It was half-past five in the afternoon. Bud Cole was sitting in the bar at his favorite corner table when Zachary Muldane walked in. "Over here, Zach," he called. Muldane smiled and came toward him, gesturing to a young waitress that he was thirsty and wanted a beer. He sat down across from Cole and looked around the noisy, smoke-filled room.

"How'd the day go, Bud?"

"So-so. How about you?"

"I'll tell you later."

"That bad, huh?" They both chuckled. The waitress brought their beers. As she bent over to set them down, her low-cut peasant blouse revealed her round breasts.

"Looks like we have some new talent," Muldane commented, indicating the waitress.

"Probably just another Stasi plant."

"I wouldn't mind planting her," Muldane said with a leer, keeping his eyes on the waitress as she maneuvered around the room. They sat without talking for a moment, sipping their beers, enjoying their military comradeship. Jazz music blared over the intercom, adding decibels to the general high noise level.

They traded office gossip and talked about the latest promotions. "We're out of the goddamn loop in this godforsaken place," Muldane grumbled. "The personnel at Headquarters in Wiesbaden don't even know we exist, let alone have us in mind when promotion time comes along." Muldane had been told that the Berlin assignment would assure, and perhaps even accelerate, his promotion. He was no longer so sure.

"Don't worry, Zach—if anything can get screwed up, the Air Force will find a way to do it."

"Very funny," Muldane said and signaled for another beer.

Cole held up two fingers to indicate he wanted one too. "By the way, Zach," he said, "General Swenson has asked me to have the 575th host the next reception for the Intelligence Missions."

"So the Old Man wants you to organize the gathering of the spooks, huh?" Muldane chuckled.

"That's right," Cole agreed. "It's our turn to send the invites."

These Inter-Allied get-togethers were monthly occasions, held on a rotating basis in each of the city's four military sectors. They were intended by the West to demonstrate that Berlin remained a single city and to undermine East Berlin's claim to be the capital of the GDR. Why the Russians continued to attend as well as to host these functions was the subject of numerous discussions and hypotheses. To keep the East Germans in their place? To keep tabs on the Western intelligence services? Because no orders had been received to curtail these contacts? No one knew for sure.

"When's the party?"

"A week from Wednesday."

"That's less than two weeks away."

"Yeah, I know. The General warned me to be damn careful because of the Russkis—one false move and we could create a diplomatic incident."

"That's always the risk you run," Muldane agreed.

"I want you to pull this together for me, Zach."

"Me?"

"Yes. We'll hold it here at Harnack Haus, of course. I want you to plan the hors d'oeuvres and the entertainment. I'm sure

you can put on a good show. But nothing political, you understand? Nothing that could offend our goddamn heroic wartime
ally."

"All right, I'll do my best." Muldane moved his chair next to
Cole and, talking softly so that no one could overhear, said: "Bud,
we've got to get rid of Zandt at the Meisenstrasse safe house."

"Why is that?"

Muldane recounted how ineffectual Zandt had been that day
in failing to persuade the refugee to return to Frankfurt/Oder. "That
was not exceptional," he said. "That was one of his typical performances. We need someone who's motivated, aggressive in that slot."

"I agree. Any thoughts about a replacement?" Cole asked.

"Well, ideally we ought to have someone who is enthusiastic
about our mission, who is bright and speaks good German, who
can inspire confidence and be a good judge of people."

"That's the ideal, Zach. Now let's come back to earth. We've
got to work with what we have."

"Yeah, I know. Basically, a lazy bunch of civilians." Muldane
paused for a moment. "I suppose Norman Liebman comes closest
to the ideal."

"Haven't you tried in the past," Cole asked, "to move him over
to covert work?"

"Yeah, I did last year, but he refused. Said he couldn't square it
with his conscience."

"That's a hard answer to argue with."

"Fuck his conscience," Muldane said angrily, loud enough for
the two lieutenants at the neighboring table to hear and look up.
He continued more softly: "If I were you, I'd tell him that's how
he could really be useful, and if he's not interested, he can get the
hell out of our outfit. We shouldn't have any yellow-bellies in our
unit."

Cole understood that Muldane was just blowing off steam. It
was difficult for career officers to adjust to civilian subordinates
who were not compelled to obey orders. Cole himself was more
sensitive and flexible on the point.

"Liebman may not be yellow, Zach," Cole said quietly, "just stubborn, and in his own view a man of principle. He's doing a good job as an overt interrogator. Why the hell force him into something he doesn't want to do?"

Muldane scowled.

"How about bringing Pritzer up to the safe house," Cole suggested, "and letting Zandt do the original screening at Marienfelde?"

Muldane thought that over. "That may work, Bud, even though nobody likes the man."

"I know. Pritzer's a little hot under the collar."

"But he speaks good German," Muldane said. "He's no dummy and seems ambitious. Let's give it a try."

"Isn't his wife an East German refugee?" Cole asked.

"Yes."

"Wouldn't that be a security risk?"

"We checked her out and then double-checked before Pritzer got permission to marry her," Muldane replied. "She's as clean as a whistle. The only problem 'ole Jutta ever causes is a heat wave."

"All right," Cole said. "Let's run this change by Herter in the morning. I think it's probably the best we can do."

*   *   *

On his way back home from Marienfelde, Pritzer stopped at the 575th office and handed in his report of the day's screenings. The officers had left for the day. An elderly civilian cartographer was bent over his maps and was clearly not interested in starting a conversation. No one else seemed to be interested in chit-chat, so Pritzer drove home to his villa in the neighboring district of Zehlendorf.

He pulled into the gravel driveway, slammed the door of his black Opel, and entered the large marble hallway of his house. He called out for Jutta, but obtaining no response, realized she must be out, even though this was not one of the three days a week she worked at Amerika Haus.

"Where did my wife go, Frau Engelhart?" Pritzer asked his housekeeper.

"I do not know, Herr Pritzer," she replied.

"It is your duty to know where your mistress is," Pritzer barked. The elderly housekeeper had learned that the best way to handle Pritzer's bad moods and absurd commands was to ignore them without, however, giving any appearance of rudeness. She also knew that his temper had worsened since his marriage. In her opinion, he was suffering from a typical old man/young wife syndrome.

Pritzer settled down in the living room and poured himself a Scotch. He wondered where Jutta could be; probably out shopping again, he thought. She was a spendthrift, always wheedling him for more money. But he would be willing to forgive her today for any extravagant purchases as long as they could forget about last night's argument.

He leaned back in his easy chair and thought again of the moment when, two years earlier, he had first seen Jutta in the Marienfelde waiting room. She no longer wore bright red lipstick or tight-ribbed sweaters, but her current expensive clothes and makeup were no less alluring. He recalled the many security checks and countless written requests that preceded his obtaining permission to marry her. It had been an exceptional case, but who could blame the paunchy forty-four-year-old Pritzer for moving heaven and earth to wed the beautiful twenty-year-old Jutta? Nor did anyone question her motives, for to marry an American, any American, was an East German girl's dream. A dream not of love, sex, or companionship but of chocolates, nylons, and cigarettes.

I have a beautiful wife, Pritzer now reminded himself. Of course she's going to be admired, and being young and sensual, she is going to respond. I must get hold of myself, he thought. I'm lucky to have such a desirable wife. But do I really have her? After all, she locked me out of the bedroom last night. And that wasn't the first time.

It was already dark when Jutta returned home, more than an hour past their usual dinner time. She was laden down with packages and in ebullient spirits. She took off her coat and twirling in a pirouette said, "Look at my new short skirt, *Liebchen*. Like it?"

What Pritzer wanted was an embrace, but when he rose and moved toward her, she ran upstairs with her packages, laughing and shouting to Frau Engelhart that dinner could be served in ten minutes.

Dinner was a somber affair. The meal was overcooked due to Jutta's late arrival, the lamb chops too tough and the vegetables mushy. Pritzer ate in silence while Jutta spoke enthusiastically about her best friend's latest lover, a movie they just had to see, a car accident on the Kudamm with three ambulances. "And what was your day like, *Liebchen*?" she finally asked.

He muttered, "I spent the day talking to refugees who were grateful to have made it to the West. You remember, the way you felt two years ago."

"Yes, yes, I know," she replied. "A poor, lost East German maiden saved by a gallant and handsome American. What a fairy tale come true! I'm not good enough for you, that's all. You should get rid of your ungrateful wife. Say the word, Mutiger, and I'm gone." She had invented this taunting nickname, which meant "the courageous one" in German and resembled his first name, Helmut.

Nibbling on small chocolate éclairs, Jutta remarked: "You're in a rut, Mutiger. You do the same thing day after day. Can't you get another job? Maybe one that will pay more?"

"Jutta, you know I've tried to get out of the screening job."

"You should. You've already met me." She thought her remark clever; he ignored it.

"The trouble is Muldane. He has no use for civilians. If he could, he'd fill all the good jobs with military personnel."

"Don't be so meek, Mutiger." She smiled at the inadvertent juxtaposition of the meek and the brave. "Go over his head and see Colonel Cole. He is a charming man. Tell him you are too valuable to be sitting around all day asking dirty refugees the same stupid questions."

"They're not always the same questions, and they're not stupid. And as for calling the refugees dirty . . ."

"You know what I mean," Jutta said. "Anyway, we could certainly use some extra money."

"No matter how much money I'd make," Pritzer grumbled, "you'd always want more."

"And then a new job might make you more . . . interesting." She said the last word slowly and moistened her lips. "More attractive to a young wife like me. Why not tell him that you'd like to run agents—you know, send refugees back to gather information? I'm sure that would pay more than screening at Marienfelde. You'd be good at that, I think. With any luck you could recruit a few sexy girls like me. That should perk you up."

Pritzer was aghast. "What are you talking about?" he said in a frightened voice. "What do you know about things like that?"

Jutta laughed. "Don't be naive, Mutiger. If I didn't know, I'd be the only one in West Berlin not to know that the Allies send refugees back to spy for them."

"I don't want to talk about that. It's classified."

"I don't care what it is, but if you got into that line of work, you might stop being such a boring sourpuss when you come home in the evening."

Later that night, as they were lying awake in their separate beds, Pritzer remarked that if he were offered a new job, it might not be in Berlin. Jutta sat up straight. "You wouldn't leave Berlin?" she asked anxiously.

He didn't answer. "I see," she said. "You're just trying to frighten me." She got up and sat on the side of Pritzer's bed, her lithe body beneath the sheer gown clearly outlined in the moonlight. "They don't run agents from anywhere else, do they? Tell me we won't leave here," she pleaded.

"That depends on what I'm offered—if I'm offered anything. But I'm afraid that once they know I want to change jobs, they'll take that opportunity to get rid of me."

Jutta climbed into bed with him and pressing close, whispered: "Don't say you want to leave, *Liebling*. Just ask if there isn't anything else—something more important—you could do to be helpful to the organization. But remember it will have to be in Berlin. I couldn't bear to leave this wonderful city." She gave him an intimate caress and quickly slipped back into her own bed.

Day 2 Saturday

Though little Manfred had slept soundly at the safe house, his parents had spent a disturbed and sleepless night. Hans Weber could not stop talking about Muldane's proposals. Getting out of East Berlin had been simple, he reminded Anna; going back should be even easier. No one in Frankfurt/Oder knew of their escape. If anyone spotted him there, he'd say that he had come back to pick up something they had forgotten and that he was returning to Finsterwalde.

"I don't like it," Anna said fearfully. "I'm sure the police will find out that we're not visiting my cousins in Finsterwalde."

"Even if they do," Weber reassured her, "by then I'll be back safely with you in West Berlin."

"We're safe now," she insisted. "We've made it across. Why take this crazy risk?"

"Because it's the chance of a lifetime. Now stop crying and listen to me. All I have to do is go back, look out our kitchen window, and come back to report what I've seen. That will just take just a few hours. And for that the Americans will give me DM 2500. Imagine—DM 2500—more than I can earn in months back home. They also said they'd help me find a job. Think of that! In forty-eight hours we'll be able to start a new life—for both of us and little Manfred. And we'll have DM 2500 in our pockets."

But Anna was unconvinced. "I don't believe it. It's too easy. If it were that simple, they wouldn't give us all that money."

"It's a lot of money for us, but it's just pennies for the Americans. It also happens that our apartment looks right out on something they want to know about."

"What?"

"The bridge and the anti-aircraft batteries."

Anna gasped. "My God, they want you to be a spy! They can lock you up for life or even shoot you for that!"

"Only if they catch me." He tried to sound light-hearted, but she again burst into tears.

"Don't get hysterical," he said forcefully, holding her shoulders and shaking her. "I'm just going to go to our apartment and look out our kitchen window. They can't shoot me for that."

The more Anna objected, the more Weber became persuaded that going on the mission would be "a piece of cake." As dawn was breaking, he had convinced himself that he had hit the jackpot.

The housekeeper had laid out a substantial breakfast: apple juice, scrambled eggs, *Aufschnitt* or cold cuts, dark bread and creamy sweet butter, and a large pot of hot coffee. She had even gone out early that morning to buy some baby food. The Webers were still eating as Major Zachary Muldane arrived at exactly eight o'clock.

Anna had dark circles under her eyes from tears and lack of sleep. She refused to be taken in by the charm Muldane tried to summon for her, but fearful of all officialdom, she remained quiet and did not voice her anxieties. Muldane drank a cup of coffee with them and went downstairs, asking Weber to join him after he had finished breakfast. One last impassioned plea by Anna was disregarded. Weber, a stubborn man, had made up his mind.

When he went downstairs, Weber had a request. "Mr. Jones," he asked, "please be good enough to repeat the various promises that you and the other man made to me yesterday."

"I would be happy to," Muldane replied, indicating an easy chair next to his desk where Weber should sit down. "We will pay you DM 2500 for information you can obtain by looking out your apartment window."

"One trip only?"

"One trip."

"And your help in finding a job?"

"And on your return we will assist you in your job search in West Germany," Muldane confirmed.

"Mr. Jones," Weber asked, "would you put that in writing?"

"I'm afraid that's impossible," Muldane answered curtly. "You will have to take my word for it."

Weber hesitated. "If I am going to risk my life, I should have your promise in writing," he insisted.

"I said that was impossible," Muldane repeated, "but I can let you have some of the money in advance."

"How much?"

"How about DM 500?"

"That's only twenty percent of what you promised me," Weber replied. "I think I'm entitled to at least fifty percent. Let me have DM 1250."

Muldane's tone became severe. "You're entitled to nothing, Herr Weber. I will let you have DM 1000, and that will be the end of the discussion."

Muldane removed a small metal cash box from a lower desk drawer, opened it, and counted out DM 1000. Weber's eyes bulged. Muldane saw his reaction and was satisfied that Weber was committed. Deutsche Marks, he had learned, would do it every time.

"What if I don't come back?" Weber asked.

"What do you mean?"

"The remainder. Would Anna get it?"

"Of course."

"Can I have that in writing?" Weber asked.

"Trust me," Muldane said. "Americans, you know, keep their word." He looked at his watch. It was ten minutes to nine, time to get down to business. "There is a 12:42 train from Friedrichstrasse that you ought to be able to get," he said. "Now let me show you a few things."

Muldane reached into his black zippered folder and took out pictures of the latest Soviet radar equipment. One apparatus, mounted on the back of a truck, had been photographed during transport from behind curtained windows. Another installation was in place near a series of oil tanks, but the picture was fuzzy, probably having been taken from a moving train or car. Aerial photos were interesting for showing the radar's distinct diagonal emplacements.

"That's what we're looking for," Muldane said. "Have you ever seen anything like these near the bridge, Herr Weber?"

"No. I told you that yesterday."

"I thought that perhaps the pictures would have changed your mind. Well, all we want you to do is return to your apartment and look out of your window very attentively. Here is a small pair of East German binoculars. Hide them while you're on the train. They might be hard to explain. Take a good look at the anti-aircraft batteries near the bridge. Pay special attention to the land around them. That's where the radar would be."

"That's all?"

"That's all, and then come right back. Oh, by the way. Try not to be self-conscious. No one but you knows that you're on a mission. Don't start imagining that the police are on to you. If you begin to think that way, you'll act suspicious and that might well attract attention. Act normally and forget your assignment until you're in the apartment. Understood?"

"Yes, sir."

It was now nearly ten o'clock. Muldane gave Weber some East German money. "My driver will take you to our secure crossover point to East Berlin," Muldane said. "I'll wait for you here while you say goodbye to your family."

Weber went back upstairs and gave Anna the DM 1000. She clung to him as he assured her he would be back that night. "Stop worrying," he said, smoothing her hair from her face and kissing her. "All will be well. This is the beginning of our wonderful new life."

*   *   *

The 575th Air Supply Squadron held a weekly staff meeting every Saturday morning at 10:00 a.m. Cole sat at the end of a long table in the so-called Map Room with the unit's three other commis-

sioned officers seated to his left and right. Herter was at the opposite end with the cartographer and a few other senior civilian employees. A number of military enlisted personnel were seated in
the middle on both sides of the table. Folding chairs, placed along
the room's walls, were reserved for the remaining civilian personnel. That morning, as usual, Liebman and Pritzer both sat against
the wall.

Cole called the meeting to order. To his immediate right,
Muldane's chair was unoccupied. First, they proceeded to the weekly
review of the unit's target list. Each target had a designated seven-
digit code number, identifying its location, its type (airfield, ammunition dump, oil storage facility, rail junction, etc.); the priority assigned to its coverage, and the frequency of reports to be
generated. In addition, the code names of the agents responsible
for the target in question were highlighted.

Next, they reviewed the list of active agents, each identified by
his code name and the name of his handler. Currently, the 575th
Squadron had some two dozen agents in the field. About half of
them were "short-timers"—that is, refugees doing two or three
runs before "retiring"; the other half were steady "long-timers,"
who reported from time to time on specific targets in proximity to
their place of residence within the GDR. Over ninety percent of
the useful intelligence gathered came from these long-timers, who
were in the main supervised directly by Herter.

Cole was calling attention to revised due dates for reports to
the 2050th Air Support Wing in Wiesbaden when Muldane came
into the room and quietly slipped into his seat. Cole read out a few
of the latest Berlin Command bulletins, one of which recommended
a general tightening of security measures.

"This bulletin," Cole commented, "is prompted by a careless
slip-up by the Army. It should remind us all, and I can't repeat the
point often enough, that in our line of work there is zero tolerance
for carelessness. It can lead to breaches of security, and that in turn
can endanger our missions."

Apparently, the week before, a maid in an Army billet had

been found in possession of an Army Intelligence report. The CIC was investigating the incident. Stories of mishaps occurring in brother services were always well received.

Cole nodded at Carlton Herter and asked for his covert operations report. Herter began, as he always did, with a word of caution. "Since those present at this meeting possess varying degrees of security clearance and because in any event the need-to-know rule always applies to details of individual mission assignments, I will remain relatively general in my remarks. Nonetheless, I will disclose target priorities so that both our covert and overt operations can be coordinated."

Herter enumerated the targets—in the main the principal Soviet airfields and their support facilities in the GDR—that were now "well covered," either by agents sent into the field or by reconnaissance trips of the U.S. Military Mission in Potsdam. "No refugees need to be screened for any of these targets in the coming week," he advised. He then listed the targets that were of current interest. "In particular," he stated, "there are two to which I am assigning the highest priority: the airfield in Cottbus, where we believe that a squadron of FISHBEDS—the latest version of the Mig fighter—may have been spotted, and the bridge in Frankfurt/Oder, where the anti-aircraft defenses are perhaps being upgraded."

The soft-spoken cartographer showed slides of new maps of East Germany he had put together based on the latest intelligence reports; they indicated the locations of airfields and other military targets. He had been coaxed out of retirement because of his minute knowledge of East European geography, and led a contented, secluded existence with his charts.

"I would urge you all," Cole said, "to make good use of these new materials. All our efforts are worthless if we don't take advantage of our own output." He then asked, "Is there any other business?"

A sergeant spoke up. "I have put together a new schedule for night-watch duty, Colonel, which should take care of some recent complaints by both the civilian and enlisted personnel."

"That's fine, Sergeant," Cole said. "I assume the schedule has been posted on the bulletin board." The Sergeant confirmed that it had been.

As the meeting was breaking up, Pritzer approached Cole. "May I see you for a moment, Colonel?" he asked. Cole nodded, and Pritzer followed him and Muldane into Cole's office.

"What is it, Pritzer?" Cole asked, sitting down behind his desk. Muldane sat in a chair near the desk, while Pritzer awkwardly remained standing.

"I'd like to talk about a new assignment, sir," he said. "I'm getting a bit bored just screening refugees at Marienfelde."

"How long have you been at it?"

"Three years. Three long years."

"What else would you like to do?" Cole asked.

"Other than screw that sexy little wife of yours?" Muldane interjected.

Cole frowned while Pritzer forced a smile in pretense that he had not taken offense. "I was wondering if I couldn't be more useful to the unit"—Pritzer had learned that the military always talked in terms of the squadron or the unit—"doing something else, something more important."

"Like what?"

"I think I would enjoy working on the covert side. I have the necessary background, and I think it would be more interesting. I would hope that it might also mean a pay raise. I haven't had a raise in a long time. It would be a good change for me, I think, and," he added quickly, "for the unit."

Cole looked over at Muldane as if to ask whether he had briefed Pritzer on their previous evening's discussion. Muldane shook his head.

"Frankly, Pritzer, this is a coincidence. Major Muldane and I were talking about you just last night—about making such a change. However, I see two difficulties in assigning you to covert. First of all, you have a reputation of being a bit of a hot-head—too prone to fly off the handle, perhaps, to be a responsible handler."

Pritzer felt the blood rush to his head. He was about to deny the charge heatedly, but stopped short to avoid proving the allegation. Instead, he responded evenly. "I think it would be only fair for me to be given the chance."

"Yes, well. The second reason," Cole said, "is your wife. As an East German, she presents a potential security risk. She is no problem when you're screening incoming refugees. But if you were to work on the covert side, sending some of them back to the East on spying missions, well . . . that might be a different story." Cole looked over at Muldane, who nodded his agreement.

"You can't imagine anyone hating the GDR more than Jutta does, Colonel," Pritzer said vehemently, beads of perspiration forming on his forehead. "She has no family left there who could be used to pressure her. She was thoroughly checked out before we were given permission to marry. Anyway, I would never talk about my activities. I don't do that now." Even as he said it Pritzer realized that the statement was inaccurate, since he often regaled Jutta with stories, many of them exaggerated, about refugees he had seen.

"All right, Pritzer," Cole said. "I'll consider your request and let you know." Pritzer left the office, and after a few moments Cole and Muldane asked Herter to join them. "We're thinking of moving Pritzer into covert work," Cole said. "What do you think?"

Herter bridled. "Just because he speaks German and may be bored interviewing is no reason to make him a handler," Herter protested. "The job requires sensitivity—how far one can push an agent; judgment—what type of mission an agent can and can't do; patience and understanding—to establish a relationship of trust. Do you think that Pritzer has any of those qualifications?"

"Not really," Cole admitted, smiling at Herter's vehemence.

"You're describing an ideal, Carl," Muldane said, echoing Cole's remark the evening before. "We've got to deal with the poor specimens we have at our disposal."

This was an unpleasant truth that Herter, the perfectionist, did not wish to recognize. Muldane continued his argument. "How well do you think Zandt is now doing at Meisenstrasse?" he asked Herter.

"Not very well."

"You're damn right. I had to step in yesterday and turn some-one around to go back to Frankfurt/Oder. He couldn't do it him-self. Isn't it possible that Pritzer might do better?"

"Sure it's possible," Herter agreed. "But it's also possible that the moon is made of green cheese."

Muldane's jaw tightened. Carlton Herter had to be given due deference as an intelligence specialist, but as far as Muldane was concerned, the 575th was a military outfit and that meant that officers had the last word. "I say let's give him a chance," Muldane countered. "One thing going for Pritzer is that he's eager to get into covert work. He'll try hard to prove himself."

"Major," Herter replied, "it's not usually a good idea to let someone enter covert work who is eager for it. Doing that can lay the groundwork for a very unpleasant future surprise."

They continued their debate. In the end Cole decided to al-low Pritzer, under Muldane's close supervision, to handle not more than two agents for a three-month probationary period. During that time, Zandt would be removed from Meisenstrasse—to "shape him up"—and assigned to refugee screening at Marienfelde.

*   *   *

It was a sunny Saturday afternoon, with the kind of April sunlight that finally promised the end of Berlin's long, dark winter season. The perfect day, Cole had suggested to Brigitte Halder, for a stroll in the Grünewald, the large forest within Berlin's city limits which held a special meaning for them both. Cole walked out to his pride and joy, a small red MG convertible, and, though it was still cool, the bright afternoon sunlight inspired him to put the top down. Brigitte was bound to like that, he reflected.

As Cole began the short drive to Brigitte's home in Dahlem, where she lived with her father, he thought back to their first en-

counter. It had been a chance meeting one Sunday afternoon, en-
gineered by Graf, Brigitte's black labrador. Cole had been walking
in the Grünewald along a well-trodden path lined with tall trees
and strewn with pine needles when Graf, in a headlong dash after
a tennis ball, suddenly hurtled into him, momentarily throwing
him off balance. Brigitte ran up to Cole.

"I am so sorry," she said, a little out of breath. "I hope my dog
didn't hurt you."

With a twinkle in his eye, Cole replied, "Let me check. No, I
think I'm all right, Fraülein, but frankly, I can only really forgive
you if you'll join me for a cup of coffee."

Brigitte broke into a wide grin.

"Halder," she said, holding out her hand to shake. "Brigitte
Halder."

"Bud Cole," he replied, taking her hand and noting her firm,
cool grip.

"You are an American, I suppose," Brigitte said in very good
English.

"And my guess is that you are German," he responded.

They both laughed and set out slowly for the Waldhuette, a
popular small café at the end of the woodland trail, each taking
turns throwing the ball for an excited Graf to chase. It was too
chilly to sit on the Waldhuette's outside terrace, so they entered
the large rustic dining room and were shown to a small booth near
a window, where Graf settled down under the table.

"What will you have, Fraülein Halder? " Cole asked.

"I think I'll have a Berlin speciality, *Berliner Weisse mit Schuss*,
white beer with a dash of raspberry liqueur. Have you ever had it?"

"No, but I'll have one too."

Brigitte's laughter was frank, unrestrained, and charming as
the stocky waitress arrived with two enormous glass beer mugs,
and Cole's eyes opened wide in surprise. He followed her example
and poured his shot glass of liqueur into the mug, turning the
beer a pinkish color.

They sat for a long time, sipping their beers, chatting, both enjoying this unexpected company. Brigitte finally stood. "I should be going now, Mr. Cole," she said, again holding out her hand.

Cole rose and shook it. "It has been a great pleasure to meet you," he said. "Thank you for introducing me to Berlin beer." She turned and quickly walked away, holding Graf on a tight leash.

Cole was determined to see her again. She had given him her name, but, as he discovered, there were many Halders in the Berlin telephone directory, though no listing for a Brigitte Halder.

Not yet aware that she worked at the Clayallee Interrogation Center, Cole decided that his only hope for another meeting was to stake out the Waldhuette. He was there early the next Sunday afternoon, sitting at the same table, keeping a lookout down the forest path. Brigitte did not appear. It rained the following Sunday. But a week later there she suddenly was, with Graf bounding ahead of her. Giving Cole her broad, captivating smile, she joined him at "their table," as if this had been a prearranged encounter. They had Berliner Weisse and before leaving she accepted his invitation to dinner later that week. So it had begun, scarcely three months ago.

A year and a half earlier, Cole's fiancée had broken up with him, and her desertion had hurt. Since then Cole had lived a healthy if somewhat celibate officer's life— "somewhat celibate" because as a normal and attractive man he had little difficulty in finding willing partners for occasional sexual romps. Cole treated these as entertaining escapades, not as anything of consequence. But Brigitte, he instinctively felt, might be a different story.

Arriving at the small villa where Brigitte lived, Cole parked in front of the house, waiting, as she had asked, for her to come out. He resisted the temptation to blow the horn, which would doubtless have annoyed Brigitte's father, who seemed anything but welcoming. Brigitte soon appeared, accompanied by Graf, who rushed ahead and bounded into the back seat of the car. Brigitte, seeing that the car's top was down, began to tuck her long black hair beneath a brightly colored kerchief. She had classical good looks, with dark brown eyes that reflected her changing moods and contrasted dramatically with her white, almost translucent skin. She was tall and moved on her long legs as gracefully as a gazelle.

"It isn't summer yet, Colonel," she said as he leaned over to open the low car door for her. She was wearing a loose blue skirt and white blouse; her legs were bare, and the blouse did nothing to obscure the outline of her full breasts. She climbed nimbly into the front seat's small space and patted Graf, who was comfortably tucked in behind her. She looked lovely, Cole thought, every man's dream of a girl in a convertible.

"I have to return these books to Amerika Haus," she said. "I'm afraid they're two days overdue. Can we stop there on the way to the Grünewald?"

"It's in the opposite direction, Brigitte."

"So what? You'll have that much more time to drive your MG."

He pushed the starter and slid the floor stick shift into gear. The engine roared and with a widening grin Cole pulled out into the street.

He turned right on Clayallee, heading toward the urban center of West Berlin. The broad main thoroughfares had all been cleared of the rubble of World War II bombings, which as they approached the city center could be seen on either side, stacked in orderly piles on empty lots among the ruins. Veritable mountains of debris, overgrown by shrubs and wild grasses, dotted the Berlin landscape, providing playgrounds for the city's children on the remnants of the Thousand Year Reich.

There was little German civilian traffic except for bicycles. The speeding red MG had the road largely to itself, though Cole had to slow down as they hit the row of traffic lights on the Kurfürstendamm, known to Berliners by its affectionate abbreviation "Kudamm." A number of pedestrians looked askance at the seemingly carefree Brigitte with an American in a fancy sports car. But on the whole they were more curious than disapproving, since after the 1948 airlift most Berliners considered Americans as their friends, indeed as their saviors from the rampaging Red Army. Some even let themselves imagine that they had always been allies of the Americans against the ungodly Soviet Communists. It was a rewriting of history in which Brigitte did not participate.

Amerika Haus, a modern four-story steel and glass structure run by the United States Information Agency to promote American culture and ideas, was centrally located on Wittenbergplatz. The books in the library included American classics and lighter fare such as detective stories and romantic novels. The periodical section, with its array of magazines and newspapers, was particularly popular with a generation of Germans unaccustomed to being exposed to differing points of view. In addition lectures, exhibits, and movies were always well attended, since the postwar Berliners were starved for information and entertainment. Though all the programs were intended to show the States in the best possible light, their propaganda function was treated as anodyne compared to what Berliners had experienced a mere decade earlier.

Cole pulled into the parking lot behind Amerika Haus, and Brigitte tied Graf to the flagpole, the American flag fluttering at its top. Then she and Cole entered the library from the rear entrance on the ground floor.

Jutta Pritzer had been a recent and lively addition to the Amerika Haus staff. Three days a week, she checked library books in and out and in her spare time replaced them on the shelves. She was quick and efficient in her work, friendly and popular with her co-workers and with visitors. She seemed to reserve her aggressive qualities for her husband.

Brigitte and Jutta had met on a few social occasions, most recently at a cocktail party for some of the 575th Squadron staff. "I have an instinctive aversion to her. Call it my German female intuition," she had told Cole at the end of the evening.

"I call it your German jealousy," Cole had replied. Like most men, he found Jutta attractive and sexy. "You're jealous because she's a blonde. Or maybe," he teased, "because she's managed to get an American to marry her." Brigitte had given him a light tap on the head for that remark.

Brigitte now returned her books to Jutta, and the two chatted briefly. "Yes, Fraülein Halder, your name is still on the waiting list for that recent book on German immigrants to America," Jutta assured Brigitte. "I will put it aside for you the moment it is returned."

"Are you enjoying your job here?" Cole asked Jutta.

"I love it, Colonel," she said winningly. "Everyone is so nice. I get to meet so many interesting people. It's so much better than sitting around waiting for Helmut to come home." She laughed.

Cole and Brigitte left the building, untied an eager Graf, and climbed back into the MG. As they drove off to the Grünewald, Brigitte shook her head and then said seriously, "There's something about that girl that isn't quite right."

Cole laughed. "There's a lot about her husband Pritzer that isn't quite right either. They're a perfect match."

They parked near an entrance to the park and with Graf prancing ahead walked down the pine-needle-covered path into the forest.

"Let's stop talking about Jutta," he said, "and concentrate on a much more interesting subject."

"And what could that possibly be, Bud?" she asked, anticipating his response.

"You and me. Let's talk about you," he said, taking her hand.

"What about me?"

"I wish you'd relax a little more. Let yourself go. Have some fun. Enjoy yourself a little."

Brigitte pulled her hand away. "That's easy for you to say. You are an American colonel, and you won the war. Try to feel what it's like to be on the losing side. It's not that simple to be carefree when your fiancé has been killed in the war, and you're trying to put your life back together."

Cole put his arm around Brigitte's shoulders and spoke gently: "Brigitte, I'm sorry. I didn't mean to upset you. I'm trying to be helpful." He paused. "I'm very fond of you, you know."

They walked on in silence. Brigitte picked up a stick and threw it, and Graf bounded off, proudly bringing it back. Cole tried again: "I probably shouldn't say this, but I don't know who else will. And someone should. Brigitte, it's been twelve years since your fiancé was killed. You can't continue grieving all your life. You're a young, good-looking woman. You've got to put all this past behind you and get on with your own life."

But for Brigitte the sorrowful past remained hauntingly present. She slowly turned toward Cole and, looking straight into his eyes, spoke quietly, her voice a trifle unsteady. "Look, Bud," she said, "you are a very nice man. I enjoy being with you, going to a movie or walking in the Grünewald. It's the first male companionship . . ." She hesitated. "You are the first friend I've had in years. I've been very lonely. But please don't push me, and don't have any illusions about me either. I no longer seem to have deep feelings." Tears welled up in her eyes. "I may never have any again. I think that my heart died with Franz in Stalingrad." She brushed her tears away and looked around to find another stick for Graf to chase.

Cole put his arm around her shoulders and for a long time they walked on quietly in the calm silence of the deep forest.

*   *   *

Norman Liebman was in the PX cafeteria for an early supper; afterward he would probably take the U-Bahn, West Berlin's subway system, down to the Kudamm to see a movie. He had become a vegetarian, not because he did not relish the taste of meat but rather as a personal protest against slaughterhouses. Going down the line with his plastic tray, he settled on asparagus as an appetizer; a mixture of peas, carrots, and Brussels sprouts; and a fruit salad. He chose a small unoccupied table against the wall, sat down with his tray, and slowly began to eat, all the while scanning BZ, the Berlin tabloid, to see what movies were playing. At the same time Eugene Zandt, the interrogator from the safe house on Meisenstrasse, holding a tray piled high with food, stopped by the cashier at the end of the line. He looked around the room and, spotting Liebman, hurried over to him.

"Evening, Norman," he said. "Mind if I join you?"

"Of course not, Eugene. Sit down." Liebman folded the paper and put it aside. Other than their employer, these two had little in common—Liebman a sensitive intellectual and Zandt an insecure egotist.

The latter was eager to talk. "How about that meeting this morning?" he chortled. "I bet that maid in the Army billet got more than a classified report, huh?"

Liebman looked around. "Keep your voice down," he said.

Zandt was undeterred. "Why the hell doesn't the Stasi send me some knockout babe to finagle some classified documents? I'd sure give her the goods. Yes, sir," he repeated with emphasis, "I'd sure as hell put the blocks to her."

Liebman looked at the shrunken little man and marveled at his capacity for self-delusion. He decided that a bit of mockery would be the appropriate response.

"My friend," he said with a straight face, "the Stasi hasn't sent you any of their female agents because they've decided you'd be too formidable an adversary." Zandt did not reply; his mouth was full of mashed potatoes.

To make conversation and having first checked that no one else was within earshot, Liebman asked about the refugee from Frankfurt/Oder he had sent over to the safe house that morning. Zandt swallowed and then let loose a stream of invective about snotty officers making life unbearable for civilians. "After all," he said, "we're the ones doing all the work."

Liebman refused to be drawn into name-calling, suspecting that any adverse comment he might make would, if it served his purposes, be reported by Zandt.

"What is the latest outrage?" Liebman asked pleasantly.

Zandt recounted that morning's episode with Weber. "I tried to get him to go back to Frankfurt/Oder. He didn't want to go; he was happy to have escaped with his wife and kid. Why the hell should we coerce him to return?"

It was evident that Zandt was not objecting on any moral

grounds, Liebman thought. He was simply making excuses for his own failure.

"How did Muldane do with him?"

"I don't know," Zandt replied sullenly. "All I know is that he took over from me yesterday afternoon. Then he sent for the man's wife and kid, and they all spent the night at the safe house."

"Sounds like a done deal."

"And it probably means that I'll be judged to have screwed up," Zandt said in the hope that Liebman would contradict that assessment. But Liebman's thoughts were on the fact that another man's life would be put at risk to answer a probably meaningless inquiry.

Leaving Zandt to his anger, Liebman, deep in thought, walked back to his apartment through a wooded section behind the PX. He was no longer in the mood for a movie.

Zandt might not be alone in possessing a capacity for self-delusion, Liebman told himself ruefully. Was his own life devoid of self-deceit? Time and again, he had tried to convince himself that his overt interrogations did not cause harm. Yet he could not eradicate some lingering qualms.

He had an uneasy premonition about the refugee from Frankfurt/Oder. All he had done, he reflected, was to question him on a target he was assigned to cover, nothing more. But was his role as pure as he pretended? What if the man went back and was caught in Frankfurt/Oder? Would Liebman really bear no moral responsibility? Wasn't he the one who had deliberately started Weber on his path back to the East?

When Liebman got back to his apartment, he poured himself a cognac and selected some records of Mozart string quartets. Their divine harmony, he hoped, would assuage his restless and conflicting thoughts.

*   *   *

Earlier that Saturday morning Muldane's driver had taken Hans
Weber in a battered Volkswagen with West Berlin civilian plates to
a crossover point in the Kreuzberg district. A tunnel, constructed
of connecting cellars in a row of houses along the Sector border,
provided an exit to an East Berlin side street. Weber emerged from
that exit and took the S-Bahn to Friedrichstrasse. He easily made
the 12:42 train.

There were few passengers on the train that afternoon. Weber
had been concerned that the conductor of the previous day's morning run might be on board and recognize him. But a different
conductor took his ticket and paid him no heed. Weber then worried about how to explain the field glasses he was carrying. Of
course they were of East German origin, but what was he doing
with them? He was no bird-watcher, and he could think of no
other innocent explanation. He might say that he had just bought
them, second-hand, but how would he respond to the follow-up
questions: where? why? for how much? He got up and hid the
field glasses behind the radiator in the toilet, deciding he would
collect them at the end of the journey. Ten minutes later he went
back to wipe off his fingerprints.

The train passed through a forest of birch trees devoid of un-
derbrush, with a dizzying number of vertical columns—a natural
cathedral. A little farther on, a solitary Russian tank stood in a
field, the barrel of its turret cannon pointed skyward. Then the
train pulled into Finsterwalde. Weber felt reassured; from now on
the alibi that he was visiting his cousins would be more plausible.
Twenty minutes later the train's locomotive broke down. It took
more than an hour for a replacement to be located and put into
service. The train arrived in Frankfurt/Oder an hour late, at 15:36.
Weber retrieved his field glasses from the toilet.

Leaving the station, he retraced his steps of the morning before. Every few minutes he looked around to check that he was not
being followed. Then he remembered Muldane's caution to act

normally. Constantly turning around could attract attention. He forced himself to look only straight ahead.

He climbed the stairs and unlocked the apartment door he had secured some thirty-six hours before. It seemed like a lifetime ago, like a place he recognized from a dream. He went over to the kitchen window and stepped to the side to prevent his neighbor, Frau Brubacher, a busybody, from seeing him look out. The bridge was there—a tranquil scene in the late afternoon sun. He shook his head in disbelief. This commonplace view was worth a fortune to the Americans. He wondered what matter-of-fact scene in the West the Russians would find valuable. He suppressed a laugh; he realized he was thinking like a double agent.

Weber steadied himself by the window and began to examine the bridge carefully through the field glasses. The anti-aircraft emplacements on either side of the bridge on the east bank of the Oder were clearly visible, but there were no radar installations to be seen, either of the type Muldane had shown him or of any other kind. He continued to scan the bridge from one end to the other and also examined the adjoining area. There was nothing new or out of the ordinary, except some earth-moving equipment near the anti-aircraft battery on the south side of the bridge. Some minor excavation was in progress there, and mounds of earth that had been removed were being leveled.

That was it, Weber concluded. He could think of nothing further to do. He put the field glasses on the kitchen table and decided to leave them behind. One less thing to worry about on the trip back, and one less thing to explain.

He carefully locked the apartment door and ran down the stairs, once again avoiding an encounter with Herr Metzger, the building superintendent. With a light-hearted step he walked back toward the railway station. Easiest DM 2500 I'll ever make, he thought. Then he cautioned himself: Don't get cocky or overconfident. You've still got to get back.

He suddenly felt hungry. After all, he hadn't eaten since breakfast. He looked at his watch; it was 17:30. On weekends the trains to Berlin left at twenty-three minutes past the hour. He had enough time to get a bite to eat. Best not to go to the little snack bar in the train station, he decided. Instead, he stopped at a small Bierstube on the way and ordered a hard roll with salami and a beer. Five men, also drinking beer, were at the next table. Weber wondered what they would say if they knew he was on a secret spy mission. The beer was cold. He gulped it avidly and ordered a second glass while happily taking large bites of the salami roll.

The return trip was uneventful. The conductor was the same one who had taken his ticket earlier that afternoon, but he did not seem to recognize Weber. At least he gave no sign of any such recognition. Weber had a few anxious moments with the thought that conductors were trained to remain impassive but to alert the police at the next stop. But nothing untoward happened, and Weber dozed the rest of the way to East Berlin, where the train arrived on time at 20:11.

He took the S-Bahn back to that morning's crossover point. As instructed, he first walked around the neighborhood until he was sure he wasn't being followed. A group of young East Berlin rowdies—probably children of Party officials—were shouting and singing their way down the sidewalk, pushing everyone else aside. Weber quickly crossed the street to avoid a confrontation. Then, with no one in sight and using the codes to secure access he had been given, Weber returned to West Berlin by the same route of connected cellars.

Within the hour he was back at the safe house with Anna and the baby. She threw her arms around him, shuddering with relief. She had been frantic all day, convinced that the worst was inevitable. Weber was jubilant. The trip had been as simple as Muldane had described.

"Nothing to it," he assured Anna. He sat down and pulled her over onto his lap. She pressed close and whispered, "I don't care. As long as you're back. I've been so frightened."

"Getting money out of the Americans," he crowed, "is like taking candy from a baby."

Anna slowly calmed down. "I am a little too anxious some-times," she confessed. "I was afraid that with our dreams suddenly realized, they would just as quickly all disappear."

"No, Anna, don't worry. We've made it. We are safe in the West, and we have 2500 marks!" he said, gently kissing her cheek.

Anna gave him a weak smile. "You were right to go back quickly just once," she admitted. "Or maybe . . . maybe you were just lucky."

The housekeeper had prepared a typical Berlin meal—*Königsberger Klopse*, or large meat dumplings, in a white cream sauce with capers, boiled potatoes, and cabbage—which Weber ate with gusto and Anna with thanksgiving. They were soon in bed where their love-making was as hearty as their supper.

*   *   *

That evening when Jutta returned home, she found Pritzer in an unusually upbeat mood. "What is it, Mutiger?" she asked. "Why the big satisfied grin?"

"I'll tell you after dinner."

"Tell me now," she insisted.

He motioned toward the kitchen.

"Don't be so stupid," she said. "Frau Engelhart is as deaf as Beethoven. Tell me." She pushed an unresisting Pritzer down on the sofa and threatened to tickle him if he didn't reveal his secret immediately.

"I've been asked to work on covert operations," he whispered proudly.

"What does that mean?" she asked.

"I'm going to be engaged in secret work," he explained. "What I'll be doing will be classified."

"Are you going to be a handler?"

"Shh! Quiet."

"All right," she lowered her voice, "but will you be sending spies over to the GDR?"

"I guess so. Yes, of course."

She jumped up. "That's marvelous," she exclaimed. "You'll show those East German bastards. From now on, I'm living with a Cold War hero." Pritzer had the uncomfortable feeling that she was mocking him, but she spoke with such fervor he felt exhilarated.

"Now listen," he warned, "as far as anyone else is concerned, I just interview refugees. If what I told you gets out, I'd be fired—if not put in jail. Remember that."

"You can count on me," she promised earnestly. "I'll never tell a soul."

"You'd better not."

After a while she asked, "Are you going to get a raise?"

"Not right away," Pritzer said defensively. In fact, Cole had not said anything about more money. "Probably after a few months."

"Oh, it doesn't matter, Mutiger, I'm so excited. When we're snuggled close together in bed and no one can hear us, will you tell me about your adventures?"

"Don't be ridiculous, Jutta. You know I couldn't do that. That would be revealing military secrets."

"Oh, I don't mean telling me where you're sending people and what for. I know you have to keep that secret. I just thought you could tell me some personal things—you know, some stories about people's lives. That would be so thrilling!"

"Absolutely not, Jutta. I don't want you asking any more questions like that," he said sternly. "Just be glad that I told you of my change in jobs." Pritzer had the sinking feeling that he shouldn't have done even that.

Day 3 Sunday

Major Zachary Muldane drove his two-door black Buick sedan to Pritzer's house at quarter of eight in the morning. It was foggy and drizzling, a typical Berlin spring morning. Pritzer was waiting at the curb, holding an open umbrella. He had been awakened by Muldane's call an hour before.

"We're off to the safe house," Muldane explained, as Pritzer awkwardly scrambled into the car. "I'm going to debrief a guy, and I want you to listen in because he may be your agent from now on."

"Why? Will he be going back?"

"Probably," Muldane replied wryly, "though he doesn't know it yet. Don't say anything; just listen. I'll introduce you as Herr Steiner. OK?" Pritzer nodded.

They stopped at the 575th office and woke the guard, still asleep that Sunday morning on the cot near the barred and locked entrance door. Muldane opened the small safe in the orderly room and signed for some cash he would give Weber. He picked up the folder on the Frankfurt/Oder bridge, which contained pictures of new Soviet radar installations ringing Moscow that Herter had left for him the night before. He checked the incoming telexes and found nothing that required immediate attention. The situation board showed that three agents, including Weber, had returned in the last twelve hours.

They drove to the Meisenstrasse safe house where Weber—shaved, showered, and with his dark hair slicked back—was waiting downstairs. He greeted Muldane and Herr Steiner. He was obviously in a buoyant mood. Merely to make small talk, Muldane asked Weber what time he had come back. (The question was superfluous, since according to standard operating procedure the guard at the safe house had called the 575th office the night before to report Weber's return.)

"I returned at 9:15 last night."

"Easy, wasn't it?"

"Yes," Weber agreed with a grin.

"I told you there was nothing to worry about. Now, what did you see?"

"Nothing, really."

"The anti-aircraft guns are still there?"

Weber laughed. "Yes, of course."

"All four batteries?"

"Yes."

"On the other side of the Oder? Two batteries on each side of the bridge?"

"Yes."

"What was the weather like?"

"Overcast but bright. I had no problem seeing each gun. I could see them clearly. I used the field glasses."

Muldane consulted his folder then asked, "Nothing else to report?"

"No."

"No radar batteries?"

"No, there was nothing of the kind you showed me near the anti-aircraft guns."

"But somewhere else?"

"What do you mean?"

"Did you see any radar equipment somewhere else, not near the bridge but, for example, in town?"

"No."

"All right, Herr Weber, now take your time and think carefully. Are you sure you saw nothing out of the ordinary, nothing that was different, nothing that had changed since the last time you looked out your kitchen window?"

Weber furrowed his brow. "The only thing that was new . . ."

"Yes?" Muldane leaned forward.

"It's really not worth mentioning."

"Let me be the judge of that." Muldane's tone was severe.

"They seemed to be excavating and leveling some land on the other side of the river."

"Near the bridge?" Muldane asked sharply.

"Yes—in fact, next to one of the anti-aircraft batteries on the right . . ."

"On the right?"

"On the right side of the bridge when you look across the river; the south side of the bridge, if you like."

Pritzer coughed and was about to speak, but Muldane shook his head. Pritzer remained quiet.

"Herr Weber, what made you think there was some excavation going on? It's across the river. You're a kilometer or so away."

"There's some earth-moving equipment and a lot of sand that must have been shoveled out."

"What kind of equipment?"

"I saw two tractors," Weber replied slowly, gathering his thoughts, "and a large steam shovel and, yes, also I believe a steamroller. There might have been some others, but that's all I saw."

Pritzer, anxious to participate and unable to control himself any longer, asked, "Was anyone working on the site?"

"No. It was Saturday afternoon."

"Thank you, Herr Steiner," Muldane said pointedly. He turned again toward Weber. "Are you certain that this work you are describing had just begun? After all, you never looked across the river much, did you, Herr Weber—that is, before you were given our assignment?"

Weber smiled. "No, but that pile of sand is really noticeable. It would be hard to miss even from across the river, and then there's all that machinery."

Muldane excused himself, went to the office next door, and called Herter at home on a secure line. Herter picked up the phone immediately, and Muldane relayed Weber's report on the earth-moving equipment.

"Could this be preparatory work for the type of radar we're looking for?" he asked.

Herter was hesitant. "Perhaps, but I wouldn't jump to any conclusions."

"Isn't that where the radar would be placed?" Muldane insisted.

"Yes," Herter conceded, "as close as possible to the guns and to the extent possible aligned with their trajectory."

"Could you deploy another agent in the field to monitor this target?" Muldane asked.

"Unfortunately," Herter replied, "the man who regularly covered the Cottbus airfield was arrested last week." He sighed. "Such a pity, he would have been ideal. He was an expert on air defenses."

"No one else?"

"No, no one better than this guy Weber. With his apartment he has a ringside seat on the work in progress. We've got to train him and keep him focused on the target," Herter urged. "Remember, the bridge is a Number One Headquarters Priority. We've got to find out what that digging is all about. Offer him what it takes, Major, and don't let him back out."

Pritzer and Weber both looked up as Muldane came back into the room. "Well, thank you, Herr Weber," Muldane said. "That was a most interesting report. By the way, can I please have the field glasses?"

Weber was taken aback. "I left them in the apartment," he stammered. "I didn't know you wanted them back."

"They were perfectly good glasses, weren't they?"

"Yes, of course, but I was afraid I'd be caught with them on the train." He paused, hoping for Muldane's understanding. "I wouldn't have known how to explain them."

"That's all right," Muldane replied coolly. "No harm done." Pritzer noted that Weber had been put on the defensive.

Muldane took some money out of a long brown envelope. "Here is your remaining DM 1500." He counted out the DM 100 notes meticulously under Weber's hungry gaze and handed them to him, shook his hand, and as a clear signal that the mission was terminated, said: "Thank you, Herr Weber, for a job well done."

Weber took the money, counted the bills himself, and, when he had finished, reverently folded the bank notes and put them in his trouser pocket. Never before had he possessed such wealth. Muldane watched him carefully and then, in the guise of polite conversation, asked what he planned to do now. Weber replied that he would look for a job, any job in West Germany. Muldane assured him amiably that he and his family would be flown out of West Berlin, whenever he wanted. "We owe you that," Muldane remarked grandly, "and as I promised, we will give you some help."

Weber was all smiles as Muldane stood, gathered his papers together, and then, as if voicing an afterthought, turned toward Weber and said: "How would you like to double, perhaps even triple, the money you already have?"

Startled, Weber asked, "How?"

Muldane sat down again across from Weber. "To tell you the truth," he confided, "I'm intrigued by all that digging you saw on the other side of the river. I'd like to know more about it."

"What more is there to know?"

"Maybe when they start digging again tomorrow we'll begin to understand what they have in mind."

Weber stood up. "I am not going back again," he said resolutely, staring at Muldane without blinking. Muldane returned the gaze, seriously but not angrily. "Not even for another DM 5000?" he asked softly.

Weber looked surprised and did not immediately respond. Muldane pursued the opening: "It was so easy, wasn't it? Instead of DM 5000, how about DM 10,000 for one more quick in and out? What do you say?"

Weber was speechless.

"Let's look at this logically," Muldane continued. Although his arguments were couched in reasonableness, the driving force remained the 10,000 Deutsche Marks. "Because of this week's school vacation, you won't be missed in Frankfurt for another eight days. Isn't that right?"

Weber nodded.

"Your friends and colleagues believe you're out of town visiting cousins. So where is the risk?"

"What if they see me back in town?" Weber asked.

Muldane was encouraged. The question showed that Weber was wavering. "That's simple. You just have to say that you returned to get something or do something. As a matter of fact, you might make it a point to drop by the school. Pick up a book or some homework or what have you. Tell anyone you see that Anna and the baby are still with your cousins, that you're all having a very pleasant time. A perfect cover!"

"The school is closed during vacation," Weber stated. "There is no one there."

Muldane did not pursue the invention of a cover story but sat quietly and expressionless, waiting for Weber to mull over his proposal. Pritzer looked quizzically at Muldane, who with his hands together stared intently at the floor boards.

Weber was calculating feverishly. The Americans, he told himself, had kept their word. He had DM 2500 in hand. Now he was being offered DM 10,000 more, a veritable fortune. And the American was right. It had been easy, and if he went back again now, there would be no reason to suspect him—certainly not of spying. The worst charge, if he were caught, would be of having tried to flee the Socialist Fatherland. The punishment for that was not particularly severe for professionals like him whom the State needed. There was an acute shortage of teachers; so many had already fled. He would be watched closely, of course, which would mean being separated from Anna and the baby for a while—until he could manage another escape. He wrestled silently with that possibility and concluded that there was practically no chance of being caught. In other words, the money was worth the risk.

But if he agreed to go back, he would try to get more money. After all, the Americans seemed to have an endless supply. "I'll consider going back one more time, that's all," he announced, "but only for DM 15,000. After all, you're asking me to risk my life."

Muldane's response was swift; he knew he had him. "I said DM 10,000, which as you well know is more than generous for a little day's excursion. If you don't want to go, tell me, and I'll send someone else."

Weber began to buckle. "When do you want to know?" he asked.

"Right now!"

Muldane had turned savage, and Weber wilted. "I want half the money in advance," he declared.

"Agreed," Muldane said. "Now let's get to work." He showed Weber the new pictures of Soviet radar installations. One was a drawing that had been traced from a picture in a Soviet military manual. The radar disk was oval in shape and appeared disproportionately large for its underpinnings. There was a photograph of a smiling young woman with the radar and an armed guard visible over her left shoulder. The radar portion of the photo had been enlarged, and Muldane described for Weber the amount of space that would have to be cleared to accommodate this equipment.

"I want you to see," Muldane said, "whether there is any similar excavation near the three other AAs." Weber looked puzzled. "That's what we call anti-aircraft batteries," Muldane explained.

"Couldn't one radar guide more than one anti-aircraft battery?" Weber asked.

Muldane was pleased by the question. Weber, he realized, had the makings of a savvy agent. "Technically, yes," he replied, "but we understand that the Soviets have very few personnel trained to operate the equipment in a multi-battery mode."

Muldane reached into his pocket and handed Weber what looked like a thin East German cigarette lighter with a nondescript tin casing.

"What's this?" Weber asked.

"It's a Minolta camera with a very accurate long-range lens. It's simple to operate. Look here. To take a picture, you merely press the button for the flame. The film has 64 frames; no need to focus or make any other adjustment. You do need a minimum of light, however. It doesn't take pictures in the dark." He gave a short, mirthless laugh.

"If I'm caught with that, they'll shoot me or at least put me in jail for life," Weber protested.

"So don't get caught with it. At any hint of trouble, throw it away. It will look just like an ordinary lighter that has run out of fuel. Anyway, no one in the East has ever seen a camera like this."

This was a deliberate lie. The Stasi had confiscated more than a dozen similar models. However, Muldane's purpose was to reassure Weber, and in his view agents were reassured just as effectively by lies as by the unvarnished truth. He took Weber over to the window and let him take a few photos.

Weber beamed. "This is quite a toy," he said.

"I suggest you leave early tomorrow morning," Muldane told him. "In case of rain, you should postpone your trip for a day. Bad weather might stop the excavation work and in any event I want some clear pictures."

Weber nodded his head in agreement.

"Also, you told me that you had applied to the Education Ministry for a new teaching job but that you haven't gotten a reply. Is that right?"

"That's correct."

"Good. Upon your arrival in East Berlin, stop at the Education Ministry to inquire about that job application. That should give you an iron-clad alibi for being in East Berlin."

Weber was impressed by Muldane's meticulous attention to detail.

Muldane and Pritzer got up to leave. "What about my money?" Weber asked.

"I wouldn't forget that," Muldane said smoothly. Once again he took the brown envelope out of his folder and this time counted out DM 5000. Weber's hands trembled as he accepted the money. Muldane smiled and said, "The driver will pick you up at 6:30 tomorrow morning."

"If it's not raining . . ."

"That's right. Call the driver again when you're back—and, by the way, good luck."

Weber was left alone in a dazed state. He had DM 6500 in his hands with a promise of another DM 5000 on his return the next day—almost a year's salary for a teacher in Frankfurt/Oder. Was Anna right, he asked himself? Was this too good, too easy, to be true? Yet what was more "true" in the German sense than a fistful of Deutsche Marks? One more quick trip, and their future was assured.

Weber no longer had any doubts, but he knew that he would have to persuade Anna. That would not be easy. She had all those typically female premonitions. Also, she was not adventurous. She had not wanted to leave Frankfurt/Oder in the first place. Stay put and make the best of it, had been her motto. It had taken months to convince her to seek a better life in the West for themselves and above all for little Manfred.

She was also inflexible. Now that they had made it to the West, she was terrified by any thought of his returning. She was sure that destiny would punish them for overreaching. For what was it, if not overreaching, to earn a fortune for doing practically nothing? All that money, she would say, must have come out of someone's hide and for that there was bound to be retribution. Weber had heard the litany before. He did not doubt that he would be subjected to it again.

Muldane stopped briefly at the 575th and left a short note for Herter summarizing Weber's report. He then drove Pritzer back to his house. "Sorry to have spoiled your Sunday morning," Muldane said, "but I hope it was instructive."

"You were terrific, Major."

"I'm not fishing for compliments, Pritzer," Muldane said curtly. "I want you to learn how to do this. Remember, keep agents off balance, the carrot always in front of their noses. Never give them everything they want. Tell them they're expendable, even when, like Weber this morning, they're not. Praise should always be mixed with some criticism. Always tell them to do better next time."

"I understand."

"Good. I'm going to turn Weber over to you. You handle him from now on."

"Isn't this his last trip?"

Muldane laughed as he pulled into Pritzer's driveway. "Once they've gotten this close to the honey-pot, they always come back for more."

"All of them?"

"All the ones I've ever known. I'll bet you that our friend Weber will be going back to Frankfurt/Oder for a long time to come."

"For how long?"

"For as long as we need him or . . ."

"Or what?"

"Or until he gets caught."

*   *   *

After attending the American Protestant church service conducted at The Outpost—the Berlin Command's movie theater—Carlton Herter returned to his office. He was anxious to transmit the information that Muldane's source had supplied. Stale intelligence was equal to stupidity, he liked to say. Anything new on a target, especially one that Headquarters had designated as a Number One Priority, had to be passed on at once. With no cipher clerk in the office, Herter encoded the message himself—it was good, he reminded himself, to stay in touch with the nuts and bolts of intelligence.

Muldane's report had been concise, and Herter only added his professional view on what the report did and did not signify. In sum, he concluded that further clarification of the excavations in Frankfurt/Oder was required and stated that an agent would be returning tomorrow for more detailed observations. He gave the coded dispatch to the corporal on duty that afternoon to teletype to Headquarters, the 2050th Air Support Wing in Wiesbaden.

Herter returned to his office and closed the door. Here, surrounded by his files, reports, codes, maps, safe, and locked cabinets, he felt content and at peace. It was his spiritual home, the deliberately sparsely furnished apartment in the BOQ but an impersonal resting place. Herter saw intelligence work as a means to achieve some understanding in a confusing world. To him, a confirmed bachelor with no strong family ties or outside interests, it was an all-encompassing craft, not to mention a challenging game of wits. Herter was patriotic, but devoid of any ideological commitment. He felt no personal animosity toward his adversaries, viewing them with respect, as opposing chess players.

Herter lit his pipe and sat back, letting his mind wander. This excavation at the Frankfurt/Oder bridge—there was probably nothing to it, he thought, and yet it would make some sense to bring in radar and sharpen the accuracy of the AA batteries. It would be intriguing to learn what that digging was all about. Every upgrading of the Soviet defensive posture had to be watched carefully and analyzed for its portent. An impersonal intellectual puzzle. Just what he liked best.

*　　*　　*

Jutta was at home when Pritzer returned from his meeting with Weber. She was flushed with excitement. Taking his hands and pulling him into the living room, she asked eagerly: "How did it go?"

"Very interesting," Pritzer replied reservedly.

"Better than interrogating the riffraff at Marienfelde, eh?"

"Damn right. Really rather exciting."

"Anything you can tell me? I'm *sooo* curious," she purred. They sat on the sofa where she gazed up at him expectantly.

"Actually, yes," he said, breaking into a grin. He got up and went into the hall where he had left his briefcase. Jutta watched him open it and carefully take out a small leather pouch. He returned to the sofa, unbuttoned the pouch, and to Jutta's surprise pulled out a small black revolver.

"Let me see it," she said, reaching for the gun.

He held her back. "No," he said firmly. "This is not a toy, Jutta. I need this for protection, now that I'm in covert work. But you're not to touch it. Do you understand?"

"Yes," she said meekly. She seemed astonished, he noted. He had been excited himself when the Sergeant had issued him the weapon and suggested he try it out in the pistol range in the basement of the Clayallee Headquarters compound.

"What kind is it?" she asked.

"It's a 28-caliber Beretta. You can see it's very thin and small and can easily fit into my coat pocket. I'm going to keep it in the drawer of my night table. It will always be loaded, so don't go near it."

He slid it back into the leather pouch, which he gingerly put on a side table. She snuggled closer to him. "Is there anything else you can tell me?" she asked.

"Well, not really. This is all very secret stuff, Jutta. You've got to realize that."

"Oh, I don't want to know anything secret. Nothing that you shouldn't tell me. Just some unimportant little detail that isn't secret but that can give me an idea of what your new life is like. I want to be part of your life, you know."

Pritzer knew full well that he must say nothing further, but he softened. Jutta's eager face looking up at him, and the hope it inspired that he might win back some of her admiration, made him decide to say something, something innocuous. The regulations were specific that nothing whatsoever pertaining to covert activities was to be discussed. However, Pritzer reasoned that he was smart enough to carry out the intent of the regulations without following the precise letter of the law. He would be careful not to reveal anything that might constitute a breach of security.

He put his arm around her, and she pressed closer. "We heard a report from a man who has just returned from the East," he whispered.

"Yes? Then what?"

Pritzer hesitated before replying, "We sent him back for more information."

"How exciting! Was he frightened?"

"No. There was no reason for him to be afraid."

"Why not? He might be arrested."

Pritzer replied sharply, "I'm afraid that's all I can tell you."

"Of course, I understand. How wonderful," she sighed. "My Mutiger is a spy! I am married to a spy!" She gave him an enthusiastic hug.

"Shhh!" he warned. "Stop it, or I won't ever tell you anything like that again." She quieted down and let her hand graze his face and then slowly travel down his body. She breathed softly and irregularly through open lips, her eyes unfocused. Pritzer's reaction was immediate arousal, and as Jutta's fingers unfastened his trousers and caressed his genitals, Pritzer's last thought, before he surrendered to passion, was the certainty that happiness had been restored to his life.

*　　*　　*

Bud Cole appreciated haute cuisine. Some might think this unusual for a career Air Force pilot from a small southern town. But that would overlook both the delicacies of southern cooking, for which Cole's mother was locally renowned, and his exposure in his years of globe-circling flights to a wide variety of the world's culinary dishes. He had, in short, become a gourmet as well as something of a gourmand, and had soon discovered that the best food in Berlin was, not surprisingly, to be found in the French officers' mess.

It was difficult for him to reciprocate on a social basis; his French guests had been condescending the first and only time he had invited them to the American officers' dining room at Harnack Haus. Instead, he had embarked on a plan to "liaise" with the French, intimating from time to time that he had intelligence information to pass on "unofficially" to America's oldest allies. Such a hint invariably led to a dinner invitation from Colonel Durafour, the head of French Military Intelligence in Berlin.

During these repasts, after an abundant round of apéritifs, Cole between bites would talk vaguely and imprecisely of important missions about to be launched, or of defectors about to arrive with secrets of particular significance for the French, or again—and this was always received with the greatest attention—of a plot the British were hatching against the French which he could help to thwart. Very little information was ever in fact transferred on these occasions, but the French kept taking Cole's bait because they wouldn't risk missing out on a possible intelligence nugget.

Before any such meeting Cole and Herter always discussed two questions: what would the French be interested in learning, and what might the 575th be willing to pass on? These were invariably difficult matters. On the one hand, letting the French know the American targets might lead the French to supply additional information. That, though unlikely, would be an obvious plus. However, tipping the American hand in this fashion might disclose some weak spots. Worse, it could lead to French agents doing double duty in the same sensitive areas, with obvious added risks to both sides. In the end, they usually decided that Cole should let slip some red herrings, that he should refer to one or more obvious targets that needed updating and perhaps reveal one target of actual current importance. This involved no breach in security, for the American Intelligence Services were mandated to share information of interest to their Western Allied counterparts, a mandate that as a practical matter was only complied with in exceptional circumstances.

The day was clear and sunny as Cole drove to the French Sector in anticipation of a leisurely and delectable Sunday lunch. The bridge in Frankfurt/Oder was the morsel that he would be tendering, and during the drive he considered how best to drop that hint without actually divulging the identity of the target.

The French Officers' Club was located in a handsome villa on a landscaped knoll overlooking the Tegeler See in the northern part of the city. The staff was entirely French, in contrast to the German help found in the British and American clubs. The French explained that this staffing was based on security considerations, which made sense, but many still suspected that it was the quality of service rather than any concern for security that underlay the policy.

Colonel Durafour was in the hall waiting to greet his guest. Durafour's English was approximate, Cole's French nonexistent; their conversations always had a tentative and halting quality.

They went first into the bar with its large window offering a view on the well-tended classic flower garden. They exchanged customary pleasantries. "I understand, Colonel," Cole remarked, "that you have a new commanding officer."

"That is correct, *mon Colonel*," Durafour responded. "Général de Montsouris arrived last week to assume his duties. He has a distinguished war record, you know. He helped Général Leclerc liberate Paris."

Cole wisely did not suggest that the Americans had also given a helping hand in that operation.

"A glass of champagne?" Durafour suggested.

"That would be delightful," Cole agreed.

"It is a fine Krug vintage," Durafour explained.

"That sounds German," Cole said with a laugh, "but I don't suppose you would serve German champagne, would you?"

"There is no such thing as German champagne," Durafour replied stiffly. "Krug is one of the best French champagnes. I hope it is to your satisfaction."

"Delicious. Absolutely delicious," Cole said, relishing both the aroma and the taste. They talked a few more minutes, during which Cole drained his glass. Durafour did not offer a refill.

"We are planning a cocktail party a week from Wednesday," Cole said. "Your invitation will perhaps already have arrived. I hope you will do us the honor of attending."

"The honor will be mine," Durafour replied. "Also the pleasure. I have always enjoyed American parties. They are so very entertaining." He soon led the way into the small and surprisingly intimate dining room.

They sat at Durafour's usual corner table with a view of the lawn sloping down to the lake. The table was set, as a matter of course, with stiff white linen, heavy Christofle silver, Limoges china, and finely cut crystal. The menus were presented with a flourish, and Cole studied his closely. The maître d'hôtel remarked that the turbot had been flown in from Paris that morning. They both decided on the assortment of hors d'oeuvres—a club favorite—and the poached turbot. Durafour ordered a chilled bottle of Chablis and some bottled Evian. With these preliminaries out of the way, they began their conversation.

"I assume we can agree, *mon Colonel*," Durafour began, "that there are no indications of any immediate emergency."

"You mean of an impending Russian attack?"

"Yes."

"Absolutely. No sign whatsoever," Cole confirmed.

"Moreover," Durafour stated, "it appears to us that the political situation in the GDR remains under tight control with no uprising in the offing—of the type that occurred in June 1953—that might bring Russian tanks into the streets."

"Our analysis exactly. Moreover, we believe that the level of Soviet military forces is unchanged."

Durafour nodded his agreement. These were all customary findings of fact.

The hors d'oeuvres cart was wheeled next to their table. Cole made a liberal choice among the variety of salads, cold cuts, smoked fish, and pickled vegetables being offered. Durafour took some green salad and a slice of smoked salmon. He tasted the Chablis with approval and nodded his assent for the waiter to fill their glasses. He squeezed some fresh lemon over his salmon, shook a little pepper on it, and having taken a small bite asked Cole in a restrained voice, "Anything new of any interest?" In other words, why the hell have you invited yourself out here today?

Cole became confidential. He looked around to be sure he

would not be overheard. "I wanted to let you know, Colonel," he said, "that we have just completed a top-secret analysis of the weaknesses of the Warsaw Pact."

Durafour looked perplexed. "Which of the Pact's weaknesses?" he asked. "Planes? Tanks? Supplies? Transportation facilities?"

"No," Cole replied, looking around again before speaking. "Bridges. We've been focusing on how the Warsaw Pact forces would move in an emergency"—always the synonym for war—"and have come to the conclusion that the most crippling blow we could deliver at such a time would be not on airfields or ammo dumps or oil storage tanks, but on bridges. Take out the bridges and we could stop the Warsaw Pact in its tracks."

Cole's wine glass was empty, and the waiter, who was watching from a discreet distance, quickly refilled it.

"The wine is delicious," Cole said. "What kind is it?"

"A young Chablis. Nothing extraordinary, but very refreshing. I'm glad you like it."

Their turbot was served, and for a while they ate in silence.

"Which bridges?" Durafour finally asked.

"What do you mean?"

"Which ones have you identified that would cripple a Warsaw Pact offensive if they were destroyed?"

"Those that span rivers, of course, Colonel. I can't say more than that, but I do believe that the Allies should all concentrate on the same vulnerable targets. I've told you that we're focusing on bridges. I suggest you do the same."

"Yes, of course, thank you for that advice," Durafour mumbled. There was no further professional discussion during the rest of the meal. Durafour skipped dessert and had a double espresso, while Cole ordered a small round lemon tart. Cole was satisfied that he had paid for lunch with his disclosure. Durafour remained baffled and suspicious.

In a discussion with an aide later that evening, Durafour exploded. "Either that American Colonel is a complete fool, or he takes me for one, or . . ."

"Or what, *mon Colonel?*"

"Or he's given us an indication we must examine carefully." He paused to reflect a moment, and then snapped, "Get me a folder tomorrow morning with what we have on all the bridges in the GDR."

*   *   *

Norman Liebman had a subscription to the Sunday evening concert series of the Berlin Philharmoniker. The orchestra's concert hall in the city's center had been bombed out during the war, and until a new one could be built—a project close to the heart of many West Berliners—the orchestra performed in the Titania Palast, a large movie theater in the outlying Steglitz district.

Liebman was in a small *Gasthaus* across the way from the Titania Palast enjoying a preconcert snack with a crowd of other ticketholders. He shared a long wooden table with three high-spirited middle-aged couples. He had ordered a bowl of vegetable soup and a glass of Franken wine. Life was strange, he thought, not for the first time. Here he sat, served and surrounded by good, solid burghers, who only a decade earlier had supported a regime bent on killing him. In those days they would have chased him from their table with insults instead of raising their glasses in an occasional friendly *prosit* as they were doing just now.

He felt a kinship toward them, though he knew it was largely a one-way street. In truth, Liebman felt a kinship to all men, indeed to all living creatures. He held life of any kind to be most precious—not because of any religious belief, for he was a confirmed agnostic, but rather as a reaction to the recent carnage to which he had been a witness and to which he had nearly succumbed. He accepted the fact that some people were undeniably violent. Many considered this to be man's natural state. Liebman had a different view of humanity. He strove for the good and beautiful, the harmony of music instead of the sounds of gunfire.

But that was probably sentimental prattle, he reflected. No

well-meaning person could question the moral justification of root-
ing out the Nazi pestilence, no matter what violence was required.
I am too soft, he admitted to himself, too tender-hearted. Perhaps
I am the coward that Muldane thinks I am.

The program for that night's concert featured a Brahms sym-
phony, one of the hallmarks of the land of *Dichter und Denker*—
their land, as Germans prided themselves, of poets and thinkers.
The audience, which listened in respectful silence with but little
critical judgment, was in the main composed of the elderly, trying
to reach back to an earlier and better time. But, Liebman wondered, had those earlier times really been better? Hadn't the same
music been played, and played as well, during the dark years? In
fact, some of the world's masterpieces were created in the cruelest
times, whereas, to quote Orson Welles, the Swiss after centuries of
pacific democracy had to their credit only the cuckoo clock. The
connection between art and bestiality remained a conundrum.

Liebman abandoned these disturbing thoughts and lost himself in the romantic soaring of the Berlin Philharmoniker's strings.

*   *   *

Brigitte and her father, Professor Halder, were just finishing dinner when the telephone rang. Brigitte answered while her father
watched apprehensively.

"Halder," she said.

"It's Bud, Brigitte," Cole said. "How about catching the late
show at The Outpost?"

"What's playing?" she asked.

"A Fred Astaire and Ginger Rogers movie. Come on; it'll be
fun."

Ignoring her father's disapproving look, she quickly accepted.
"Don't bother picking me up. I'll meet you in front of the theater," she said. She cleared the table hastily, ran upstairs to put on
a sweater and, telling her father not to wait up for her, rushed out
of the house breathing in the cool night air.

The film had been pleasantly entertaining and as they left the theater, Cole suggested they stop at the PX for some ice cream. "That's how we always ended our movie dates back home," he said, then added, "when we were sixteen." It was an unspoken understanding that he would not invite her up to his apartment, and Cole was careful not to press her on that point.

She laughed and took his arm. "Have we regressed all that much?" she asked. Oh my God, she thought, sixteen! When I was sixteen, the war was about to start, and at that age he was eating ice cream with his girlfriends.

The PX cafeteria was filled with the movie crowd. A 575th Staff Sergeant was seated in a corner with his arm around a petite brunette who worked in the PX beauty parlor. Cole and Brigitte sat across from each other at a small table in the middle of the room. Cole looked with tenderness at Brigitte's strong and classically chiseled face and was amused by her first tentative spoonfuls of the banana split he had persuaded her to order.

"Like it?" he asked.

"It's different."

"Does that mean yes or no?"

"I'm still deciding," she answered, delicately tasting successive bites of banana, whipped cream, and vanilla ice cream. Cole had ordered his favorite butterscotch sundae.

"How blessedly ordinary this all is," she suddenly remarked, looking around the noisy cafeteria. "There is no fear or even awareness of the suffering and despair so close to us."

"So close?" Cole inquired.

"Yes, close both in time and territory." She shook her head sadly, and then smiled at him guardedly.

The night was clear and cool, the light from the half-moon silvery and bright. Cole left his car in the PX parking lot as he walked Brigitte home. They strolled slowly, his arm around her shoulders and hers around his waist.

"I'm sorry about yesterday, Bud," she said suddenly.

"What do you mean? Didn't you enjoy our walk in the Grünewald? I did."

"Of course I did. I meant I'm sorry about my outburst. You know, about your not having any illusions about me. And me not having feelings any more. All of that. I'm just very high-strung and upset at times."

"Could it be," he asked gently, "that you're afraid of anyone getting too close?"

"Perhaps," she agreed a little unsteadily. "I suppose that could be it."

"That wouldn't be so bad as far as I'm concerned." They came around the corner of her street, and Cole slowly and firmly turned her around to face him. She stepped back against the trunk of an old elm tree. They looked into each other's eyes, and then Cole leaned forward and brushed his lips against hers. She trembled, but did not withdraw. He kissed her hard; she moaned softly and then with a shudder of abandonment fiercely returned his embrace, locking her arms tightly around his neck and pulling him close.

They did not speak again until they had reached her door, where they both quietly said good night.

*　　*　　*

That night in his bed with Pritzer relaxing in contented repose, Jutta turned toward him and, twirling the hairs on his chest with her fingers, asked, "Did you also give him a Beretta?"

"Who?"

"Your agent."

"Of course not. Now stop asking me these questions. There's nothing more at all I'm going to say about my work."

He rolled over and soon fell asleep. Jutta returned to her bed but remained awake for some time.

Day 4 Monday

It was raining on Monday, so Weber's mission was postponed. Anna had been pleading with him not to return, but he had remained adamant.

"One more trip," he had insisted, "just one more, and we'll be rich. Our future will be golden."

"I don't care what color it is," she had replied. "I just want a future. Remember, Hans, that's why we came over. To have a better life for ourselves and little Manfred. Not to get rich."

"But *Liebling*, with DM 12,500 in our pockets we'll have a much easier start. Trust me. Everything will turn out just fine."

To cheer her up, Weber suggested that they take advantage of their free day and go into the city to do some shopping. Anna insisted that she didn't want to go out in the rain, but Weber replied with an old German proverb to the effect that rainwater wouldn't melt her since she wasn't made of sugar. The fact that little Manfred needed a few things overcame her reluctance. The housekeeper promised to look in on the baby, and so they set off, bundled up in raincoats, with Weber holding an umbrella over Anna's head. He was ebullient, Anna full of foreboding. He was confident that seeing all that they could now afford would raise her spirits.

They took the U-Bahn down to Wittenbergplatz. By the time they emerged onto the street, the rain had stopped and the sun was trying to pierce through the mist that still hung over the city. To the eyes of an East German, accustomed to the drab, colorless privation of the GDR, the glittering windows of the food stores on Tauenzienstrasse—with their bewildering array of cold cuts, sausages, cheeses, chocolates, cookies, and cakes— constituted an extravagant provocation.

They took the escalators to the top floor of Berlin's famous

KaDeWe department store, and worked their way down one floor at a time. The abundance and variety of clothes and other consumer goods on display were overwhelming. The baby department was on the third floor, and Anna picked out a pair of blue pajamas.

"Manfred really needs these," she said.

"Get him a second pair," Weber declared proudly. She looked at him doubtfully. He had always been very tight with money, and she had to account for every *Groschen* of her weekly housekeeping money.

"Go ahead," Weber said. "Pick out a second one or a third one, if Manfred needs it. We can afford it now." He looked around, hoping that some passerby might have heard him, but none of the other shoppers seemed interested.

The KaDeWe's women's section was on the second floor, and Weber tried to get Anna to buy something for herself, but she refused. "We're going to need that money," she reminded him prudently. "Let's not waste it now on any unnecessary luxuries."

Despite that injunction, Weber was able to persuade her to have some coffee and cake on the terrace of the Café Kranzler. Anna gaped at the well-dressed window-shopping crowd parading in front of them on the Kudamm, and felt shabby and out of place. Not so Weber. He reveled in the general bustle and excitedly kept pointing out different foreign car models.

An old man in a shabby brown suit and knit tie was playing the accordion on the sidewalk while a young boy, presumably his grandson, moved among the tables with a tin cup, begging for change. Weber proudly dropped a DM into the cup. As the accordionist played an old Berlin ballad about the uniqueness of the city's atmosphere and a waitress brought a platter of cakes for them to choose from, Anna momentarily forgot her fears and began to think that she was living a fairy tale.

*   *   *

As on every Monday morning the refugee ranks had swollen at Marienfelde, and Eugene Zandt, resentful at the downgrading of his former status at the Meisenstrasse safe house, was pursuing his new screening assignment with a vengeance. Anyone with even the most tenuous connection to Frankfurt/Oder was referred to the Clayallee Interrogation Center, with the result that by noon Liebman was flooded with candidates, most of them unsuitable for even rudimentary questioning. The Center was full, the other intelligence services using the building were protesting, and Brigitte, as a last resort, had to ask the new arrivals to sit on the stairs and wait.

Liebman called Zandt to complain. The latter replied that he was only following orders and that it was up to Liebman to separate the wheat from the chaff. Liebman then called Muldane, who took the call in Cole's office. Liebman explained the logjam being created and asked that Zandt be told to screen more efficiently.

"Isn't it up to you to tell him?" Muldane asked.

"Yes, sir. That's true, technically. But he doesn't listen to me," Liebman admitted. "It would be better for an officer to give him that instruction."

Muldane said he would take care of the matter and hung up.

"What's up?" Cole asked.

"Zandt is obviously pissed off at being at Marienfelde, so he's clogging the refugee pipeline."

"How do we know?"

"Even the Army and Navy spooks are complaining. It seems we've got refugees from Frankfurt/Oder hanging from the rafters down at Clayallee. The real problem is Liebman. He can't assert himself. He's the one who should be regulating the refugee flow."

"As far as I can make out, he's the best interviewer we've got."

"Bud, he's a goddamn pacifist. He doesn't belong in a military outfit."

Cole was silent for a moment. "Give Marienfelde a call, Zach, and tell Zandt to let up," he said. "But listen, that doesn't mean we don't want to see every possible source on that damned bridge. That's Wiesbaden's priority at the moment. Understand?"

Muldane nodded, acknowledging the contradictory order he was being asked to execute.

The fact that everyone from Frankfurt/Oder—whether young or old, with bad eyesight or weakness in the head—was being "processed" did not go unnoticed by the Stasi spies at Marienfelde. That American interest in Frankfurt/Oder had increased dramatically was a fact quickly reported to East Berlin.

*　　*　　*

Kommissar Dieter Zeunert at last had a corner office in the massive building on East Berlin's Normannenstrasse, which housed the dreaded Ministry for State Security—the *Ministerium für Staatssicherheit* (MfS) or, as it was commonly called, the Stasi. Zeunert worked in the *Abwehr,* the counter-intelligence section of the Ministry's Central Intelligence Directorate—the *Hauptverwaltung Aufklärung* (HVA). He had had to wait five years, until his ineffectual superior had lost his last rear-guard action to delay retirement, to receive official recognition for the duties he already performed. A large map of the GDR behind his desk indicated the military targets he was charged with protecting against Western saboteurs and spies who were intent, as he frequently reminded his subordinates, on trying to impede the GDR's march toward the Inevitable Victory of Socialism.

Zeunert, a man in his mid-forties, had easily made the transition from the Third Reich's *Abwehr* to its GDR's namesake. After all, he continued to serve in the secret police of a "disciplined" state with very similar methods and procedures. Also, with one exception, the enemies were the same—the decadent democracies: the Americans, the British, and the French. True, the dominant ideology had changed, but one had to be flexible, Zeunert told himself, and courageous enough to recognize that one's former

faith had been placed in a flawed deity. Communism was the only
true and pure path—it was a road along which he intended to
travel unswervingly and relentlessly until the promised goal had
been reached.

It did irritate Zeunert that Germans were not masters in their
own house. Of course the war had been lost, that couldn't be denied. But that was now so many years ago. Others seemed to continue dwelling in the past; he had put all that behind him.

Zeunert had to answer to a Russian lieutenant—Anatoly
Ossipov. A mere lieutenant! He, Zeunert, who in his previous
Abwehr days used to brief German Generals. Zeunert would have
preferred to have a German superior like certain Stasi officials who
were concerned with political internal security. But his domain of
military counter-espionage was a reserved area under the direct
supervision of the so-called Soviet Military Friendship Force.

His desk was covered with messages that Monday morning. A
number of Western spies had been apprehended over the weekend, all of them assigned the usual military targets. A U.S. Military Mission car had trespassed inside the restricted area near
Dessau; that was to be expected in view of the fighter aircraft stationed there. The Americans were undoubtedly checking up on
the rumor (deliberately planted) that the planes on the runways
were but wooden decoys.

Zeunert's secretary brought in a cup of coffee. She was an un-
attractive middle-aged spinster with thick glasses, unshaved legs,
and a distinct body odor. Why, Zeunert thought, not for the first
time, must we send all of our attractive East German girls over to
the West? It would be a sure-fire morale booster to keep a few of
the lively, sexy ones in our own offices. Without a word, the secretary placed on his desk the coffee, along with a report that had just
arrived from Marienfelde.

Routine reports from Stasi sources at Marienfelde were due
every Wednesday, although any unusual activity was to be reported
at once. The special message was brief and advised that suddenly
Frankfurt/Oder had become a priority target for the American Air

Force interrogator. The specific target had not yet been identified, but all refugees with a Frankfurt/Oder connection were being given special attention. This was puzzling. Zeunert knew of no point of interest in that city for the U.S. Air Force. He called his assistant.

"Check the file on Targets to be Protected," he ordered, "and determine which ones are located in or near Frankfurt/Oder. And make sure nothing has happened these last few days, or is about to happen, that would arouse the curiosity of the *revanchists.*" It was disconcerting; at times, he had to admit, the West had a better grasp than he did on what was going on in the GDR.

As he waited for a response, Zeunert walked over to the map and confirmed that there were no significant military targets near Frankfurt/Oder—no casernes, no airfields, no supply or ammunition depots. There was of course the bridge across the Oder River, the frontier imposed after 1945 between the GDR and Poland, but there was nothing new about that crossover point, nothing that should suddenly alert the U.S. Air Force.

The assistant called back fifteen minutes later. He had made a number of inquiries: there was absolutely no change or unusual activity of any kind to report. "Maintain a daily watch on Frankfurt/Oder and keep me informed," Zeunert grumbled into the telephone. The Americans must be after something, he mused.

He decided to call Lieutenant Ossipov. Perhaps he could clear up the mystery, and if he couldn't, he would at least be made aware, once again, that Kommissar Zeunert was on the job, closely anticipating U.S. probes.

"It appears," Zeunert began in the favored German impersonal bureaucratic style, "that the American services—the U.S. Air Force, to be precise—have developed a sudden interest in Frankfurt/Oder. We are trying to determine the reason for this unexpected focus, but for the moment are at a loss to explain it. I was wondering if an initiative by your forces might provide an explanation."

Lieutenant Anatoly Ossipov was an intelligent, quadrilingual Red Army officer in his early thirties, who had fought his way into

Berlin in 1945. At war's end, he had been sent to an officers' school in Leningrad, which trained elite military cadres for foreign diplomatic and intelligence assignments. After several tours of duty at a number of Soviet embassies, Ossipov had been assigned to the counter-espionage section of Soviet Military Intelligence (*Glavnoye Razvedyvatelnoye Upravleniye*, or the GRU) at Soviet Military Headquarters in Karlshorst, an outskirt of Berlin.

During the war his fifteen-year-old brother had been taken hostage and shot by the Germans, but in the performance of his duties Ossipov kept his undiminished hatred of Germans under tight control. He was aware that cooperation with East Germans was a necessity—a transitory one, he hoped. But that didn't mean that he would freely discuss Soviet military moves with his German contacts. His job was to gather information, and he was sparing in doling any out. Moreover, he considered Zeunert a functionary, to be used and kept in his place.

"Offhand I don't know of any developments in Frankfurt/Oder," he replied. "However, I will make the appropriate inquiries. In the meantime I suggest that you strengthen the surveillance of all of the important military installations in that city."

"That's just the problem, Comrade Lieutenant," Zeunert said. "There aren't any."

Ossipov's manner turned icy-cold. "There must be, Herr Kommissar, if the American Air Force is interested in the city." He slammed down the phone.

Zeunert remained seated at his desk, perplexed. Ossipov was right. There must be something in Frankfurt/Oder that had caught the Americans' attention. He put in a call to Heinz Janicek, the head of the Stasi office in Frankfurt/Oder, and explained the targeting of his city by Western intelligence. Janicek did not have an explanation.

"Any troop movements?"

"No."

"Any new military installation?"

"No, except . . ."

"Except what?"

"Except," Janicek volunteered, "the additional warehouse under construction for the parachute factory."

"Don't be stupid," Zeunert retorted sharply.

"I'm trying to be helpful, Herr Kommissar. There's just isn't anything else."

"What about the bridge? Anything new there?"

"Not that I know of."

"All right. Increase security around the bridge. Understand?"

"Soviet troops guard the bridge, Herr Kommissar, as well as our border guards on our side and Polish border guards on the other."

Zeunert did not hide his frustration. "This is an order, Janicek," he said. "Station a cordon of Stasi personnel around the bridge and keep a sharp lookout around the city for Western spies. Keep me informed."

Later that day, Ossipov called Zeunert back to say that he had been unable to discover any new development in Frankfurt/Oder. "It is your responsibility," he admonished Zeunert, "to protect whatever target the American Air Force has selected. Keep me informed."

Ossipov then turned back to preparing a memorandum for his new Commanding Officer on the cocktail party at the American Officers' Club to be held the following week on Wednesday. A smile crossed his face when he realized that the party was being hosted by the American Air Force.

*   *   *

Every morning, six days a week, Carlton Herter prepared the Morning Report, which was flashed in code to the 2050th Air Support Wing, the USAF Headquarters in Wiesbaden. Copies were placed in sealed envelopes on Cole's and Muldane's desks in West Berlin. The Morning Report summarized all information gathered during the last 24 hours (the last 48 hours every Monday morning).

At 7:00 a.m. the Staff Sergeant in charge of the Code Room would begin the encoding process, for Herter was insistent that the message be sent before 8:00 a.m.

The Morning Report's format—devised by Herter and known in both Berlin and Wiesbaden as the Hertogram—never varied. Information was identified as originating from either an overt or a covert source; date and time of observation were noted; reliability of information and of source was graded on a scale from 1 to 5; lastly, a recommendation was made on whether or not to follow up. The USAF had its standard formats for intelligence reports, but Herter, in an unusual deviation from standard operating procedure, refused to abandon his own system. It was a measure of the high professional regard in which he was held that he was permitted to continue with his Hertograms. Unbeknownst to him, these were quickly transcribed at Headquarters to conform to the USAF format.

Since the Frankfurt/Oder bridge had been listed by the 2050th Air Support Wing as a priority target, that day's Morning Report with its reference to Weber's account aroused immediate interest. The importance of this information was debated at the daily morning staff meeting of the Intelligence Evaluation Section in Wiesbaden.

A young civilian analyst who had recently joined the group and was struggling to make a name for himself expressed the view that perhaps the Russians were going to install not radar equipment, but SAMs—surface-to-air missiles—to protect the bridge. This suggestion was greeted with general skepticism and some derision. The Russians, it was recalled, had not as yet deployed any missiles outside their own borders. It seemed unlikely that if they were ever to do so, they would begin with an installation at an exposed site of secondary importance.

"Why do you think they would consider it a secondary target?" the young analyst asked heatedly, feeling compelled to defend what had been but a random shot in the dark. "We have placed it on our priority list, haven't we? And the photos we have of Russian SAMs in the Ukraine and over the Volga are all next to bridges. Aren't they?" That was true. "I say we should match those photos against the excavation work being done in Frankfurt/Oder."

The Major, who chaired the meetings of the Intelligence Evaluation Section and whose nickname was Major Overkill, decided that some further investigation was warranted. "Let's get Potsdam to check this out," he declared. "And the 575th should send some more people back to look at that bridge. Mention the possibility of a missile site, and I want some photos."

The U.S. Military Mission in Potsdam, GDR, and its twin, the Soviet Military Mission in the Federal Republic of Germany (West Germany's official title), had both been established pursuant to postwar agreements among the victorious Allies. They had originally been given unlimited freedom of movement in their respective zones of operation. However, denial of access by the two Missions to military areas had quickly been imposed as the Cold War erupted and intensified; but the Missions were maintained since even their limited operations were deemed very useful by both sides. Thus, the latest models of silver American cars—with the Stars and Stripes flying on the two front fenders—continued to crisscross the GDR, creating wherever they appeared the excitement of travelers from a forbidden planet.

One U.S. Mission car near the Baltic Sea received a radio message that afternoon to return to Potsdam by way of Frankfurt/ Oder. The assignment, transmitted in code, was to check out some new construction on the southeast side of the bridge. The Army Captain in charge of the car and his two passengers grumbled. It was pouring rain; the side roads were muddy and almost impassable. To add to their difficulties, they had had a flat tire, which caused further delay. The car had been away on its mission for three days, and the three men were looking forward to returning home to Potsdam that evening.

"Can't this Frankfurt/Oder recon be delayed a day or two?" the Captain asked.

The answer was negative; this was a priority assignment. The car pulled over, and the Captain, with the two other members of the Mission team, an Air Force lieutenant and an Army Master Sergeant driver, consulted their maps. The roads to Frankfurt/Oder were poor, and it was difficult to estimate how much time would be lost in clearing the ubiquitous checkpoints they were bound to encounter. It was evident that they could not reach Frankfurt/Oder before dark. They would have to spend the night there.

The Captain called Mission Headquarters and asked that hotel reservations be made for them that night in Frankfurt/Oder. These were arranged by the Soviet Military Coordination Office, which provided the Russians with a convenient means of keeping track of the U.S. Mission cars. The stopover in Frankfurt/Oder—a place generally bypassed by the U.S. Mission—would be duly noted by Lieutenant Ossipov.

*   *   *

Helmut Pritzer was at present installed, with three other civilian handlers of the 575th, on the ground floor of the safe house on Meisenstrasse, processing refugees referred by Liebman for possible recruitment to engage in covert work. Many of the referrals now came from Frankfurt/Oder, ever since the bridge had been assigned priority over the usual airfield targets such as Cottbus and Dessau.

Muldane routinely made a daily visit to the safe house. That afternoon he mentioned to Pritzer that HQ in Wiesbaden had suggested that the dig near the bridge might possibly be preparatory work for missile sites. He showed him clandestine photos of SAMs taken in the Moscow area as well as drawings, prepared under Herter's supervision, of the type of clearing that would take place for any such installation.

"You're concentrating on the bridge. Is that right?" Muldane asked Pritzer.

"Yes; it looks like we all are."

"Any luck so far?"

"I only started this morning, Captain," Pritzer answered defensively.

"How many bodies have you seen?"

Pritzer looked down on his referral sheet. "Three," he said.

"Not a very good average."

"Liebman is just sending us shit, Captain. Look at my referrals: a metal worker with a limp and bad eyesight; a frightened old woman bringing her granddaughter over to her mother; a high school dropout who has trouble reading. How can anyone make agents of people like that?"

Muldane sat in quietly on Pritzer's next interview and judged that Pritzer at least seemed to be doing better than his predecessor, Zandt, had done. Pritzer was certainly more motivated, and he encountered little resentment for his haughty, peremptory manner. Germans seemed to expect that attitude from all persons in authority. What they found surprising and suspicious, Muldane knew, was the more humane approach that Liebman employed. Muldane told Pritzer to keep up the good work and went to check on the progress being made by the other handlers.

*   *   *

That afternoon Colonel Durafour, prompted by Cole's intimations, was examining the folder he had requested on bridges in the GDR. There was a total of 6,023, most of them for road traffic. There were 276 railroad crossings and 12 foot bridges. What was he to make of Cole's remarks? An aide suggested that since Cole was an Air Force officer, he would be interested in bridges that were potential bombing targets. All bridges are potential bombing targets, Durafour had snapped impatiently. But, the aide persisted, some must be more important than others. Durafour grumbled his assent and together they again began to look at the map of the GDR.

"How many bridges are there over the Oder?" Durafour asked.

"A few dozen," the aide replied, looking at the report, "but the most important one—the principal road connection between Moscow and Berlin—is the large bridge in Frankfurt/Oder. That would be the main East/West crossing point for any Red Army push toward the West."

"Yes, but we've known that for a long time. Why should the bridge in Frankfurt/Oder suddenly be of special interest?" The aide had no answer and remained quiet. Durafour continued to verbalize his thoughts: "I accept that from a military point of view this is probably the most strategic bridge in the GDR. So if this is the target that Cole hinted at, there must be a new development. That's it—something new in Frankfurt/Oder."

Having arrived at this conclusion, Durafour gave the necessary instructions to send an "observer" to the bridge. He hesitated to assign top priority to the mission and instead gave it a second-tier classification. After all, he reflected, this might be an American ruse to keep French Intelligence away from other targets of greater significance.

Moreover, the French did not have the unlimited funds at the Americans' disposal and they usually had the last pickings of potential refugee informers. Consequently, they relied on a mere handful of trusted professionals they were slowly implanting in various sections of the GDR. This meant many fewer reports, but of generally higher quality.

Durafour placed the folder with the bridge information back in the wall safe behind the small Canaletto—inherited from his father and from which Durafour was never parted— and went to change for a late afternoon's sail on the Tegeler See.

*   *   *

Cole and Muldane were finishing their dinner at the Officers' Club in Harnack Haus. True to form, Muldane ogled one of the new waitresses. He was well known for his one-track mind after sundown, not an uncommon military trait. "Good legs, nice tits," he remarked.

Cole gave him a tolerant smile. "Probably a Stasi spy," he said.

"I know. The East Germans are our pimps. They pick out their best-lookers, train them to be whores, and then send them over to spy on us. We hire them because they're good lays . . ."

"And," Cole added, "because we don't have much choice. As far as I can tell, everyone in Berlin is spying on someone or other." They both smiled.

After dinner, they drove to the Daisy, the notorious nightclub that Muldane for some time had been anxious to show Cole. The latter had finally agreed to go since he was curious to see the famous spectacle, but he had warned Muldane not to count on him to participate in this German replica of a slave auction. At fairly regular intervals, usually as the result of a drunken brawl, Daisy was declared Off Limits for American military personnel. However, these restrictions did not apply to officers in the Intelligence Services, the reason advanced being that disreputable locations were promising professional fishing grounds.

Daisy, located in an abandoned warehouse, consisted of one large hall with tables set in alcoves on four different levels. Each table had a telephone and a small lamp, illuminating a sign with a large identifying number. The lamps gave the appearance of fireflies in a large meadow. The tables were placed above and around a spacious central dance floor; an orchestra played in a balcony above the entrance door. The room was fairly somber, except for the bright reflections of half a dozen spotlights trained on a globe, which was studded with bits of colored glass and revolved slowly, sending a prism of colors throughout the hall.

Men were charged an entrance fee of DM 10, whereas women were admitted free. Most of the male clientele were Allied servicemen or civilians intent on a quick pickup. There was also a sprinkling of Germans with similar plans. However, without the monetary resources of their foreign rivals, they were reduced to being voyeurs.

As usual, women outnumbered men by a ratio of at least three to one. That ratio would increase as the evening wore on and couples that had paired off had departed. The young girls sat in groups of two or three, looking avidly around for a human contact. Each one carefully sipped the single bottle of soda water the management provided per evening. All were dressed shabbily, many trying to be provocative with short skirts or low necklines. Their shoes were often bootlike. Stockings were a rarity, and too much lipstick the rule.

There were also some older women, who generally sat alone. They wore their everyday—perhaps their only—clothes, in the hope of meeting someone, anyone. Sudden garish reflections from the revolving ceiling globe would for an instant illuminate their startled faces.

Cole and Muldane were shown to one of the front tables near the dance floor. Half a dozen female couples were dancing to a slow foxtrot, looking around unabashedly for men to cut in. A middle-aged couple was executing some elegant ballroom steps. A tipsy young soldier was being led around the dance floor by a tough old harridan eager to take him off and fleece him before he could be rescued by the MPs.

"This is quite something," Cole said, looking all around the hall. "There must be more than a hundred tables."

"Yeah, it's big all right."

"What are the numbers for?"

"Telephone numbers. Each table has its own number. Look, up there," Muldane said, pointing to the sign above their table. "Ours is 43."

"I'll be damned," Cole said, grinning.

Muldane ordered a bottle of champagne—"for our unknown guests-to-be," he said with a wink.

Many eyes were fixed on them. They were obviously Americans; the professional habituées and the ever-present Stasi informers correctly spotted them as officers. Their phone immediately began to ring. Muldane picked up the receiver.

"Wouldn't you like some company?" a syrupy female voice cooed in heavily accented English. "I know how to drink champagne."

"Is that all you know how to do?" Muldane retorted archly.

"No, of course not," the voice answered with a giggle. "I have a very well-rounded education." A shopworn response, Muldane thought.

"What number are you at?" he asked.

"I won't tell, but I am looking straight at you."

"Keep on looking, love," Muldane said and hung up. The phone instantly rang again. A throaty voice announced: "My lovemaking will make you think that you're in Paradise."

"I'm there already, darling," Muldane replied, chuckling, "just by being in the same dance hall as you."

A bottle of champagne—in truth, a sweetish German white sparkling wine—ostentatiously wrapped in a large white napkin was brought to the table in a metal ice bucket. It was accompanied by a tray of small canapés with salami, cheese, and chopped eggs.

"There's more goddamn tail running around here," Muldane commented, surveying the neighboring tables, "than we could screw in a month of Sundays. The war has killed most of the young men so the women are all desperate. I tell you, Bud, with our little joysticks we're on a doggone mission of mercy."

As Muldane filled their glasses, Cole thought of Brigitte. Was she also desperate and accepting of his mercy? The phone rang again. Muldane handed the receiver to Cole. "Your turn, Bud," he said.

"We're two pretty girls," a high-pitched and obviously young voice said, "who are lonely, thirsty, and hungry. Why don't you invite us over?"

"Where are you?" Cole asked.

"Table 22."

Cole and Muldane looked over to Table 22 and saw two smiling girls; one waved tentatively with her right hand. "These aren't the usual pros. They look like young amateurs," Muldane said. "Probably their first time out. Just my meat. Let's ask them over."

"Fine with me, Zach," Cole replied. "But remember, I just came to look and you know, I don't think much of one-night stands."

"Suit yourself, Bud," Muldane said with an evil grin. "But with all the luscious women in Berlin, one night is all I can spare for any one of them."

Cole shook his head. Muldane, he thought, was a good officer with sound judgment, but as far as women were concerned—well, juvenile was a charitable characterization.

The girls were both quite young—barely twenty, if that, Cole thought. The chubbier one with blonde hair was talkative; the other with dark brown eyes was prettier, but quiet and shy. Their English was halting, but their vocabulary was sufficient for the occasion. They had come from the East the year before and were living with one of the girls' cousins. They said they were secretaries, whereas in fact they were both waitresses.

Muldane had called for two more glasses and quickly filled them for the girls. They choked on the champagne and began to giggle. The chubbier one started wolfing down the canapés, and Muldane ordered another plate. The conversation soon lagged. There really wasn't much to talk about.

Muldane pulled the blonde's chair over to his. She continued eating as he gently put his hand under her skirt. There was no resistance as he felt her moisten and relax. Satisfied, Muldane removed his hand; the bargain had been struck. The girl gave him a coy look and then laughed, squeezing her thighs together.

Her friend looked embarrassed. Cole had not made any similar moves. Instead he asked her to dance. She didn't know how and merely followed his lead, all the while pressing the length of her body against his with her head resting on his shoulder. She had a firm young body, and their joint gyrations were beginning to arouse Cole. He felt himself harden, and she smiled up at him bashfully. Cole smiled back but felt uneasy. This was indeed a slave market, he thought, rather than a dance hall.

Cole did not view himself as a conqueror. He was still taken aback by all these pliant women, ready, indeed eager, to bed any member of the Occupation Forces. Most Germans had no difficulty with an American's status as lord and master. That was the victor's prerogative, and it was one they would arrogantly have enjoyed had they been victorious. But since they had been beaten, all that was left for them was to try, each in his or her own way, to derive some profit from that subservient relationship. However, instinctively Cole wouldn't take candy from a baby. Muldane would and did.

*   *   *

It was after ten o'clock at night when the three members of the Potsdam Mission arrived at the Drei Löwen Hotel on Rosa Luxemburg Strasse in Frankfurt/Oder. The sight of the Potsdam Mission car—a new, silver Mercury with its abundance of shiny chrome and stylish fenders—was a rarity in Frankfurt/Oder and despite the lateness of the hour it quickly attracted a small crowd.

The Captain asked for the location of the garage that was to have been reserved. The desk clerk apologized but said that unfortunately all the garage spaces were occupied. Mission cars had to be protected, the Captain insisted, and threatened to call the Soviet Military Liaison Office. The threat had an immediate effect and the desk clerk hurriedly moved the hotel manager's car out of the garage. The Army Master Sergeant driver secured his vehicle with electronic alarms, demanded the keys to the garage, and locked it.

The hotel dining room had closed an hour before, but the desk clerk suggested a nearby Gasthaus that stayed open until midnight. The three men took their bags to their rooms and briefly washed up. Then they headed for the Gasthaus, taking their confidential documents with them, since they knew that in the meantime their rooms would be assiduously searched.

The Gasthaus was smoky and noisy, but a hush fell over the room as soon as the three uniformed Americans entered. They sat down at a table next to the window facing the street and ordered beers and the day's menu, the inevitable sausages and cabbage. The beer was cool, and they were thirsty, quickly ordering a second round. As word of their presence spread, more locals pushed into the restaurant just to gawk. Potsdam Mission personnel were under strict orders not to make contact with the local population, so they merely smiled and kept eating. For their part, the local inhabitants were afraid to be seen talking to Americans, fearing that there might be Stasi informers in the room. But there was no prohibition against staring.

The crowd continued to grow, and people on the sidewalk, unable to get into the Gasthaus, were beginning to jostle one another for a look through the window. The Americans decided they had better avoid an incident. They quickly finished their meal and stood up to return to the hotel. They left a generous tip and, smiling, gently elbowed their way out.

Another visitor to Frankfurt/Oder that evening did not attract such notice. Herr Juergen Nitsche, a self-styled traveling salesman for soap and toiletries, checked into a small pension and after eating in a modest neighborhood eatery, retired early. No one searched his suitcases during his absence, though he was on a similar mission, sent by Colonel Durafour.

*   *   *

That evening, curled up next to Pritzer on the sofa, Jutta nibbled at his earlobe and occasionally breathed softly into his ear. After a while she slipped her hand under his shirt and whispered: "How did my Mutiger do today? Did you win an important battle in the Cold War?"

"Not today," Pritzer replied. "I'll do that tomorrow, maybe . . ."

"You mean you were a lazy one—*ein Faultier*—who didn't earn his pay," Jutta said with mock severity. "I might have to spank you for that."

"Oh, I earned it all right. I must have seen over a dozen refugees."

"Did any pretty girls flirt with you?" She tugged at the hairs on his chest, and he winced.

"None, I promise."

She let go and fondled his chest. "Would you tell me if any girl had?" she asked, teasingly.

"I don't know," he answered playfully.

"I've been thinking of my Mutiger all day long," she whispered, giving him a peck on the cheek. "I'm doing my little part, you know, in helping the West by taking in books and checking them out at Amerika Haus, but nothing like the very important job that you're doing now."

Flattery had been a rare commodity in Pritzer's life. At war's end, after having interrogated German prisoners of war in North Africa and France, he had remained in Europe, not due to any particular enthusiasm, but rather because he had nowhere else to go. Quite unexpectedly, the prestige and power accruing to a member of the Occupation Forces filled a badly undernourished ego— a psychological makeup that Jutta understood perfectly. She alternated praise with punishment, and Pritzer craved both.

"Of course you're helping, darling," he said, reaching for her breasts, a move she deftly averted. "Our fight now is a battle of ideas, and the Amerika Haus is our outpost in the front line of that war." (This was the slogan often trumpeted by L. Cabot Pearson, the head of the United States Information Agency in Berlin.)

Jutta snuggled closer. "Tell me something about the people you saw, Mutiger."

"What?"

"Not their names, of course, silly. That would be a secret, wouldn't it? I don't want any secrets, but I'm so interested in what you do. Do they come from all over the GDR?"

Pritzer thought a moment. Nothing secret about that; there were frequent press reports on the number of refugees and their places of origin. "Yes, all over," he answered.

"I guess they're still fleeing from Dresden." Jutta had been born in Dresden.

"I suppose so. I've only seen people from Frankfurt/Oder." The moment he spoke, he knew it was a slip.

"If you ever see someone from Dresden," she said, "please ask if the *Kunz Konditorei* is still open. I sometime still think of their *Kuchen* in the night. Not even *Kranzler* has cakes as sweet and creamy as the ones at the *Kunz*."

Pritzer readily agreed that he would ask, much relieved that Jutta apparently had not noticed his indiscretion. In the future, he warned himself, he would have to be more careful.

Day 5 Tuesday

There were low-hanging clouds early that morning, but no rain was forecast. Weber's farewell from Anna was difficult, but in an unavowed way he felt relieved to get away from her angst. She had not yet learned, as he himself had quickly grasped, that to get ahead in the West one had to act forcefully and independently. She remained fearfully enmeshed in the GDR's requirement to conform silently in order to survive. He would show her how to live in liberty and freedom.

There was a breeze and, as he stood at the curb in front of the safe house waiting for the car with the wind refreshing his face, he felt exhilarated and anxious for the day's adventure to begin. The car pulled up at precisely 6:15 a.m. and again deposited him at the Kreuzberg crossover point.

"This is getting to be routine," Weber said to the driver, trying to make conversation. The driver remained tight-lipped. His instructions were not to speak to any of the passengers, other than to caution them to be silent.

Once in East Berlin, Weber first stopped at the Education Ministry and left a note at the reception desk inquiring about the status of his request for a new teaching assignment. He then easily caught the 9:41 express, which made only two stops prior to Frankfurt/Oder. The train was only half full, and Weber's mood during the trip alternated between confidence and worry, the latter principally caused by the camera he was carrying. He calmed himself by repeating Muldane's reassuring words—the Vopos had no idea that a camera could be concealed in a lighter; he could throw the lighter away with a pack of cigarettes in case of any trouble.

Weber, a nonsmoker, had bought a pack of cigarettes at the Friedrichstrasse Station. Did the woman behind the counter, he worried, notice his hesitation in deciding which brand to buy?

Did she think that suspicious? He fingered the lighter nervously. What if someone asked him for a light? Had anyone ever asked him for one? No, he had to admit. But he had never had a pack of cigarettes on him before. Nobody knew that, he told himself impatiently.

Weber's anxiety level would have been higher had he known that there were two Stasi officials in the next car. They had been sent, unannounced, to Frankfurt/Oder by Kommissar Zeunert to check on what additional security measures had been put in place.

The sky was still overcast, and it was cool as the train pulled into Frankfurt/Oder. Two full trolley cars passed the station stop with passengers standing on the running boards, holding on to outside railings. Weber began to walk back to his apartment, unaware that the two Stasi men were just a few steps behind him. They turned into the police station, while Weber continued walking through the adjoining small park.

In returning to his apartment, Weber passed Frau Brubacher on the stairs. She lived on the same floor, across the landing from the Webers.

"How's little Manfred?" she asked.

"Just fine, thank you, Frau Brubacher. He and Anna are with her cousins in Finsterwalde."

"I miss hearing the baby cry," she said. "It's lonely on the third floor without your family."

"He'll soon be waking you up again, Frau Brubacher. Don't worry." Weber disengaged himself as tactfully as he could. She would have been content to chat all morning long. He went directly into the kitchen and looked out the window. The sky had brightened, and the morning mist had lifted.

He took up the field glasses he had previously left on the kitchen table and focused on the bridge. The construction site on the opposite bank had been expanded, he noted. There were three bulldozers and a crane at work; trucks were hauling away the sand and stones that had been excavated. Weber positioned himself at the side of the kitchen window, where he could not himself be observed, and over the next two hours took pictures of the bridge and its construction site. At one point, a car horn seemed to have become stuck. The bridge traffic began to back up, while a number of cars raced along the side of the river-bank road. But matters returned to normal a little while later. A squadron of Mig fighters flew overhead, and Weber playfully aimed his camera into the sky and snapped a picture.

*   *   *.

Earlier that morning, Juergen Nitsche, the soap and toiletries salesman, had gone down to the river bank, but had found the Oder still covered by a thick blanket of fog. He returned to the pension for breakfast, and was served a stale roll, but good butter and strong *ersatz* coffee. The manager was having his breakfast at the same time, which Nitsche noted included eggs and ham. There was no one else in the small dining room, and Nitsche tried to start a conversation.

"What's new in town?" he asked.

"Nothing that would interest a foreigner," the manager replied rudely.

Undaunted, Nitsche tried again. "How's the local football team doing?" he asked.

"Same as ever. Losing."

Writing off the manager as a possible source of information, Nitsche finished a second cup of coffee, excused himself, and went upstairs to pack. He was fiftyish, short and trim of stature, with quick and sharp movements. He left the pension and walked to the train station to check his suitcase. Then, with his sample case of toiletries in hand, he went to the information counter and asked where the city's pharmacies were located.

"Why do you want to know?" the heavy-set woman sitting behind the counter asked.

"That's hardly a state secret, is it?" Nitsche said in an attempt at humor. The woman did not seem amused, so Nitsche added quickly, "I sell soaps and toiletries." He opened his sample case to prove it.

The woman softened her tone. "Go to the Konsum," she advised. "That's where I buy my soap. They have a much larger choice."

"That's true, but unfortunately the Konsum is a large State organization and you know, Madam, they won't buy from a small family supplier like me."

The woman acknowledged this fact with a sigh and pulled out a city map. She was marking the location of various pharmacies as the Berlin train arrived, and Weber, followed by the two Berlin Stasi officials, walked through the station.

"Good luck," she said to Nitsche, who thanked her for her help.

One of the pharmacies was near the bridge, but Nitsche decided it would be more prudent to call on a few others first. The toiletries company that Nitsche allegedly represented was a front set up by French Intelligence. The soaps and other articles were manufactured in France with German wrapping and labels and an East Berlin letter-box address. Having made two unsuccessful calls—"No one buys soap from us anymore," he was told by both—Nitsche headed for the pharmacy near the bridge.

A car with two men sitting inside it was parked up the street from the pharmacy. One man got out as Nitsche approached, stopped him, and asked to see his papers. These seemed to be in order. The man handed the papers back and asked Nitsche to explain his presence. Nitsche said he hoped to make a sale in the pharmacy and showed his sample case. The man waved him on, but warned him to get out of the area as soon as his business was done.

The pharmacy was run by an elderly couple. Nitsche showed them his wares. "They're beautiful," the woman said, "but we can't afford them."

"What my wife means," the man added, "is that the few customers we have left can't afford them."

"I really have to make a sale," Nitsche said earnestly. "My prices are very flexible. I can let you have some soap at a real discount."

The man shook his head.

"Or let you pay after you have made some sales."

"I'm sorry," the man said, as his wife looked on nodding her head sadly. "We just don't have the money."

"Business is that bad?" Nitsche asked.

"Ever since they set up that road block down the street," the woman said, "even our old clients seem to be afraid to come here."

"When did they do that?" Nitsche asked.

"A few weeks ago," she replied, "and then . . ."

"Shhh, mama," the man interrupted. "You know we shouldn't be talking about those things." The woman fell quiet.

"Well," Nitsche said, "I'm afraid business won't get much better with that car parked up the street."

"What car?" the man asked.

"Some sort of official car. Parked about fifty meters from here. A man got out and stopped me. He examined my papers and told me to get out of the area as soon as possible."

"That's the end of us," the woman moaned. "I've told you. We should close up shop and take our leave."

"Take our leave, you say. And go where, you silly goose?" the man answered angrily. "Who would buy our shop under these circumstances? Here at least we have a roof over our heads." The woman began to cry softly.

"I'm not from here," Nitsche said hesitantly, "but it's hard to see why this should be such a heavily guarded area."

"We can't understand it either," the woman replied, wiping away her tears with a large knotted handkerchief. "All we know is that from time to time there are suddenly police and soldiers everywhere, and we're told to stay in our houses and not look out the windows."

"Shhh!"

Wrought up by their predicament, she turned on her husband. "Why are you shushing me?" she asked irately. "I'm not saying anything that everyone in this town doesn't know. What we're told to do is not a secret."

"Do you ever look out the window?" Nitsche asked.

"We're law-abiding citizens," the man replied.

"And slowly starving to death," the woman added bitterly.

Nitsche left the shop and went down the street toward the river. Access to the bridge was blocked by a Vopo checkpoint; behind it was a Russian military post with a machine-gun emplacement. Nitsche stopped and, looking around to the left, saw a Gasthaus on a small hill. He walked up to it and settled on the outside terrace, which afforded a direct view of the bridge. The fog had lifted, but the sky was still overcast with low-hanging clouds. He ordered a beer and tried to decide what his next move should be.

There was a sudden commotion. A silver car, the American flag flying on its two front fenders, came racing down toward the bridge, then screeched to a halt at the Vopo checkpoint. The barrier was down, and the car's driver was gesticulating out his window to have it lifted. The Vopo on guard duty did not budge. The American driver began to blow the car's horn and then to lean on it. A Russian soldier left his station and went inside the small hut at the Vopo checkpoint. A few minutes later, he returned to his post.

The incident had caused all traffic on the bridge to stop. The American car horn kept up a constant clamor, but no other horn was heard. GDR traffic regulations forbade the use of horns except in dire emergencies. The impasse had now lasted a full twenty minutes, with traffic steadily building on both sides of the bridge. Then, a Russian military vehicle drove up along the soft shoulder of the river-bank road. A Red Army officer got out of the car and went inside the guard post. He reappeared shortly thereafter accompanied by two Russian soldiers. Together, they walked briskly over to the American vehicle, whose passengers did not get out. Nitsche could see the Russian talking to the Americans through the car windows. A few moments later, the Russian officer signaled the Vopo to raise the barrier and saluted as the American car passed through the checkpoint. The Vopo did not salute.

The Oder River was the frontier between the GDR and Poland, and the Potsdam Mission cars had no right to enter Poland. Therefore, in planning how best to observe his assigned target, the Captain had given instructions to drive along the Western river banks on both sides of the bridge. Traffic blocked the river-bank road, but the American car swerved onto the road's soft shoulder next to the river so as to have an unobstructed full view of the bridge.

Photographing military installations was technically forbidden, but doing so was the very essence of the Potsdam Mission's duties. Both the Captain and the Lieutenant were busy filming the bridge, zooming in on the eastern and southern side with its construction area. A half-mile down the road the car made a sharp U-turn and came back on the same shoulder, both officers continuing to photograph the bridge and its surroundings. The road passed under the bridge, and the car would have repeated the process on the other side, but a Russian military vehicle ahead blocked its path. Quickly and with practiced efficiency, the American officers extracted the films from their cameras, hiding them in the removable panels of the car doors and replacing them with unexposed cartridges.

A Red Army Major walked toward them accompanied by a soldier carrying a submachine gun. "It is forbidden to take pictures of military installations," he said sternly.

"Are there any military installations here?" the American Captain answered with mocking innocence. "We just saw this beautiful river and . . ."

"Don't be arrogant," the Major warned, "and give me your cameras."

"All right, if you insist," the Captain said, handing over both cameras. "But just take the films and give us back the cameras."

"My orders are to confiscate the cameras," the Major replied, breaking into a wide grin. Western cameras always brought a hefty price on the black market. "Now get out of this restricted area," he ordered, "and no more funny business."

All this time, Nitsche at his table on the terrace had been taking in as much as he could of the comings and goings around the bridge. After the American car had left, he went inside and tried to elicit some information from the bartender. But the latter was totally uncommunicative. A truck pulling a flatcar piled high with thick steel rods drove into the Gasthaus parking lot. Two drivers got out and sat down at a table on the terrace. Nitsche returned to his outside table. The truck drivers ordered beers, *würstel,* and potato salad.

Nitsche watched them out of the corner of his eye. One was garrulous, the other, busily eating and drinking, responded by nods and shakes of his head. After a while, Nitsche stood up and ambled over to them.

"Did you have a long trip?"

"Long enough," the talkative one replied.

"Where did you come from?"

"Rostock."

"That's not so far," Nitsche said, sitting down at a table next to theirs.

"Try driving on those roads with our load. You'll see how far it is." The other driver gave an ugly laugh.

"What are you carrying?" Nitsche asked.

"Steel rods, as you can see."

The bartender came out on the terrace with a second round of large steins of beer.

"Where are you taking them?" Nitsche asked.

"Just to the construction site at the other side of the bridge. Next week will be worse; we're scheduled to bring in some heavy platforms. I sure hope to hell they'll pay the bonuses they promised; I'm counting on it. Aren't you, Kurt?"

The other man, his mouth full, just grunted.

"What are these rods and platforms for?" Nitsche asked.

The second driver looked over at him suspiciously. "What is this?" he asked gruffly. "A fuckin' interrogation?"

"Sorry," Nitsche apologized. "I don't mean to be nosy. Just trying to pass the time of day until my next appointment." He gave an ingratiating smile, which was not returned. The drivers were concentrating on their food.

The bartender had stayed by the door, listening to Nitsche's inquiries. He went back inside and called the police to report that a stranger was asking a lot of questions about construction work at the bridge.

Nitsche began to feel uncomfortable. He counted out the money he owed and got up to leave. The bartender came back outside. "How about another beer?" he suggested.

"No, thank you," Nitsche replied, leaving the Gasthaus hastily before the police arrived.

*   *   *

In the afternoon, Weber headed back to the train station. The sun was now shining, matching his confident and elated spirits. He had a calm and uneventful trip back to Berlin, carrying his precious lighter and unopened pack of cigarettes unconcernedly in his outer coat pocket.

*   *   *

Brigitte's father, Professor Friedrich Halder, a staunch anti-Communist, had left Berlin's prestigious Humboldt University at war's end because of its location in the Russian Sector and had moved to the recently established Freie Universität in West Berlin. As a disciple and biographer of Heidegger, he was a well-known, if controversial, teacher of philosophy. His antipathy to Communism and his disdain for the Nazis did not, however, mean that he embraced the Western Allies. Yes, the American airlift in 1948 had saved West Berlin, but, as he often reminded Brigitte and anyone else who would listen, this was not done for any love of the West Berliners. The Americans were driven by their own global strategic interests; otherwise, he maintained, they would nonchalantly have let us starve.

"Let us not forget that we are Germans," he would proclaim proudly. "We have been defeated, although it took the whole world to bring us to our knees. Now, we must have dignity in our defeat, work hard, and in time regain our rightful place in the society of civilized nations."

Ever since the death of Halder's wife from cancer five years earlier, Brigitte had kept house for her father. This was a cozy arrangement for the elderly man, which he feared would not last, for Brigitte, now 31, would in time put the grieving for her dead fiancé aside and rebuild a normal life for herself. A few weeks ago she had brought a young man to the house, who to her father's dismay turned out to be an American officer.

"Can't you find a good German to keep you company?" he had exploded after Cole's first visit.

"The one I found is dead, father," she had replied calmly.

"There are others."

"There will never be another Franz," she said, ending the discussion by leaving the room.

Professor Halder was at it again as Brigitte sat in the salon waiting for Cole to arrive. "Would you go out with a Russian?" he asked.

"I don't know," she answered, realizing that her reply would provoke her father even further. "I don't believe in national guilt. I try to judge people as individuals."

"You're an idealist and a dreamer," Halder said angrily. "We Germans can't afford ideals right now. We need to be tough and realistic so that we can reconstruct our shattered society."

Cole rang the front doorbell in the middle of this altercation. Professor Halder greeted him with icy courtesy and quickly excused himself, saying that he had a lecture to prepare. Brigitte and Cole left the house soon thereafter.

"I'm taking you out for a good meal," he said, holding the car door open for her.

"Are your intentions purely culinary?" she asked mischievously, looking up at him and crinkling her nose as she slipped into the soft leather-cushioned seat.

Cole grinned. "Time will tell," he said, getting into the driver's seat and starting the car for the drive into town. He had made a dinner reservation in the posh dining room of the Hotel Kempinski. The hotel was located at the corner of the Kudamm and Fasanenstrasse, and Cole parked the car next to the remains of what had been Berlin's largest synagogue. They got out of the car and, walking the short distance to the Kempinski's outside terrace, sat down at a white metal table under a large cream-colored umbrella. Brigitte's long, graceful legs drew admiring glances from men at the nearby tables and passersby on the Kudamm.

"Your father doesn't like me very much, does he?" Cole said.

"It's nothing personal. He just hasn't gotten around to thinking of Americans as friends."

Cole thought about that for a moment. "I hope that isn't an inherited trait," he said.

Brigitte smiled. "No, of course not. I judge people one by one. I have seen the consequences of the other kind of thinking."

"How many Germans are like you," Cole asked, "and how many think like your father?"

Brigitte laughed. "Stop! Before we get into those deep waters, how about a drink?" She ordered a glass of Rhein wine; he had a dry martini, which despite his explicit instructions was lukewarm and anything but dry.

Brigitte looked down the Kudamm at the imposing ruin of the Kaiser Wilhelm Memorial Church with its jagged steeple jutting into the darkening evening sky. She remembered seeing the fires still burning the morning after the church had been bombed. Now its blackened hulk, amidst the glitter of West Berlin's luxury boutiques, was a reminder of the dark, yet recent, past.

"I don't know," she finally said in answer to Cole's question.

"I've never counted noses. My guess is that my father and I are fairly representative of our generations." She thought it best not to add "our class." She had learned that Americans did not understand or appreciate European class distinctions. She went on: "The older ones can't fully accept blame, while we're too young to feel any sense of guilt. And yet we know that the outside world considers us all to be Nazis. That's true, isn't it?"

"I suppose so, but only by people who don't know you."

"But that's always the case," Brigitte exclaimed, raising her voice. "Generalizations about other people are always believed by people who don't know. And these know-nothings usually form a majority, and that's how tragedies come about."

The couple at the next table had turned around at Brigitte's outburst. It was getting dark, and Cole suggested they go in to dinner. They were shown to a window table in the somber wood-paneled dining room. When they were seated, Cole took Brigitte's hand.

"Listen, Brigitte," he said. "We're not going to solve the world's problems tonight. Let's just relax and enjoy each other's company."

Brigitte did not pull her hand away. Instead, she looked intently at Cole and tried to smile, while at the same time her eyes filled with tears. They sat quietly for a minute or two and then, when Brigitte had recovered her composure, she declared that she was ravenously hungry.

Whereas most Berlin restaurants only offered the traditional "good burgher" German cooking, the Kempinski's menu was elaborate. Cole was pleased to show off his culinary expertise by describing in some detail a number of the French dishes. Brigitte listened with amusement. To her, after the deprivation of the war years, food was still but a remedy for hunger pangs. She had not yet had time to develop a discriminating palate, but she was more than willing to learn. They both decided to start with a duck paté followed by a coq au vin, which they were assured was one of the chef's specialties. After perusing the wine list, Cole chose a bottle of Saint Emilion, which he thought would go well with both dishes.

He made sure to keep the conversation light and Brigitte's glass well filled. After dinner, they strolled down the Kudamm and went to see a brainless movie filled with pratfalls, police chases, and beds with unexpected occupants.

It was drizzling when they came out of the movie and, laughing like young teenagers, scampered back to his car. For the last two days Brigitte had asked herself how Cole would behave after Sunday night's kiss. How did she want him to act? What signal had she sent? All these musings had been superfluous. As they settled into the dry comfort of the car, Cole put his arm around Brigitte, slowly turned her wet face to his, and gave her a gentle kiss, which with no hesitation she returned eagerly. They held each other tightly for a minute or two, without speaking. Then, Cole started the car and headed back toward Dahlem.

Brigitte thought he would probably drive back to his apartment and if so, she was ready for love. She nestled her head against his shoulder as he drove slowly through the rain-drenched streets. Though Cole sensed her compliance, he wanted to be careful not to rush her. Brigitte was becoming important to him. She was a great girl, not a one-night stand. Brigitte had her eyes closed and as the car came to a halt, she was surprised to find herself in front of her own house. Not only surprised but also disappointed.

Cole was grinning at her. Had he read her thoughts? she wondered. She leaned over for a quick good-night kiss, which turned into a long embrace. Her breathing quickened, and she pulled away. I'm acting like a bitch in heat, she scolded herself. That clever American is letting me seduce him. She jumped out of the car and, blowing Cole a kiss, loped into the shelter of her front veranda. Cole looked after her, admiring the animal grace of her movements. I'm falling for that woman, he said to himself as he drove away. The thought was a pleasing one.

Back in his BOQ, Cole stretched out on his bed in the dark and thought about Brigitte. She had been through the fire, he mused, but had come out of it a decent human being.

He looked out the window. The show in the top-floor maids' rooms in the neighboring apartment house was in full swing. Young German girls were provocatively posing and undressing in the windows with the lights on behind them. These striptease performances were a nightly entertainment, and due to the rapid turnover in domestic personnel, the sport was to be the first to spot and try out the new talent. A blinking of lights in the BOQ would bring the performers over for a closer inspection. The standard price was a carton of cigarettes.

Just an extension of the Daisy slave market, Cole muttered to himself as he got up to get a beer out of the fridge. Yet what right, he asked himself, did he have to be so self-righteous? What about the covert missions he was running? How different were they on moral grounds from the sexual spectacle he was witnessing? Weren't the refugees who were being pressured to spy his own slaves? These thoughts made him uncomfortable as he sat in the dark, watching the show across the way and sipping his beer.

Lives are put at risk and even sacrificed in military operations, he reflected. That is certainly true in war. But in peace? Can part of a society, the one carrying on espionage activities, be at war while the rest is at peace?

Cole got up and shook his head. His father—the mayor of the small southern town where Cole had grown up—would undoubtedly call these questions "wooly-headed nonsense." He took the empty beer bottle back into the kitchen. He was a soldier, Cole reminded himself, an American officer and proud of it. He had an important mission to accomplish with whatever effective means were available, which certainly included recruiting refugees. Idealism was a noble sentiment, but most idealists were free to dream only because they were protected by those with less refined sensibilities. Those like himself who were willing to get their hands dirty.

*   *   *

It was late in the evening when Pritzer returned to the office of the 575th, after completing his debriefing of Weber. Herter was still at his desk, compiling reports, and Pritzer handed him the camera that Weber had returned.

"How did Weber do?" Herter asked.

"The photos should tell the story. He took a whole roll of film."

"Good," Herter said. "I'll have it developed first thing in the morning. It would be helpful to have your summary of Weber's report at the same time." The phrase "it would be helpful" was Herter's typical introduction to a command. "Didn't you also send a second agent to look at the bridge?"

"Yes," Pritzer replied. "He should have come back this evening too. I hope nothing happened to him."

Herter shrugged. To him, agents were pawns in the intelligence-gathering game. They could be put at risk or sacrificed on the basis of the value of the information to be obtained.

"Don't worry, Pritzer. He'll be back. They always come back for their money."

"Speaking of which," Pritzer confessed, "I forgot to stop by earlier this evening to pick up Weber's money."

"That was a mistake," Herter said. "Never forget payday. After all, money is our only hold over these people. Don't put any stock in their professed love of liberty and democracy. That's just crap they think we like to hear. What they want is the almighty Deutsche Mark."

"I promised to pay him in the morning."

"How did he take that?"

"He was pissed."

Herter smiled. "No great harm done, Pritzer," he said. "After all, it is also essential to keep agents on edge. Let's have a look at the photos and review your report before you see Weber in the morning."

"Are you suggesting we might hold out on him? Not pay him? You just said never to forget payday."

"What do you think this is?" Herter replied, with an edge to his voice. "The goddamn Salvation Army? There's no bond of loyalty between a handler and an agent. There is no moral obligation to keep promises. It's all a question of control. All our actions must be directed to that end. Keep them under pressure at all times. The moment an agent thinks he's got something on you, it's over. Understand?"

"Yes."

"Never forget it," Herter said, putting on his glasses and beginning to review another report.

After putting his scribbled notes of Weber's debriefing in the office safe, Pritzer left the office with the distinct feeling that he was being treated like an agent himself.

Day 6 Wednesday

Pritzer returned to the office of the 575th at 7 a.m. to prepare his summary of Weber's report. He found Herter and Muldane together examining the photos that Weber had taken.

"Where's the report on the Weber mission?" Herter asked.

"I've come in early to write it up," Pritzer replied.

Muldane turned to Pritzer and said, "You know, our man has really brought in some extraordinary stuff." Pritzer thought of Weber as "his" man now, but didn't say so.

"Of course," Herter said, "these photos were taken from across the river and at a low altitude, from a third-floor flat. But Muldane is right. They're quite something."

Herter had spread out the photos on his long table, discarded the few that were either overexposed or out of focus, and sorted the remainder in accordance with the particular views they depicted. Herter was restrained, but clearly keyed up. The contours of the construction work seemed to match the outline of the terrain required for SAM installations.

"I've enlarged the sites pictured on the Weber photos," he explained, "and superimposed them over pictures of SAM installations outside Moscow. Of course, the latter have the SAM batteries installed, so we can't compare empty terrains, but take a close look at the circumference. The angles and contours are remarkably similar, and the depression left of center at the Frankfurt/Oder site is where the principal support of the command module could be located. It's hard to believe that this is all a mere coincidence."

Muldane was fascinated. "Let's get Bud in here," he said, leaving Herter's office to find Cole. Herter kept studying the photographs, and Pritzer edged in for a closer look.

Herter turned to him. "I want that mission summary, Pritzer," he said. "On the double!"

Pritzer retrieved his notes from the office safe and, sitting at an empty desk in the hall, began to transcribe Weber's report. He saw Cole and Muldane enter Herter's office and close the door behind them, and he felt a flash of anger. He was again being treated unfairly. After all, it was his agent who had brought back the photos. He was now writing the report that would doubtless accompany the transfer of those pictures to Headquarters. Yet his principal role was being ignored; no, not ignored, erased. Perhaps, he thought, Weber would be taken away from him, now that he had proved his worth. That would be typical of the military. A bunch of bastards!

"This could be a matter of grave importance," Herter said, as Cole and Muldane entered his office. "If the Russians are beginning to station SAMs this far forward, it may signal that they are expecting or preparing for hostilities."

"Why would that be?" Cole asked. "They may only be protecting their military installations. A reasonable precaution, wouldn't you say?"

"No, Colonel, not really," Herter expounded, "because we know that the Russians don't have enough SAMs to protect their vital targets inside Russia, their oil fields, tank and airplane factories, and the like. The Russian military is desperate to mount these defenses inside Mother Russia. Now, if they were to begin to use part of this precious supply this far forward on the western Polish border, we'd better take due note."

Herter showed Cole the photos and the comparisons he had made. The similarities were striking, though of course it took a bit of imagination to picture the missile batteries on the Frankfurt/ Oder construction site.

"Is it possible that we are overreacting here?" Cole asked, guardedly. It was rare that he would question any of Herter's conclusions. "In fact, all we have at the moment for sure," he added with a chuckle, "is a sand pile near a bridge."

Muldane looked anxiously at Herter, anticipating that he would take the remark as a rebuke. But Herter, a true professional, appeared to welcome the inquiry. "You're right, Colonel," he said, "all we have is a sand pile. What we must have now is more information on that sand pile. If it's for Russian kids to play in, fine; no danger to us. But if . . ."

"OK, I understand," Cole said, "we have to keep a watchful eye on that bridge. By the way, let me see the report on that mission."

"Pritzer's writing it up right now," Herter said. "Let's see if he's finished." As Herter moved toward the door, Pritzer knocked twice and came in, his report in hand.

"Good timing. We were just talking about you," Muldane said, taking the report from Pritzer. "Sit down. We're about to discuss your man's new mission."

Muldane quickly read Pritzer's short summary. "Nothing new here," he said, handing the paper to Cole. He glanced at it and passed it on to Herter, who read it quickly and without comment placed it on the table next to the photographs.

"What agents do we have covering Frankfurt/Oder?" Cole asked.

"Weber, who returned last evening with the photos," Muldane answered, "and we're waiting for another one to return."

"They're both my agents," Pritzer interjected proudly.

"Frankfurt/Oder," Herter remarked, "has never before been a place that we've paid much attention to."

"Is this worth activating one of your agents in place?" Cole asked.

Herter hesitated. He had a dozen or so agents—moles, in the accepted jargon—living unobtrusively in the GDR, with moneys paid monthly into West German bank accounts in their cover names. They awaited his signal to become active. The problem was that their activation destroyed their safe anonymity. Moles were like rockets. Once the fuse was lit, they were generally only good for a single mission. Given the time and expense required to secrete moles, Herter was always most reluctant to sound the call to active duty.

"Before we do that, Colonel," he said, "let's wait for the second agent to return and see what he has to say. Also, I want some better pictures. The Minoltas are good, but they don't have the detachable telephoto lens the small Leicas have. Let's send Weber back with a Leica and have him focus"—Herter looked over at Cole with a grimace—"on the sand pile."

Pritzer spoke up. "Gentlemen," he said, "I'm not sure that Weber will agree to return. We've already had him go twice. I doubt that he'll risk his neck a third time, particularly if he's supposed to carry a fancy camera."

"I understand that we haven't paid him for that second trip yet," Muldane remarked.

"That's true. We still owe him half, DM 5000," Pritzer confirmed.

"We can use that as a pressure point," Herter said with satisfaction. "Also, we can be very generous in what we offer him for this trip. The Leica photos are indispensable. They will give us a very clear picture of what's going on. He can tape the telephoto lens to his leg, and we can sew the camera into his jacket. He'll be perfectly safe. He'll have no reason to worry."

"This is important, Pritzer," Cole said, as Pritzer got up to leave. "We'll all be watching your performance." After he had left, Cole asked Muldane to assist Pritzer in his handling of Weber. "We can't afford to have this mission screwed up," he said.

*   *   *

The Stasi office was located on the second floor of Frankfurt/Oder's Central Police Station. The local Stasi chief, Heinz Janicek, was not pleased to see the two Berlin emissaries.

"Why are you here?" he asked gruffly. "Your time would be better spent plugging all the Berlin escape routes. The border is leaking like a sieve."

Janicek was a lifelong dedicated Communist, now in his sixties. He was bald and rotund with a ruddy complexion and a no-nonsense manner. Imprisoned for Communist activities by the

Nazis, he had been able to flee to the Soviet Union in 1939 during the brief Russo-German honeymoon. He returned to Germany in 1945 with the advancing Red Army and devoted himself to the fulfillment of his dream—building Socialism in the Fatherland. He was honest and, protected by the Party hierarchy as an "Old Comrade," not afraid to speak his mind.

"Kommissar Zeunert sent us," one of the emissaries explained, "to see if we can be of any help."

"You mean he sent you down here to spy on me," Janicek retorted. "I have taken all the measures I consider necessary. My assistant will give you the details. Now please excuse me. I have important work to do." Without another word, the Berlin agents were ushered out as Janicek turned his attention to some papers on his desk.

But Heinz Janicek was concerned. He had been informed of the Potsdam Mission's presence at the bridge the day before. That was troubling. The Mission's cars rarely paid Frankfurt/Oder a visit. It could of course be a coincidence, but Janicek knew that was unlikely.

He could not explain the Americans' sudden interest in the bridge. He picked up the telephone and called the engineer in charge of the bridge, but learned he was out of town. All his assistant could say was that some excavation work was being undertaken by the Russians.

"Do you know the purpose of this work?" Janicek asked.

"No," the latter replied. "Our fraternal comrades-in-arms are often rather tight-lipped about their projects. But it doesn't look like a big deal to me. Perhaps a small building for the anti-aircraft crews."

"Is that just your guess?"

"Yes."

"I don't want guesses when I'm asking for information," Janicek shouted and slammed down the receiver.

He decided he could no longer delay a call to Kommissar Zeunert, the Stasi chief of counter-intelligence in Berlin, who had asked for daily reports on the security measures being taken in Frankfurt/Oder. After a moment, Zeunert came on the line and without interrupting listened to Janicek's account. He paused a moment to reflect.

Then he inquired with mock disbelief, "Do I understand you correctly? The Americans are sending the Potsdam Mission to look at an excavation near the bridge whose purpose you, in charge of the security of the city, totally ignore?"

"That is twisting my words, Herr Kommissar," Janicek responded heatedly.

"Let me put the question another way," Zeunert continued. "Would the Americans be wasting the time of the Potsdam Mission unless they suspected that there was something of value they wanted to learn at the bridge?"

"No, I suppose not."

"Therefore, they either *do* know something we don't, or at least they *suspect* something. And we don't know what that is either. Do you follow me, Janicek?"

"Yes, Kommissar," Janicek replied grudgingly. He bitterly resented Zeunert's condescension. What right, Janicek asked himself, did that young pup have to lecture him, an Old Fighter who had sat in a Nazi prison for the sake of the World Triumph of Socialism when Zeunert was still in diapers?

"I suggest," Zeunert admonished Janicek, "that you clarify this situation immediately. Understood? Immediately."

"Yes, Herr Kommissar."

*   *   *

"Wiesbaden Headquarters. General Norcross on the line," the switchboard announced.

What the hell does the Old Man want now? Cole wondered as he sat down at his desk to take the call. "Yes, General," he said.

"Bud, is that you?"

"Yes, sir."

"How're things goin'?"

"Just fine, General."

"Anything new or out of the ordinary I should know about?"

"Not that I can think of, sir."

"I've been gettin' some questions on that bridge construction . . ."

"In Frankfurt/Oder?"

"Yeah, that's the one. Can you give me an update?"

Cole took a deep breath. "Well, sir," he replied, "as you may have heard, one of the 575th sources . . ."

"Can the self-congratulations, Bud. Just the facts, please."

"A few days ago we had a report on some construction work near the bridge, one of your Headquarters' priority targets. We're checking it out."

"I've heard," General Norcross said, "that this may be preparatory work for missile installations. Anything to that?"

"As I said, we're checking it out, sir."

"That could be very serious. You realize that, don't you, Bud?"

"Yes, General, I sure do."

"Have you put sufficient resources on this?"

"All my available agents, General, but frankly, I don't have that many. And I'm working with some second-rate handlers. If I could get some more experienced personnel, I might be able to produce . . ."

"Stop belly-achin', Bud. You've got the largest number of USAF civilian employees in Europe as it is. Munich is always after me to take some of them away from you. I'm protecting your ass as it is, my boy, but I can't send you any more. Move your people around. Give them new assignments. Maybe they're just getting stale in their old jobs. And keep me informed on that damn bridge. I'm taking a personal interest, y'hear?"

As was his habit, General Norcross hung up abruptly. He's running true to form, Cole reflected. Never any help or praise; just demands. Move people around? He may be right on that.

Cole buzzed the switchboard and asked that Liebman report

to his office immediately. In the meantime, Cole took Liebman's personnel file out of a lower desk drawer and began to review it. Liebman arrived some twenty minutes later.

"You wanted to see me, Colonel?" Liebman said, a bit out of breath.

"Yes, Liebman. Come in and sit down. I've been going over the civilian personnel records. You know, it's almost time again for annual reviews. I've examined yours and thought we should have a little talk."

Liebman had no doubt about what was coming. He had had a number of "little talks" before. "I hope that you are satisfied with my performance," he said evenly.

"Very much so. You are an able and conscientious interrogator."

"Thank you, sir," Liebman answered. There was a pause. Liebman waited, careful not to give Cole any opening.

"Don't you ever get bored," Cole asked, "asking the same damn questions, day in and day out?"

Liebman smiled. "Frankly, sometimes, a little, yes."

"Wouldn't you like a job with more variety, more excitement, more suited to your talents and intelligence?"

"Colonel," Liebman answered, "I'd be pleased to take on a more challenging job. But if none is open, I'm happy to continue as I am. I trust that I am contributing my fair share to the Squadron's overall mission."

"You could contribute a helluva lot more," Cole replied softly.

"How?" Liebman asked, knowing full well what the answer would be. Cole was just being more circuitous than his predecessors had been. One colonel had barked at him: "Goddamn it, I want you to run agents. Understand?" Liebman had understood and had refused to do so, despite threats that his stubbornness would damage his career. In the end, the 575th needed a good interrogator, which there was no doubt he was. So he was left in place and relative peace, until the next time. "How?" he asked again.

"I want you to reconsider your refusal to engage in covert work," Cole said in a quiet, reasonable tone. "We're short of able personnel in that area. We need a man of your talent and experience."

"I'm sorry, Colonel," Liebman replied with equally measured inflection, "but I have made it abundantly clear whenever that subject has been raised with me that covert work is against my principles."

"What are those principles that stop you from helping to preserve the Free World against the danger of Communism?"

This was sensitive ground. Liebman could not deny that stopping Communism was a practical as well as a moral imperative. "I'm not questioning the purpose or the necessity of covert work, Colonel. It's just that I can't do it."

Cole's tone became harsher. "So you agree it's a job that has to be done. The rest of us do it and try not to be too squeamish about it. What's so special about you?"

"There's nothing special about me," Liebman protested, "but I've been a witness to so much useless killing that I can't bring myself to put anyone else's life at risk."

"So what you're saying is that you just want others to do the dirty work. Is that it?"

"No, Colonel," Liebman replied softly, "what I'm saying, I suppose, is that I've become a pacifist."

Cole reacted firmly. "Liebman, you're in a military unit, even if you are a civilian. A military outfit is no place for a pacifist."

"Colonel, you have just told me that I'm performing well in my job. Why not just leave me there, instead of trying to push me into one I can't do?"

Cole changed tactics and though his voice was lower, the thrust of his argument was sharper. "I think you're either dumb or a hypocrite, Liebman. And you don't strike me as being dumb."

"Why do you say that, Colonel?"

"Why do you think that setting a refugee up for being sent back is that much purer than sending him back yourself?"

"It's not purer, Colonel. It's different."

"What do you think you're doing when you refer him to the safe house? You're setting him up, Liebman. You're the Judas goat, for Christ's sake. Stop kidding yourself. You're engaged in covert activities already."

Liebman did not respond, and the two men continued to stare at each other.

At length, Cole said: "You have a week to request a formal transfer to covert operations."

"And if I don't?"

"Then, Liebman, I'm afraid that your days with this outfit are numbered."

*   *   *

Muldane was discussing with Pritzer how to deal with Weber. He discouraged him from using Herter's heavy-handed tactic of withholding money due. That, he said, would only create resentment when what was needed now was cooperation. Also, Muldane suggested a less clumsy alternative to Herter's idea of sewing the Minolta camera into Weber's clothing. And finally, Muldane advised Pritzer to employ a mixture of praise, continued emphasis on the minimal risk involved, and above all a promise of lots more money in prospect.

"How much more will we be willing to pay?" Pritzer asked.

Muldane reflected a moment. "I would think that you could go as high as DM 25,000," he said. "But try and have him go for less."

Pritzer found an anxious and frustrated Weber waiting for him at the safe house. All night long he had been convinced that Herr Steiner would renege on coming up with the remaining DM 5000. The more Anna tried to calm him by saying that he should be glad to be back safe and sound and satisfied to have all the money he had already been paid, the more furious he became at the thought of having been cheated.

Consequently, Pritzer's opening gambit hit a bull's-eye. "I'm so sorry, Herr Weber, that I forgot to bring your money last night. Here it is."

As Pritzer counted out the crisp DM 100 notes, a nonplused Weber mumbled some incoherent phrases of thanks. Anna had been right; he had become exercised for nothing.

"I've brought the photos you took. They're really very good. Do you mind going over them with me?"

"No of course not. I'd like to see them," Weber said.

They sat down at a table in the corner of the large room and studied the photos together. Pritzer asked Weber to identify some of the houses in the foreground, inquired about the various small boats moored on the river banks, and questioned him on the strictness of the security measures in force around the bridge and the anti-aircraft batteries. There was little Weber could add on any of these points.

"Did you learn anything about these excavations?" Pritzer asked.

"No."

"We're intrigued," Pritzer explained, pointing to one of the enlarged photos, "by that hole here, near the middle on the left side. Any idea what that might be for?"

"Not the slightest."

"Let me show you something else." Pritzer took a large aerial reconnaissance photo out of a thick manila envelope marked SECRET SENSITIVE. "This," he said, "is the picture of a Russian missile battery."

Weber was wide-eyed. "I've never seen anything like that!" he exclaimed.

"We wonder whether the excavation near your bridge might be preparatory work for a similar installation. Do you see this large central metal structure in the middle?"

Weber nodded.

"It could fit very nicely into that hole I just pointed out to you on the left side of the dig." Weber stared in amazement from one picture to the other. Pritzer looked at him with satisfaction.

"What are they?" Weber asked.

"Russian surface-to-air missiles, called SAMs. Much faster and more accurate than the anti-aircraft guns currently defending the bridge. You do see now, don't you, the importance of your having returned to look out your kitchen window?" Pritzer was satisfied with his formulation, but Weber kept looking at the photos and did not respond.

"Well, Herr Weber," Pritzer said, gathering up the photos and carefully putting the aerial reconnaissance picture back into the manila envelope, "two quick trips and suddenly you're DM 12,500 richer. You see we keep our word." Pritzer waited for that to sink in and then asked, "What are you going to do now?"

"Start a new life for myself and my family."

"That money should be a big help."

Weber smiled, clutching his DM 100 notes tightly.

Like a toreador smoothly guiding in his stiletto-like sword, Pritzer asked softly, "How would you like to make one last, one final trip?"

The question had been asked so quietly that Weber's negative response was equally muted and restrained.

"Not even for DM 25,000?"

"How much did you say?"

"DM 25,000. Twenty-five-thousand Deutsche Mark."

Weber hesitated. "To do what?" he asked.

"We need a clearer picture of the excavation."

"The ones you showed me looked very clear to me."

"We want one taken by a telephoto lens, and we're prepared to pay you DM 25,000 for that."

Pritzer thought he had him, but Weber surprised him. "No," he replied. "It's a tempting offer, Herr Steiner, but I won't push my luck. I don't want to risk my neck a third time. DM 12,500 will give me a good enough start."

Pritzer was disappointed. His impulse would have been to press the point, but Muldane had foreseen this contingency and instructed Pritzer to give a tactical magnanimous response.

"Fine, Herr Weber," he said, "we would never want to force

you to do anything against your will. It's just that a quick trip would be such an easy thing for you to do, and, as I just showed you, such an important one. A mere three or four hours and you'd be truly a rich man." Pritzer eyed Weber closely and noted his momentary vacillation.

"Thank you, Herr Weber," he said quickly, walking over to Weber and shaking his hand in an unmistakable gesture of dismissal. "We'll let you know about the arrangements for flying you and your family out to West Germany."

"When would that be?"

"In a few days, I hope." Pritzer had sat down at the table again and, barely looking up, said, "Good-bye."

Weber left the room and climbed the stairs to the second floor apartment, feeling strangely off-balance and trying to put the thought of DM 25,000 out of his mind.

*   *   *

The best restaurant in West Berlin was unquestionably in the Maison de France. That evening, for no particular reason other than that he had nothing else planned and felt in need of a solitary recharging of his batteries, Major Muldane had decided to treat himself to a fancy dinner. The restaurant was on the top floor of a concrete-fronted building on the corner of the Kudamm and Uhlandstrasse, which housed various French cultural and information services and a movie theater at street level featuring French films.

The restaurant was reserved for Allied officers and their guests, though German guests were pointedly not welcome. Monsieur Max, the German maître d'hôtel, ceremoniously showed Muldane to a table near the picture window on the Kudamm. Monsieur Max was proud to be in charge of a non-German dining room; it somehow made him less German, an ardently sought-after quality in postwar Germany. At times, a French officer would complain about the lack of a French maître d'hôtel, but he would be advised that Max did his job exceedingly well, spoke but slightly accented French, and was available at wages no self-respecting French maître d'hôtel would accept.

During the day Muldane had received the list of the Russian guests who would be attending next week's cocktail party. There were comments by the CIC, the Army's Counter Intelligence Corps, next to the names of some persons on whom it had files. The CIC officer who had given Muldane the list had admitted that the comments would not be very helpful.

"Our information," he had said, "is mostly based on the largely fictitious biographical data that the Russkis give us, and in the rare cases where we know better, we can't tell you because that information is classified."

"I suppose that we supply the Russians with a similarly phony list," Muldane had remarked.

"Not at all," the CIC officer had replied. "Our policy for these social functions is to give the Russians our real names; it's our 'cover names' that we don't supply."

"You mean to say that we give them real names, and they give us cover names?"

"That's right," the CIC officer had confirmed. "But after you've been in Berlin for a while, it's hard to know which name has the greater substance."

Muldane was reflecting on this strange interchange when the waiter's discreet cough caught his attention. He ordered a Scotch and soda and began to nibble on the assortment of peanuts, potato chips, and olives he had been served.

The cocktail party was now only a week away, and Cole had already twice asked Muldane for a report on the program that he was planning. Acceptances had been received from the heads of the three other Intelligence Missions. Moreover, General Swenson, the U.S. Commanding General, was slated to put in a short appearance.

"Let's do a bang-up job," Cole had urged, "but remember, nothing 'political.' I don't want any diplomatic incident."

"What if I show some Mickey Mouse cartoons?" Muldane had suggested mischievously.

"This is serious business, Zach," Cole had replied earnestly. "Don't let me down."

His earlier flippant remark had made Muldane consider showing a Disney nature film. He was sipping his drink and turning that idea over in his mind when a tall, distinguished-looking man in a blue pin-stripe custom-tailored suit deliberately walked over to his table, put his hand on Muldane's shoulder, and smilingly asked if he could join him.

L. Cabot Pearson was the USIA representative in Berlin in charge of Amerika Haus and other U.S. "re-education" efforts. A former war correspondent for *The Washington Post*, he was both a pseudo-intellectual and a social snob. Muldane was not alone in trying to avoid him whenever possible, but tonight there seemed to be no escape.

"Sit down, Cabot," Muldane said, "and have a drink."

Pearson settled his large frame into the smallish chair. "The usual, Mr. Pearson?" the hovering waiter asked when Pearson was seated. Pearson nodded and was quickly served a double Beefeater martini, straight up, in a chilled crystal glass.

"I don't often see you here, Major," Pearson said. "If you haven't ordered, let me recommend the rack of lamb. It's delicious." Pearson's voice was deep and resonant. His British-tinged accent was a source of amusement at the British Officers' Club. However, Pearson maintained that it was a Boston, not an English, accent.

Muldane let Pearson order for both of them, which he did with authority in serious consultation with Monsieur Max. They agreed upon a menu of warm foie gras on toast, rack of lamb, and a mixed salad. Pearson then studied the wine list and after some deliberate hesitation chose a Sauterne for the foie gras and a Pomerol for the lamb.

As the foie gras was served, Pearson launched into a series of complaints about recurrent staffing problems at Amerika Haus, at the same time grumbling to Max that the foie gras was cool and not lukewarm. Muldane listened patiently and then decided he might as well put this unfortunate encounter to some use by picking Pearson's brain.

"Any thoughts on how to entertain the Russkis?" he asked. "I'm in charge of planning events for the four-power get-together next week."

"So they have you doing that too, have they?" Pearson smiled. "Is that the party next week at Harnack Haus?"

"Yes, next Wednesday evening."

"So I'm to help plan my own entertainment. Is that it?" The lamb was being brought, and Pearson tasted the Pomerol and declared it potable.

"I've been told," Muldane mentioned, "not to come up with anything that might be considered political propaganda. I believe the Russians have a rather broad definition of that term."

"Yes, indeed," Pearson confirmed. "The last incident, if I remember correctly, involved a Jimmy Stewart movie. The Russians objected to the fact that every family was shown to own a car. Clearly capitalistic propaganda!" Pearson guffawed, brushed his lips with his napkin, and took another sip of wine.

"I suppose," Muldane said with a grin, "I shouldn't be asking the head of the USIA for some neutral nonpropaganda material, but frankly I'm stumped. Particularly since the Colonel . . ."

"Bud Cole?"

"Yeah."

"He's a good man."

"Yes, he is," Muldane agreed. "He's a straight-shooter. Anyway, he wants a program for the party that will knock their socks off. Got any thoughts?"

As they talked, Pearson was of the view that music was the perfect—in fact, probably the only—answer to Muldane's problem. "Have a string quartet," he proposed. "It will show them we're cultured. Have them play some Shostakovich. That would be a nice touch." He paused and took another sip of wine. "A jazz concert is a possibility, too, of course, if a string quartet is too high-brow—for our people, not the Russkis; they're musically quite literate." Finally, he suggested a singer of popular American songs or a dancer or a combination of any of the above.

Muldane listened to this litany and asked Pearson if he could recommend any performers. Pearson could not. Unfortunately, Amerika Haus had no upcoming musical events. Muldane thanked him for his suggestions and said he'd come up with something.

"Surprise me, Major," Pearson said, surveying the cheese tray that he was being offered. "I look forward to it." He selected a generous portion of Reblochon. Then, turning back to Muldane, he asked a surprising question: "Tell me, Major, how are you bearing up in our historic struggle between good and evil?"

"Is that what the hell you really think we're up to?" Muldane replied.

"Of course. It's our Great Crusade against Godless Communism, known more familiarly around Amerika Haus as GCGC." Pearson paused. "Don't you agree?"

"I'm no stranger to war, Cabot," Muldane said testily. "You may remember that I picked up some shrapnel during a bombing raid over Schweinfurt. But I'm not sure that slogans present a very accurate picture."

"All great struggles must be presented in terms of black and white," Pearson insisted. "Whoever heard of going over the top to die for a particular shade of gray? Answer me that."

"I would say that talk is a lot cheaper than bullets."

Pearson persisted. "But which is the more effective?"

Muldane did not reply. The two men finished their espressos, and Muldane declined to join Pearson in an after-dinner cordial. Saying he had a date, he excused himself and wandered up the Kudamm with its shop windows lit and its café terraces still crowded late in the evening. What a stuffed shirt that Pearson is, he thought, but I must admit he does know his food and wines.

On the sidewalk in front of a café near the Fasanenstrasse, a young man was drawing a remarkable likeness of the Mona Lisa with different-colored chalks. A small crowd, mostly young couples with their arms around each other, were watching him without tossing any change in the small circle he had drawn for "Contributions to the Artist." Muldane stopped a moment to look and then walked on.

L. Cabot Pearson dawdled at the restaurant for some time, enjoying his Courvoisier. At length, he strolled out into the fresh air of the still bustling Kudamm. It was too early by Pearson's night-owl standards to return home. Without further ado, he headed to Mommsenstrasse, a street paralleling the Kudamm, and entered what appeared to be a nondescript, three-story family residence, actually the domain of the city's fabled madam, Fräulein Kitty. Pearson considered her house Berlin's most exclusive club, whose rules of entry were based not on wealth or family lineage but on that most prized of all Berlin's commodities—the potential for providing intelligence information.

Day 7 Thursday

Weber's eyes were bloodshot. He had been up most of the night and had come to the conclusion that Steiner was right. It would be easy; there was nothing to it. His absence would not be noticed until school started again in four days. A few hours on the train; some pictures from his kitchen window; and then almost DM 40,000 in his pocket. You have to take some risks in life, Weber told himself. This appeared to be a small risk worth taking.

Anna had of course been against it. She was superstitious. "You've been lucky twice. Don't be foolhardy," she had warned. "The third time things always go wrong. Think of me and our little Manfred."

"I am thinking of you," Weber had replied irately. "Another DM 25,000 would really set us up."

"We have more than enough already," she pleaded. "It's a fortune we never expected to have just a few days ago."

"I can double it."

"Or be sent to jail, and then what would become of the baby and me?"

The more Anna argued throughout the night, the more Weber became firm in his conviction that he must go one more time. He felt instinctively that he would be following his lucky star, and Weber had more faith in his instincts than in a woman's superstition. He would go, but he would ask for more money.

After breakfast, Weber sent word that he wanted to see Herr Steiner. Pritzer arrived at the safe house fifteen minutes later, determined not to show his excitement at Weber's expected change of heart.

"I've thought it over, Herr Steiner," Weber said.

"Yes?" Pritzer answered as nonchalantly as he could.

"I'm willing to go back one last time, but I absolutely must have more than DM 25,000."

"You are getting greedy, Herr Weber. A very bad sign," Pritzer said. It was standard operating procedure never to accede to an agent's demand for additional pay. "You know very well that DM 25,000 is very generous for a short day's excursion. If you won't take it, I can find someone else who would be pleased to go in your stead."

The two men stared at each other. Pritzer was bluffing. Not only did he not have a substitute to send, but he was highly anxious because the second agent he had dispatched to Frankfurt/Oder had not yet returned. The latter was now overdue by twenty-four hours.

"Well, Herr Weber," Pritzer said firmly, "make up your mind. I have other work to do."

Weber looked at Pritzer and realized there was no more money to be had. "All right," he grumbled, "I'll go. Where is my advance?"

"I can let you have DM 10,000."

"I want half; I want DM 12,500."

"Stop bargaining. What do you think this is, a Turkish bazaar? You'll take the DM 10,000 and get the rest when you return. Now, here are your instructions."

"What do you want me to do?" Weber's tone was surly but resigned.

"Just about what you did before, but this time you're going to work with this." Pritzer opened a small leather case and removed the small Leica camera with its telephoto lens.

Weber was alarmed. "It's too big," he objected. "I'll be spotted with that."

"Be quiet, and let me show you," Pritzer said. He demonstrated, as Muldane had shown him, how to detach and collapse the lens and to tape it to his leg. The Leica itself was to be placed inside the tin casing of a cheap GDR camera which, Pritzer assured Weber, would be just the kind that he would be bringing home from vacation. The Leica was already focused on the distance to the bridge from Weber's apartment, and Pritzer made

Weber practice loading the film, attaching and detaching the lens and taking some pictures.

"Your mission," Pritzer said at the end of his briefing, "is to take the photos. But if you happen to come across anyone working on the site, or anyone who knows about it, we'll give you a premium for additional information."

"How much?"

"That depends on what it's worth. We want to know what the construction is all about. Concentrate on that."

Pritzer reached into his breast pocket and took out a thick brown envelope. Under Weber's hungry gaze, he counted out one hundred DM 100 notes and handed them over.

"It's raining today, Herr Weber," Pritzer said. "Be prepared to leave early tomorrow morning, if the weather is clear. The driver will pick you up at 6:15 a.m. The usual routine. Call me as soon as you get back."

Pritzer left, Weber noted, without wishing him the customary "Good luck." I'm getting to be as superstitious as Anna, Weber rebuked himself.

*   *   *

Pritzer's second agent, a nervous middle-aged accountant, was overdue because he was now sitting in the Stasi jail in Frankfurt/Oder. He had been picked up the previous day, unable to explain his presence near the bridge. It took very little muscular interrogation to crush the frightened man. In a torrent of words he described the mission in Frankfurt/Oder he had been assigned. Janicek listened skeptically. Radar stations? Missiles? Absurd. Was the man deranged or an *agent provocateur*? And yet Zeunert himself had pointed out that the American Intelligence Services were concentrating on the bridge at Frankfurt/Oder.

"You are lying," Janicek said harshly. "The mission you describe is not believable. It is obviously an attempt—a fairly clumsy

one, I must say—to divert us from safeguarding the real targets of
American Intelligence. We'll get the truth out of you, even if we
have to use stronger measures." Turning to the guard, Zeunert
said: "Put him in the tub."

Located in a sound-proofed bathroom on the same floor, the
"tub" was a large metal bathtub with a number of steel grips on
both sides. The man was stripped and dumped into the tub face-
down with his ankles strapped to the sides. Alternating ice-cold
and scalding water was poured into the tub as the man flailed
desperately with his hands to keep from drowning. A half-hour
later, dressed in a cheap prison robe and still not fully dry, he was
again back before Janicek.

"Well," the latter asked sardonically, "are you ready to tell me
the truth instead of that fairy story?"

"I'll tell you anything you want, only please don't put me
back in that tub."

"I'm glad you're being reasonable. Now, will you admit you
were sent over to fool us?"

"I'll admit that. I'll confess to anything," the man was trembling. "Only you must know it wouldn't be the truth. What I told
you before is the truth."

A stubborn ox, Janicek thought, as he told the guard the take
the man back to his cell. I've got to get to the bottom of this
puzzle. Radar stations or missiles near the bridge here in town?
What the hell can this all mean?

*   *   *

In his office in the French military compound in Tegel, Colonel
Durafour was pondering the same puzzle. He had Nitsche's report
before him: increased security around the bridge; the Potsdam
Mission's car making a pass at the target; steel rods being delivered
to the construction site. It was a mystery. One thing, however, was
clear. Cole's veiled hint had turned out to be a valuable tip. Not
enough as yet to form the basis for a report to the *Quartier Général*—

they always wanted every angle covered and disdained hypotheses—but certainly enough of a lead to pursue.

The Americans obviously knew more. Another dinner invitation to Cole? No, Durafour decided, that would be tiresome. Instead, he would send an IAIC (an Inter-Allied Intelligence Communication) which should give a certain official status to their
cooperation on this target.

Cole received the coded IAIC a few hours later. It read in part
as follows: "Have followed up on your valuable suggestion. Our
sources confirm substantial and unexplained activity at Frankfurt/
Oder bridge. Steel rods are being trucked in from Rostock to the
site. Heavy platforms to be delivered next week. Security around
the bridge recently tightened. Will continue observation and would
appreciate liaison to coordinate our respective assessments."

Cole brought the IAIC in to Herter, whose eyebrows shot up.
"Was it necessary, Colonel," he asked archly, "to disclose our target
to the French?"

"I didn't," Cole replied. "As we had agreed, I just mentioned
our general interest in bridges. Durafour must have hit upon Frank-
furt/Oder by accident."

Herter considered this. "Or perhaps they've had their own
suspicions about the work at the bridge and are pretending that
we're the ones who have led them to Frankfurt/Oder," he said.
"Hiding their sources, while trying to pump us for ours. How
does he put it? 'Would appreciate liaison.' A typical Frog maneuver."

"Any thought on how to respond?" Cole asked.

"I want to check out this lead about steel rods from Rostock.
Let's wait until we get some more information ourselves, Colonel.
Then we can pass on something that's fairly routine so as not to
compromise any advantage we may have. We've got to dangle some-
thing out there, though, to have any chance of learning what the
Frogs have got."

"OK," Cole responded, "that sounds about right."

*   *   *

Lieutenant Anatoly Ossipov sat in his office in Karlshorst late in the evening, perplexed, staring at various reports he had just reviewed. His own inquiry regarding the excavation work around the bridge had become snarled in red tape and interservice rivalry. Sent by his superior, Red Air Force Colonel Fitin, to his counterpart in Red Army Intelligence, the request for information had been answered by a short reply asking in turn the reason for making the inquiry. Colonel Fitin had explained and was then reminded that it was the responsibility of the Red Army, not the Red Air Force, to assure the security of ground installations. Colonel Fitin with some heat had asserted that the Red Air Force had joint responsibility over anti-aircraft batteries and consequently he demanded a prompt reply to his original request.

To date, there had been no further response. An unexplained reason for this lack of cooperation was that the Red Army's preliminary investigation had failed to turn up any information regarding an alleged construction activity near the Frankfurt/Oder bridge. This was not a reply that the Red Army wanted to make to a Red Air Force query. It might give the unfortunate impression that the Red Army was not well informed.

Colonel Fitin had told Ossipov that he would make an official appeal to General Headquarters, stressing his "need to know," but Ossipov was not encouraged. Such an appeal would take months to be heard, and the outcome was uncertain.

There was no longer any doubt that the bridge at Frankfurt/Oder remained a target for Western Intelligence. Tuesday's reconnaissance by the Potsdam Mission car was one indication, the interest shown in refugees from Frankfurt/Oder another. But why? Was this, Ossipov considered, merely a carefully orchestrated diversion to mask an intelligence effort elsewhere? That was a hypothesis without a shred of evidence.

He placed a call to Zeunert, which the Stasi switchboard transferred to Zeunert's home. Zeunert was in the middle of dinner.

He took the call in his library, carefully closing the door behind him.

"Kommissar Zeunert here," he said.

"Lieutenant Ossipov speaking. Any news to report on the Frankfurt/Oder bridge?"

"Not really, Lieutenant. We've arrested a man who maintains that he was sent over to look at the excavation at the bridge. He talked about the installation of radars and missiles. That's obviously a lot of nonsense, but we'll get the truth out of him."

"Keep me informed," Ossipov demanded.

"I will, of course, Lieutenant," Zeunert replied. "By the way, have you by any chance learned the purpose for the excavation work?"

"For the moment," Ossipov replied tersely, "that information is a military secret. When I obtain the necessary clearance, I will be more specific. However, you can assume that the work in progress at the bridge is in preparation for a significant military installation."

So, maybe the arrested agent was telling the truth, Zeunert thought. Yet Ossipov did not object when I said that the man was lying. Zeunert returned to his now cold dinner, thoroughly confused.

*   *   *

Pritzer was troubled as he returned home that evening. He had been proud of his manipulation of Weber in the morning, but no one had been particularly interested in his achievement. Instead, Herter had only asked about his second agent who was overdue.

Jutta was waiting for him in the living room, wearing a sheer blouse with no bra. Vulgar, Frau Engelhart had said to herself, *keine Manieren*.

Pritzer went over to the liquor cabinet and poured himself a large Scotch. Jutta was pleased to see that he was agitated; it made him easier to manipulate.

"A glass of white wine, please," she said sweetly, curled up on the sofa with her legs tucked under her. He poured some Mosel wine into a traditional green-stemmed glass and handed it to her. She gave him a sexy smile and took a sip.

"How did my Mutiger do today?" she asked as Pritzer sank into an overstuffed armchair next to her.

"Just so-so," he answered.

"My little Mutiger's all upset," Jutta said, putting on her baby voice. "What's the matter?"

"The damn military. They treat us civilians like dirt."

"You know, Mutiger, you work for the military," she said reasonably, like a good wife trying to be helpful. "Maybe you should try to get on their good side instead of always rubbing them the wrong way."

"Why do you say that?"

"From what you tell me, you're always on the outs with the officers, with the Colonel and Muldane."

"They don't treat me with respect. They're down on civilians."

"All civilians?"

"Most of us."

"But not all, no?"

"No, not all, that's true," he admitted. "Herter's held in awe and even Liebman, whom they don't like, they do respect."

"I get along with all of them just fine," Jutta said, stretching her legs and lifting her arms, accentuating her bare breasts under the diaphanous blouse.

"My problem," Pritzer said, smiling, "may be that I don't have your anatomy." He walked over to the couch and tried to embrace Jutta, who slipped away. "Mutiger, remember Frau Engelhart," she said with mock primness.

Pritzer sank back into the armchair. Jutta came up behind him and gently began to massage his neck and upper back. Pritzer leaned forward, luxuriating in her touch.

"You're just having trouble getting started in your new job," she said soothingly. "Handling agents must be nerve-wracking, especially at first."

"Shhh! Don't talk about what I do."

"You're silly," she said lightheartedly. "Nobody can hear us."

"Frau Engelhart, remember?"

"She's in the kitchen, and I'm practically whispering in your ear."

"Your talking like this could cost me my job," he said nervously.

"Don't worry, you can trust me, Mutiger. But you are naive if you don't realize that everybody knows what you're all doing here. The minute I got to Marienfelde two years ago, I was warned that the Allies would try to send me back. No big secret!" She continued her gentle massage.

"Are you still only seeing people from Frankfurt/Oder?" she asked matter-of-factly.

Pritzer sat up, startled and frightened. "How do you know that?" he asked, inadvertently confirming his mission assignment.

"You told me."

"I did not."

"Now, Mutiger, would I make that up?"

Pritzer was dumbfounded. So she had remembered his slip of the tongue Monday night. Damn it!

"It seems like such a dull, uninteresting place to want to see people from," Jutta continued.

"What do you know about Frankfurt/Oder?"

Jutta had come back to the sofa and was sipping her Mosel wine. "Not much," she replied, "but it always had the reputation of being a dull town, no excitement, ugly girls. Muldane probably gave you that assignment as a test before giving you a real target." She giggled. "They're all probably laughing at you trying to get some worthwhile information out of Frankfurt/Oder."

Her calculated mockery got under his skin. "Poor Mutiger," she teased, "everyone takes advantage of you. And that's the husband that I, a beautiful girl, end up with? The butt of everyone's jokes."

"Stop that!" he snapped.

She grinned up at him, kicked off her shoes, and stretched her scarlet-painted toenails toward him.

"I can't talk to you about any of this," he said quietly, looking toward the kitchen.

"I know," Jutta replied, "it must be so embarrassing."

"It's not embarrassing," he retorted. "It's a military secret, but I can tell you this. I'm not the butt of anyone's jokes. I've been given a most important assignment. One that now has the highest priority. What do you think of that?"

Jutta kept up her taunting comments all through dinner, but as Pritzer became more disoriented, she was careful to limit his drinking. She purred that it would interfere with their bed-time fun. "I'm going to give Mutiger a good spanking tonight," she promised. "You've been a very naughty boy."

The prospect of their mild bondage games excited and momentarily distracted Pritzer. Jutta was well-versed in this erotic specialty that rendered this big hulk of a man helpless.

Soon after dinner and Frau Engelhart's departure, Jutta grabbed Pritzer's tie and solemnly led him upstairs. He was made to undress and carefully fold his clothes, while Jutta, fully dressed, sat in an easy chair with her legs crossed, strictly observing him without saying a word. When he had finished, he lay down naked on his back while in quick, practiced movements she tied his wrists tightly to the two bedposts.

She leaned over him, her eyes shining. "Tonight," she announced in a throaty voice, "you're going to be the U.S. agent that the cruel East Germans have kidnapped and are holding captive in their dungeon. I will be the interrogator and you're my helpless victim."

She began a slow strip-tease and noted with satisfaction, but no surprise, Pritzer's steadily mounting arousal. She took a small whip from their little leather bag of bondage playthings and let it whistle through the air. At once, Pritzer became fully aroused.

"So, Frankfurt/Oder is your priority target?" she hissed. "Your whole body is my priority target for tonight." She slowly and methodically caressed the length of his body with the laces of the whip. "What it is that interests you in that dull town? Tell me," she commanded, giving his chest a light flick of the whip.

Pritzer protested. "Please," he said weakly.

"Speak up," she insisted, lightly whip-lashing his legs. Pritzer clenched his teeth. "You think you won't talk, is that it, you American swine? Well, we'll see about that." She began to rain blows on Pritzer's body, many uncomfortably close to his erect penis. He tried to loosen his bound wrists, but he was securely tied.

Pritzer began to fear that this was no longer a game, that he was really being interrogated. "I've had enough," he said, as his erection began to subside. "I don't want to play anymore."

Jutta changed her approach accordingly. She began to lick his chest. Pritzer squirmed as she tongued the nipples, and his erection returned.

"Tell me," she said, "is the target, for example, the railroad station?"

"No," he whispered.

"Are there any oil storage tanks or military barracks?" Pritzer shook his head. He was beginning to relax as she continued her licking and little love bites. Suddenly she asked, "Is it the bridge?" She felt him flinch. "The bridge," she said triumphantly, "it's the bridge, isn't it?"

"No," Pritzer exclaimed. "No, it isn't."

"Yes, it is Mutiger. You know it is. And so do I. You can't keep a secret from me."

She slipped off the bed and walked over to Pritzer's night table. He watched in horror as she opened the drawer and took out the Beretta pistol. Caressing the revolver between the palms of her hands, she climbed back onto the bed, straddling Pritzer's stomach. He was voiceless, transfixed by fear. She opened the safety latch and carefully laid the Beretta on the bed, its muzzle pointing at Pritzer's temple.

"Now," she warned him, "tell me what it is that you're so interested in about that bridge. I just hope," she added with a laugh, "that the pistol won't go off."

"Don't move," a terrified Pritzer screamed. "That pistol fires very easily. I'll tell you what you want, but get that pistol away from me."

Jutta picked up the Beretta and pointed it at the ceiling. "I'm waiting," she said.

"You're right," he gasped. "It is the bridge we're after."

"But why?"

"There's some new excavation nearby we want explained."

"Is that all?"

"Yes," he said, exhausted and drained, "that's all."

Jutta stood up and put the Beretta back in the drawer of the night table. Then she untied Pritzer's hands, caressed the length of his body, and gently eased his sex between her lips. She licked and kissed for a long time, but Pritzer was too tired for any love session.

Eventually, Jutta settled down with him in his bed, and when they were ready for sleep, she turned to him and very quietly said, "I really scared you with my interrogation, didn't I?"

"You mean it was all in fun?"

"But, Mutiger, what do I care where you send your agents and what you ask them to look for?"

She snuggled close and fell asleep, leaving Pritzer bewildered and still very much afraid. He felt that he was sinking.

Day 8 Friday

Pritzer spent a tormented night. The beautiful woman sleeping soundly and seemingly without a care next to him had made him reveal top-secret information. If anyone found out, he'd be ruined. He'd also be in jail. Moreover, he had the express duty to reveal the fact that classified information had been compromised. Keeping silent would compound his crime. He began to sweat.

But there was no need to panic, he tried to tell himself. After all, she had just been playing. She might not even have paid much attention to what he was saying. But what about the fact that she had remembered his slip of the tongue the other night about only seeing refugees from Frankfurt/Oder? He turned over, trying without success to find a comfortable position.

Why would she do this, he asked himself? Of course, she was just the good-looking type the Stasi sent over to latch on to Americans. But Jutta a spy? Ridiculous. She was just flirtatious, mischievous, and very curious. A typical young female refugee. She was cunning, though, he had to admit, and she had come from the East. But she had been thoroughly vetted before they were allowed to marry, and she had received a clean bill of health. Yet those clearance procedures were spotty at best. It was difficult to verify East German information. He groaned and again turned over.

It was true, he had to concede, that from the very first she had always wanted to dominate him. But that was her nature, just as wanting to be subjugated was his. It was also, he knew, a classic espionage trick. Nonsense, he told himself, we just enjoy sex games. Nothing wrong or even very unusual about that. I've got to stop dramatizing all this, he tried to tell himself. I'm a good judge of human nature. I would surely have noticed something wrong these last two years if she were a Stasi plant. Wouldn't I?

Pritzer looked down at Jutta breathing regularly and sleeping by his side. She looked so pretty and innocent. *Jutta is not a spy,* he repeated to himself. And yet one fact was incontrovertible. Jutta, whatever she might be, was now in possession of highly classified information, and what she did with it, either deliberately or inadvertently, could determine his future.

*   *   *

The weather was clear, and the same civilian driver picked Weber up in front of the safe house at precisely 6:15 a.m. This time Weber suppressed the urge to remark that this was getting to be routine. The telephoto lens was taped to his right leg, but it neither showed nor impeded his movements. He bought a one-way ticket to Frankfurt/Oder and waited on Platform 3 for the 7:41 express. *Just like last time,* he encouraged himself. *No big deal.*

*   *   *

Pritzer was anxious as he went to work that morning. He sat quietly at a desk in the 575th Squadron Office, ostensibly reviewing the latest GGDRTs (Guidelines for GDR Targets) that for security reasons could not be removed from the premises. He looked furtively at the faces of some of his co-workers. How placid they all looked. What would they say, he wondered, if they knew that last night, while tied up by his wife, he had revealed their top priority target? He shuddered. It was all too ludicrous. If he could only take that one moment back! He continued to stare at the same GGDRT without registering its information.

Muldane stopped by the desk and asked, "Has your second agent come back?"

"No, not yet, Major."

"Any word from him?"

"No."

"Perhaps," Muldane suggested, "he has decided that spying

wasn't for him." With a laugh, he added, "If he has, I can't say that I'd blame him."

Herter came out of his office and joined them. "Glad you're together," he said. "I followed up on the Frog report about steel rods from Rostock. I've just determined that the Lenin Iron and Steel Works in Rostock provide the underpinnings for Russian military installations, including rocket launching sites. What do you think of that?"

"One more piece to our puzzle," Muldane volunteered. Pritzer said nothing.

"Possibly. Keep this very confidential," Herter said. "It may be a breakthrough. I'm going to brief the Colonel."

But when Herter entered Cole's office and told him the news, Cole was not unduly impressed. To Herter's annoyance, Cole maintained that so far they still had only a hole in the ground, now with steel rods being delivered to it.

"I need more than that before sending up the balloon," Cole remarked. Herter was unaccustomed to having Cole dismiss his theories in so cavalier a fashion. Yet, Herter had to concede, Cole had a point. So far he had only theories. Some hard evidence was lacking to make his speculation credible. In fact, the Lenin Iron and Steel Works produced steel rods for many purposes other than rocket sites. Herter returned to his office determined to solve the mystery of "the hole in the ground."

*　　*　　*

As head of the United States Information Agency's Mission in Berlin, L. Cabot Pearson had a spacious office on the top floor of the five-story Amerika Haus. Its large picture window overlooked the mountains of rubble that bordered the Tiergarten, the city's prewar fashionable residential area.

Pearson was disdainful of the standard government office furniture and had, at his own expense, brought over some English antiques that he favored. On the far wall was his prize possession, a small Cézanne painting of Mont Saint Victoire. These furnishings were not particularly in keeping with his duties as the salesman of American culture, but they did reflect his personal tastes. He had secured his post through influential family connections and was not prepared to let anything—certainly not his official duties—interfere with his accustomed lifestyle.

He had placed the recent, largely unread, USIA directives in his outbox and was chuckling over the latest cartoons in *Punch* when his secretary buzzed that he had a visitor. He told her to ask the high school principal, whom he was expecting, to wait a few minutes.

"It's not the principal," she informed him.

"Who is it?"

"A police officer."

Surprised, Pearson asked her to show him in.

The West Berlin Police Captain who entered was a man in his fifties with thick gray hair, sharp features, and a ruddy face. He held himself stiffly and spoke fluent, if heavily accented, English.

"I am sorry to disturb you, Mister Pearson," he said, "but I have some confidential information to impart."

Pearson asked the Captain to sit in one of the two armchairs flanking a low coffee table and went over to shut the door. He then sat in the second armchair and looked expectantly at his visitor.

The Captain pulled out a photograph from a folder and showed it to Pearson. "Do you know this woman?" he asked.

Pearson looked at the picture and answered, "Of course. It's Mrs. Pritzer. Mrs. Jutta Pritzer. She works here."

"How long has she been with you?"

"I'm not exactly sure. We can check our records. I would say about six months. Why? What's the problem, Captain?"

"We're not sure there is a problem, Mister Pearson," the Captain replied, carefully choosing his words. "It is too easy in this town to throw suspicion on perfectly innocent people. You said Mrs. Pritzer. Is her husband alive?"

"Yes. He's a civilian employee of the U.S. Air Force here in Berlin."

"By any chance is Mrs. Pritzer German?"

"Yes, she is, but she has applied for American citizenship, which she will be granted automatically as the wife of an American." Pearson was becoming a bit testy. "Look here, Captain," he said, "you'd better tell me why you are asking all these questions. I don't need to remind you that we are in the American Sector and that customarily we are the ones to ask questions rather than answer them."

After thirty years in the police force, the Captain was not easily intimidated. "Of course, Mister Pearson. I will explain everything to you immediately, but first, if you please, tell me two more things. How long have the Pritzers been married, and was she originally from the GDR?"

The thrust of the Captain's inquiries was becoming apparent. "Yes," Pearson replied. "Mrs. Pritzer was a refugee from the GDR. She and her husband first met, I would say, two to three years ago. It was apparently love at first sight. They were married about six months ago when all the necessary authorizations had been obtained. Damned attractive woman. Lucky fellow, that Pritzer."

"How old is Mr. Pritzer?" the Captain asked.

"In his mid-forties, I believe." Love at first sight began to sound a little hollow. "Captain, you should know that her background was thoroughly investigated before Pritzer, a U.S. government employee, was given permission to marry her. On top of that, we ran our own security check on her before taking her on at Amerika Haus. She is clean as far as we're concerned. Now, what do you have to tell me?" The question sounded more like a dare than a query.

"I hope that the trust you have in her will be justified and confirmed."

"Please, get to the point," Pearson said impatiently.

The Captain took a deep breath. "As you know, because of recent threats we have been watching Amerika Haus very closely," he said.

"Yes, yes. We very much appreciate the protection you are providing."

"Mrs. Pritzer was seen coming out of Amerika Haus"—the Captain consulted his notes—"at 9:54 this morning. She seemed nervous and kept looking around. Then she spotted a man standing in front of the Wittenbergplatz U-Bahn station and hurried over to him. They had a quick conversation, and then, again looking around furtively, she reentered Amerika Haus at 10:07 a.m. We followed the man for an hour and took some photos of him. He employed the classic tactics utilized to shake off pursuers, hopping on and off buses and U-Bahns and heading in opposite directions." Something struck the Captain as amusing, and he stopped for a second and smiled before continuing his remarks. "I perhaps shouldn't have said 'hopping,' since the man has a pronounced limp. We last saw him heading for a crossover point to East Berlin."

"Is that all?" Pearson asked, somewhat perplexed.

"I wish it were," the Captain sighed. "We have studied the photos of that man and, although we are not certain, we have good reason to believe that he is a Stasi operator, with the cover name of Schumpeter, who runs a network of spies in West Berlin."

"Well, I'll be damned," Pearson said. He and the Captain looked at each other for a moment. Then Pearson spoke. "It seems to me," he said, "that I should immediately alert our Counter-Intelligence Corps."

"You are free to do what you feel you must," the Captain replied, his literal translation from the German resulting in rather stilted English. "As you reminded me, we are in the American Sector. However, I would propose that we merely follow Mrs. Pritzer's movements closely for the next few days. Let us see what develops. After all, this might just have been a private meeting."

"What are you trying to say? Do you think that this man might be her lover?" Pearson asked. That thought had not really occurred to him.

"It is possible," the Captain replied. "Young attractive German woman married to a much older foreigner. Why not? On the other hand, Schumpeter, or whoever it is, is no Don Juan. He's seedy-looking, not that young himself, and on top of that, he limps. No, I very much doubt that this is a romance." The Captain paused and looked at Pearson, who remained silent. "Still, for the moment we have little to go on, and I mustn't forget all those American 'clearances' you told me about."

Pearson looked up to determine whether the Captain was being sarcastic. It was hard to tell. The Captain rose, and Pearson walked with him to the door. With Pearson's hand still on the door handle, the Captain asked for a few days to pursue his investigation. "If she is indeed a spy, she could lead us to bigger fish."

"I'll see what I can do," Pearson replied.

When the Captain had left, Pearson sank back into the armchair. The Captain was right, he reflected. Not much to go on as yet. But Jutta's behavior was suspicious and if, perish the thought, the man she met was a Stasi handler . . .

In the end Pearson decided to hold off advising Counter-Intelligence for twenty-four hours. That was within the parameters. No sense jumping the gun. But, oh my God, he reflected, it would be damned embarrassing to have a spy scandal in Amerika Haus. This had all the makings of a congressional investigation! Uncle Robert, who had gotten him the Berlin job, would not be pleased.

Yet Pearson was uncomfortable keeping this information to himself even for twenty-four hours. He needed a reliable and discreet sounding board. Someone like Bud Cole. In the meantime he asked his secretary to bring in Jutta's personnel file.

*   *   *

Hans Weber was back in Frankfurt/Oder on his third mission. The routine had dispelled some of his initial nervousness, but he cautioned himself not to become either overconfident or sloppy. As he made his way on foot from the railway station to the apartment, he stopped and bent down a number of times, ostensibly to tie his shoelaces. In fact, he was checking to make sure that the telephoto lens remained firmly fastened to his leg.

He entered his apartment building quietly and climbed the stairs to the third floor. It was a bright, sunny day, and the view of the bridge from his kitchen window was sharp and clear. He had some trouble fitting the lens to the camera. It did not slide in as smoothly as it had in his practice session the previous day. He sat down on the floor, trying to screw the lens into the camera's aperture. So preoccupied was he that he failed to hear the building superintendent open the front door and enter the apartment.

"Anyone here?" Metzger called out from the small entrance hall.

Startled and frightened, Weber threw his coat over the lens and camera and quickly got to his feet as Metzger came into the kitchen.

"Sorry, Herr Weber," he said. "I didn't know you were back. Since you were going to be away this week, I thought it would be a good time to fix the leak in the toilet you've been complaining about. But I can come back some other time."

"No, no, Herr Metzger," Weber stammered. "Don't let me stop you. Go right ahead. I've just come back to pick up a few things for the baby that we forgot to take along."

Metzger looked inquisitively at the coat on the kitchen floor. Weber scooped it up, being careful to pick up the camera and lens as well. He went into the baby's room and threw some diapers, baby bottles, and baby clothes into a small suitcase. Turning to be sure that Metzger was out of sight, he also slipped the camera and lens into the suitcase.

"Good-bye, Herr Metzger," Weber said as he was leaving. "Thanks for taking care of the leak. We will be back from Finsterwalde on Sunday night. Back to school again on Monday, you know," he added with what he hoped was a carefree chuckle.

Like most East German superintendents, Metzger was a police informer on the people in his building. The Webers had always been a quiet couple, never any suspicion or trouble. But Weber had clearly been disturbed to be surprised in the kitchen. Metzger had heard him scramble to his feet, so he must have been sitting on the floor. Metzger went over to the window. Nothing special; nothing at all to see except the bridge.

The thought crossed his mind that the Webers might have fled to the West. He looked in the closets; they were full of clothes. He went over to the desk and pulled open the drawers. He took a savings book out of the middle drawer. Weber had taken out almost all of his savings the day before he left. That was unusual, but the bank would have demanded an explanation. As he worked on the toilet's plumbing, Metzger continued to be puzzled by Weber's reaction. He was more than surprised to see me, Metzger recalled. He appeared afraid, as if he had been caught committing a crime.

In the meantime Weber, thoroughly disoriented, was on the street with his suitcase. That had been a close call, he realized. In another second or two, Metzger would have seen the camera and the telephoto lens. He could not return to Berlin without a single photo, but he felt uncomfortable going back to the apartment after what he had told Metzger. He wandered through the streets trying to make up his mind what to do, feeling exposed and vulnerable.

He entered a small restaurant near his school where he was well known. The room was small with dark oak paneling. A large chandelier fashioned out of numerous bucks' antlers hung low, casting a diffused light in the smoke-filled air.

"*Guten Tag, Herr Weber,*" the owner called out to him from behind the bar. "It is not often that you honor us with your presence anymore." The reproach was good-natured and brought Weber gratefully back to his previous, more normal way of life.

"My wife and baby are visiting her cousins in Finsterwalde," he offered by way of explanation. The owner suggested that Weber join some other men at the *Stammtisch*, the round corner table reserved for regular patrons. With the suitcase clamped between his legs, Weber ordered a beer. At first he paid scant attention to the conversation going on around him and concentrated on his own predicament. One of the men at the table complained that the construction schedule that had been imposed was unrealistic. Weber's ears pricked up.

"We can't get it done in that time frame. It's impossible," the man grumbled.

Attempting to sound merely polite rather than interested, Weber asked, "What job is it you're working on?"

"The one for the Russkis."

Weber stayed at the table for another hour, joining the others in multiple beers. A few times, he thought quite innocently, he tried to find out more about the Russian construction job. But one man became suspicious of Weber's questions and after Weber had left, questioned the owner about him.

"His name is Weber," the owner replied. "He's a teacher in the neighborhood school. A good guy."

"He certainly was very curious about our job."

"Probably just trying to make conversation. I wouldn't worry about him. He's OK."

But the man, like so many others, was a Stasi informer with recent instructions to increase his vigilance. Frankfurt/Oder was becoming a target for Western spies and every suspicious character was to be reported. Later that evening, the man called his police contact and informed him of Weber's inquiries.

Weber had left the restaurant a little befuddled by all the beers he had consumed. It was getting late, and he did not want to go back to Berlin empty-handed. He decided to return to the apartment and take his pictures early in the morning.

In the middle of the night, Metzger looked out his bedroom window and saw a light on in the Weber apartment. Cursing to himself that he must have left it on, he got dressed, climbed the three flights, and let himself in with his passkey. But it was Weber who had forgotten to turn the kitchen light off. He woke up with fright as Metzger came in.

"I thought you said you were going back to Finsterwalde," Metzger grumbled, annoyed that he had gotten out of bed for nothing.

Weber, still half-asleep, gave an incoherent explanation about missing a train.

"Will you be staying now or going back?" Metzger asked.

"I don't know," Weber said, sitting up in bed. "I mean, I'm leaving in the morning. Thank you, Herr Metzger. It's good of you to take such good care of our building."

Metzger went back downstairs, shaking his head. There's something fishy going on, he said to himself.

*   *   *

Cole had taken Brigitte out for dinner at Richter's, still Berlin's most fashionable German restaurant. The fact that the Führer used to frequent the establishment no longer lent the prestige it had previously conferred. But neither did the restaurant suffer from that history, the excellence of its German *Küche* assuring it a devoted clientele.

There was a moment's confusion when Cole and Brigitte arrived because the headwaiter could not instantly locate their reservation. He then found it listed under the K's, spelled Kohl, instead of the C's, and with a wave of the leather-bound menu ceremoniously led them to a good table in the select, and more intimate, side dining room.

Brigitte was in a happy and relaxed mood, and in Cole's eyes looked prettier than ever. She was wearing a simple straight blue skirt and a scoop-necked silk blouse. Her hair fell in a graceful wave onto her neck and shoulders, its blackness a pleasing contrast to her bright yellow blouse.

She agreed to let Cole order for both of them, which he did in earnest consultation with the head waiter. They decided on what the Germans called a "good burgher" repast. Bismarck herring in sour cream, with slices of apple and onion, to start. Then as the main course *Gänsebraten*—roast goose—with red and green braised cabbage leaves and lightly salted boiled potatoes. A cool Franken wine to lighten the main course. A mixed vegetable salad, served with a simple vinaigrette, and some mild cheese to provide a finishing touch. An ample and spicy meal, Cole thought, akin to the Southern cooking on which he had been raised.

"Why are you smiling?" he asked.

"I was thinking this is so much more enjoyable than last night," she said.

"Who was my competition last night?" he asked.

"My father," she replied, laughing. "I took him to the Stachelschweine—you know, the political cabaret. I had hoped that the irreverent skits would lighten his dour mood."

"Did they?"

"No," she answered. "The performance infuriated him. 'Lack of respect,' he thundered. 'Our defeat should have convinced the Germans that what we need is discipline, hard work, and faith in our country. Not all this foolish criticism and consorting with the conquerors.'" Brigitte shrugged and took a sip of the Franken wine that had been poured. "He is a burden," she sighed, "but one I have to bear."

"I wish that I could be of some help," Cole said.

"You can," Brigitte responded, looking at him intently. "You do. I feel happy and relaxed with you, Bud. These are feelings for a man I have not had for many, many years." Tears welled up in her eyes, and she momentarily stopped speaking.

Cole reached over and took her hand. She held his tightly while a few tears trickled down her cheeks. "When Franz was killed at Stalingrad more than a decade ago, I thought my life was over. Instead of comforting me, my father kept insisting that I should grieve for Germany's loss as well as my own. I nearly went mad and then gradually retreated into a solitary life with Graf as my sole companion."

"I see," Cole said, gently trying to lighten her mood, "my competition is a dog. That's a new challenge for me which I'm not sure I can meet."

She smiled and brushed her tears away.

"I know," Cole remarked, now speaking earnestly, "that my

real competition is your fiancé's memory, with which I would be foolish to try to compete. But I wonder how long he would have wanted you to stop living a normal and healthy life."

Brigitte swallowed hard and did not respond. Cole is right, she thought. Franz would never have demanded that she stop living. And were her father's strictures wholly disinterested? Wasn't he perhaps motivated by a concern that he might lose her company and assistance? After all, if she left him, he would have to hire a housekeeper.

She brushed these thoughts aside as the waiter served their demitasses. She glanced over at Cole, who was studying her face.

"Looks like some pretty heavy thinking going on over there," he teased. "Are you trying to figure out how to make a quick getaway?"

"No such luck, Bud," she replied. "You're stuck with me for another few hours."

"That's a punishment I'll just have to endure. Where do I get to serve my sentence?"

"How about your apartment?" she answered evenly, watching Cole's surprised reaction with a sparkle in her eyes.

"It's not that much of a place to see," Cole responded. "Wouldn't you rather go dancing . . . or how about a late movie?" he asked, maintaining a straight face.

"What do you want me to do, beg?" Brigitte said, her eyes narrowing in feigned anger. "It's up to you. You can also take me home, if you prefer."

"A difficult choice, you must admit," Cole said with a grin. "I suppose I'll have to choose the BOQ. It's the lesser of two evils." She raised her hand to slap him, but he caught her wrist, pulled her hand to his lips and kissed it.

Cole's apartment was on the second floor. He turned on a few lights in the living room and switched on the radio. The Brahms Violin Concerto was being broadcast on RIAS. Just what the doctor ordered, Cole thought as he went into the small kitchen to bring in some cognac. Brigitte kicked off her shoes and settled down on the sofa. Cole sat next to her, and they clinked snifters.

Brigitte was slightly tipsy already. "Were you surprised that I would suggest coming up here?" she asked.

"Frankly, yes. But also very glad." He turned her face to his and kissed her.

"Mmmm. That's nice. I might have some more of those a little later," she smiled.

"They're very reasonable—in fact for you, tonight, they're free." They kissed again, this time a long and deeper kiss.

Brigitte straightened up. "I don't understand," she said, "why you are surprised to have me here. Don't you know that all German girls are eager to have an American lover? Especially a high-ranking officer!" She glanced at him provocatively.

"Stop it, Brigitte. I don't think of you as a German girl."

"No? What am I? A poor stateless person?"

"Of course not."

"You'll just have to face it, Bud," she declared, with apparent seriousness. "I'm just another one of hundreds of thousands of available German women in this poor defeated country whose men have been killed." She had never spoken to him—or to anyone else—in this vein before. Cole was caught off-guard by her sudden change of mood. He listened to her quietly, trying to fathom her deep feelings, but was incapable of deciphering the forces that were driving her.

All at once, Cole felt her sob and burst into bitter tears. He kissed her softly, telling her to stop crying, that all would be well. They both gently eased down onto the sofa and lay close beside each other. They held each other silently, listening to the music. Brigitte's tears stopped, and it seemed as if nothing on earth existed, except the two of them, and that was wonderful.

"I've been so lonely," she whispered in his ear.

"You don't have to be lonely any more," Cole said, wiping a few tears from her face.

He put the palm of his hand on her breast and let it rest there, feeling the mounting irregular cadence of her breathing. He tenderly began to unbutton her bright yellow blouse, all the while kissing her still tear-stained cheeks. She rolled over on her back, moaning softly and looking up at him with yearning. Her blouse was open. He kissed her neck and as he reached behind her to undo the clasp of her bra, the doorbell rang.

They both sat up, startled. Cole cursed. It was past midnight. Brigitte was frightened. "Who is it, Bud?" she whispered.

"I haven't the faintest . . . let's hope whoever it is goes away." They held their breath and waited. The doorbell sounded again, a loud, insistent ring.

Cole got up. "Pick up your things and go into the bedroom," he told Brigitte, "and be quiet." He closed the door to the bedroom after her and then opened the front door. Pearson was standing in the hall.

"Good evening, Bud," Pearson said. "May I come in?"

"Evening, Cabot. It's a bit late. Can't this wait until tomorrow?" Cole remained standing in his doorway blocking the entrance.

"I know it's late," Pearson replied with annoyance. "I wouldn't have come now unless it were damn important. Can I please come in? I've got to talk to you."

Cole moved aside and steered Pearson into the living room. "I've got company," Cole explained. At that moment, Brigitte appeared, fully dressed, with her coat over her arm.

"It's high time I went home, Colonel," she said brightly. "Thank you so much for dinner. It was delightful."

Pearson did not show any surprise at Brigitte's presence. "*Guten Abend, Fräulein,*" he said suavely. Women were not allowed in the BOQ, but that rule was honored in its constant breach.

Cole was upset. "Brigitte, let me drive you home," he said.

"Don't worry," she answered. "I'll get a taxi at the Clayallee station." She gave him a little wink and was gone.

Cole returned to the living room and glared at Pearson. "This had better be good," he said.

"Attractive girl," Pearson remarked, sitting down and carefully crossing his legs so as not to disturb the crease in his trousers. He glanced at the bottle of French cognac. "May I please have a taste of that?" he asked, then added, "Some of these German girls are really outstanding. I've got one working at Amerika Haus—fabulous legs."

"Cabot, I assume you didn't come here in the middle of the night to expound on your obsession with German women," Cole said as he poured Pearson's cognac.

"You're wrong, Bud. I did come here to talk about at least one German woman."

"Who?"

"Jutta Pritzer. You know her?"

"Of course. She's married to Helmut Pritzer, one of my civilian employees."

"What else do you know about her?"

"She's a helluva tease, but a damned good-looking one. Pritzer's got his hands full."

"Not just Pritzer. Maybe we all do," Pearson said gravely and with emphasis.

"What do you mean?"

Pearson told Cole of the Berlin Police Captain's visit that afternoon.

"Have you informed the CIC?" Cole asked.

"No, not yet. I thought I would first discuss it with you. After all, Pritzer is one of your employees."

"I'm not in the counter-intelligence business. You know damn well that our orders are to inform CIC immediately whenever we suspect an enemy penetration. This is serious, Cabot. We've got to tell CIC right away."

"Hang on a minute, Bud, will you?" Pearson answered. "I know it's serious. That's why I'm here. But I also know that once we inform those clowns, they'll bollix it up to a fare-thee-well. I've seen them do it—a bunch of amateur Dick Tracys."

"I don't agree with any of that," Cole said. "The people I've worked with at CIC are competent."

Pearson tried another tack. "There may be another explanation for Jutta's behavior."

"For instance?"

"Maybe the man is her lover."

"Perhaps," Cole replied. "But that's not for us to find out."

"Why not? Why don't we ask her why she stepped out of Amerika Haus this morning?"

"Cabot, if she's a spy, we'd be tipping our hand and giving her a chance to get away."

"Not if we interrogate her in a safe house."

"And what would we do afterward?" Cole asked sarcastically. "Lock the door and keep her there? For how long? What if we believed some cock and bull story she told us and she then slipped back into the GDR after we let her go. We'd be in serious trouble ourselves. Why the hell should we do this? Why not simply inform the CIC?"

Pearson put down his glass and leaned forward. "Bud," he said earnestly, "I'm trying to avoid a scandal at Amerika Haus. I'm under a lot of pressure and criticism right now for my handling of that organization. Some congressional staffers have reported that I don't have the right kind of books in our library. 'Too liberal' they say, 'not America First enough.' The last thing I need right now is a spy in our midst. It would be the end of my tenure. God knows what other posting I would get. Probably Zanzibar." He laughed without mirth and reached for his glass, gulping the last of the cognac.

"Frankly, Bud," he continued, "it wouldn't do you any good either. The wife of one of your employees an East German spy!" Cole shrugged. "I just thought that if we could quickly clear this up ourselves, we'd all be better off. For God's sake, I can't believe that Jutta's a spy. Promiscuous, yes; deceitful in her personal life, probably—but a Communist spy? She likes her capitalistic luxuries too much for that."

Cole looked at Pearson and felt a mixture of contempt and pity. "Sorry, Cabot," Cole said firmly. "I can't go along with what you suggest. I'm glad you told me, and now the two of us are going to pay a call on the CIC."

"Now? It's after one o'clock in the morning."

"Right now. There may not be any time to lose."

* * *

At the Berlin safe house, Anna Weber was becoming frantic. Weber had promised to return that day. He was not back yet, and she began to fear that her forebodings were coming true. Wide awake all night long, she cradled the sleeping Manfred in her arms, listening with increasing hopelessness for Weber's footsteps on the creaky stairs.

Day 9 Saturday

It was 6:00 a.m. in Frankfurt/Oder when Weber was awakened by a loud banging on the apartment's door. He heard a shout of "Police. Open up." Before he could get out of bed, the police were inside the apartment. Metzger, standing on the landing and peering in curiously, had given them the key. In the early-morning hours he had called in a description of Weber's curious behavior. Prompted by reports from both Metzger and Weber's fellow diner, the police had decided to act.

*   *   *

Captain Mark Loring of the Counter Intelligence Corps was tired. In the middle of the night he had been awakened with the information that Pritzer's wife might be a GDR agent. Cole and Pearson had acted strictly in accordance with the regulations, which called for immediate notification of any such suspicion. Nonetheless, Loring thought that had they waited till morning, the regulations would not have been stretched to the breaking point.

He did not treat the report on Jutta with equivalent urgency; he received dozens of such notifications each week. Every German female who associated with Allied personnel was suspect, and there was no doubt that a substantial number of these were in at least occasional contact with the Stasi. Since it was impossible to limit relations between American personnel and willing young German women, the essential security measure—the only practical safeguard—was to persuade the Americans to keep their traps shut about their official duties.

It was now eight-thirty in the morning, and he and Cole, seated in a small conference room in the American Command compound, were again conferring on the allegations against Jutta Pritzer.

"We can't arrest her," Loring said. "We don't have any grounds for that as yet. But we'll keep her under surveillance."

Loring, a thirtyish career officer, impressed Cole. He had a brisk, no-nonsense manner and seemed to be well-versed in the spy-catching business. He was of average height, trim, pleasant looking, and with dark hair, which he parted down the middle.

"What are you going to do about her husband?" Loring asked.

"I don't think he's a spy," Cole replied.

"We can't exclude that possibility, though, can we?"

"I suppose we can't," Cole admitted.

"In any event, Colonel," Loring said emphatically, "he must not be told of our suspicions. Whether he's a spy or not, he would be likely in some way to alert her, which would give her a chance to flee."

"If indeed she is a foreign agent," Cole added.

"Yes, of course. But that is an assumption we must make until it is demonstrated to be false."

Cole nodded.

"What does Pritzer do?" Loring asked.

"He's a handler for agents we send over to the East."

Loring stood and walked over to the room's single window. With his hands clasped behind his back, he looked out on the branches of the tall oak trees that flanked the building on both sides. Cole saw him slightly shake his head.

Loring turned around to face Cole. "That's too much of a security risk, Colonel," he said. "I strongly recommend that you relieve him of those duties for the moment and assign him to a nonclassified desk job."

"How would I explain that, Captain?" Cole asked.

"Find the most plausible reason you can, Colonel. I'm sorry I can't be of more help to you on that."

Cole had another thought. "Wouldn't removing him abruptly set off just the kind of warning signal that we're trying to avoid?"

"Those were exactly the conflicting considerations I was weighing a minute ago," Loring said, sitting down at the conference table again. "On balance, I think we must avoid compromising the safety of our people."

Loring's position made sense, and after all, Cole thought, the matter was now out of his hands. He got up from his chair and asked, "Anything else, Captain?"

"Yes, Colonel, two more things. First, I would redouble the security precautions of agents that have been entrusted to Pritzer."

"Any suggestions?" Cole asked.

"Yes. I would keep his agents in the West for a while and hope that those who are now on missions will return safely."

"Understood."

"And second, keep this entire matter very close to your chest. Share it on a strict need-to-know basis with no more than one or two other persons, preferably officers. After all, there may be more than one mole in your outfit."

"Or none at all," Cole said a little too quickly.

*   *   *

Saturday was one of the week's busiest days at Amerika Haus and also the most difficult to staff, since most employees tried to save the weekend for themselves. To help out, Jutta had volunteered to work two Saturday afternoons a month. In one of her new bright-blue dresses, she walked gaily to the Onkel Toms Hütte U-Bahn Station on her way to work. She was unaware of the young woman in a loden-green trench coat trailing about a half a block behind her.

When he did not want to be disturbed, L. Cabot Pearson left his top-floor office and used an unmarked ground-floor hideaway, from which he could see the book checkout desk. It was always a pleasure to watch Jutta's lithe figure in action. Not one of Fräulein Kitty's protégées moved with such exciting animal grace. What he wouldn't give to spend a risk-free *moment intime* with her! But that was just the point—it wouldn't be risk-free, and Pearson's inbred priority had always been to avoid a scandal. What a frightful mess he'd be in now, he realized, if he had let himself go with Jutta. He sighed with relief and consoled himself that after all, Fräulein Kitty gave him a sufficient outlet for his active libido.

Pearson's fear of having his reputation besmirched by a spy scandal had been erased during last night's meeting at the CIC. Captain Loring had assured him that he would be held blameless and had enlisted his help in keeping a sharp eye on Jutta. No problem, Pearson had replied. Henceforth, his voyeurism would be part of an intelligence operation.

Jutta arrived right on time and quickly settled down on the high stool behind the checkout desk. A spy? Pearson wondered. It seemed ludicrous. And yet . . . He sat back in a comfortable armchair with Jutta clearly in sight and picked up the latest Olympia Press book. It would not be placed on the Amerika Haus shelves and its import to the United States was prohibited. It was a good thing, Pearson thought, that the British had not lost their taste for elegant pornography.

*   *   *

Dieter Zeunert was feeling smug. Everything was under control. He had good news to report to Ossipov, news of the efficiency with which his organization was pursuing its mission.

"Lieutenant Ossipov, Kommissar Zeunert calling."

"Yes?"

"I have some news to report."

"I am listening."

"We have caught another American agent. He was photographing the Frankfurt/Oder bridge from his kitchen window."

"What was he looking for?" Ossipov asked.

"I don't know. He is being brought down to me this afternoon for questioning. There can be no doubt, Herr Lieutenant, that the Americans are very interested in that bridge."

"Yes, I agree."

"It would be a great help," Zeunert ventured, "if we had some idea of what in fact is being built near the bridge."

Ossipov's rejoinder was short. "I've told you that is classified information, but I can say that you are proceeding correctly."

"May I assume nevertheless that some sort of new military installations are planned for the bridge?"

"I forbid you," Ossipov replied angrily, "to make any assumptions about Soviet Army plans. I have told you that you are proceeding in the correct manner. That should be enough for you."

"Of course. I understand, Herr Lieutenant," Zeunert said, resignedly.

"By the way," Ossipov asked, "have you received our Instruction concerning the production of anti-imperialist propaganda?"

"No, Herr Lieutenant. What about?" he inquired.

"Soviet Army Headquarters," Ossipov explained, "is becoming annoyed by all these pin-pricks, these enemy agents swarming like gnats over the GDR. At some point, we're going to have to seal the border with West Berlin." Zeunert noted with interest that Ossipov was no longer following the previous Soviet line about "liberating" West Berlin. "For now," Ossipov continued, "what would be welcome is some publicity on these illegal incursions, these nefarious sabotage and spying missions, something that would embarrass the West and strengthen the image of the GDR as a peace-loving society. See what you and your comrades can come up with."

"Yes, Herr Lieutenant," Zeunert said, and then somewhat desperately added, "Please, Herr Lieutenant, understand that I am not trying to obtain classified information. However, the Americans must know what is being planned at the bridge; otherwise they wouldn't be sending their agents there. But I don't know what it is I am being asked to defend. It is difficult to carry out my assignment under these circumstances."

"Don't complicate matters, Zeunert—your duty is to protect the bridge and its surroundings," Ossipov snapped and hung up.

At the end of that conversation Zeunert was in a less buoyant mood. It isn't easy, he reflected, to work for someone who still considers us as enemies. He mentally checked himself. No, that was too harsh. Ossipov was just exhibiting the Russian mania for secrecy. I'll just have to solve this riddle alone, he determined. I wonder what our new prisoner will have to tell us this afternoon.

Across the city in the suburb of Karlshorst, Ossipov was just as frustrated. He had not yet received any reply to his own inquiry about the bridge. He sat down to draft a short memorandum to Colonel Fitin. "The Americans," he wrote, "appear to suspect the imminent installation of military facilities at the Frankfurt/Oder bridge. Radar and missile installations have been evoked. Please advise whether their suspicions are correct." Ossipov reread what he had written. It was short and to the point, but he was not optimistic about receiving a precise response.

Ossipov gathered his papers together and carefully placed them in the safe behind his desk. I'll just have to wait and see what the Germans come up with, he concluded. How humiliating to depend on that self-satisfied, toadying Stasi functionary! In annoyance, Ossipov slammed his fist on his desk and walked out.

*   *   *

As Commander of the 575th Air Supply Squadron, Cole felt a responsibility to inspect the unit's various safe houses, which he did conscientiously once a month. When he reached the villa on Meisenstrasse that afternoon, the housekeeper was waiting anxiously to tell him of the terrible state of the woman upstairs with her baby. Cole rightly considered that the woman's safety and well-being were the responsibility of her husband's handler. But he had a good heart, and the housekeeper's description of Anna's pitiful condition made him climb the stairs to try to calm her down.

The housekeeper had not exaggerated. Anna was in a frenzy. "I'll never see him again," she wailed. "I begged him not to go, but you sent him back. Oh, why did you send him back?" She collapsed on the bed in a fit of coughing.

"When was he scheduled to return?" Cole asked gently.

"Yesterday," she whimpered.

"That's not very long. He is sure to return today. Stop crying," Cole said, searching for soothing words.

She stared at Cole and repeated: "He is never coming back. He's been caught. He's in jail. I know it. I feel it."

"Perhaps he had an accident," Cole suggested, "and is in the hospital. He will come back when he's better." Anna stopped crying for a moment. In her anxiety she had not focused on that possibility. "You see," Cole continued, "that may be why he's not back yet and can't communicate. He will return soon."

"When?"

"I don't know. You must be patient."

Little Manfred, who had been playing on the floor, stubbed his toe against the bedpost and began to cry. Anna picked him up and comforted him with kisses and a gentle rocking in her arms.

Somewhat calmed by this distraction, Anna turned to Cole and asked in a more controlled voice, "If instead of being in the hospital he has been arrested, what will they do to him?"

"That is hard to say," Cole admitted.

"But that must have happened to others you sent over, hasn't it?" she asked grimly.

Cole didn't respond.

"Hasn't it?" she insisted.

"Yes."

"And what happened to them? Did they shoot them?" Her voice trembled.

"No."

"What then?"

"A prison term."

"How long?"

Cole paused, then answered in a whisper, "A long time."

Anna crumpled into a ball on the bed, racked with sobs of despair, as Cole looked on helplessly. After some time, she sat up. "I have heard of swaps," she said. "Can't you swap Hans for a Stasi spy you've got in prison? You must have many of them. Please, swap him."

Cole remained silent.

"We will give you back all the money you have given us. We don't want your money," she said fiercely. "Take your dirty money. But give me back my husband. I want my husband back," she wailed.

"You must calm down, " Cole said earnestly. "We will see what can be done. Believe me. Now rest."

With sudden fury in her voice Anna shouted, "Rest. How can I ever rest again? We were so happy. We believed your propaganda about a new life in the West. Freedom. Liberty. Now, here I am. I've lost a husband and our baby has no father, just when we thought we were safe. There is no difference between you and the Russians. Both of you are playing some sort of a game, and we're the ones that get hurt. What for? What do we get out of this? Nothing. We are ruined. Give me back my husband!" she begged. "I want my husband."

Shaken, Cole tried to put his arm around her. She broke away angrily. "Don't touch me," she hissed. "Oh, I wish we had never laid eyes on any of you. Look where your false promises have led us."

Cole disengaged himself with difficulty and went back downstairs. He told the housekeeper to be sure not to let Anna leave the house. He would send a doctor to administer a sedative. Then, he called his switchboard and asked that arrangements be made to have Anna and the baby transferred back to Marienfelde.

"I want her to be treated well," Cole ordered. "I want her assigned one of those single rooms usually reserved for VIP's before flying them out."

*   *   *

After leaving the safe house Cole hurried to attend a BCISCG (Berlin Command Intelligence Services Coordinating Group) lunch and briefing. He did not return to his office until mid-afternoon. When he did, Herter and Muldane were waiting for him.

"How was lunch?" Muldane asked.

"Lunch was OK," Cole replied. "The briefing was a goddamned waste of time."

"Why was that?" Muldane asked. He had been impressed when once in Cole's absence he had attended a BCISCG meeting as the 575th Squadron representative.

"Just the usual spooks strutting their stuff, trying to impress the competition."

"Did anyone mention the Frankfurt/Oder bridge?" Herter asked.

"The Potsdam Mission referred to the bridge as one of the targets they had recently visited."

"That's all? No other comment?"

"No," Cole said wearily, sitting down behind his desk. "By the way, I had a hysterical woman and her baby transferred back to Marienfelde from one of our safe houses."

"Which one?" Herter asked.

"Meisenstrasse," Cole replied. "Her husband is overdue. Who's his handler? He should be informed of the wife's transfer."

"It's Pritzer," Muldane said.

"Let me double-check," Herter volunteered. He consulted his blue Agent Assignment ring binder. "Yes, it is Pritzer," he confirmed. "Her name is Anna Weber, and her husband Hans Weber is the one Pritzer sent back to take pictures of the Frankfurt/Oder bridge."

"Doesn't Pritzer have another agent who's overdue?" Muldane asked.

"Yes," Herter said, "that's right. He was also sent to Frankfurt/Oder."

"Does Pritzer have any agent in the field who's not overdue?" Cole asked warily.

"No," Herter replied. "Only those two."

Cole took a deep breath. "Gentlemen," he said, "this seems to be the right time to tell you about a very confidential matter." After Muldane had closed the double doors to Cole's office, Cole informed the two men of the allegations against Jutta and of Captain Loring's recommendation that Pritzer be taken off covert work. Herter and Muldane were shaken by the news.

"Loring also said," Cole remarked in conclusion, "that we should pay special attention to the safety of the agents that Pritzer has been running."

"Holy shit!" Muldane exclaimed. "They may both have been betrayed."

"Hold on, Zach," Cole said. "Don't be ready to string him up."

"Remember how hard he pushed to get into covert work," Muldane persisted. "Put that together with his wife under suspicion as an East German spy, and it isn't very reassuring."

"I don't see Pritzer as a mole. He's not the type," Cole argued.

"They make the best moles," Muldane countered.

"Why would he do it? What would be his motive?" Cole queried.

"One of the usual ones, I suppose," Muldane said. "Money, sex, or ideology."

"All right, let's take them one at a time," Herter suggested. "Pritzer a Communist zealot? Not very plausible." Cole and Muldane smilingly agreed.

"Sex? He's got his hands full with Jutta." Again the other two nodded, Muldane with a leer.

"Money? That's always a possibility, but he's well paid in U.S dollars here in Berlin, living the good life," Herter remarked. "Not a likely candidate, I would say, to risk jail for some extra money. What else should we consider, gentlemen?"

No one could think of a ready answer.

"At least there's one bright spot," Cole remarked. "It'll now be easy to switch him out of covert work. We can blame the fact that his agents haven't returned."

"He'll protest," Herter said.

"Sure, he will," Cole agreed, "but he won't suspect why we're really doing it."

"Unless, of course," Muldane said, "he's really a spy."

Cole gave Muldane an annoyed look and, turning to Herter, asked, "What do we do now with that damned bridge?"

"We'll keep chipping away at the mystery of that excavation. But you know, Colonel, I'm beginning to think that we might be barking up the wrong tree. All we still have, as you said some time ago, is a hole in the ground."

"We have the French IAIC," Muldane reminded them both.

"True," Herter said, "but if it were up to me, I'd downgrade the priority assigned to that target."

"You know damn well that Wiesbaden sets the priorities," Cole replied.

Herter shrugged. "Anyway, we'll keep looking. Is that all, Colonel?" he asked.

"Yes, thank you," Cole said, standing up and stretching. "This has been most enlightening." Herter returned to his office.

"A quick game of golf, Bud?" Muldane inquired hopefully.

"I wish I could, Zach," Cole said with a wan smile, "but I've got a pile of paperwork to get out this afternoon. By the way, how are you coming on Wednesday's cocktail party?"

"Everything is under control, Bud," Muldane replied reassuringly. "It's going to be great." He would be meeting with the Harnack Haus chef on Monday to go over his suggestions for hors d'oeuvres. He had also decided to show a Walt Disney nature film. That would surely be noncontroversial. Let the Russians find some political propaganda to complain about in that!

*   *   *

Weber was brought to Berlin from Frankfurt/Oder that afternoon, blindfolded and with an armed guard beside him in the back seat of a black Stasi sedan, which had raced along the Autobahn with its sirens blaring. Dumped into a windowless cell with a single weak bulb in wire-mesh netting, a stinking tin toilet bowl in the corner, and a damp straw mattress on the floor, he had the frightening sensation of having been buried alive. He pounded his fist against the heavy iron door, which produced little sound and no human response.

Weber had not been questioned after his arrest in Frankfurt/Oder for, as Zeunert told Janicek, he wanted to interrogate a "virgin." Furthermore, leaving a prisoner in a dark cell for twenty-four hours anticipating the worst was an effective softening-up technique.

Weber was crazed by remorse. Why had he gone back a third time? Why hadn't he listened to Anna? What would happen to him now? He shuddered at the likely prospects. What would become of Anna and little Manfred? He wept at the misery that his foolhardiness had brought about.

In calmer moments Weber tried to plan what to say to his captors. His first impulse was to deny any wrongdoing. This would be difficult, he realized, since he had been caught with a Western camera and telephoto lens in his possession. Then, he thought he would confess and plead for mercy. He would argue that he hadn't hurt the GDR; he hadn't even had time to take any pictures. No, he decided, that admission might make matters worse. As if they could be worse! Unable to frame a convincing story, he decided to devote his energies to accomplishing one goal: to be reunited with Anna and the baby. Nothing else mattered. He would be prepared to do anything to achieve that end.

That decision taken, he calmed down somewhat. Toward evening the panel in the iron door was pushed open. Weber was handed a plastic tray with a bowl of watery barley soup and a slice of dark bread.

"Ten minutes to eat," a rough voice announced, as the panel again clanged shut. Weber was famished; he had not been given any food or drink since his arrest. But anxiety at his predicament had suppressed his hunger pangs. Now, he eagerly slurped up the soup, using the bread to soak up the remaining liquid. He was still hungry, but the meal, sparse as it was, showed that he had not been forgotten. He was reassured that at least he would not be left alone to die. He lay down on the mattress and fell into an exhausted sleep.

*   *   *

Cole prided himself on his persuasive powers and thought he should give that talent another try with Liebman before the one-week deadline he had given him ran out. After all, as Cole reminded himself with a smile, Liebman was a civilian. Consequently, a reasonable discussion instead of a military command might prove effective.

Both men lived in the same BOQ building in the tree-shaded development behind the PX dubbed the Golden Ghetto. Though they sometimes crossed in the stairwell, neither had ever been in the other's apartment. But that was not surprising; military and civilian personnel rarely mixed socially, particularly when there were pronounced differences in rank.

It was after dinner, and as Cole returned home he saw the light on in Liebman's apartment. He dialed his number, and Liebman answered.

"This is the Colonel, Norman," Cole said. "If it isn't too late for you, I wondered if you'd like to have a nightcap."

"That's very kind of you, Colonel," a surprised Liebman replied. "I'm in the midst of a drink myself and have some cheese and crackers out. Would you care to join me?"

"I'd be delighted," Cole said. "I'll be right down."

When Cole arrived, there was music playing on the phonograph. A quarter-wheel of French Brie and crackers were on the coffee table. Cole asked for a Scotch and soda; Liebman was drinking sherry. They sat down in stuffed armchairs across from each other in Liebman's book-filled living room.

"Cheers, Colonel," Liebman said somewhat warily.

"Cheers," Cole replied amiably.

Liebman began to spread some Brie on the crackers, as Cole asked, "What's playing?"

"It's Beethoven's Spring Sonata for Violin and Piano. Do you know it?"

"I'm afraid I don't," Cole replied.

"There's wonderful music in Berlin, Colonel," Liebman said, passing him the small wooden platter with cheese and crackers. "Have you had a chance to hear any of it?" "I'm afraid I'm an ignoramus as far as music is concerned," Cole admitted. "I do enjoy listening to classical music, though, even if I don't know what I'm hearing." Liebman nodded and an awkward silence ensued.

Cole took a sip of his whiskey. "I'm sure you're wondering why I'm down here, Norm," he said.

"I'm pleased to have you here, Colonel, whatever the reason."

"I thought I might have been a bit too harsh in our talk last Wednesday," Cole explained. "You are a very valuable member of our outfit, Norm, so I thought an informal talk away from the office might allow us to understand each other better."

"I see," Liebman replied, now very much on his guard.

"I'd be interested," Cole began, "to hear how you think our unit, the 575th, fits into the general scheme of things."

Liebman hesitated before replying, searching for an appropriately anodyne answer. At length, he said, "We're trying to gather intelligence to give us advance warning of a Soviet attack and perhaps even the means to forestall one. It's a necessary precaution in the present circumstances."

"If you agree it's necessary, Norm," Cole asked, leaning forward, "why do you refuse to participate fully? Why not get directly involved in our covert work?"

Liebman replied steadily, "Not everyone is qualified to do what is necessary. We could all agree that an operation is necessary to save a patient's life, but even if I had the medical training, I wouldn't have the stomach, the guts, to slice into the patient's body."

Cole was not to be put off so easily. "Let me rephrase my question. On the assumption that you agree that our objective is necessary, do you object to the way we are carrying it out?"

Liebman looked at Cole and decided that the time had come to express his views. "There is no doubt, Colonel," Liebman stated, "that gathering intelligence is necessary, but not the way we are doing it."

"Why not?" Cole asked in surprise.

"Because, Colonel, frankly we're a bunch of clumsy amateurs," Liebman answered with a touch of anger. "We Americans are known to be wastrels; we throw away more goods than others produce. But in this case our outfit throws away lives, and I can't stand that."

"What if the sacrifice of one life assures the survival of many others?" Cole asked.

"That's the usual excuse given for putting lives at risk," Liebman replied less heatedly. "You're right, Colonel, there are ideals and values worth dying for and sending others out to die for. But, I ask you, does our haphazard approach meet that test? Right now, we're sending back all but the maimed and the blind to look at an excavation near a bridge. Is that professional? Efficient? Does it even make sense?"

"They might be digging the foundations for an important military installation."

"They could also be digging a latrine."

Cole laughed; they had evidently reached a verbal impasse. Liebman was concerned that he had allowed himself to be carried away and that he had spoken too freely. He glanced at Cole but did not detect any feeling of outrage, just a puzzled knitted brow.

"If you feel that strongly, Norm," Cole asked, "why do you stick around?"

"A perfectly fair question, Colonel. I ask it of myself constantly, particularly since I owe an answer to your ultimatum in a few days' time."

"What answer will you be giving me, Norm?" Cole asked earnestly.

Liebman stood and walked over to one of the two large windows looking out at the fading daylight. The streetlamps on the broad Argentinische Allee had just been switched on and bathed the neighborhood in an orange glow. As he answered, he seemed to be talking as much to himself as to Cole.

"I don't know, Colonel. Like so many others I can talk a good game, make ringing declarations about principles. However, I wonder if I'm not just posturing, building myself up by pretending to be on some higher moral ground. Whereas when it really comes down to the nitty-gritty, it's all just a copout."

The music had stopped, and Liebman turned off the phonograph. He asked Cole if he wanted another drink, but Cole refused. Liebman poured himself some more sherry and sat down again. "You know, Colonel," he said quietly. "You may be right. I'm just kidding myself. I'm already working on the covert side."

Cole stared at Liebman intently.

"I'm feeding refugees into the covert pipeline just like the railroad engineers who scheduled the trains to the Nazi death camps. You were right," he said his voice quaking, "to call me a Judas goat."

"I'm sorry. That was a little too rough," Cole offered.

"No, you were right," Liebman insisted. "I've just been unwilling to face facts."

Cole looked with compassion at Liebman, who seemed distraught. "I'm not much of a hero, really," Liebman said, continuing his self-analysis. "I told you I was a pacifist, but perhaps I am only spineless. And also selfish."

Cole looked puzzled.

"Yes, Colonel. I'm egotistical. Life is good here. The pay isn't great, but the dollars go a long way. And the work, whatever else one can say about it, isn't hard. Repetitive and dull, yes. But not hard. Anyway," he sighed, "I have nowhere else to go. I'm alone in the world. My family, you know, all perished in the war."

Cole nodded; yes, he knew.

"Yet strange as it may seem," Liebman went on, "I still feel that I belong here, that this is my home—from which I was lucky to escape with my life. But who says that a home must be warm and loving?" Liebman let out a bitter chuckle. "It's still my home."

Liebman's eyes started to moisten. "Colonel," he said, "I can't shake a certain affinity I feel to Germany, to this familiar space and its customs, its music, its literature, its food, its way of life . . ."

"But not to its people, I gather," Cole commented.

"No, not to certain of its people, that is true." He paused. "Although I do feel a kinship to refugees, a compassion for any displaced person." Liebman fell silent, sitting back in his chair, staring ahead. Cole waited a few minutes, but Liebman remained immobile. And Cole quietly took his leave.

Deep in thought, he climbed the stairs back to his apartment and poured himself another Scotch. It was hard to assess whether he had made any progress with Liebman. Without doubt, he had roiled the man's emotions, but it was unclear what effect that turmoil would have. The man was in a very fragile state. Was that an appropriate frame of mind for a covert assignment?

A bunch of clumsy amateurs, Cole recalled, that's what Liebman had called the unit's covert operations. But no nation's military had ever been a model of efficiency. And even if Liebman were right that there was much room for improvement, that would be no reason to undermine the 575th covert effort. Draining his glass, Cole decided that what Liebman and that hysterical woman, Anna Weber, could not accept was the old adage that you had to break eggs to make an omelet. They couldn't accept it because they happened to be the eggs.

Day 10 Sunday

Weber, bleary-eyed and with a two-day beard, was brought into Zeunert's office. His joints ached from the damp mattress on which he had fallen asleep. It was early in the morning, but Weber had lost track of time in his darkened cell. He was pushed into a chair, while a light was adjusted to shine into his eyes.

"Who sent you over to take pictures?" Zeunert's voice was sharp. Standing behind the lamp, he was but an indistinct shadow to Weber.

"The Americans," Weber answered shakily.

"What did they want you to photograph?"

"The bridge," Weber replied. There seemed to be no point in denying that.

"What about the bridge?" Zeunert demanded.

"Please turn out the light," Weber asked, trying to shield his eyes with his hands. The guard behind him gave him a hard slap and pushed down his hands.

"Just answer the questions and keep looking into the light."

"It hurts my eyes," Weber objected.

"More than that will hurt before we're through with you." The guard gave a coarse laugh.

"What part of the bridge are they interested in?" Zeunert asked.

"The excavation on the East side. On the southern side of the East bank," Weber answered. He had decided that he had no choice but to be as cooperative as possible.

"Why? What do they want to know about the excavation?"

"They want to know the reason for it."

Zeunert went back to his desk and looked again at his Frankfurt/Oder file. Then he strode back toward Weber. "Did they give you any hint of what they're looking for?"

Weber squirmed in his seat, and the guard, warning him not to move, pushed down on his shoulders. "I was asked to pay particular attention to the depression in the middle of the excavation."

"Is that all?"

Weber hesitated. Zeunert nodded to the guard, who punched Weber in the small of his back. Weber cried out in both surprise and pain.

"I said is that all?" Zeunert repeated calmly.

"They can't explain the purpose of that hole," Weber answered quickly, "that depression. That's why they sent me to take pictures of it."

"I'm just going to ask you one more time," Zeunert said threateningly, "did they give you any hint of what they think you might find?"

Weber was frightened. He had planned not to admit that his mission was to spy on military installations. He would limit his admissions to being asked to photograph the work being done around the bridge. Two more blows, harder this time, hit him again in the back, and he shrieked with pain.

"Well?" Zeunert asked. "I'm waiting."

"Please don't hit me again," Weber pleaded. "All I know, I swear it, is that they showed me pictures of rockets or missiles, I don't know the difference, and asked if I had seen anything like that."

"What did you say?"

"Of course I've never seen anything like that."

Zeunert turned off the lamp. "We're going to take a short break," he said. Weber was given a hot cup of bitter-tasting coffee and allowed to stretch his aching limbs.

Zeunert was intrigued. Weber was confirming the prior agent's report about the bridge. It wasn't possible, Zeunert thought, and then corrected himself. Everything was possible. But it wasn't probable that both had been sent over with the same disinformation.

So the Americans believe that the Russians may be installing missiles, Zeunert said to himself. Maybe they are; we'd be the last to know. It would make some strategic sense for the Russians to move their front lines forward. In the event of a war—a limited one, of course, to spare the Big Powers—the atom bombs would only fall on us, the Germans. After all, we're obviously expendable to both the Russians and the Americans. If that is the Russian plan, it would explain Ossipov's reluctance to reveal it. But I'll puncture that "classified information" gambit of his, Zeunert thought. I'll report to him what the Americans are beginning to suspect. That should flush out the truth.

Weber coughed, and Zeunert looked up. Weber was slouching in his chair, his head down and arms folded across his chest, the guard standing behind him. Zeunert rose and walked over toward Weber, again turning on the light.

"Describe the man—it was a man wasn't it?—who sent you over," he said.

"Middle-aged, medium height, heavy-set, balding," Weber said.

"Any distinctive features?"

Weber thought a moment and then said, "Protruding eyes."

"What name did he give you?"

"He called himself Steiner, Herr Steiner."

"How's his German?"

"Fairly fluent, but with an American accent."

Zeunert took a folder from his desk and handed it to Weber. It contained photographs of American personnel. Many had been clipped from *The Stars and Stripes,* which featured pictures and listed the players on the Berlin Command's baseball, football, and bowling teams. Pritzer, no athlete, did not show up on any of these. Then there were random shots of Americans taken by Stasi operatives on West Berlin streets or in shops, restaurants, or parks. A picture of a smiling Jutta and Pritzer, taken on the terrace of a restaurant overlooking the Wannsee, caught Weber's attention.

"That looks like the one," Weber said.

"Are you sure?" Zeunert asked.

"No," Weber replied, studying the picture further, "but it looks like Steiner."

"That's enough," Zeunert suddenly snapped. "Take him back to his cell," he said to the guard. "Put him on Regime Number 2." That meant relatively decent food and treatment; Regime Number 1, the best, was reserved for important prisoners like former high Party officials.

When Weber and the guard had left the room, Zeunert walked to his corner window and looked down at Normannenstrasse, deserted on a Sunday morning. So, Herr Steiner, he said to himself, I intend to find out if this missile craze is your own personal obsession or if it's a matter that American Intelligence is actively pursuing. In the latter case we would take it much more seriously.

The register of Jutta and Pritzer's photograph identified her as one of Schumpeter's agents. Zeunert asked his switchboard to get Schumpeter on the line. Zeunert worked seven days a week, and if regrettably he could not impose the same work schedule on all his subordinates, he did insist that they be readily available at all times.

While waiting for the call to be put through, Zeunert reread the Russian Instruction on negative propaganda Ossipov had mentioned and that had finally landed on his desk. It demanded that the East German media publish stories that would warn the population against Western spies. At the same time they should ridicule the futile efforts to sabotage the country's Socialist achievements and to undermine the strong bonds of friendship between the peace-loving Russian and German peoples. An idea on how to comply with this order was beginning to form in Zeunert's mind when the telephone rang.

"Schumpeter here, Comrade Kommissar."

"Good," Zeunert replied. "You have an agent, Jutta Berkenbusch, I believe, who's married to an American called Pritzer. Is that right?"

"Yes, Comrade Kommissar."

"I assume Pritzer is a handler of agents sent into the GDR."

"Yes, Comrade Kommissar."

"Schumpeter, I must know immediately," Zeunert's tone of voice was insistent, "if Pritzer uses the cover name Steiner and, if possible, whether he sent a certain Weber to take pictures of the bridge in Frankfurt/Oder. Immediately, do you hear?"

"Herr Kommissar," Schumpeter said nervously.

"What is it?"

"She may have trouble getting that information quickly. She's been doing well getting useful bits and pieces, but if she pushes too hard too fast, she's likely to blow her cover and . . ."

"I don't want excuses, Schumpeter," Zeunert thundered. "We have agents in the West to supply information. I don't give a damn if she blows her cover. I've told you what I want to know and I don't care what it will take to get it. That's your problem."

Schumpeter hastily promised to do his best, and Zeunert's last words were that that had better be good enough.

It was getting to be lunchtime, and after a morning well spent Zeunert looked forward to a satisfying meal, a welcome change from the menus served during the week in the Stasi canteen. As he walked slowly toward Alexander Platz and his favorite small restaurant, a real Berliner *Kneipe* where he would order his favorite *rouladen*—thin slices of beef rolled around a filling of bacon, chopped onions and pickles—he began to consider again how best to implement the latest Russian Instruction. Show Western Intelligence in a bad light! That shouldn't be difficult and might be quite amusing. If certain assumptions proved correct, someone like Weber could fill the bill. Zeunert chuckled. Yes, Weber might just possibly be the one to help him pull off a real coup.

*   *   *

It was early Sunday afternoon. Pritzer was taking a nap upstairs. Jutta, playing solitaire in the downstairs living room, could hear his loud snoring. The telephone rang, and Jutta answered.

"Can you talk?" Schumpeter asked.

"Yes, briefly," Jutta replied.

"Meet me at the Mexiko Platz S-Bahn Station in thirty minutes."

"But . . ."

"No buts. Thirty minutes." Schumpeter hung up, leaving Jutta holding the receiver with a dead line. To Jutta's relief, Pritzer's snoring continued unabated. She quickly scribbled a note, which she left on the kitchen table, saying that she had some errands to run. She would be back within the hour.

Mexiko Platz was a fifteen-minute walk from the Pritzer villa. It was a sunny afternoon, and the other Sunday strollers, ambling with their families or sweethearts, would have been surprised to learn that the pretty young woman walking quickly toward them was a spy heading for a rendezvous with her handler. The only ones not surprised were the CIC agents on a 24-hour vigil, following Jutta at a safe distance in a nondescript Volkswagen. The Pritzers' telephone calls were being monitored, and the agents had just received word on their car radio of the Mexiko Platz meeting.

Schumpeter was sitting on the green bench next to the candy and tobacco store at the S-Bahn entrance. Jutta looked at her watch. Schumpeter was early; it had only been twenty-six minutes since his call. There was always traffic, even on Sunday, around Mexiko Platz, and Jutta waited impatiently for the light to change so that she could cross the street.

When she had crossed, Schumpeter motioned Jutta to sit down next to him. He seemed jittery, which was unlike him. Jutta was tense herself. Though she didn't dare say so, she thought these public meetings risky, particularly since these last few days she had had the uncomfortable feeling of being followed. The Volkswagen was parked nearby. One CIC agent radioed in to report their position, while the other snapped pictures of Jutta and Schumpeter.

No one else was sitting on the bench, and the traffic and pedestrian bustle around them appeared to provide adequate cover for their conversation.

"Listen carefully," he whispered. "Two things we must find

out right away. First, does Pritzer use Steiner as his cover name? Second, did he send an agent called Weber to take pictures of the Frankfurt/Oder bridge?"

Jutta started to protest, but he told her fiercely to keep her mouth shut. He needed answers to those questions within the next twenty-four hours. Was that understood?

"I'll never get him to tell me that," Jutta said. "Certainly not within the few hours you've given me."

"That's your assignment," Schumpeter replied. "You've always assured me you have your husband under control. Now prove it. If it will help you any, Weber came over to the West a week or so ago with his wife and little baby. Also, if you have to, you can blow your cover to get those answers. I will be waiting for your call at exactly 10 a.m. tomorrow morning. Just say yes or no to question 1 about the cover name and question 2 about pictures of the bridge. I won't take 'I don't know' for an answer. Is that clear?"

Jutta nodded.

"Don't worry about security," Schumpeter said. "Speed is the main point of this assignment. Don't forget. Ten o'clock tomorrow."

While the two of them had been talking, the CIC agents had gotten out of the Volkswagen and together were slowly walking toward them. Both had their hands in their trench-coat pockets, gripping their pistols. A sixth sense made Schumpeter look up; he saw the two men heading toward them. He rose from the bench, and the CIC men quickened their pace.

Schumpeter ducked into the S-Bahn station building, and the CIC men began to run after him. Despite his limp, Schumpeter was remarkably agile. Grabbing the steel handrails with both hands, he swung himself four or five steps at a time down the staircase to the station platforms. He was in luck and managed to squeeze into a departing train. The train doors clanged shut just as the CIC men reached the platform and the train with Schumpeter aboard pulled out, leaving them behind.

Jutta had witnessed the beginning of the chase. She was still sitting on the bench in a state of shock as the CIC men came back to the street and got into their car. Jutta watched them drive off, her thoughts in shambles. It took her a little while to pull herself together. Then she rose and began to walk back home, carefully assessing her own situation. Obviously, someone was after Schumpeter, probably the Berlin police or one of the American Intelligence Services. In their trench coats and from their general demeanor, they could be either Germans or Americans. The fact that the two had gone back to their car without Schumpeter probably meant that he had gotten away.

The other obvious point was that she had been spotted with Schumpeter. It was odd that the two men hadn't accosted her before driving off, if only to get more information on Schumpeter. The likely explanation was that they knew exactly who she was and where to find her in case they wanted her. She had her cover story prepared: Schumpeter was her uncle from Dresden, who had come over to the West to ask for money because his wife was in the hospital. Jutta did have an uncle in Dresden, which fact was conveniently recorded in her background check. Pritzer might believe the "uncle" story, but the police wouldn't. For why had her "uncle" fled at their approach?

She stopped at a grocery store to buy some bread, cheese, and wurst to prove that she had gone out shopping. She barely looked at what she took off the shelves, now totally preoccupied with how to extract the answers to Schumpeter's two questions. Schumpeter was crazy, she decided. He had given her an impossible assignment with an unachievable time frame.

*   *   *

Anna Weber and little Manfred had been assigned a small room in the family barracks at Marienfelde. This was no mean feat at a time when, due to a shortage of seats on outgoing flights, the camp was severely overcrowded. But with the priority always assigned American requests, a family of four being housed by the

BND, the West German Intelligence Service, was evicted to make room for Anna and her baby.

But the move from the safe house back to the camp had only increased Anna Weber's fright and despair. Even the private room she perceived as more of an isolating prison than a relative luxury. She had spent much of her first full day in camp crying on her bed while Manfred, unperturbed by his mother's unhappy state, played on the floor with his teddy bear.

That morning the camp's social worker had visited Anna. There had been a number of suicides recently at Marienfelde, and the camp authorities were keeping an anxious watch on all severely depressed residents. She urged Anna to come to the canteen for lunch, but Anna said she wasn't hungry. "All I want is my husband back," she said. "That's all. Please help me." These were pleas with which the social worker was familiar, and her mechanical assurances that all would turn out well were, as usual, ineffective.

Upon leaving, the social worker deliberately left the door to Anna's room open as an invitation for some neighbors to start looking in. These visits did force Anna to try and pull herself together. One young woman in particular was unusually accommodating. She listened with interest and sympathy as Anna related the story of her misfortunes. She sat on the floor, holding the teddy bear up for a delighted Manfred to clutch back into his arms. She stayed with Anna much of the day, making polite conversation and engaging in mindless chit-chat. She asked about the Webers' life in Frankfurt/Oder, their escape from the GDR—a story, she said laughingly, that everyone in Marienfelde could duplicate with their own personal variations—and seemed particularly interested in the safe house where the Webers had been put up for over a week. She took Anna's hand to comfort her, and at one point put her arms around her shoulders as Anna broke down recounting her husband's last leave-taking.

By evening Anna was feeling more composed. The talk with her new friend had been a help. It would be no less useful to the

Stasi, which received a summary of Anna's remarks as part of the daily report made by its assiduous agent in Marienfelde, the friendly young woman who had so kindly played with Manfred and his teddy bear.

*　　*　　*

One of Norman Liebman's preferred spots for relaxation and contemplation was the Egyptian Collection in the Dahlem Museum. His favorite, of course, was the stunning bust of Queen Nefertiti, with its symmetrical and perfectly proportioned face, long, graceful neck, and tastefully applied makeup. Carved more than three thousand years before, it was a dispassionate symbol of the unchanging perception of female beauty.

He was about to leave for the museum when the telephone rang. It was Cole, saying that there was a confidential matter he wished to discuss; could he come by Liebman's flat for a moment?

Cole apologized for the intrusion on a Sunday morning, and with a smile promised that this was not the beginning of daily visits. However, he said that the previous evening he had forgotten to mention a sudden personnel change to be made on Monday. Liebman thought he could see the guillotine blade descending on his neck.

They walked into the living room, and Liebman asked if he would like a cup of coffee. Cole declined, saying he would only be staying for a minute. "Please sit down, Colonel," Liebman said, and they again settled in the two armchairs.

"I understand you have been swamped lately," Cole began genially, "so I'm going to send Helmut Pritzer to give you a hand."

"It's very good of you to try and help me out," Liebman said, "but frankly, I think that I can handle the load fairly well myself. Moreover, our room at the Interrogation Center is quite small. I'm not sure that two of us . . ."

Cole interrupted him but not harshly. He explained that he wanted Pritzer to get more experience on the overt side of the business and that Pritzer could certainly learn a lot from Liebman. "After all," Cole said, "you're our undisputed expert on the overt side." So much of an expert, Liebman thought ironically, that you're forcing me out.

"The reason I'm here, though, Norm," Cole said with an embarrassed smile, "is to inform you that Pritzer is to be denied access to classified information. I cannot explain the reasons for this limitation, but I will count on you to see that it is observed."

"How can he be helpful in our interrogations if he doesn't know the targets we have in mind?" a baffled Liebman asked.

"That shouldn't be too hard," Cole answered blithely. "Just let him see those refugees who come from areas we're always interested in—you know, like airfields and rail junctions and oil storage facilities. Also, and I can't stress this point strongly enough, you must make sure that he has no contact, none whatsoever, with any refugee we hope to recruit. He is not to know those you may be sending to a safe house. That part of your job is absolutely *verboten* to him. That's essential."

Cole rose to leave. "By the way," he said, "Pritzer doesn't know yet of his new assignment. So if you should happen to run into him today, don't say a word. I'll be speaking with him tomorrow morning."

Liebman walked Cole to the door. "This is a very ticklish business, Norm," Cole said as he left the apartment. "I'm counting on your discretion and good common sense."

Liebman's first reaction had been that Pritzer was being introduced as his replacement. But as Liebman left the apartment and began his walk to the museum, passing through Dahlem with its villas set back, mostly behind iron fences, the more he thought about it, the less likely this appeared. Cole must be aware that Pritzer was a poor interrogator, as his tour at Marienfelde had shown. He had neither the patience nor the human touch necessary to elicit information from frightened, disoriented people. Then, this remarkable restriction on classified information! How in the devil's name, Liebman asked himself, could Pritzer be useful asking questions if he didn't know what they were looking for? Cole had finessed the point without answering it.

Liebman climbed the familiar stone front steps of the Dahlem Museum and immediately went up to the second floor, where Berlin's famed Egyptian Collection had found temporary postwar housing. He walked by the seated limestone figure of Hetep-ni, the ancient Egyptian revenue office official, and stopped a moment to enjoy a colorful wall painting of two men in a boat on the Nile, hunting hippopotami.

Then he hurried on to the room where the bust of Queen Nefertiti was displayed on a center glass-enclosed pedestal, with soft spotlights illuminating it on all sides. He sat down on a chair near the wall and gazed with inexhaustible admiration at the classic profile. The multicolored floral necklace and the tall, green-beribboned, flat-topped crown formed the perfect frame for the Queen's elegant features. Liebman let his thoughts wander; annoyingly, they returned from the aeons of the past to the present day.

Though Cole had not alluded to it today, his ultimatum still stood. That had been made clear the night before, and Liebman had no idea how he was going to respond. Liebman looked back at Queen Nefertiti. Her sculptor, Tuthmosis, had never inlaid her left eye, which stared out blank and unseeing. With his thoughts in turmoil, Liebman felt that he too must be afflicted with partial interior blindness. He rose and walked over to the Nefertiti. How serene she was! Looking at her, he began to shake off his despairing mood. I'm overdramatizing, he told himself. I have no fundamental objection to intelligence-gathering. As I told Cole, I'm just against the sloppy, unprofessional way we do it.

But it wasn't sloppiness in procedures that troubled him, He knew that was a rationalization. It was having to persuade a refugee to return that he found unbearable. Not the principle of using refugees as a source of covert intelligence, but his own involvement in the means to that end.

Liebman's World War II experiences had hardened his reactions to misfortune, but he was thick-skinned only to general misfortune, not to individual tragedy. The concept that returning refugees were caught as spies—*c'est la guerre.* Yet he doubted that he could withstand the guilt of having one of his own agents caught. There was no denying the power of Nefertiti's ethereal beauty. Here was the affirmation of an eternal positive force. He continued to stare in wonderment at the different aspects of this three-thousand-year-old masterpiece: the royal upward tilt of the head, the tawny hue of the smooth feline face, the outline of the crimson upper lip, the full and tapered arch of the eyebrows. This meticulous veneration was as close as Liebman could come to a religious experience.

On his way home, with his mind clear and feeling strangely liberated, Liebman easily came to a decision. He would not become a handler; he would not coerce the helpless or unwary into dangerous situations. His refusal would not be totally logical since his activities already had a covert nexus. He could discern no moral imparity between Judas and the crucifier. But why did one have to be logical in making a personal choice? He had a good record, he had put some money aside, and being fully bilingual he should have no trouble finding another civil service job in Berlin or somewhere else in Germany.

However, he would have to be careful in his dealings with Cole, a very clever and to him a potentially dangerous man. A black mark in his personnel file could be a handicap in finding future employment. That's what he would focus on now, Liebman told himself: how best to neutralize Cole.

*   *   *

Brigitte had arrived at Cole's apartment in late afternoon, laden down with a bag of groceries. She had promised to cook a real Berlin meal and had refused his offer to go shopping with her. "It's going to be a surprise," she had said lightly. "All you have to do is promise there will be no more late-night visitors."

She now busied herself in the kitchen and would not let Cole enter. "Don't be so curious," she called out from behind the closed door. "Go read a magazine or take a nap. It won't take me more than forty-five minutes to get everything ready."

Cole smiled and returned to the living room. He stretched out on the couch and relaxed amidst the clattering of pans and dishes. It was comforting to hear her bustling about in the kitchen.

It seemed that he had just closed his eyes when Brigitte came out of the kitchen with beads of perspiration on her upper lip. She took off her green apron, sat down in an easy chair, and smiled at the reclining Cole. "It's all prepared—the meat's in the oven, and the cook is thirsty," she declared.

Cole sat up and, swinging his legs to the floor, slipped on his moccasins. "What does your ladyship desire?" he asked.

"I'll have a cool glass of Mosel, which I saw you had in the icebox. The cook would also like a kiss," she said turning her face to his.

"What?" Cole asked in mock surprise. "Before I've tasted dinner?"

"I may not get one after you do," she said. "So pay up now."

Cole went over and bent down to kiss her. What started as a light peck quickly turned more serious. Their lips never parting, Brigitte put her arms around his neck, and he slid down onto the chair beside her. She turned the length of her body toward him, their lips pressed together, then slowly opening to give their tongues full play. Cole's hand moved up to caress her breasts, and she shuddered in quick response.

With an effort, she sat up and disentangled herself. "If we don't stop now," she said, smoothing her dress and passing her hand through her tousled hair, "my dinner will burn."

"I'm suddenly not hungry," Cole said, grinning and trying to pull her back down.

"That's gratitude for you," she answered, pretending anger, "after I've slaved over a hot stove. It's obvious that the way to your heart is not through your stomach. You're a sex-starved beast, that's all you are, and"—softening her tone to a throaty whisper, she added— "I'll feed you first and take care of your other appetite later."

She jumped up out of his grasp, laughing, as he looked at her with longing and affection. What a pleasure, he thought, to have her around and what a welcome relief from the headache of his unit's mounting troubles.

"All right, you win, you heartless creature," he said, pouring out a glass of Mosel wine for her. "Can I do anything else to help?"

"Yes, Colonel," she replied, "you can set the table." He did as he was told and even managed to find some candles, which he lit ceremoniously.

Brigitte had prepared some Berlin specialties—*Kassler Rippchen*, a smoked pork loin, with boiled potatoes and spinach. "Looks great, honey," he said, holding out a chair for her. "Back home, I'm what is known as a meat and potatoes man."

They clinked wine glasses, and Brigitte watched as Cole took his first bites. He grinned broadly and pronounced everything delicious. They ate in silence for a few minutes. Several times, he looked over at Brigitte as she ate in the European manner, never letting go of her knife or shifting her fork from the left hand to the right. She was truly lovely, he thought with wonder. Cole knew that fraternizing with German women was frowned upon, but he was confident that his relationship with Brigitte created no security risk. True, the Jutta episode had given him a momentary twinge. But even though Brigitte worked at the Refugee Interrogation Center, which gave her quite an insight into the American refugee dragnet, they had never discussed anything even remotely connected with their work. It was an unspoken agreement between them.

It was he who that evening began to break it. Cole remarked that he was puzzled by the spectacle of citizens of the same nation, presumably living in harmony with each other a little more than a decade earlier, now at each other's throats, each embracing a rival world system not on the basis of personal belief but of geography.

"It's really quite simple," Brigitte said, holding out her glass for more wine. "We were one nation and we were defeated. All together we shared the same problems, which right after the war meant doing everything in our power to find enough food to eat and a roof over our heads. That's the normal fate of losers. No complaint! But something unusual also happened. We found ourselves divided. Those in the West were encouraged to become 'good democrats'—that is, capitalistic burghers, and those in the East were urged to become 'good democrats'—that is, Communist comrades. In the West we were told that the Communists in the East were part of a totalitarian world conspiracy, and in the East they were taught that people in the West were a bunch of fascists. The adults, who had survived the war and had been through years of Nazi brainwashing, give little credence to either side."

So engrossed was she in what she was trying to convey, Brigitte had stopped eating. Now, somewhat embarrassed at her vehemence, she looked down at her plate, picked out a bite of pork loin, and dabbed it with mustard. As an afterthought, she said, "What effect all this will have on the younger generation, who knows? Most of us in the East and the West just try to pick up the pieces, avoid politics, and get on with our lives."

Cole was taken aback at the fervor that his simple question had loosed. "So, if I understand you correctly," he said with gentle irony, "you too are just trying to get on with your life, without having to commit to either side."

Unintentionally, he had touched a raw nerve, and Brigitte flared up. "Why do you say that?" she demanded angrily. "You have no right to accuse me of being an indifferent bystander. I know what the Red Army is like. They raped half the women in Berlin and sent many of the men who were still around to die in Siberia. I know the difference between Communism and the West. I tried to give you an answer to a very general question, and you twisted it to misrepresent my personal feelings."

She stopped a moment, her eyes blazing. "I wouldn't work for you," she said, "if I didn't believe in freedom, in respect for the individual, all that the West supposedly stands for."

"Supposedly?"

"Yes, supposedly, because there are a number of things that go on here that don't live up to all those high ideals."

"I'm sorry to have upset you," Cole said. "Please calm down." He reached across the table and gave her hand a squeeze. She looked at him and soon her eyes softened. She smiled, and he knew he was forgiven. She began to clear the table.

"It was delicious," he told her. "Thanks for making it." While she was in the kitchen, Cole refilled their wine glasses. Brigitte returned with her favorite dessert, two large coffee éclairs, bought in her neighborhood pastry shop. She had a craving for sweets and quickly finished her dessert. Cole laughed and gave her the last bite of his éclair.

A little later they resumed their conversation. "Is it conceivable," Cole asked, "in today's circumstances, for an intelligent person in the West to refuse to stand up to Communism?"

"There are intelligent people in the West who are Communists, Bud," she answered. "Some out of opportunism, I'm sure, but very many out of deep conviction."

"I'm talking about people who are not Communists, but who would shy away from standing up against Communist aggression."

"You mean Better Red Than Dead."

"Yes. Exactly. I've got a guy in my outfit who seems to be leaning that way. It seems to me to be just plain cowardice, wrapped up in a moral justification."

"That may not be fair," she said thoughtfully. "There are some reasonable voices who say that anything is better than another war. There are people who are convinced that to survive, humanity must find a better way to settle disputes. Your man may hold that view, and I would think it takes some strong moral fiber to express it to you."

"I think it's a coward's copout," Cole replied defensively.

"Sure there are cowards who find this opinion a convenient

excuse," she said, methodically scraping up the last remnants of coffee icing on her plate, "but you can't call everyone in the West a coward or a Communist if he refuses to enroll in an anti-Communist crusade. Many people are afraid that heating up the Cold War will turn it into a hot war."

"That doesn't make sense. We're just defending ourselves—not only ourselves, but the entire West—against the Russian threat. Everyone should see that. Don't you?"

"Have you ever thought about how the Russians see you?" she asked. "You know: capitalist Americans, ringing their country with atom bombs—a pretty frightening adversary."

"But we'd never be the ones to start a war," Cole retorted. "We just have to be strong enough to have a second strike capability to wipe out anyone who would dare attack us."

"Oh my God!" she exclaimed. "We've just finished a war that killed some thirty million people and ruined our nation along with many others. And here we sit talking about the next one." She put her head between her hands and began to cry.

Cole stood up and walked around the table. He put his arms under Brigitte's elbows, helping her out of the chair, and guided her back to the sofa. "Let's leave politics to the politicians," he said softly, "and concentrate on love for lovers."

She turned her tear-stained face up to his, and they kissed for a long time, very gently. Then Cole stood up and dimmed the lights. He put on some popular dance music at a low volume. The night was clear and the rays of the nearly full moon were shining in through the window. Brigitte had stretched out on the sofa, waiting for him. Cole lay down next to her. The length of their bodies touched, their arms closed about each other, and their lips melted in a deep embrace. She sighed with relief. They remained motionless, cleaved to each other in the moonlight. Cole slid his hand inside her blouse and began to caress her breasts. Brigitte whimpered as her breathing quickened. She pressed herself closer to his arousing maleness.

Cole sat up and pulled her up with him. "Come with me,

darling," he whispered and led Brigitte, willing and excited, to his bedroom. He helped her as she quickly shed her skirt and blouse. He pulled back the bed covers and put his own clothes on a chair against the wall. When he turned around, she was smiling. He came to her, and she enveloped him in a tight embrace, locking her arms around his neck. They lay down together on the bed, and she entwined her strong, long legs around the small of his back. They rolled over, compressing their bodies into a single loving organism. Brigitte was strong, her passion giving her extra force, but she could not match Cole's six-foot athletic frame. Cole easily turned her on her back and straddled her, holding her wrists above her head. Feeling helpless and with mounting excitement, she bucked her hips violently, trying to dislodge his clasp. He grinned, and continuing to hold her firmly, he kissed her mouth, her neck, and her shoulders in quick unexpected forays. He gently nibbled at her breasts, the points of which immediately began to harden.

Brigitte trembled. Tossing her head from side to side, she let out squeals of protest and desire. Her hips no longer bucked now but shuddered in an uncontrollable rhythm. She moaned, becoming warm and moist, ready for Cole. He let go of her wrists, and she wrapped her arms about him. He smoothly slid into her and was engulfed.

They moved together, Brigitte with abandon trying to force the pace and Cole holding back to draw out their pleasure. Her passion soon made Cole lose his control. He started to ravage her. She clutched at him and cried out as he continued his assault. Their hearts pounding, they rose up together, breathless in a simultaneous orgasm and collapsed, exhausted, into each other's arms.

*   *   *

It was a quiet Sunday night at the Pritzers. They were both preoccupied. Pritzer was brooding over the fate of his two missing agents. Jutta was no more talkative. She kept turning over in her mind how she could get Pritzer to divulge his cover name and confirm the assignment he had given Weber. The bondage trick clearly wouldn't work a second time; he wouldn't allow himself be tied up again, and there were limits to what could be extracted in a "game." What she had been asked to find out went far beyond those limits. Moreover, she had to work fast.

They both retired early. Before falling asleep two hours later, Jutta had hit on a plan. Yes, that should work, she said to herself happily, and with regained confidence, she quickly fell asleep.

Day 11 Monday

When Pritzer came downstairs at 7:15 a.m., he was
surprised to see Jutta in the kitchen, sitting at the breakfast table. She had still been in bed when he had gone in to shave
and shower. She greeted him with a cheerful "*Guten Morgen, Herr
Steiner!*"

At first, Pritzer did not react, so she repeated the greeting.
Suddenly comprehending, he stared at her and in a shaking voice
asked, "What did you say?"

"I said good morning, Herr Steiner. That's one of your cover
names, isn't it?"

Pritzer sat down, holding on to the table for support. "What
are you talking about?"

"Can I call myself Frau Steiner from now on?" Jutta prattled
on gaily. "I think Steiner is so much nicer and easier to pronounce
that Pritzer. It was a good choice for a cover name."

Pritzer slammed the table with his fist. "I absolutely forbid
you ever to call me that again."

Jutta laughed. "Don't get so excited, Mutiger. You call yourself Steiner to others, why not to your lawful wife?"

"Who said I call myself that?" Pritzer asked defiantly.

"Herr Weber told me. He's such a nice man, coming over to
the West with his wife and baby. He told me you called yourself
Steiner."

Pritzer stared at her in disbelief. This must be a nightmare
from which he would soon wake up.

"What I don't understand," Jutta continued in her best unconcerned and chatty manner, "is why you would want to separate
him from his family; no, more than that, risk his life just to take
some pictures of a bridge. Tell me, Mutiger, why did you do that?"

Pritzer now sat very still. He could feel his heart pounding in his chest; he became slightly dizzy, with Jutta not quite in focus. "What do you want?" he asked hoarsely.

She stopped her little act and speaking intently, said, "I want to know whether Steiner is your cover name and whether you sent Weber to take pictures of the Frankfurt/Oder bridge."

"Why do you want to know?"

"That's my business, but if you tell me, I'll never again ask you another question. In fact, Mutiger, I will disappear from your life."

"You're a spy. My God, you're an East German spy."

Jutta looked at Pritzer almost with pity. "Yes, Mutiger, I was sent over to trap you. It was not difficult, you know."

"You bitch!" he shouted and lunged at her.

She moved back, holding a chair in front of her for protection. "Don't touch me," she said. "If you so much as lay a finger on me, I'll reveal all the secrets you've told me, including the mission you gave Weber, which I note you haven't denied. That should get you a nice long jail term."

Pritzer stopped, held at bay not so much by the protruding chair legs as by Jutta's threats. "But," she continued, "if you're a good boy and answer my two questions, I'll disappear from your life today without giving you any further trouble."

"How can I rely on that?" Pritzer asked, sitting down again, his anger replaced by an all-pervasive fear.

"You'll just have to, Mutiger," Jutta replied in a reasonable tone. "You have no choice. Unless of course, you want to turn me in now, and I can tell Colonel Cole what a blabbermouth you've been."

Pritzer knew that he should have Jutta arrested, but he was deathly afraid of going to jail himself. He also knew that Jutta would find ways of blackmailing him in the future. Torn between these conflicting views, he remained seated and immobile.

"Well, Mutiger," Jutta asked, putting aside the chair and taking hold of his hair to pull his head back, "I don't see you reaching for the telephone. You're still my little slave, aren't you? Now tell me: am I right on Steiner and Weber?"

Pritzer looked up at her and nodded. As she let go of his head, she saw that he had tears in his eyes.

"Thank you, *Schätzchen*," she said. "That's all I wanted to know. If you ever get tired of the American Way of Life, come on over to the GDR. I'll find you a nice little Socialist cubbyhole."

She went upstairs to pack, leaving Pritzer alone with his life in ruins.

*   *   *

It promised to be a busy morning for Colonel Cole. He had driven Brigitte home shortly after dawn and stopped at the PX cafeteria for a doughnut and a quick cup of coffee. When he reached the 575th Squadron Office at 7:20, he had a message that General Norcross from Wiesbaden Headquarters had called ten minutes earlier. He asked the switchboard to get the General on the line.

"Bud," General Norcross asked, "anything new on that damn bridge construction?"

"No sir, not really. Why?"

"Believe it or not, I've had an inquiry from that prissy Frog who sits on the Intelligence Coordination Council. He thanked me for that 'veree useful tip' about the Frankfurt/Oder bridge. Now he wants to compare notes so that we can both get up to speed. What the hell is that all about?"

Cole silently cursed himself. "Well, General," he said, "we liaise here with our brother Allied services and give each other pointers."

"You mean to tell me, Bud," the General shouted, "that you spilled the beans to the French about that bridge, a current Number One Intelligence Priority?"

"No, General, of course not," Cole answered. "During a review of our joint efforts, I mentioned that we were looking at bridges. I did not pinpoint the Frankfurt/Oder bridge."

"Well, then, how the hell did he focus on Frankfurt/Oder?"

"I don't know, sir," Cole replied. "They've probably developed some info on their own."

"You mean something we don't know about?"

"General, if you ask me, I don't think there's much there at that bridge for us to worry about."

"Why do you say that?" the General asked suspiciously.

"All we have at the moment, frankly, is a sandpile."

The General was not convinced. "I'm going to ask the Potsdam Mission to take another look. I want a thorough briefing on that fuckin' bridge before seeing the Frog later in the week." The line went dead.

What a lousy way to start the day, Cole thought. He took a deep breath and decided he might as well get the Pritzer matter settled first. But for some time Pritzer could not be located. Bewildered and frightened, he had been wandering aimlessly in the streets of his suburban district of Zehlendorf. Finally, however, having arrived at the 575th and been told that the Colonel wanted to see him, he turned up at Cole's office door.

"Sorry to keep you waiting, sir," Pritzer apologized. "I've been over at the safe house." He looked haggard.

"Doing what?" Cole asked.

"Just looking, or rather checking," Pritzer said nervously, "to see if the Webers left anything of interest in their room."

"Did they?"

"No."

"As a matter of fact, it's your agents I want to talk to you about, Pritzer," Cole said. "Close the door, will you, and sit down." Pritzer, moving mechanically, sat down heavily.

"It's beginning to look as if you lost both of your agents," Cole said, frowning at Pritzer in order to provoke him to talk.

Pritzer took the bait. "It's not my fault, Colonel," he protested. "Agents get caught sometimes. You can't blame it on the handler. Anyway, who knows if they're caught? They may just be late."

"Having both agents 'late,' as you say, at the same time is disturbing, Pritzer."

Abashed, Pritzer bowed his head. All the while, he could not stop thinking of Jutta and fantasizing what Cole would say if he knew that his wife was a spy. But that was an admission he had resolved not to make. He had decided instead to take the chance, however slim, that Jutta would keep her promise to disappear from his life. It was a desperate gamble, but one in harmony with his current deranged temperament.

"I believe you need some more training, Pritzer, before I can let you continue with covert operations," Cole said, not unkindly.

"Please, Colonel," Pritzer pleaded, "don't take me off covert work. I know I'm new at this, but I'm sure I can do this job. In fact—you may think this is funny—I feel that I was made for covert work. Please let me have another chance."

Cole looked at Pritzer, a pitiable figure, but hardly a Soviet mole. Cole smiled as he thought of what Muldane would say, that those were the best kind of moles. "This isn't child's play, Pritzer," Cole said. "We can't afford mistakes, and untrained people make mistakes."

"Everybody makes mistakes, Colonel," Pritzer replied under his breath.

"Untrained people make more mistakes," Cole said tersely. "As of now, I'm taking you off covert and as a precaution I've also temporarily—only temporarily, mind you—suspended your security clearance."

"What?" Pritzer asked in disbelief.

"Just a temporary measure."

That morning Pritzer had no fight left in him. "No, Colonel," he begged, "please don't do that."

"I'm afraid I have no choice."

"I've had a security clearance all through the Second World War. Why take it away now just because my agents have not returned?"

Cole did not answer, and Pritzer in desperation took another tack.

"What do you expect me to do in an intelligence outfit, Colonel, without a security clearance?" he said weakly.

"I want you to go to the Interrogation Center and give Liebman a hand. He's swamped. Help him gather overt information, but stay away from referrals to a safe house. Liebman's been told of these limitations."

"How is this giving me the training you say I need for covert work?" Pritzer asked.

"Don't worry. I'll make the appropriate arrangements for your training, Pritzer," Cole replied. "In the meantime, Liebman needs your help. That's all. Dismissed."

Pritzer shuffled out. Cole was satisfied. Pritzer was upset and obviously felt humiliated, but that was to be expected. The important point was that he could not have guessed the real reason for being removed from covert work.

Cole called Liebman and told him that Pritzer was on the way. "Keep your eye on him," Cole said, "and report anything suspicious or unusual." Liebman said nothing, but considered that last remark both suspicious and unusual.

"By the way, Liebman, you have three more days, I think, to reply to my suggestion for a job change."

"I know, Colonel," Liebman replied. "You'll hear from me in a timely fashion."

*   *   *

Jutta had been sitting in the living room waiting for the time to report to Schumpeter. At precisely 10:00 a.m. she called his West Berlin contact number. She called from home, seeing no further reason to observe the usual security procedures. Her message, "The answer is yes to both questions 1 and 2," was duly recorded and relayed to Schumpeter's Stasi line in the East. It was also monitored by the CIC.

Then Jutta picked up her two suitcases and with a light heart set off toward the Argentinische Allee, where she intended to hail a taxi. She had walked but a block and a half when a car that had been parked near the Pritzer villa pulled up beside her. Two men jumped out. They grabbed and pushed her, kicking and screaming, into the back seat of the car. One of the men picked up the suitcases Jutta had dropped and threw them in back as well. The doors were slammed shut and locked automatically; curtains blacked out the car's back windows. The entire incident—a not uncommon sight in postwar Berlin—had taken less than two minutes. The car quickly pulled away and drove to a nearby CIC safe house.

*   *   *

Zeunert was always at his desk by 7 a.m. At that hour he was alone, except for a few cleaning women down the hall, on the fourth floor of the Normannenstrasse Stasi Headquarters building. He savored the solitude, alone with his dossiers and the control of human destinies they signified. Within the hour, footsteps and the opening and closing of doors would indicate other early arrivals, all of them aware that Kommissar Zeunert was already on the job. But for the moment all was quiet as he took up the pile of memoranda that had come in over the weekend.

Years of practice had allowed him to scan reports and as if by a sixth sense to pick out the relevant bits of information. His eye fell on the name of Weber in Sunday's dispatch from Marienfelde. He read carefully the report from the woman agent at Marienfelde who had befriended Anna Weber. Then he slapped the top of his desk in glee. Yes, indeed, this was precisely what he needed to put his plan into effect. At times like this Zeunert felt that life was but a treasure hunt in which destiny would plant clues for him to discover. He called the basement prison warden and asked that Weber be brought up.

"I am trying to decide what to do with you," he told Weber when the latter was again seated across from him, with a beefy guard standing behind him. "Let's see now, photographing military installations for the Western *revanchists*. That should get you twenty-five years at hard labor . . ."—Weber stared at him in panic—"if we're lenient." Zeunert enjoyed the cat and mouse game with prisoners. "Of course, since you were spying on a Soviet military installation, we might turn you over to our Socialist brethren, and you could experience the delights of the Siberian winters."

Weber was silent and hung his head in hopelessness. Zeunert studied him closely and then in a low, reflective tone remarked, "Or, if to atone for your treachery, you would want to help the Fatherland . . ." He paused, and Weber looked up. "If you were to prove cooperative . . ." Weber listened attentively. "If you wanted to see Anna and the baby again . . ."

Weber's eyes filled with tears. "How?" he asked incredulously.

"Ah, I thought that might get your attention."

"How do you know about them?" Weber asked frantically. "Where are they?"

"They are back at Marienfelde. Anna is crushed, hysterical. She blames you and your stupidity for having ruined all of your lives."

Weber broke down, burying his head in his hands.

"She is right, of course," Zeunert continued. "Your lives, at least your lives together, are over. You will rot in one of our jails or freeze in the Siberian Gulag, and she'll have to make a new life for herself. She will try to marry again, I suppose, if only to give the baby a father."

"No," Weber groaned.

"It won't be easy to find a husband. So many of the men her age were killed in the war, so that a woman with a child will probably have to settle for some older man, perhaps a cripple or, if she's lucky, a widower. It won't be a love match, but if she takes good care of him, he may be kind to her. It will take her some time to forget you, and I'm sure she'll tell the baby about you. The foolish man who wrecked their lives."

Weber gripped his chair and in a subdued voice asked, "Why are you torturing me like this?"

Zeunert came out from behind his desk and, standing in front of Weber, said, "I'm just pointing out what a dreadful position you have created for yourself and your family. You all face a very sad future unless . . ." He left that word hanging.

"Unless what?"

"What would you do to be reunited with Anna and the baby?" Weber's reply was immediate. "Anything," he shouted.

"And to return to your teaching in Frankfurt/Oder and your apartment near the river?"

"Oh, please! I would give anything, I would do anything to start again."

There was no reason to prolong the session. Weber was committed. "We'll see," Zeunert said, returning to his desk. "I'll expect absolute obedience."

"What do you want me to do?" Weber asked warily.

"Very little, in fact. You see, we in the GDR are getting tired of having our citizens—like you—abused by the West and their Fascist running dogs. We've decided to call attention to their clumsy methods of trying to undermine our Socialist progress. Publicity, you know, is a good disinfectant."

Weber was puzzled. "I don't understand what you want me to do."

"Why, you will be the stars of our little production—Anna, you, and the baby. You will bear witness to the shameful acts you were forced to undertake."

"No one forced me," Weber said candidly. "I did it for money."

"That's not the kind of cooperation I expect from you," Zeunert retorted sharply. "Think again what happened to you. Arriving penniless in the West, you were offered amounts of money that appeared fabulous to you. Momentarily dazzled and bewildered, you recklessly allowed yourself to be recruited as a spy, putting your family and yourself in mortal danger. That's what I want you to say. Understand?"

Weber nodded. Zeunert had Weber write a note to Anna, which he did eagerly. He begged her to come back and reassured her that they would be permitted to resume their lives together. Zeunert read the note and was satisfied.

"It will be in her hands in a few hours," Zeunert said, taking a small envelope from his desk drawer and carefully placing the note inside it. "We will need her cooperation as well for our little drama." He looked at Weber and smiled. "You are a bit confused. I'm not surprised. As if by a miracle, you're going to escape jail and be reunited with your family. But I warn you. One false step and it's Siberia!" Zeunert laughed as Weber was led away.

The telephone rang, and Zeunert picked up the receiver. It was Schumpeter. "My agent has confirmed that Pritzer uses the cover name Steiner and that he sent Weber to take pictures of the Frankfurt/Oder bridge."

"Excellent!" Zeunert responded. "Good work. Exactly what I need."

Schumpeter was pleasantly surprised. In the two years he had worked for Zeunert, he had never before received the slightest word of praise.

*   *   *

There were more than a dozen refugees—holdovers from Friday afternoon—in the waiting room when Pritzer opened the front door to the Refugee Interrogation Center. He nodded absentmindedly to Brigitte, who was seated at the reception desk with Graf curled up at her feet. She gave him a crisp "*Guten Morgen*." She had never bothered to conceal her antipathy for him, but in view of her well-known friendship with Cole, Pritzer always treated her with wariness and exaggerated politeness. This morning, however, Pritzer had other things on his mind than whether Brigitte might be poisoning Cole's mind against him.

Liebman was just finishing his interrogation of a young woman, who was relieved to be excused as Pritzer, a bit out of breath from his climb up the narrow stairs, walked in. A small table and two chairs had been set up in an adjoining alcove.

"Sorry there's not much extra room for you, Helmut," Liebman said apologetically.

"This is just fine, Norm," Pritzer said, ducking to avoid hitting his head against the supporting beam. "After all, this is just a temporary arrangement." He squeezed in behind the table and sat down.

"Yes, that's what I've been told," Liebman replied. The two men looked at each other, both of them embarrassed.

"I appreciate your coming over," Liebman said. "It's been very busy. I can sure use your help."

"What do you want me to do?"

"I want you to interview sources coming from areas near airfields. You know the questions: Anything unusual happen recently? New types of planes? New military units in town? Any rumors?"

"Yes, I know the drill."

Liebman handed Pritzer some yellow sheets of paper. "Here are some questionnaires to fill out," he said.

"What if I spot a likely recruit?" Pritzer asked.

"Cole told me," Liebman answered, "that you're not supposed to be involved with covert referrals."

"He told me the same thing," Pritzer admitted. "But that's my profession, Norm. What do I do if I find one?" There was an awkward pause.

"I suggest you ignore your instinct and stick to overt questioning."

Pritzer's temper flared. "But that's crazy," he said. "Good agents are goddamned hard to find. What about if I find one, I'll pass him on to you and you send him over to the safe house?"

"No. That would be going against Cole's orders."

"No it wouldn't," Pritzer insisted. "I wouldn't be referring him to the safe house. You would."

"That's the same thing."

"No, it's not."

They glared at each other.

"No, Helmut, no deal. You stick to overt work and forget about the covert side."

"You're making a serious mistake," was Pritzer's surly answer.

"Shall we discuss the matter with the Colonel?" Liebman said. But the last thing Pritzer wanted was another conversation with

Cole. Liebman handed him the folder of a retired tramway conductor from Erfurt. "Take a look at this one," he suggested.

Pritzer called Brigitte and asked her to send the man up.

*   *   *

"Captain Loring of the Counter Intelligence Corps calling," the switchboard announced.

"All right. Put him on," Cole said.

"Is this line secure?" Loring asked.

"Yes," Cole replied.

"Are you alone?"

"Yes. What's up?" Cole asked, sensing that the answer was going to be another pack of troubles.

"We have Jutta Pritzer in custody," Loring said flatly.

"What?"

"We picked her up this morning leaving her house in a hurry with two suitcases."

"Where is she now?"

"In the cellar of one of our safe houses, screaming bloody murder. She's about to be a U.S. citizen. She wants her husband and a lawyer. We can't do this to her."

"Can you?"

"Of course. This is still a military zone, and we operate under the Military Code, something like martial law, you know."

"Have you gotten anything out of her?" Cole asked.

"No. She denies any wrongdoing. Keeps insisting that the man we saw her meet on the street was her uncle from Dresden."

This was getting mighty sticky, Cole thought. "Shouldn't we tell Pritzer?" he asked.

"That's what I wanted to discuss with you," Loring replied. "If he's clean, he could obviously help us. But if he's not . . ."

"You mean if he's a spy too?"

"Exactly. If he is, he'll have some advance warning to take evasive action. But even if he's not, if she has something on him, he'll want to protect her. In both of those cases, telling Pritzer could screw up our investigation."

"Pritzer will soon realize that she's disappeared, won't he?" Cole suggested.

"She was headed out the door on foot with two suitcases."

"Like she was leaving him?"

"Possibly."

"But if they've had a fight, why would she be asking for him?" Cole asked.

"They've probably just had one of their domestic spats. From what I hear, she gives old Pritzer enough reason to be angry. That wouldn't stop her from calling him for help once she's landed in the soup. She may also simply have been going on a trip. In any event, this gives us a little time."

"What a friggin' mess!" Cole remarked.

"Yes, it is, Colonel, at least potentially," Loring agreed. "On balance, my judgment is to tell Pritzer and give him a chance to see her. We can eavesdrop on their conversation and then grill Pritzer. That should give us some idea of the magnitude of the problem we face."

"That sounds right, Captain," Cole responded. "I suppose that you would like me to break the good news."

"Thank you. That would be helpful, Colonel, and I'll take it from there."

Cole called in Herter and Muldane and told them of Jutta's arrest.

"I say boot him out of the outfit," Muldane urged. "His wife's a spy, for Christ's sake."

"We think that, Zach," Cole corrected him. "We don't know. Anyway, he may be completely innocent, so we'd have no reason to fire him. And he's protected under Civil Service rules."

"They don't count for squat when the security of an intelligence operation is at stake."

"Let's not go overboard here," Cole warned. "Pritzer may be able to help us dismantle Jutta's spy cell, if she really belongs to one. I'm going to tell him of Jutta's arrest and then CIC will be monitoring both of them very closely."

"The risk, of course," Herter said gravely, "is that he's a Soviet agent and alerting him will cause him and all of his colleagues to dive for cover."

"Yes," Cole said, "Loring mentioned that risk, but on balance he thought we should tell Pritzer."

As their meeting broke up, Cole asked Herter, "Anything new on that damn Frankfurt/Oder bridge?"

"Not really. A couple of reports about ongoing construction."

"I see. Keep me informed, will you?"

After Herter left, Cole continued to mull over the quandary presented by the Frankfurt/Oder bridge. It was taking an inordinate amount of time and resources without any credible indication of its intelligence value. Nor was Cole insensitive to the potential waste of human lives. As a pilot, he had always considered the safety of his crew a paramount responsibility. Did not the agents, endangered by the missions his subordinates assigned, deserve some measure of similar concern?

*   *   *

Lieutenant Anatoly Ossipov had lost all patience. He had just received another report from Zeunert elaborating on the American suspicions that missiles were being installed at the Frankfurt/Oder bridge. Ossipov knew this was absurd, but why had it been impossible to obtain an official denial? Who was hiding what? He was being fended off in the same manner that he was keeping Zeunert at bay. It was humiliating. He decided to go to see Colonel Vladimir Fitin personally. After all, he reasoned, Fitin was the head of Soviet Air Force Intelligence in the Berlin area and should be able to break this logjam.

Colonel Fitin was a very heavy-set, beribboned warrior, brought out of retirement in the early 1950s to help staff the Soviet Occupation forces. Fitin, always more a politician than a soldier, had managed to survive the recurring military purges by avoiding all types of confrontations.

"You know, Ossipov," Fitin lectured, "we must not push these inquiries. That would be interfering with our brother Services, and before you know it, they will start interfering with us." He grinned, showing a mouthful of irregular, tobacco-stained teeth.

"I am not trying to interfere, Comrade Colonel," Ossipov replied respectfully. "But the Americans are sending agents to the bridge in Frankfurt/Oder, where they think we are establishing a missile site."

Fitin guffawed. "Let them think that," he exclaimed. "We spend a lot of effort attempting to send them on wild goose chases. Here they've made one up for themselves. They are doing our work for us." Once Fitin started on a certain track, he was hard to deflect. "That's wonderful! Let's encourage them to follow up on this brilliant idea. Let's begin excavations of the same type at every bridge all over the GDR. That will keep them busy." He thumped his desk joyously. Then, more somberly, he added, "Idiots! As if we'd allow our German brothers anywhere near our missiles or other new weapons."

"But don't you see, Comrade Colonel," Ossipov remarked, "that it would be most helpful for us to know the reason for the excavation. We could mislead the Americans much better if we weren't as much in the dark as they are."

Fitin turned serious. "You don't realize, Ossipov, how complicated this inquiry of yours has become. Why, it's turned into an international incident."

"A what?"

"An international problem, Ossipov," Fitin replied. "We now have a border dispute on our hands. As you know, the Oder River is the border between the GDR and Poland, our two great brother Socialist Republics."

"I don't see . . ."

"I agree, Ossipov, that the border should have no meaning for our victorious armed forces, but there are diplomatic niceties which we as a great superpower must be careful to respect. The excavation you're inquiring about is on the East side of the river, right?"

"Yes, Comrade Colonel."

"Therefore, it is in Poland and not in the GDR," Fitin exclaimed as if this were a revelation, "and the matter must be raised with our Polish brethren."

"Comrade Colonel," Ossipov stated, barely containing his annoyance, "I am inquiring about a Red Army installation."

"Located on Polish soil. We must not overlook the fact that our heroic Polish allies would want to be consulted about any information regarding their territory that might come to the attention of their German Socialist brothers, for whom, it must sadly be admitted, they feel little fraternal warmth."

Fitin gave him a complacent smile, which Ossipov took to mean that there was but a slender chance he would receive an answer to his inquiry. "I'll just have to use my imagination, Comrade Colonel," Ossipov said, taking his leave.

"That's it, Ossipov," Fitin replied, pleased to bring an awkward discussion to an end, "a little Socialist ingenuity will do the trick. In the meantime, let's keep the Americans very busy searching for missile installations. Set up some decoys around the Frankfurt/Oder bridge. Get the rumor mill working."

*   *   *

Anna Weber was sitting in her room in the Marienfelde barrack, staring blankly out the window, an unread newspaper on her lap. She had shed all her tears and now instead of pain felt only a futile numbness. Manfred was on the floor playing with his teddy bear.

The young woman who had befriended her came in and closed the door behind her. She had an excited glint in her eyes.

"I have a message for you, Anna," she said, handing her Weber's letter.

Anna took the envelope and opened it with trembling hands. There was no doubt; the letter was in Weber's handwriting. Thank

God, he was alive. And he wrote of her coming back to East Germany and of their being reunited! But the emotional shock was too sudden, too unexpected. Eagerly, she read the few lines over and over again, searching for any underlying meaning. Had Hans written this of his own free will? Of course not. He must be in prison and so he was writing her not only with his jailer's knowledge, but obviously at his behest. Was this a plot to lure her back? She looked for a warning in the communication, an indication that this was a trap she must avoid, but found nothing remotely threatening. She looked up and saw the young woman watching her intently.

What, she wondered, would become of her back in the GDR? Fleeing the country—*Republiksflucht*—was a punishable crime. Would she be heading back only to be put in prison? Hans' note was reassuring, but of course it would have to be, to entice her to return. She felt irresolute. There was no one to turn to for advice. If she asked the Americans or the camp officials, they were bound to try to dissuade her; they might even prevent her from leaving.

"Shall we go?" the young woman said in a brisk tone of voice, bringing Anna out of her tangled thoughts.

"I'm not sure," Anna said slowly.

"Not sure?" the young woman mimicked sarcastically. "Not sure of seeing your husband again? You want to stay alone with your baby and rot in a refugee camp? Are you crazy?"

"I am afraid of going back," Anna protested. "They will put me in jail."

"Of course they won't," the young woman replied tartly. "Didn't your husband write you that all would be well?"

"How do you know what he wrote me?" Anna asked suspiciously.

"I have reunited couples before," the woman answered glibly. "Stop imagining things. Here, now let me help you put your things together."

The young woman dragged Anna's suitcase out from under the dresser and threw it on the bed. She opened the dresser drawers, while Anna, still undecided, watched her pack without objecting. It only took a few moments to gather Anna's and little Manfred's belongings. The young woman went over to the wash basin and put the toilet articles into a plastic bag, then closed the suitcase and pulled it off the bed.

"Ready to go," she announced, taking the suitcase in one hand and helping Anna to her feet with the other. Despite Anna's lingering fear, her hope of being reunited with Weber, combined with the young woman's forceful manner, propelled her forward.

At the door she pointed to another suitcase in the corner. "What about Hans' things?" Anna asked.

"You take that suitcase," the young woman said, anxious to get under way.

"It's too heavy for me. I have to carry the baby," Anna objected.

The young woman gave her an annoyed look. "Let's go," she said sharply, picking up the second suitcase. Anna picked up Manfred, while he kept his arms around his teddy bear into whose lining Anna, upon her return to Marienfelde, had sewn the money that Weber had been paid for his spy missions.

The young woman knew the German guard at the camp gate. She told him that she was taking her sister and her little nephew home with her for a few days. He laughed and waved her on. An old car was parked nearby, and after Anna and Manfred were seated in front and the suitcases piled in the rear seat, the young woman drove quickly to the garage of a seemingly deserted three-story house in Kreuzberg alongside the East Berlin border.

Schumpeter was waiting for them. "What took you so long?" he asked irritably.

"I came as quickly as I could," the young woman replied evenly.

He shrugged his shoulders and simply said, "Follow me." Holding a flashlight, Schumpeter led the way down some stairs and then along a narrow corridor with steam pipes dripping water. At length they re-emerged up a steep staircase into a courtyard in East Berlin. A driver in a black car was waiting for them.

*   *   *

It was late in the afternoon, and Pritzer had interviewed twelve refugees, none of whom he was satisfied could possibly have qualified for covert work, so that the restriction he chafed under had so far been merely theoretical. As he interrogated, listened to replies, and wrote down the sparse bits of useful information, he was able to put aside the terror that Jutta had inspired. But only momentarily, for then the palpitations would recur.

It was, Pritzer knew, an impending disaster that would devastate his life unless . . . unless what? . . . unless she disappeared back into the GDR and was never heard from again. Yes, that was his only hope. He recalled that she had said he would have to trust her. The bitch! But she was right. That was all he had left: to trust the woman who had made such an utter fool of him. He again considered making a clean breast of it all to Cole, but had to face the fact that he was too cowardly, also too devious, for any such straightforward course of action.

He told himself that the disappearance of his only two agents was enough of a black mark to have to live down. He would have to work diligently to dig himself out of that hole. He had even decided to ingratiate himself with Liebman. A favorable report in his personnel file by Liebman on his interrogation technique would not hurt. He felt like Sisyphus, always having to start over again, just when he seemed on the threshold of professional advancement. He was sinking into maudlin self-pity when Liebman called out, "Phone call for you, Helmut."

"Who is it?"

"The Colonel."

Pritzer went to Liebman's desk and took the receiver. "Yes, Colonel, Pritzer here," he said and then, "Of course, sir. Right away." He put down the receiver and with a tinge of self-importance told Liebman, "The Colonel wants to see me."

"It's getting late," Liebman said kindly. "Don't worry about coming back. I'll finish up here. See you in the morning."

As he walked up Clayallee to the American Command compound, Pritzer tried to guess what Cole had on his mind. Cole's voice over the phone had been neutral——not unfriendly, Pritzer thought, not threatening. He fumbled for his wallet to show his pass at the gatehouse, then entered the building and went directly to Cole's office.

"Good afternoon, Pritzer," Cole said, looking up. "Close the door and sit down. I'm afraid what I have to say is not going to be pleasant."

Pritzer felt a tremor traverse his body as he sat down, gripping the metal armrests of the chair. He stared at Cole apprehensively.

"Your wife," Cole announced, "is being detained by CIC."

"What?" Pritzer exclaimed, half rising out of his seat.

"Let me repeat. She is being held by CIC."

"But why?"

"She is suspected of being an East German spy."

"Oh my God," Pritzer groaned. "That can't be."

"Have you had any reason to suspect her loyalty?" Cole asked. It was Cole now who stared at Pritzer.

Pritzer's instinct when pressed had invariably been to lie. This instinct was deeply ingrained. He would talk himself out of any jam later on with, if necessary, additional prevarications. He had learned early on that it was only the truth that one had difficulty talking oneself out of.

"Of course not," Pritzer replied shakily, clutching the armrests to stop his hands from trembling. "This is ridiculous. Jutta comes from the East, but she has always talked about Communism with contempt. She has lots of faults, Jutta," Pritzer added with a nervous laugh, "but a spy, no. Certainly not."

Cole saw that Pritzer was genuinely shocked by word of Jutta's arrest. Whether the shock also covered the charge of espionage was unclear.

"I assume you want to see your wife," Cole said.

In truth, Jutta was the last person on earth Pritzer wanted to see. "Of course I do, Colonel," Pritzer said quickly. "As soon as possible. I'm sure there's a very simple explanation."

"I hope so," Cole said, buzzing the switchboard to get Captain Loring on the line.

"Captain Loring?" Cole said after they had been connected, "Colonel Cole here . . . I've got Pritzer with me. Yes . . . He wants to see his wife as soon as possible . . . Oh, I see. Well, tomorrow morning then . . . At CIC Headquarters. OK. Ten o'clock in your office? . . . I'll tell him. Thanks."

Cole hung up. "It's too late today, Pritzer. Right now your wife's at a CIC safe house, and they haven't finished their interrogation yet. They'll be bringing her to CIC Headquarters later tonight. You can see her there tomorrow morning at 10 o'clock. Ask for Captain Loring."

The news that she was being interrogated sent Pritzer into a panic. "Colonel, I've got to see her tonight," he entreated, his voice rising. "Why can't I see my wife after the interrogation is finished? I'm sure she's asked to see me. She must be in a terrible state. She's about to become an American citizen, you know. They can't just lock her up like that."

"Listen, Pritzer, I'm not a lawyer, but Berlin is a military zone, and I'm pretty sure that CIC can hold anyone suspected of spying." Seeing Pritzer's stricken face, Cole softened a bit. "I know this is tough, Pritzer," he said. "Have a stiff drink and go to bed. You'll get to see your wife in the morning."

Without another word, Pritzer shuffled out of the 575th Squadron Office and began to walk home in a daze. So Jutta had not disappeared into the GDR; she had not even made it to East Berlin. Her threat to expose him rang loudly in his ears; he felt more cornered than ever.

He suddenly understood why he had been removed from covert work and had even been denied access to priority targets. He was obviously under suspicion himself. He laughed out loud, startling a woman passerby. There was nothing to that charge; he wasn't a spy; he hadn't passed information to the enemy, except . . . except what Jutta had wormed out of him. That was classified. She was a spy, and she had undoubtedly relayed that information to her handler. Pritzer broke out in a cold sweat. There was no way around it; he faced years in jail.

He waited with other pedestrians at a red traffic light before crossing Argentinische Allee. It seemed odd to be in the proximity of ordinary people with their common worries while he, unbeknownst to them, had a cataclysm with which to contend.

Get hold of yourself, he admonished himself. What good would it do for Jutta to expose you? None at all. In fact it would be an admission of her guilt. It would confirm that she was a spy, trying to extract information from him. The only way to save herself, Pritzer reasoned, was for her to deny everything and pretend she was a devoted little wife. Well, with her reputation that characterization might be pushing it, but she could vigorously deny spying. Jutta was tough; Pritzer could testify to that. Whatever they had on her, there was no doubt that she'd come up with an excuse. It might well be premature to panic.

Pritzer looked up and for a moment didn't recognize where he was. Then he saw that he had walked more than a kilometer past his own house. He allowed himself the luxury of a smile and retraced his steps. Cole was right. He'd have a stiff drink and try to get some rest.

But despite the drink, his night was sleepless and filled with terror. The CIC might not have the goods on her, but he did. He knew, on the very best authority, that she was a spy. So what should he do, he asked himself. Try to get her out of jail, or turn her in? As he considered the consequences of these alternatives, he could come to only one conclusion. Either way, he was lost.

*　　*　　*

At first glance, Mommsenstrasse had nothing in particular to recommend it. Despite its location near the Kurfürstendamm, it could boast of no luxury shops or movie theaters. Instead, it appeared to be a street of staid, drab middle-class dwellings, with but the occasional small shop or eating establishment. And yet at number

28 Mommsenstrasse, near the corner of Knesebeckstrasse, there was a three-story house whose nondescript exterior had for decades provided a discreet curtain to conceal the city's most extravagant debauchery.

Number 28 was the kingdom of Fräulein Kitty. Now in her mid-fifties, she had arrived in Berlin in 1922 from her native Pomeranian village, barely twenty years old, with a small suitcase, her savings that would scarcely have covered a night's lodging in a good hotel, a beautiful body, and a fierce will to succeed. She quickly put her body to profitable use and was soon the most requested of the denizens in one of Berlin's swankier brothels. But whereas the other girls concentrated all their attentions on the male clientele, Kitty decided early on to befriend the Princess, the madam of the establishment, known more commonly to the police as Frau Irmgard Sippenheimer.

It did not take Kitty long to learn the tricks of the trade, for which she seemed to have a natural bent. Within a year, having put a neat little bundle of money aside and collected the names and telephone numbers of the more generous clients, she bade farewell to a very angry Princess and set up shop on her own. Her establishment was an instant success, not only because novelty is always welcome in the oldest profession but also because Kitty and her band of youthful companions, many of whom had also deserted the Princess, brought verve and a sense of fun to what had traditionally been the stiff and stodgy atmosphere of a Berlin bordello.

The turbulent times of the Weimar Republic soon opened up the possibility of profit from activities other than the pleasures of the flesh. As tired politicians in power and those hungry to accede to power crossed paths at Fräulein Kitty's, she became a patient and attentive listener to their various troubles. At first, the clients merely spent time with Kitty as they waited for the woman of their choice to be ready to receive them. But gradually the understanding and compassion that Kitty provided—as well as the challenge of being the only unavailable attractive female on the premises—became as much of a drawing card to her harried clientele as her more traditional carnal offerings. The disparateness and prominence of many of her visitors made Kitty a unique fount of information, and she soon discovered that this intimate knowledge of current affairs could, if handled carefully, give rise to an additional source of income.

Within a short time, not only politicians but journalists, spies and diplomats, the rich and curious, would-be blackmailers and innocent gossips, playboys and con artists—in fact, representatives of all the myriad classes of Berlin's active night life—all would find their way to Fräulein Kitty's. There, many of them would just sit all night in the small downstairs bar adjoining the entrance, talking, arguing, and exchanging the latest jokes while keeping a glazed eye on the staircase to try to identify those climbing up to, or descending from, the upper floors where Kitty and her handmaidens held court.

Though political plots and conspiracies were the essence of Kitty's intangible offerings, her business was curiously unaffected by the violent political changes in Germany during the first half of the twentieth century. Throughout the slow and agonizing death-knell of the Weimar Republic with its bloody street clashes, the rise and fall of the Nazi Thousand-Year Reich, the conquest of Berlin by the Red Army, and the postwar division of the city, Fräulein Kitty remained open and extended her unique blend of welcome to any who could afford the price, with payment accepted in cash or valuable information.

Lieutenant Ossipov had arrived early that evening—that is, at eleven o'clock, early by Fräulein Kitty's standard. He looked briefly into the downstairs bar, which at that hour had only half a dozen habitués including Colonel Durafour at a corner table in earnest conversation with L. Cabot Pearson. Ossipov did not enter the bar but went directly upstairs. Most of the girls, still unoccupied, were sitting, as Kitty had taught them, quietly and primly in the overstuffed chairs of the large salon. They were all quite young, generally in their early twenties, with pretty faces, little makeup, and carefully brushed hair. They were dressed in simple but revealing garb. Their aspect was that of the graduating class of a respectable finishing school rather than of the roster of Berlin's classiest whorehouse.

Ossipov nodded to a blond Czech girl with whom he was well acquainted and headed for the salon's back door, its glass panel covered by a lace curtain that allowed Kitty to look out without being herself observed. Fräulein Kitty liked Ossipov. He was a handsome figure of a man—witty, invariably polite, and, if the Czech girl was to be believed, a talented and resourceful lover. He was also a valuable and rare source of information, since the Russians, fearing defections, were quite sparing in the number of their officers allowed to visit the fleshpots of the West. And the monthly stipend the Soviet Intelligence graciously provided was far more generous than similar offerings Fräulein Kitty collected from its Western counterparts.

Ossipov knocked on the door and opened it upon being invited in. Kitty was sitting at her small desk and smiled at him as he entered. She was wearing a close-fitting emerald-green shantung suit and an elaborate ivory necklace, both of which dramatically set off her dark eyes and jet-black hair.

"Lieutenant Ossipov," Kitty said in her famed deep and dulcet voice. "It is always a pleasure to welcome you to my humble establishment. A glass of champagne?"

"Thank you very much. That would be delightful." Kitty crossed the room and took two fluted crystal glasses from a little side bar. She filled them from an opened bottle of Mumm champagne, resting in a silver ice bucket on a side table, and handed one to Ossipov. They clinked glasses and Ossipov sat down in an armchair across from Kitty, who settled into a small two-seated sofa.

"What will it be tonight, Lieutenant," Kitty asked mischievously, "business or pleasure?"

"Perhaps the right mixture of both," Ossipov responded smoothly.

"The Americans have a saying: business before pleasure. Should we follow their lead tonight?"

"In general, I prefer the Americans behind us, rather than in front," Ossipov said. "But I never have any trouble, Fräulein Kitty, following wherever you might want to lead me."

Kitty's smile broadened. "It has been a quiet month, Lieutenant," she said, reaching for the black leather-bound notebook that was never far from her side. Moistening her forefinger with her tongue, she leafed through a number of pages, apparently searching for a particular item. "Ah yes, here it is," she said, and recounted detailed plans of a supposedly imminent reduction in the British military presence in West Berlin.

"Can you give me the source of that report?" Ossipov asked.

"I can tell you that one of my girls learned this quite by accident . . ."

Ossipov's eyebrows shot up. There was never anything accidental in Fräulein Kitty's activities.

"No—really," Kitty said, laughing, "the young man was quite heartbroken at being transferred back to England. He was pleading with Elise to come back with him and marry him."

"Anything else, Fräulein Kitty?" Ossipov asked.

"Just the usual, I'm afraid. Nothing out of the ordinary." She identified some of the Western military units or intelligence services to which her recent visitors belonged without revealing their names, which it was understood would have been unprofessional. The French were adjusting with some difficulty to the exacting personality of Général de Montsouris, who had recently arrived to take over the French Berlin Command.

"He seems to be a fierce disciplinarian," Kitty said, chuckling. "The poor little dears are most unhappy." Referring from time to time to her notebook, she summarized a number of her own conversations with the French officers as well as the reports that the girls were obliged to make after each *rendez-vous*. Morale was high among the Allied troops and their relations with the West Berliners had never been better. There was little concern about Berlin's isolated status.

"I haven't earned my stipend this month, Ossipov, have I?" Kitty inquired, which was intended as a gentle reminder.

"Very interesting report," Ossipov responded quickly, taking an envelope from his inside pocket and giving it to her. "It is important for us to have a hand on the pulse of West Berlin and no hand is more delicate for that task than yours, Fräulein Kitty."

Kitty smiled contentedly and slipped the envelope into her notebook. There was obviously something else on Lieutenant Ossipov's mind, and she waited quietly for him to speak.

"Has anyone mentioned a bridge?" he asked.

"A bridge?"

"Yes, a bridge over the Oder River."

"Where?"

"In Frankfurt/Oder."

"No, I don't think so," Kitty answered. "Just a moment, let me check." She leafed through her notebook again, running her finger up and down several pages, checking various passages. "No, not a word about a bridge in Frankfurt/Oder. Why?"

"No reason; no reason at all," Ossipov answered blithely. "But if anyone should mention the bridge, I'd be interested to hear of it."

"I could be of more help," Kitty said, "if you told me a little more, Lieutenant."

Ossipov hesitated a moment, as if undecided. "All right," he said, "but this is for your ears only, Fräulein Kitty." Kitty nodded, and they both understood that this was information she was intended to pass on. "The Americans seem to have the crazy notion that we're about to install missiles near that bridge. We'd like to know where they could have gotten that absurd idea."

His mission completed, Ossipov took his leave of Fräulein Kitty and, seeing his Czech girl sitting in one of the alcoves of the salon, went over to sit with her. She had been waiting for him and had been granted permission by Fräulein Kitty to turn down other suitors in the meantime. Her name was Olga. She had a pleasing, flat Slav face, with large brown eyes and curly light brown hair. Her thin waist served to exaggerate an ample bosom and wide peasant-girl hips. She made love simply, with little artifice but with a natural animal ferocity that Ossipov could match but could not tame.

They quietly shared a split of champagne, compliments of the house, Ossipov anticipating with mounting excitement his favorite forms of lechery. All at once Olga's breathing quickened. Ossipov wondered whether this was genuine or contrived behavior. Not that it mattered. She gave his hand a squeeze and whispered, "Let's go up." He emptied his glass, rose, and let her lead him across the salon to the stairs on the other side. On the way up, he noticed a man—undoubtedly an American—knocking at Fräulein Kitty's door. He smiled and followed Olga to the third-floor Versailles room, his preferred exotic trysting place. There were mirrors on its four walls, on the ceiling, and around the edges of the floor. The reflections from the bed were astounding, and the pictures taken by the hidden cameras no less startling.

Day 12 Tuesday

Bud Cole was at his desk when the telephone rang. The switchboard announced that Eugene Zandt was on the line from Marienfelde.

"Put him on," Cole said.

"I thought you might be interested to hear, Colonel," Zandt remarked, "that our house guest has left."

"Who? What house guest?"

"The woman with the baby you requested VIP quarters for last week. She's slipped out of Marienfelde."

"With the baby?"

"Yes."

"When did this happen?"

"Yesterday, probably."

"Why are you reporting this only now?" Cole asked, clearly annoyed.

"Because, Colonel," Zandt replied emphatically, "I only found out about it myself five minutes ago."

"Aren't there room checks at the camp every few hours?"

"Technically, yes."

"What does that mean?" Cole demanded.

"What that means, Colonel," Zandt answered, not in the least abashed, "is that there are so many damn people here that it's impossible to keep track of them. If you check a room and there's no one there, the person could be in the bathroom or at the camp store or socializing with a neighbor. As a practical matter, it's only at night that you can get any kind of an accurate count."

"OK, I get it," Cole said. "Any idea how she got out?"

"Not sure. A guard remembers two women, one of them with a baby, leaving in the afternoon. One of the women said she was just taking her sister home for a few hours."

"He let them out without an exit pass?"

"West Berliners often come to the camp to take their friends or relatives out for a meal or a short visit. That's not unusual."

"All right, thanks," Cole said. "Let me know if she comes back."

"Don't hold your breath, Colonel," Zandt commented before hanging up.

Cole walked into Herter's office. "Weber's wife and baby have disappeared from Marienfelde," he announced.

Herter looked up from the report he was reading. "I take it, Colonel, that Weber is still overdue," he said.

"Yes. He should have been back Saturday at the latest."

"Maybe he's changed his mind," Herter conjectured, "and decided to return to the GDR. And now he's sent for his wife and baby."

"Do you think that's what's happened?" Cole asked skeptically.

Herter put down his report. "No, not really," he said. "I suspect that he's probably been picked up, and they've put the squeeze on him to bring his family back."

"Will that create an additional problem for us?" Cole wondered.

"I wouldn't think so, Colonel," Herter declared with assurance. "There's nothing she knows that he doesn't; in fact, she probably doesn't know anything at all that could embarrass us." Herter picked up his report again.

Herter's indifference disturbed Cole. "Just two more lives down the drain. That's all, I guess," he said, trying to get a rise out of Herter.

"Three, actually, counting the baby," Herter corrected.

"You're right, three," Cole agreed, shaking his head.

Herter continued to read and, compressing his lips in annoyance, picked up a pencil and forcefully crossed out a word in the report. Cole observed him for a moment and then asked, "Don't you feel any responsibility, let alone sympathy, for these poor people?"

Herter put down his papers and looked at Cole. "There are a

lot of unfortunates on our globe, Colonel," he lectured. "Some are struck down by disease or natural disasters. Others have themselves to blame for their misfortunes. The Webers fall into the latter category. Herr Weber was too greedy."

"That's not quite accurate," Cole commented. "We're the ones that did everything possible to push him into going back."

"I don't have to tell you, Colonel, that our unit has an important job to do," Herter said, "and we need agents to carry out our mission. Weber is an intelligent adult. He was fully aware of the dangers involved. Why should I feel any compassion for his fate? It's the luck of the draw, that's all."

Herter was not totally devoid of compassion. It was only in carrying out his intelligence duties that he distanced himself from the human dimension. Cole would probably have been surprised to see Herter help a blind person across the street, a not uncommon occurrence in postwar Berlin, with its abundance of cripples and handicapped.

Cole left Herter's office and returned to his desk. He shook off his annoyance at Herter's condescension and tried to see the humor, or rather the gallows' humor, in the situation. What a strange bunch of people I've got in my outfit, he ruminated. On the one hand, that cold fish Herter and on the other Liebman, wearing his bleeding heart on his sleeve. And then, he reminded himself, there's that damn cocktail party we have to throw tomorrow. It's surprising we ever get anything done.

*   *   *

CIC's Berlin Headquarters was located in a 1930ish stone office structure on the broad Hohenzollerdamm; it was a building that had housed the Interior Ministry during World War II. Pritzer had arrived an hour early for his ten o'clock appointment and had been forced to cool his heels in the street-level waiting room before being escorted to Captain Loring's third-floor office at the appointed time.

"What have you been told?" Loring asked, as Pritzer sat down in a straight-backed chair across the desk from him.

"Only that you've arrested my wife, Captain. This is a terrible mistake . . ."

Loring interrupted him. "We haven't arrested her, Mr. Pritzer," he said calmly. "We have merely detained her for questioning."

"Captain," Pritzer insisted, "I'm sure my wife has done nothing wrong. It's absurd to think that she's a spy."

"Who told you that we suspect her of spying?" Loring asked pointedly.

"Colonel Cole. He said that she's being held as an East German spy. Captain, that's just not possible."

Loring observed Pritzer as he rambled on and concluded like Cole before him that Pritzer's excited demeanor revealed nothing. "May I please see my wife?" Pritzer was saying. "I'm sure there's a very simple explanation for all this."

"Yes, you can, Mr. Pritzer," Loring replied. "But first let me give you a few relevant facts. First of all, she has been seen twice meeting a man we are pretty sure is an East German handler of Stasi spies in West Berlin. She maintains that the man is her uncle from Dresden. Does she have an uncle in Dresden?"

"Yes," Pritzer answered guardedly, "she's mentioned an uncle in the GDR."

"Have you ever met him or seen him?"

"No, I haven't."

"Were you aware that she was meeting this uncle in West Berlin?"

"No, I wasn't," Pritzer admitted.

"We tried to apprehend him on Sunday but he gave us the slip. I must say that the uncle is very adept at evading capture. Then, when we saw her leave your house yesterday with two suitcases in hand, we thought it best to detain her and ask a few questions."

Pritzer was relieved; Jutta must have held her own. "If there's nothing else, may I see her now?" Pritzer asked, hoping that his slackening tension was not apparent.

"Of course. By the way, were you aware that your wife was leaving on a trip?" Loring asked. "Do you know where she was going?" Pritzer hesitated. "No, I don't," he said nervously. "I'll ask her, if you like."

"I must warn you, Mr. Pritzer," Loring admonished him, "that assistance given a foreign agent, even if she is your wife, would be a serious criminal offense."

*   *   *

There were four small prisoners' cells in the basement, a remnant of the former Interior Ministry's accoutrements. Jutta was brought upstairs to a ground-floor meeting room, where Pritzer was waiting for her. For once she looked slovenly; her blonde hair, which she kept pushing back behind her ears, was stringy and disheveled; her dress was rumpled; her flushed cheeks replaced her lack of makeup. Only her eyes were vibrant—fierce and defiant.

She tried to rush over to Pritzer, but the female guard held her back and ordered her to sit down at the table in the center of the room. Two chairs on either side constituted the only furnishings. A plastic foot-high shield in the center of the table and a plywood partition beneath prevented any physical contact. The guard told both of them to remain seated; they would have fifteen minutes to talk and would be watched from the adjoining room through a glass panel. There was no need to tell them that their conversation would also be monitored. That was taken for granted.

Pritzer was agitated, but Jutta was in fine form. "Mutiger, darling," she exclaimed in joyful greeting. "I've been so upset about your worrying about me. Are you all right?"

"Of course I am, darling," he said uncertainly, "but what the hell is this all about?"

"I don't know, Mutiger. As I was leaving the house on Monday, I was pushed into a car by two men and taken to a villa somewhere. I was terrified at first that the East Germans were trying to kidnap me."

"What happened?"

"They kept asking me about Uncle Friedrich from Dresden."

"What about him?"

"Well, I didn't want to trouble you, Mutiger," she explained demurely, "but Uncle Friedrich is in bad shape. He's been forced to retire from his assembly-line job and now with his meager pension he barely has enough money to live on. I've seen him a few times and have given him a little money, which I saved out of my housekeeping allowance. I'm sorry I didn't tell you. I never thought it would lead to this." She laughed nervously.

Jutta had outlined her defense, being careful at the same time to exculpate Pritzer, giving him deniability for her acts. Her message was clear. If they both stuck to the same story, she would be let go and then he had nothing to fear. Jutta had counted on Pritzer's silence, but it was reassuring to have it confirmed.

Suddenly, Jutta changed tactics and began to whine and plead. "Get me out of here," she wailed. "I haven't done anything wrong. I'm going to be an American citizen, your wife, Mutiger. They can't keep me locked up just because I've seen my uncle. I bet not even the Stasi would act that way." She realized that this was pushing the point.

Pritzer promised that he would do everything in his power to get her out as quickly as possible. He was relieved that she had not implicated him in any way, suppressing the realization that he was her guilty accomplice for not denouncing her.

"I want to go home," she sobbed. "I just want to cuddle with my little Mutiger." Pritzer thought she was putting it on too thick, but beneath her helpless pleading he detected an ominous threat. "I can't stand it here another night," she sniffled. "You know I have claustrophobia, Mutiger. I'll become hysterical if I'm locked up again. Please, do something." Translation: Get me out of here, or I might still implicate you.

The guard entered the room; the fifteen minutes were up.

Pritzer slowly climbed the stairs back to Loring's office. Loring himself had just returned from the ground floor, where he had watched Pritzer's meeting with Jutta. He sensed that the encounter had been staged. Jutta had been well trained and had performed faultlessly. The question now was whether Pritzer was in league with her or an unwitting dupe. Under the circumstances, he had decided to release Jutta, but to keep both of them under surveillance.

"Come in, Mr. Pritzer," Loring said. "You will be happy to hear that we have decided to release your wife."

"That is good news," a surprised Pritzer mumbled.

"Yes," Loring went on somewhat laconically, "we may have overreacted. Sorry about that. But you can't be too careful in Berlin where espionage is concerned—right, Mr. Pritzer?" Loring gave Pritzer a searching look.

"No, no, of course not," Pritzer agreed, avoiding his gaze.

"Please convey our apologies to your wife. I think she'll tell you that she was treated well."

Jutta, radiant and very affectionate, greeted Pritzer in Loring's outer office a few minutes later. A guard carried her two suitcases to Pritzer's car, and they quickly drove away.

As soon as they had turned the corner, she broke out into laughter. *"Mensch,"* she exclaimed. "Did we fool them! You were very good, Mutiger. A concerned husband freeing his falsely accused wife. I'm going to tell the Stasi that you'll make a very good agent."

Trembling, Pritzer pulled over to the curb. He turned to her angrily. "Stop that talk, Jutta. I'm a loyal U.S. Government employee . . ."

"Except," she interrupted, "that you have a darling little wife who is an East German spy to whom you disclose classified information . . ."

Pritzer gripped the steering wheel and gritted his teeth. "You bitch," he hissed.

" . . . and whom you have just gotten out of jail so that she wouldn't reveal your secret." She looked over at Pritzer, now bent over the steering wheel, and saw that she had regained complete control.

"Let's not park here all day," Jutta scolded. "I want to get home and take a nice long soak in the bathtub. If you're a good boy, Mutiger, I might let you sponge my back." He started the car's engine and slowly began to drive back home.

"That was smart of you, Mutiger, to get me out," she remarked as they reached Zehlendorf and turned into their street with its villas and well-tended gardens. "You know that just a few words from me and you are a ruined jailbird. You'd better never forget that."

For Pritzer, his private hell was starting again. The slim chance that Jutta would disappear was shattered. They entered their house, she going upstairs to bathe while he sank into one of the living-room armchairs. Later she announced that under the circumstances she had decided to stay in West Berlin a little longer. She would have to wait for further orders, she explained. In public, they would be "lovey-dovey," but in private,"between us the comedy is finished. I'm not your wife, but your superior in the Stasi Secret Service. In other words, Mutiger, from now on you're my submissive and obedient agent. And if you step out of line, one false move, and you're through."

Pritzer listened to her in silence. He did not doubt her determination. Nor did he protest, but he felt in his rising anger that she might have overplayed her hand. She had pushed him to the point where his instinct for survival was more powerful than his compliant nature. He would play a patient waiting game, but he would find a way out. Hopefully, short of killing her.

*   *   *

After the Pritzers had left, Loring called Cole. "I've released Jutta Pritzer," he told him.

"Why?"

"Her response to our interrogation—very smooth and focused—indicates that she's probably a Stasi plant, but we can't prove it. It's her husband I'm interested in. After all, he's the guy with the classified info."

"Do you think he's in cahoots with her?" Cole asked.

"Probably not, but there's something's wrong with him."

"What do you mean?"

"I can't put my finger on it. I may be all wrong, but I watched him as Jutta was first brought into the room by the prison guard. His anxiety seemed to be more that of a guilty party than a worried husband. Also, he never did question her on where she was heading yesterday with her suitcases, though we had asked him to find out. Bottom line, I'm sure he knows a lot more than he's telling us."

"What do we do now?" Cole asked.

"We're going to keep the pair under surveillance, but to make them relax, and perhaps drop their guard a little, you should give Pritzer a little more slack."

"You mean put him back on covert work?"

"No, that would be too risky, Colonel," Loring replied. "But you might let him have some of our target priorities to help in his interrogations. That should send him a reassuring message."

"I'll do as you say Captain," Cole said doubtfully, "but I would appreciate your confirming that in writing. You know, I'm damn uncomfortable about the possibility of having a spy in my outfit."

"Welcome to West Berlin, Colonel," was Captain Loring's cheery rejoinder.

*   *   *

Juergen Nitsche was back in Frankfurt/Oder that morning because Colonel Durafour's superior had requested additional information. As he made his way toward the bridge on foot, he was surprised that the security cordon that had previously guarded that area had apparently been removed. He entered the pharmacy he had visited last time and greeted the old couple, who were sitting together behind the counter.

"Can I interest you today in my cosmetic line?" he inquired hopefully.

"No, I am afraid not," the old man replied.

"Hasn't business picked up?" Nitsche asked. "No one stopped me this time to ask for my papers."

"It just happened this morning," the wife said, eager to impart the latest news. "Last night the roadblock was still up, and the car with the two men in trench coats was still parked up the street. And today, they're all gone."

"Be quiet, mama," the old man said fearfully.

"I'm just saying what any fool can see with his own eyes," she replied stubbornly.

"Do you have any idea why they've left?" Nitsche asked.

"No," the old man replied.

"Just as we have no idea why they came in the first place," his wife added.

"Well, I hope they'll stay away," Nitsche said lightly. "Then your business will improve, and the next time I'll be able to sell you some of my goods."

Nitsche left the pharmacy and walked to the Gasthaus, which overlooked the bridge. No one stopped him or asked to see his papers. In view of the suspicions he had aroused the last time, he decided not to go inside, but as he turned the corner of the building, he was startled to see two large trucks in the parking lot. Each was loaded with three large metal platforms that were uncovered and secured by chains.

He had a small camera in his cosmetics case, but after a quick look around, decided it would be too risky to remove it and begin taking pictures. There were large numbers stamped into the side of the platforms. He hurried away, repeating the numbers to himself and stopping in a dark doorway some distance away to write them down. His memory was excellent and with the specialized training he had received he was able that evening, once safely back in West Berlin, to sketch the platforms, the trucks providing the necessary scale.

That same afternoon, the Potsdam Military Mission car drove through Frankfurt/Oder on its way back from a routine sweep of the Brandenburg area. Its occupants spotted the same trucks in the parking lot and were able to take numerous photos before being chased away by a Red Army patrol car. However, the chase seemed desultory, not up to the frenetic pace to which the Potsdam Mission personnel had become accustomed. The senior officer in the car made a point of this in his report.

"It was almost as if they wanted us to take those pictures," he wrote. "The platforms were just sitting there, uncovered and without any guard. That is unusual for Red Army equipment and seems suspicious to us."

*   *   *

Anna had not been allowed to see Weber the night before when she had been hustled to Stasi HQ on Normannenstrasse. Despite her desperate pleas to be with her husband—"You promised me," she kept repeating—she had been told roughly to shut her trap— "*Maul halten*"—and had been locked with a crying little Manfred in a narrow, windowless room. It had a cot, an unstable wooden table, and a single chair. There was no running water, and she was obliged to call the guard for an escort down the hall to a stinking toilet. A bowl of thin barley soup, a crust of bread, and some watery milk for the baby constituted supper. Not a word about when she would see Weber. She had cried herself to sleep; a naked lightbulb hanging over the table shone all night.

She was awakened at six by a middle-aged matron, a welcome improvement over the previous evening's coarse male guard. The woman brought a small tray with weak but hot coffee, a hard roll with a dab of cherry jam, and a biscuit and glass of milk for the baby. In mid-morning Anna was taken to Zeunert's office, having been forced to leave the baby with the prison matron.

"Welcome home, Frau Weber," Zeunert called out jovially as Anna was led in and the door was closed behind her. "We have been waiting for you. Come over here and sit down." He motioned to a pair of upholstered chairs near the window and sat down in one himself.

Her heart pounding with fear, Anna did as she was told. She was too frightened to speak and with her head down waited quietly to hear her fate.

"There is no need to be afraid, Frau Weber," Zeunert declared. "You and your husband are young, and you have both made a youthful mistake in leaving the Fatherland. No doubt you were influenced by the lying, deceitful Western propaganda. Well, I hope you've learned your lesson. All that drivel about the streets over there being paved in gold. Ha! You saw what that all meant. Didn't you?"

Zeunert waited for Anna to respond. "I asked you, Frau Weber, didn't you?"

Anna, still frozen with fear and unable to speak, just nodded.

"Good," Zeunert said. "You saw that all those pretty pictures and lovely stories were all damned lies. You agree, don't you, Frau Weber?" Again, Anna nodded.

"Being exploited is what Western capitalism is all about," he lectured, his tone becoming harsher. "Your husband was exploited. He was tempted with their dirty money to become a spy and harm his Socialist homeland—his *Heimatland*. He could have been shot while following their orders to photograph a military installation."

Anna gasped. Leaning menacingly toward her, Zeunert warned, "He could still be shot for spying, you know. That is the law." He let that threat sink in, watching Anna's face contort in terror.

Zeunert was a close student of human reaction to sudden stress. He was not a sadist and, unlike some of his cohorts, did not thrill to the pain inflicted on helpless prisoners. On the other hand, he felt no empathy for any suffering imposed. Instead, he was dispassionate in calibrating the correct amount of pressure required in any particular situation. Anna's symptoms were commonplace and what he had expected.

"But," he announced theatrically, "we have decided to be merciful." Anna, startled, looked up through tearful eyes. "We need good young people like you and your husband to help build Socialism in our country, and if you truly repent, we will let you resume your constructive lives. What do you say to that, Frau Weber?"

"What do you want us to do?" she asked weakly.

Zeunert got up and walked over to his desk. "Do you smoke, Frau Weber?" he asked.

"No, thank you," she replied softly. He took a cigarette from an ornate silver and ivory box and lit it. He inhaled deeply and let the smoke escape slowly through his nostrils. To Anna he conjured up a picture of a fire-breathing dragon.

"We want very little, Frau Weber," Zeunert said, sitting down again near her. "As I have already told your husband, we would like you both to speak about your experiences in the Golden West, those eleven days you spent in the so-called Land of Freedom. We want you to tell what really happened to you over there, as a warning to others of the misery and danger they would face if they were to leave the GDR."

"But I have nothing to tell," Anna protested. "I spent most of the time with our baby on the second floor of a house."

"How were you treated?"

"Very well, really," Anna blurted out without thinking. "I didn't want Hans to go back and spy. I begged him not to do it. But he went anyway."

"Do you mean to tell me," Zeunert said, his voice turning ugly, "that he went back voluntarily? of his own free will? without being forced to go? and that you just wanted to stay over there?"

Anna began to cry. "I didn't want him to get mixed up in spying," she sobbed. "Please understand, sir, we are little people trying to live our lives quietly, without stirring up trouble. Whenever people like us are put in the spotlight, we end up getting hurt. But Hans wouldn't listen."

Zeunert stood, went over to the window and looked out, while Anna wiped her eyes with the handkerchief she always carried tucked in her sleeve. It was a foggy, drizzly day with the gray of the sky melding seamlessly with the ruins and poorly maintained structures of the East Berlin skyline.

Zeunert turned around. With his back to the window and his face in shadow, he spoke slowly and earnestly. "Now listen to me, Frau Weber," he said. "You and your husband are in a very difficult position, and I am the only person in this world who can help you. Remember that! If you cooperate, I will let you resume your quiet lives. If not . . ." Zeunert let the threat hang in the air, and Anna's entire frame was convulsed by a tremor.

"Do you understand?" he snarled.

"Yes," she whispered.

"You and your husband will follow my instructions to the letter. Do you agree?"

Anna looked down at the floor and nodded. Zeunert decided that she was sufficiently cowed. Adopting a more benign tone, he said, "Now I have a pleasant surprise for you, Frau Weber." He walked over to open a side door. Hans Weber was standing in the adjoining room with outstretched arms and tears in his eyes. She ran to him, and he enfolded her. They kissed rapturously, and to Zeunert's cynical amusement, paid no attention to their lack of privacy.

"Hans! Oh Hans!" she wept. "Thank God, you're alive. I've been so lonely. And so afraid."

Weber tried to kiss her tears away, all the while reassuring her that they would not be separated again. Zeunert grew impatient. "Enough of that," he ordered. "Sit down, both of you."

They sat quickly on a small bench set against the wall in the other room. Weber squeezed Anna's hand to reassure her. She had calmed down, and they both listened attentively to Zeunert's detailed instructions. When he had finished, he asked them to repeat what they had been told. He listened to their responses, made one or two corrections, and added a few new items. Then he said,

"Fine. I think you have it. Now don't make any mistake. Remember, a mistake could cost Herr Weber his life."

*   *   *

Professor Halder was angry. Brigitte was fixing his supper and trying to ignore his foul mood.

"Are you going out again tonight?" he asked.

"Yes, father."

"Where are you going?" he demanded. Brigitte didn't reply.

"As if I didn't know," he murmured darkly.

Brigitte turned down the flame on the gas stove, wiped her hands on her apron, and went over to her father, who was sitting at the kitchen table.

"Now, father," she said, "calm down. Colonel Cole is a perfect gentleman, and we enjoy each other's company."

"Until dawn yesterday morning," he spat out.

"I'm not sixteen," Brigitte responded, returning to her cooking and keeping her temper under control. "I am thirty-one and no longer need a chaperone, you know."

"That doesn't mean you have to turn into a camp follower."

She ignored the remark. There was no point in fighting with the old man.

"What would your poor mother, let alone Franz, have said if they saw you behave this way?" he asked.

"They would both be pleased that after all these years of self-sacrifice I was beginning to have a little fun," she answered evenly.

"Fun? I have another name for it," he grumbled.

Brigitte turned off the stove and put the boiled beef, Brussels sprouts, and potatoes on a plate. She had set the table for her father in the dark oaken dining room. An open and chilled bottle of Rhein wine rested on an ornate silver trivet, and his linen napkin was rolled in the initialed ivory napkin ring that he had been given as a child. She brought the plate into the dining room and called out to the kitchen: "Your supper is ready, father. Come and eat before it gets cold."

Professor Halder came in slowly; he suffered from arthritis in his knees and had trouble walking. He sat down, poured himself a glass of wine, and began to eat. Brigitte sat across from him but did not eat.

"Will you be seeing your American every night now?" Professor Halder inquired, suddenly betraying his anxiety.

"Are you worried about my virtue, father," Brigitte replied, "or afraid of being left alone?"

He didn't answer, and as she looked over at him, eating supper with difficulty because of his ill-fitting false teeth, he suddenly struck her as very old and fragile. She got up and went over to him. Putting her hand on his shoulder, she said kindly, "Don't worry, father. I won't desert you."

He looked up at her with tears in his eyes, and she bent down to kiss him on the forehead. "And also," she added, "please believe me. I know what I'm doing."

Reassured that he wouldn't be abandoned, Professor Halder continued to eat his supper while Brigitte took Graf out for a walk in the small neighboring park. As she returned, Cole pulled up in his car.

She quickly let the dog back into the house, grabbed a coat and kerchief, and hurried out. Cole held the car door open for her, and she gracefully slid in, leaning over to give him a kiss.

"Where to, Brünnhilde?" he teased. It was a new nickname he had coined Sunday night after her energetic love-making.

She blushed. "Wherever you say," she answered.

He drove to an old-fashioned, typical Berliner *Kneipe*, off the Kudamm, where they had been once before. It was called *Die Schildkroete*—the Turtle—and had the replica of a large green turtle hanging over its street entrance. The interior, a long, narrow room with a brick floor, was quite dark. A bar on the left was covered by a thatched roof with a mirror behind its display of bottles and glasses. The dozen-odd tables in the back each had a small copper lantern with a bright red shade hanging down low from the ceiling. All around the room ran a high shelf with stuffed turtles and empty beer mugs. The three waitresses, stocky and of indeterminate age, fitted in perfectly with the rest of the décor.

Brigitte and Cole sat down at a table against the back wall. They looked at the menu made up of traditional Berlin dishes. Cole asked Brigitte to choose for him.

"Surprise me," he said.

"I always try to," she answered impishly. She ordered two bowls of curry soup, and as the main dish, *Sauerbraten*—a pickled, spicy pot roast—with red cabbage and potato dumplings.

"We'd better have some beer with all that," Brigitte suggested, and they ordered two small *Berliner Kindls*.

Cole drained his glass and ordered another. He seemed nervous and preoccupied. He was relieved to have Brigitte's company, but was noticeably not his usual carefree, teasing self.

"Tough day?' she asked.

"Yeah," he answered. "We're in the middle of a rough patch."

She reached over to pat his hand; he took hers and held it. She was quiet, content in this guarded physical contact. Unexpectedly, Cole began to talk in a general rambling way. "You know, it's funny," he said, "I'm an officer in the military so I'm used to following orders. I'm trained not to question orders by superiors, and I'm not used to having my own orders questioned. That all works pretty well in strictly military situations, like combat or maneuvers. But here in Berlin I'm dealing with more of a mixed bag."

"What do you mean?" she asked. Only once before had he spoken about his official duties. Tonight, she saw, he obviously needed to talk, to get some concerns off his chest.

"I'm trained to perform a military mission. I'm a pilot. I can handle an airplane—all different kinds of planes, actually—and I know how to fly to the place I've been assigned, to command a crew to get the job done. I'm good at that." He paused, and Brigitte remained silent.

The waitress brought the soup, and Brigitte began to eat. Cole continued to talk. "But I have trouble getting the same sort of fix on the mission I've been given here in Berlin. You know what we do." Brigitte nodded. "It isn't clear-cut; it's complex and convoluted. The objectives are ill-defined. You never know whether you're doing fine or being led around by the nose. It sure isn't like flying a plane from Point A to Point B."

"Why don't you eat your soup, Bud," Brigitte suggested. "It's going to get cold."

He took a few spoonfuls and then continued with his train of thought. "Moreover, I've got to deal with a bunch of civilians, and I can tell you they don't respond to orders in the same way."

"There's a big civilian world out there," Brigitte remarked, "which doesn't automatically obey orders. That's not necessarily a bad thing. We Germans, you may remember, got into a lot of trouble by never questioning orders."

Cole reflected on that remark as the waitress removed the soup bowls and served the *Sauerbraten*. He ordered some more beer for them both; the curry soup had made them thirsty. He didn't think much of the *Sauerbraten;* it was too heavy, but he assured Brigitte that it was delicious. Brigitte had no developed palate, he reflected. A true child of World War II deprivations, she was immensely grateful for any and all food.

"You know," he said, "I have asked a civilian to take on a certain job and, believe it or not, he has refused."

"Why did he do that?"

"He said it was a matter of principle. I've given him a few days to think it over. I'm pretty sure he'll come around. But that's what I mean about civilians not obeying orders. It's a real discipline problem, trying to run a military outfit with people like that."

"I'm not sure I agree with you, Bud," she said gingerly. "I admire that man. The world needs more people like that, who will stand up for their beliefs."

"What if I told you," Cole replied, defensively, "that I think the man is motivated by cowardice, not principle."

"That may be true, but you have to be careful not to besmirch a good man. That's so easy for a person in authority to do."

Cole looked at Brigitte thoughtfully. She did not avert her gaze.

"All right, Brünnhilde," he said, "let's lighten up. Whatever roles we've got to play all day long, right now we can write our own script. And my lines say . . . let's see now . . . oh yes, here they are . . . I greatly enjoy your company."

"You've got a lousy scriptwriter," she answered lightly, relieved to see him relax. "Much too bland."

"How about . . . I love"—he paused—"I love being with you."

"Much better, and so do I," she said seriously.

"We haven't met under the most auspicious circumstances, have we?"

"You mean the ban against fraternizing with enemy civilians?" she asked, smiling.

"To hell with that!"

"But it would have been simpler if we had met back in Minnesota, and I was just the girl next door."

"I suppose so, but fate has decided otherwise." They looked at each other across the table with affection and desire. They decided to skip dessert and just ordered coffee.

"On the other hand," Brigitte suggested teasingly, "perhaps you would not have found me as attractive back there."

"Oh, yes I would," Cole assured her.

"Or maybe I wouldn't have been as impressed if you weren't a colonel and I a poor defeated German civilian."

"Careful, Brünnhilde, you're pushing your luck."

They left the restaurant and drove back in silence to Cole's apartment. They ascended the stairs and once inside hungrily made love. Brigitte's cry was one of fulfillment—with any concern about where this impetuous affair might be leading momentarily set aside.

Day 13 Wednesday

The sun was shining in a clear blue sky, and Jutta walked with a springy step to the U-Bahn. Her blonde hair was combed out, and she had put on her bright red suit with its short skirt that always drew admiring glances. She felt relaxed and confident.

The evening before had gone relatively well, as far as she was concerned. It had been one of Frau Engelhart's days off, so Jutta had prepared her own supper. "I'm no longer cooking for you," she had announced to Pritzer. "We're just two strangers temporarily sharing living quarters. Understood?"

Pritzer had settled in the living room and had poured himself a drink. "Careful, Mutiger," she had taunted. "Don't turn into a lush. I'm not sure the Stasi will want a drunk as an agent. If you don't watch out, you'll become an outcast on both sides of the Iron Curtain."

Pritzer had picked up an ashtray and thrown it at her. Jutta ducked, and the ashtray hit a framed lithograph on the wall, shattering its glass. She decided it would be best not to provoke him further and went upstairs to the guest room, locking the door behind her. She heard Pritzer come upstairs an hour later and go into the bedroom. Within minutes, he'd begun to snore.

She arrived at Amerika Haus ten minutes before opening time. Pearson was in his downstairs office, and Jutta was amused to see the surprised look he gave her. He was also unabashedly staring at her long bare legs. Always aware of his susceptibility, Jutta had kept up Pearson's interest by a studied combination of innocently friendly behavior and a sprinkling of erotic stances and knowing smiles.

"Good morning, Mr. Pearson," she purred.

"Good morning, Jutta," he answered.

"Sorry not to have been here on Monday," she said, coming

into his office. "I had a family problem that I had to deal with."
She leaned on his desk with the palms of her hands and looked
straight into his eyes.

"So I understand," Pearson said uneasily. He had been advised
confidentially by Cole that Jutta was being detained.

Unfazed, Jutta went on, "My uncle from Dresden was in town,
and I had to see him. He has all kinds of trouble. I'll make up that
lost day anytime you like." She gave him one of her ingratiating
smiles and straightened up.

"Thank you, Jutta," he said. "I'll let you know."

Pearson watched her walk back to the checkout desk. He was
puzzled. The last he had heard, she had been locked up as an East
German spy, and here she was back at work, seeming perfectly
normal. He closed the door to the office and called Cole.

"What's the story on Jutta?" he asked.

"There's no proof against her, but we're keeping her under
surveillance," Cole explained.

"Look," Pearson said nervously, "if she's still a suspect, I want
her the hell out of here. I can't afford a scandal. Particularly since
we've had some warning signs."

"Keep your shirt on, Cabot," Cole advised. "CIC is running
this investigation and their instructions are to act naturally and let
things run their course."

"I don't know . . ."

"Don't worry, Cabot," Cole interrupted, "I'll protect your ass
if there's any trouble. Now please let me get back to work."

Pearson fumed. Protect my ass! Not a chance, he said to himself. Cole will be invisible if there's any real trouble. I can hear the
official military spokesman now: "No comment. Sorry. Classified."
Meanwhile, I'll be crucified in Congress and in the press: "Leggy
spy in Amerika Haus." Pearson shuddered at the thought. There
seemed to be no one he could turn to for help, and he concluded
that he would have to figure this one out by himself. He opened
his door and peered out at Jutta, calmly checking books in and
out. Could she really be a spy? he wondered. Perhaps if I had a

long talk with her, I'd get a better idea of the situation. Take her to lunch. No, he decided quickly, that could be misinterpreted, could prove embarrassing if a scandal ever broke. I'll talk with her here. That's the natural thing to do. Just what CIC wants. Act natural, let matters take their course.

"Yes, Mr. Pearson," Jutta said later that afternoon. "You wanted to see me before I left?" She gave him her wide-eyed innocent look.

"Yes, Jutta," Pearson said benignly. "I was wondering if I could be of any help with your family problem."

"How very kind of you, Mr. Pearson," she replied. "I'm not sure what I could ask you to do."

"Why don't you sit down," Pearson suggested, "and tell me about your uncle."

He got up to close his office door and then sat on the small sofa. Jutta settled into a nearby chair and crossed her legs so that her short skirt rode up high on her thighs. It was the oldest trick in the book, but it was still effective, especially with older men. She kept her eyes on his and began to recount a sad chronicle, first about her uncle in Dresden, then concerning her own deprived youth and the misfortunes of other members of her family, always staying within the parameters of the cover story that had been drilled into her. She told her tale so convincingly, with the occasional well-timed sob and tear, that Pearson, moved by the narration and the nearness of her body, went over and put his arm around her shoulders to comfort her. She rose slowly and brushed her cheek against his chest before raising her head up to look at him. She was perfectly positioned for a kiss when alarm bells went off in Pearson's head. He quickly stepped back.

What an idiot I'm being, he said to himself. One minute I want her out of here as a security risk and the next she's practically in my arms. If I'm not careful, I'll soon have a spy in my bed, let alone in Amerika Haus. This woman is dangerous.

Jutta smiled. "Thank you for your kind understanding," she said. "Sorry I got a little teary. I'm very attached to my family."

Which, Pearson reflected, evidently does not include your

husband. "Well, let me know," he said coolly, "if I can be of any help."

As Jutta left the building, she was in no mood to return home. She felt like having an apéritif on the Kudamm. Unconcerned by the fact that she was being followed, she ambled down Tauentzienstrasse toward the Kudamm. It was time, she told herself, for a little relaxation.

She chose one of the front-row tables at Café Kranzler—not far from where Hans and Anna Weber had sat the week before— flirted briefly with a man at an adjoining table, ordered a *Berliner Weisse mit Schuss*, and watched the world go by.

*   *   *

The film taken the day before by the Potsdam Mission of the trucks in Frankfurt/Oder had been flown to Wiesbaden during the night and was being analyzed at USAF Headquarters. Since the car had been able to stop, the pictures were in focus, a distinct change from the normally blurry results of shots taken at high speed while the car was being hotly pursued.

The Air Force analyst who had first speculated that missile launchers were being installed was in the photo lab, impatient to learn whether his supposition might be confirmed.

"It's just a wild guess," he had told his boss the evening before.

"Sometimes the most important intelligence breakthroughs have been the result of hunches," his boss, a major in his fifties, had answered approvingly. The major was an avid reader of spy stories and had been delighted to be assigned to intelligence duties the year before his impending retirement. "Instead of a wild guess, it might be an inspired one. Yes, inspired is the right word if your guess turns out to be true."

The analyst could barely contain his excitement. "When will the prints be ready?" he asked.

"Another forty-five minutes or so, if you let me work in peace,"

came the reply. The lab technician was now viewing enlarged photos of SAM facilities outside Moscow and focusing on the platforms on which they were mounted. The platforms, close to ground
level, were difficult to distinguish with any precision, even when
greatly magnified. In fact, only two corners, jutting out, could be
seen with any clarity. But these corners, when compared to those
of the platforms on the trucks in Frankfurt/Oder, displayed striking similarities.

The lab technician put together three sets of photos and wrote
a covering note setting forth his conclusions. "The Frankfurt/Oder
platforms," he wrote, "are similar to, and possibly the same as,
those supporting the SAMs in Moscow. They are not, however,
part of the weapons system and thus, there is no assurance they
may not also be used for other purposes. We have no information
on other uses to which they can be put, but this alone is not
determinative."

The analyst eagerly put his own comments on the batch of
photos. He pointed out that (a) the excavation near the bridge
resembled preparatory groundwork for missile batteries; (b) the
construction work was being undertaken next to an important
military target; and (c) platforms used in missile sites were identified as being transported to the area. All this, the analyst argued,
makes our (he suppressed the desire to say "my") suspicion increasingly credible.

*   *   *

Bud Cole was staring at a stack of documents flown over earlier
that day by courier plane from Air Force Headquarters in
Wiesbaden. Scrawled across a small memo sheet in large handwriting was the following message from General Norcross: "Bud, I
want more confirmation. Give this top priority."

Cole looked at the set of photographs and read the Potsdam
Mission report with the covering memos from the lab technician
and the analyst. He pushed his chair back in frustration. It all

seemed inconclusive. There were no hard facts beyond the indubitable hole in the ground. And now, suddenly, he was faced with a spate of pictures and reports. Cole was becoming increasingly wary of the entire Frankfurt/Oder investigation. He called in Herter and showed him the photos and documents.

Herter returned to his office for his magnifying glass to get a closer look at the photographs. Cole watched in wry amusement as Herter, in what resembled a Sherlock Holmes pose, examined the pictures with his customary intensity.

After some time, Cole asked, "Well, Herter, what do you make of all that?"

"Very interesting, Colonel. Good stuff."

"The General wants us to redouble our efforts in solving this bridge excavation mystery. What do you think?"

Herter recognized the ambivalence of the question. "I guess we'll have to comply with the General's wishes," he replied blandly.

"Don't avoid my question by telling me to follow orders," Cole said irritably. "I want to have your professional appraisal of this whole matter."

"I told you last week that I thought we might be barking up the wrong tree. But what is it that's worrying you, Colonel?"

"I don't like the looks of it," Cole confided. "I'm beginning to think we're being set up."

"Why do you say that?" Herter looked at Cole intently.

"Let's examine the facts. Two of our agents sent to reconnoiter the excavation near the bridge have probably been caught and their assigned missions extracted from them. The Potsdam Mission car has made a pass at the bridge, and a French agent has presumably been in the area. The Russians . . ."

"Or East Germans," Herter interjected.

"Please stop interrupting. Someone on the other side has put these incidents together and concluded that we must be serious about this target. Fine, they say. If that's what they're hungry for, that's what we'll feed them."

Cole stood and, deep in thought, paced back and forth, duck-

ing each time he turned so as not to hit his head on the low
crossbeam. "OK," he said, stopping next to where Herter was sitting. "If all we had to go on were our missing agents, I wouldn't
feel so uneasy. But damn it, look at these photos. When have we
ever had pictures as clear as these before?"

"It is unusual," Herter agreed.

"The Potsdam Mission report comments that it looked as if
the Russians wanted them to take these shots. Does it make any
sense for the Russkis to allow anything as secret as platforms for
missile installations to be left unguarded in a public parking lot?"

"Not unless the platforms were to be used for some other,
unimportant purpose," Herter commented.

"Or unless it was part of a plan to lead us down the garden
path," Cole said, becoming more satisfied with his own analysis.
"Then there's Muldane's latest Fräulein Kitty report. Have you
had a chance to read it yet?"

"No, Colonel. It just landed on my desk this morning."

"A Russian asked Kitty if anyone had shown an interest in the
Frankfurt/Oder bridge or had told a 'far-fetched' story about missiles being installed there. Now, that's an obvious plant."

"I would say so."

"I say let's ease up on Frankfurt/Oder. Devote less time and
manpower to it. I'm afraid I can't yet tell the General that we're
being diddled, but by God, I think we are."

When Herter had left, Cole looked at his calendar. The reception he would be hosting for all the Allied Intelligence Services
would take place that evening. He saw that it was also time to have
his talk with Liebman. The week's deadline had run out without
Liebman having requested a transfer to covert operations. Cole
picked up the phone and said to the operator: "Tell Liebman I
want to see him right away."

The operator reported back a few minutes later. "Norm
Liebman wants to know if he should leave Pritzer alone at the
Interrogation Center."

"Yes, he can," Cole replied. Liebman's question reminded him that Pritzer's case remained another bit of unfinished business. Oh, for the relatively simple life of an Air Force pilot! He wrestled with more paperwork until Liebman arrived some twenty minutes later.

"Sit down, Liebman," Cole said amiably. "Have you given my suggestion to undertake covert work any further thought?"

"Yes, Colonel, I have," Liebman replied calmly. "A lot of thought. You're right, of course, that I'm already involved, indirectly, in the covert side of our mission."

"Exactly," Cole agreed. "I'm glad you've been able to come to that conclusion." Cole was encouraged.

"All I can tell you, Colonel," Liebman continued, "is that something deep inside me recoils from sending—no, not from sending . . ." Liebman paused, searching for the right word, "from enticing, persuading, coercing a person into harm's way."

"Don't you believe in what we're doing?" Cole asked, disappointed.

"Colonel, I'm a loyal American, a World War II veteran, and received an honorable discharge with commendation. I stayed on in Europe and have been working for the military in one capacity or another ever since. Of course I believe in our mission."

Cole stood and resumed his pacing. He had to drain the emotion out of this discussion. Liebman couldn't be bullied; but he might listen to reason. "How would you define our mission?" Cole asked.

"To stop Communism, like we stopped the Nazis, from taking over Europe."

"Isn't gathering military intelligence an important part of that battle?"

"Yes," Liebman agreed quickly, "and that's what I've been doing every day these last four years, culling information of potential military use from refugees who come over."

"So you're in favor of one type of intelligence-gathering, but not another. Can you explain the logic of that distinction?"

Liebman felt cornered. "Colonel," he said, taking a deep breath,

"I don't have any illusions about the Russians and am convinced we must fight them with all the means at our disposal. And that includes gathering intelligence in any way we can."

"Both overt and covert, right?" Cole asked.

"Of course."

"Well then, what's the problem?"

"The problem, Colonel," Liebman said, "is the way we go about it. No balance is ever struck between the high personal cost involved and the meager results achieved. I ask you, Colonel, how much valuable intelligence have we gleaned from our agents these last six months?"

"We've been able to maintain a continual watch on all the airfields in the GDR. That's nothing to sneeze at," Cole replied.

"The Potsdam Mission can generally accomplish whatever we do a lot more efficiently and at no personal risk. It would be my guess that any assignment the Potsdam Mission couldn't carry out could be handled better by the CIA than by a bunch of military outfits trying to be spooks. There are times, Colonel, when I think that our covert activities are just in place to keep some people employed who have nowhere else to go . . ."

"Calm down, Liebman," Cole said, unperturbedly. "I appreciate a man speaking up and giving me a piece of his mind. Also— and this may surprise you—I agree with much of what you say. What I don't have and badly need is a bunch of savvy intelligence operatives. Sure, there's Herter, and he's great. But most of the rest—I'm talking about the civilians, the permanent staff, not the military who rotate—they're not up to scratch, to say the least. Many have been hanging around since the end of the war. They've gotten lazy and sloppy and are just putting in their time until they can retire. On top of that, I have a Commanding General in Wiesbaden who's screaming at me to develop more intelligence information. So, faced with these problems, what do I do?"

Cole looked at Liebman to see if he was ready for what he hoped would be his clinching argument. Liebman's face was impassive. Answering his own question, Cole explained: "I look around in our outfit and try to place the most capable men in the most demanding jobs. That's why, Liebman, I want you to take on covert work. You're right. We've got a bunch of duffers there now. I'm counting on you to upgrade the quality of our team. What do you say?"

Liebman recognized that he had been elegantly outflanked. "Thank you for the compliment, Colonel," he said. "But I'm afraid I'd be a duffer myself. I've never been a spy. I've had no training in covert work and don't think I'm cut out for it. I'm too soft-hearted to send men on a wild goose chase."

"What do you mean—wild goose chase?"

"Well, for example, that hare-brained idea that the Russians are going to put missiles next to the bridge in Frankfurt/Oder."

"You think that's a phony, do you?"

"I don't know," Liebman replied carefully, "but it sure sounds far-fetched. I couldn't see myself sending someone over to check it out."

"Why the hell not?" Cole demanded with a flash of anger. "It may well be a wild goose chase, but what if it isn't? What if they are in fact planning to install missiles? Can we afford not to try and find out?"

"Colonel, I just don't believe that anything of importance, like a new missile build-up, would ever be discovered by the untrained refugees we manage to recruit. On the whole they're uneducated and not too bright, and the smarter ones regularly turn us down once they've made it safely to West Berlin. Our recruits often have trouble grasping even some rudimentary instructions. Try to teach them the difference between a FRESCO—a Mig-17—and a FISHBED—a Mig-21. Stack these poor agents of ours up against the Russians' well-known mania for secrecy, and what do you think our chances are of coming up with anything of value? My guess would be that whatever our sources turn up is either of so little significance that it isn't concealed or is something the Russians want us to discover."

Cole found these remarks disturbing. They echoed his own

frustration. Liebman was probably right about the bridge, Cole conceded; in all likelihood it was a wild goose chase. But the Potsdam Mission couldn't be everywhere, all the time. Agents, on the other hand, could slip back into their communities and with a network of family and friends might well gain access to information that would be unavailable to a Potsdam Mission car.

"So the answer is no, is it, Liebman?" Cole asked evenly.

"I'm afraid so, Colonel," Liebman replied just as composedly.

The two men stared at each other without hostility. Each was taking the other's measure. Liebman understood that a handler was more important to the 575th than an interrogator, so Cole's attempt to shift him to a more productive position was very much in keeping with good management practice. The question now was whether Cole would be willing to lose him as an interrogator as well if he could not persuade him to transfer to covert work. That would be a poor management decision, but a likely reaction by a military man whose orders were not being obeyed.

Cole suppressed his annoyance and realized with grudging respect that he wouldn't be able to budge Liebman. He was a good interrogator, the best the outfit had. What was the point of losing him?

"All right, Liebman," Cole said with a resigned tone. "Go back to your job. I'm disappointed in you. I think there may be more cowardice than principle in your attitude. But go back to work. As far as I'm concerned, the issue is closed."

As an astonished Liebman left the room, two disparate thoughts flashed through Cole's mind. Muldane would think he had been spineless. Brigitte would be pleased, if she were ever to know.

*　　*　　*

Lieutenant Ossipov was in high spirits as he traversed the central courtyard of the Russian military compound in Karlshorst, the Berlin suburb where the Russian Military Headquarters was located. Ossipov had just learned that he had been awarded an apartment in the officers' billets—with a private bathroom! Two years before, when he had first arrived in Berlin, the use of indoor plumbing on a communal basis was considered a luxury.

It was a warm day, and the first buds of spring brought the promise of some color to relieve the dark and white hues of Berlin's long winter. As he walked toward Colonel Fitin's office, he went over Zeunert's propaganda plan in his mind once again. It was ingenious—so simple, which was why it was ingenious—and also very amusing. Colonel Fitin would be pleased.

Ossipov was to accompany Colonel Fitin to the reception being given by the 575th Air Supply Squadron, which was well known, at least to all secret services, to be the Berlin intelligence bureau of the U.S. Air Force. An official black Zis, with the red flag on its front fender, stood in front of Colonel Fitin's office building. The driver, an enlisted man, was standing at attention next to the right rear door in readiness to open it for the Colonel. The soldier saluted as Ossipov opened the left rear door and let himself into the car's back seat. Then Ossipov waited for twenty minutes; it was *de rigueur* in the Red Army to keep junior officers waiting.

Finally, Colonel Fitin appeared. "Good evening, Comrade Lieutenant," he said, awkwardly settling his bulky frame into the back of the car. He reached forward to make sure that the window separating them from the driver was fully closed.

"I have some news for you on your Frankfurt/Oder inquiry," he imparted with self-importance. Ossipov's ears perked up. "You know, your question as to the excavation near the bridge."

"Yes, Comrade Colonel. What is it?"

Fitin shifted to seek a more comfortable position; the back seat of the Zis was too narrow for the comfort of passengers of Fitin's generous size. "This information was not easy to come by," Fitin confided. "As my grandmother used to say, like trying to wash a bear without getting its fur wet. It originated with our Corps of Engineers working with both East German and Polish subcontractors. Their report was forwarded to our headquarters in Warsaw because, as you remember, the work is being done on

Polish territory. From there the information was sent to Moscow, where it was examined by three interested departments in the Defense Ministry. At last, it was made available to us in Karlshorst."

"What is the purpose of the excavation, Comrade Colonel?" an impatient Ossipov inquired.

Speaking slowly and savoring the disclosure of the mystery, Fitin informed an astonished Ossipov of the purpose of the excavation work in progress next to the Frankfurt/Oder bridge.

They rode on in silence, Fitin settling back with a satisfied smirk and Ossipov contemplating the unexpected information he had received. They soon crossed into the American Sector of West Berlin at Checkpoint Charlie. The American MP waved the car through, saluting smartly. The neglected ruins along the Sector border were soon left behind and the car was quickly engulfed and slowed down in the early-evening West Berlin traffic.

"Comrade Colonel," Ossipov asked. "May I share the information you've just given me with our German Socialist brothers?"

Fitin continued to look at the bustling crowds and the smart store-window displays. "I don't want our brethren to get in the habit of receiving information from us," he said at length. "It must always be the other way around. Their job is to keep us informed."

"The Stasi is planning a very effective propaganda coup to begin as early as tomorrow morning, Comrade Colonel," Ossipov remarked. "This news that you have given me could be quite useful to them."

Fitin groused his approval. "Are the Americans still running around looking for missile sites?" he asked.

"Indeed they are, Comrade Colonel," Ossipov assured him with a broad smile. "We've made the whole Frankfurt/Oder bridge area very accessible. It has become a veritable tourist attraction. All kinds of amateur photographers."

Fitin let out a loud belly laugh and changed his position again. "Fine," he said. "Now let's go and drink some of their liquor. I don't know why they always put out a lot of vodka. That's one of the few things we have enough of ourselves. What I like is their bourbon . . . and their women."

"Yes, Comrade Colonel, they're damn good-looking. Most of them are East Germans, you know, and quite a lot of them are working for us."

Fitin laughed again. "Why can't we have good-looking East German women working for us at our headquarters, instead of the drab, sexless specimens I see around?"

Ossipov stole a glance at Fitin. He had never before seen him so relaxed, almost human. He must remember to get him a bottle of bourbon next May Day.

*   *   *

The principal reception room of Harnack Haus was still called the Bismarck Halle. Periodic suggestions to change the name to the Washington or the Eisenhower Room never bore fruit. Six columns divided the room's large expanse, the front section facing the two large interior entrance doors, the back portion surrounded by tall windows and glass doors with views on a well-kept lawn and gardens. The bar had been set up between two of the central columns; a buffet table was placed against a side wall under a large gilt mirror, which reflected a fountain playing in the garden.

Two dozen fragile gilded chairs were arranged along the walls and between the tall windows. No one ever sat down on them, which was fortunate, since they had undoubtedly been conceived for dainty females rather than hefty Cold Warrior types.

Major Muldane had been there most of the afternoon, checking and double-checking all the arrangements. This was his first time in charge of a formal reception, and Cole had reminded him that if anything went wrong, "Your ass will be in a sling."

Cole walked in ten minutes before five o'clock and inspected the hors d'oeuvres. In addition to the two ever-present American specialities—potato chips and a number of sour cream "dips"—there was a variety of German sausages and cheeses. A little heavy and unimaginative for Durafour, Cole thought, but just the ticket for the Russians.

Muldane checked with one of the bartenders. "Is there enough vodka?" he asked.

"I've got three extra bottles under the table, sir," the bartender replied.

"That should do it," Muldane said. "After all, we've only got two Russkis coming."

The British contingent was the first to arrive—always punctual and usually the first to leave after the standard forty-five minutes of protocol congeniality. Cole greeted his counterpart in RAF Intelligence, Brigadier Malcolm, with a firm handshake, which the impeccably dressed Malcolm returned stiffly, as befitted the continued strained relations between the two "cousin" services. Throughout World War II, there had existed a mixture of suspicion and irritation between the two, with the Americans convinced that the first aim of the British was to preserve the Empire and the British concerned that the Yanks were, in Churchill's phrase, out to "pick up the pieces of the British Empire."

Cole and Malcolm were exchanging banalities about the weather—always the opening British gambit, "beastly time" or "glorious day," whichever came closest to the mark—as the American Commanding Officer, General Swenson, entered the room. With a high forehead and a prominent hawk nose, Swenson was a no-nonsense military type who had been assigned to Berlin as one who would call any Russian bluff, a man whom, it was thought, the Russians would hesitate to try to bluff.

"Evening, Malcolm," Swenson said.

"Good evening, General," Brigadier Malcolm replied.

"What goodies have you prepared for us this evening, Cole?" Swenson asked.

"Come and see for yourself, General," Cole said, leading Swenson to the buffet table.

"Which Russkis are coming tonight?" Swenson inquired.

"As you might expect, it's the Air Force contingent, General.

Colonel Fitin and his assistant." Cole consulted the guest list. " A Lieutenant Ossipov."

"I know Fitin," Swenson remarked. "A slimy bastard." Cole turned around to make sure that no one had overheard Swenson's remark.

"Anything in particular I should be aware of, Cole?" Swenson asked. "Anything special that might come up tonight?"

"Not that I can think of, General."

"Fine. I can only stay about three-quarters of an hour," Swenson informed Cole, helping himself to a number of small canapés being passed around by a respectfully smiling waitress. "I have a dinner in town. What entertainment have you planned?"

"We're going to show a movie."

"That's a novel idea. What kind?"

"A nature film; a Walt Disney nature film."

Swenson chuckled. "That should at least be non-controversial."

"Our very thought, General," Cole concurred.

"Next time I'll stay a little longer if you promise to show a Bugs Bunny cartoon," Swenson said, giving Cole a pat on the shoulder and walking over to the bar.

Colonel Durafour came in like a small terrier, looked around the room and, spotting Cole, went right up to him. "How veree pleasant!" he said, effusive as ever. "It is always a deelight to come to an American party, always so entertaining."

"Good evening, Colonel. A pleasure to have you here," Cole responded. "I'm afraid that you will not find our buffet up to your French standards, but we do the best we can."

"What nonsense!" Durafour replied. "I always enjoy the greatest delicacies at your receptions." They walked toward the bar, and Durafour asked for a glass of champagne. He frowned as he was poured a glass of German sparkling white wine. He tasted it gingerly and decided that, though a bit sweet, it was drinkable.

"What amusement are we to be offered?" he asked Cole.

"We're going to show a movie," Cole said. "Something neutral. We don't want to provoke our Russian friends."

"Oh, really," Durafour remarked with a twinkle. "I thought surely that we would be playing bridge." He emphasized the last word, but Cole looked at him with a blank expression.

"It was my belief, Colonel," Durafour insisted, "that you were working on your bridge game. Do you follow me?"

Cole broke into a wide grin. "Yes, now I do, Colonel," he said. "As you say, I'm working on it, and you've just trumped my ace with that remark." Durafour smiled with satisfaction.

The room was beginning to fill up with representatives of other military intelligence services, the differing dress uniforms of the four occupying powers giving the gathering a colorful and festive aspect. Civilian employees were generally excluded from these affairs, although L. Cabot Pearson, never one to miss a party, usually managed to be present as the USIA representative, in particular because this one was taking place at Harnack Haus, his own stamping ground. Also, a second-ranking CIA official attended to keep an eye on the foreign, as well as the domestic, military competition.

Muldane had been watching for the arrival of the Russians. As soon as he saw them, he went over to advise Cole and together they went to greet them. Colonel Fitin, laden down with six rows of medals, including the Star of Valor and the Hero of the Revolution, and Lieutenant Ossipov with but a single row of ribbons, mainly administrative awards, were standing somewhat woodenly just inside the entrance doors.

"Welcome," Cole said. "Colonel Fitin and Lieutenant Ossipov, if I'm not mistaken." Both Russians came to stiff attention while Cole held out his hand. Fitin took it gingerly and then shook it vigorously.

"This is my Executive Officer, Major Muldane," Cole said, shaking hands with Ossipov. "He is in charge of this evening's entertainment. So if you have any complaints about that, take it up with him." He smiled to show that he did not seriously think there would be any problem.

Ossipov's English was fluent, and with Fitin's grasp of the language rather tentative, Ossipov acted as his translator, at times both interpreting what was being said and conveying Fitin's remarks to others.

"I'm so glad you could come, Colonel," Cole said. "Let me get you both some refreshments and then introduce you to General Swenson."

"I have already once met General Swenson," Fitin said dourly as Cole escorted the Russians over to the bar.

"Bourbon, *spasiba*," Fitin said, indicating he wanted his glass filled to the brim. Ossipov ordered vodka. A comely young waitress carrying a large silver tray of hors d'oeuvres came up to them. Fitin unabashedly ogled her, all the while helping himself liberally to a variety of canapés. Cole and Muldane watched him with amusement. Ossipov contented himself with a single small sausage dipped in mustard. Then Cole walked the Russians over to General Swenson.

After the initial greetings, there was an awkward silence. It was broken by General Swenson. "How long have you been in Berlin, Colonel?" he asked.

"We are in Karlshorst, General," Fitin replied.

"I see. Well, I thought that was part of Berlin. Let me rephrase my question, then. How long have you been in Karlshorst, Colonel?"

"Quite some time, General," Fitin replied guardedly.

"Do you like it?" Swenson asked.

"I enjoy fulfilling my responsibilities wherever I am assigned to do so," Fitin said.

"Of course, Colonel, we all do," Swenson said. He gamely tried again. "I assume that like the rest of us you'd prefer to be at home. Where do you come from?"

Fitin was not sure he had understood the question and turned to Ossipov for clarification. Then he said, "My last assignment was in a different country."

While Fitin slowly drained his glass, Swenson looked over to Cole for help. Muldane offered to get Fitin a refill, an offer that was acknowledged by Ossipov with a grateful nod. Ossipov was under instructions never to leave Fitin's side. (It was prudent for Russian officers always to have a witness to their conversations with Westerners, in particular Western intelligence personnel. Ossipov would be up late that night writing up a summary of Fitin's conversations.)

Cole stepped into the breach. "We have planned some entertainment for you tonight, Colonel," he said, "which we hope you will enjoy."

"Dancing girls?" Fitin asked, letting out a broad guffaw.

"No, I'm afraid not," Cole answered. "We're going to show a movie."

"With dancing girls?" Fitin inquired, laughing again. He could not resist repeating his remark, which he alone found amusing.

"No, Colonel," Cole said. "It's a nature film, which has been very popular in the United States. Audiences have loved it."

"Our Socialist tastes are often very different," Fitin pontificated, looking over to Ossipov to indicate that he should include that remark in his report. "Very different indeed from current Western styles."

"We would hope," Cole said, "that this film can be enjoyed by all peoples, whatever their political systems or beliefs."

Swenson excused himself and went back to the bar for another drink before leaving. Cole introduced his Russian guests to Durafour and Malcolm, both of whom were similarly stymied in attempting some inconsequential small talk. Surprisingly, it was Pearson in blue blazer and yellow foulard—an amusing caricature in Fitin's mind of exploitive capitalism—who was finally able to draw him out.

"I am most impressed by your rows of medals, Colonel," Pearson exclaimed. "I am sure that together they tell quite a story. Would you be good enough to tell that story to me, a poor civilian?"

Flattery was one of Fitin's weak points, alcohol and women the others. Starting with the medal on the left of the first row, he began to recount his military career, his halting and broken English no obstacle to his enthusiastic and loud story-telling. Ossipov stood by nervously as others glanced over at Fitin's performance in some astonishment. Fitin either didn't notice or didn't care.

A little later Cole, shouting to make himself heard above the din, announced that the film was about to start and invited the guests to move into the small theater that adjoined the Bismarck Halle. Fitin had reached the medal for his participation in the battle at Kursk where, he said, Soviet Air Force Intelligence had assured the victory of the Red Army in one of history's largest tank battles. Pearson promised to hear the rest of Fitin's personal saga later and gently steered him to the auditorium.

The nature film showed the variety of life on an acre of desert land in the southwestern United States. The desert colors were dazzling and the closeups of animal life fascinating. While the film was still in progress, Cole leaned over to Muldane, who was sitting nearby, and whispered, "Great choice, Zach."

Back in the Bismarck Halle after the film, Fitin, with a full glass of bourbon as a nightcap, was in an expansive mood. "Good film," he said to Cole, "and so correct politically."

Muldane, who was standing next to him, asked, "What do you mean correct politically, Colonel? It was a nature film. How does that involve politics?"

"Yes," Cole chimed in. "I am also puzzled by your remark, Colonel. We tried hard to find a movie with no political connotations whatsoever."

Fitin, realizing that he had trespassed on the forbidden ground of politics, tried to change the subject. But Muldane persisted.

"Please, Colonel," Muldane requested, "tell us what political message you thought the film conveyed."

With a shrug of his shoulders and making sure that Ossipov was at his side, Fitin explained. "Do you remember," he asked, "the vicious fight between the eagle and the rattlesnake?"

"Of course," Cole answered. "A brilliant piece of photography."

"Well, it seemed to me," Fitin said, "the perfect demonstration in nature of the forces of progress and reaction being locked in a death struggle from which after a bloody fight the forces of progress emerge victorious."

Bloody Communist jargon, Muldane thought. He barely suppressed the remark that the victorious eagle was the symbol of the United States.

Cole nodded and merely said, "I see." What a waste of time, he reflected, to try to find a nonpolitical film. Everything was seen through a political prism by a Communist-indoctrinated mind. It probably would have been simpler to show Fitin some dancing girls.

Day 14 Thursday

The story was splashed over the entire front page of *Neues Deutschland*, the official SED Party organ and the GDR's only large circulation newspaper. In the center was a photograph of Hans and Anna Weber, smiling, with the baby in Anna's arms. The caption read "Saved from the Ruthless Wiles of American Spies." On the left side was a picture of Pritzer—cropped from the snapshot taken on the Wannsee restaurant terrace—entitled "The so-called Herr Steiner, who sent Herr Weber on his wicked mission." And on the right, a picture of the Frankfurt/Oder bridge carried the mocking title "We give this picture, which Weber risked his life to take, to the Americans for the price of a single copy of our newspaper."

A three-column article recounted the story of the Webers: how in a moment of mental stress Hans had been cleverly inveigled to return and spy upon the GDR. The interrogations at the safe house, the cellar route used to cross the dividing line between East and West Berlin—referred to as the GDR frontier—all was written up in detailed prose. The vigilance of the Stasi in safeguarding the achievements of Socialism was heralded. The sincere regrets of the Webers for momentarily straying from the path of Socialist virtue and duty were amply recorded. Their joy was unbounded at being welcomed back into the comradeship of a peaceful democratic society. The article gave discreet, but for the initiated, high praise for the role played by Kommissar Zeunert in this affair.

There was also a first-page editorial entitled "Why Not a Wall?" which called for more energetic measures to stop the invasion of those who would seek to destroy the GDR's Socialist gains. The construction of a wall between East and West Berlin was put forward as a possible means to put an end to these nefarious intrusions.

As he was shaving, Carlton Herter heard a report of the *Neues Deutschland* articles on the 6 a.m. RIAS news broadcast. He dressed quickly and drove downtown to Bahnhof Zoo to get a copy of the paper. *Neues Deutschland* was not available in the chic West Berlin suburbs of Dahlem or Zehlendorf. He was stunned as he looked at the paper's front page and bought all of the kiosk's fourteen copies. He called the night-duty clerk at the 575th Squadron Office from a station pay phone, asking that an all-hands emergency meeting be called for nine o'clock that morning. He then drove to the office and, for once neglecting to write up his Morning Report, began to translate some of the more important sections of the newspaper articles.

"What's up?" Cole asked as he arrived ten minutes before nine.

"This!" Herter said, handing him the newspaper.

Cole took the paper and sat down at the Map Room conference table, on which Herter had laid the other copies of the paper. As Cole stared at the pictures, the remaining papers were picked up as one by one the 575th Squadron members began to assemble.

Cole briskly called the meeting to order at 9:07. There was a deadly silence as Herter summarized the various articles and read out his translation of some of the more telling passages. The civilians, who were all fluent in German, were in the process of reading the paper themselves. There were audible periodic gasps.

"Let me have your attention, please," Cole said, looking around the room. "The first order of business is damage control. Obviously Weber has been caught and has spilled the beans. What contacts has he had with any other agent or handler?"

There was a general shaking of heads. "I've pulled Weber's folder," Herter said, opening a light cardboard blue file with Weber's agent number penciled on the cover. "He first saw Pritzer at Marienfelde. The paper only refers to Pritzer as Steiner, his handler."

"By the way, that's a real flattering picture of you, Pritzer," Muldane commented. Pritzer did not react, and Cole gave Muldane an annoyed look. No one laughed.

"He then saw Liebman," Herter said, "but no need for damage control there. That's not a covert operation. Our Interrogation Center on Clayallee is well-known to everyone, and we don't hide or make any excuses for the fact that we interrogate refugees as they come over."

"On the covert side," Herter went on, "it appears that he met Zandt and Muldane. Neither is referred to in the paper, which of course doesn't mean they haven't been identified."

"Let's move on," Cole remarked. "Our safe house on Meisenstrasse is obviously compromised. Weber and his wife were there for some time, weren't they?"

"Yes, they were, Colonel," Herter replied. "But the villa probably wasn't secure anymore in any event. It is clearly time to rent another one."

"I want it deactivated ASAP," Cole ordered.

"Yes, sir."

"Weber knows our crossover point in Kreuzberg between the two Berlins," Muldane commented. "We've got to stop using it. It's undoubtedly being watched."

"Right you are," Cole agreed. "Let's put that into effect immediately. That's a matter of high priority. Is anyone going over or coming back that way today?"

Two of the civilian handlers said they were expecting agents back in the next twenty-four hours, both of whom would use the Kreuzberg tunnel route. No means were available to give them any warning.

"Poor devils," Liebman muttered under his breath.

"Is any response possible?" Muldane wondered. "Do we have any ammunition to fire back?" No one could think of any.

"We can't deny the story," Cole said soberly, "nor do we have any interest, I would think, in keeping it alive."

"We should ask ourselves," Herter stated, "why the East Germans have done this. Was there a purpose other than to score propaganda points?"

"Which they've clearly done," Muldane said ruefully. "Why isn't that enough of an explanation?"

"Because," Cole remarked, "if there is another motive at work here, we should obviously try to find out what it is. Any thoughts on what it might be?"

Muldane wondered whether the newspaper reports could be an attempt to shift attention away from the Frankfurt/Oder bridge.

"An interesting suggestion," Herter said. "The East Germans would be trying out a new weapon: ridicule. Yes, it's a possibility to keep in mind."

Liebman spoke up next. "We all know," he said, "that the GDR is hurting badly with the increasing outflow of its young and skilled workforce. They must find a way to stem it or the country will go under. The *Neues Deutschland* editorial proposes the building of a wall to keep out spies. Now, a wall may be just the answer to their workforce problem, and this propaganda ploy may furnish some kind of a reason for building one. They can't admit to constructing a wall to keep their people in, so they'll build one and say it's the only way to keep spies out."

"Very perceptive," Herter commented. "I think you may have something there, Liebman."

"That's a fascinating thought, Liebman," Cole said. "I'll pass it on."

Throughout the meeting Pritzer had been in a trance, barely listening to the discussion around him. The newspaper article was on the table in front of him. He stared at his own picture and kept rereading Weber's report of the mission that he had been assigned. Ever so slowly, a plan began to take shape in his mind.

There were no further remarks of consequence. Cole looked at his watch. It was 10:15. "All right gentlemen, that's it," he said. "I've got to call Wiesbaden." He asked Muldane to convene an emergency meeting later in the day of the Berlin Command Intelligence Services Coordinating Group, saying, "I prefer that we call them before they call us."

As Cole returned to his office, the telephone rang. "Mr. Pearson on the line, Colonel," the switchboard announced.

Cole swore under his breath. "Just the man I don't need right now," he muttered. He picked up the receiver. "Yes, Cabot, what is it? I only have a few minutes to talk."

"Have you seen the *Neues Deutschland* front page?" Pearson asked in an agitated voice.

"Of course I have, Cabot. That's why I have very little time to talk. What can I do for you?"

"Bud, I'm being bombarded with questions from the press. I don't know what to say."

Pearson was a hopeless nuisance, a royal pain in the ass, but in replying Cole tried to not let his annoyance show. "Say that you run an information service on America, not the GDR. You have no idea what this is all about, probably just run-of-the-mill Communist propaganda."

"That won't satisfy them," Pearson said.

"It'll just have to, Cabot. Sorry, I've got to hang up now."

"Before you do," Pearson interjected quickly, "what do you think I should do about Jutta Pritzer?"

"What do you mean?"

"Well, her husband's picture is plastered all over the front page."

"So what?" Cole said impatiently. "The husband of one of your employees may be an American spy master. Big deal!"

"But what about . . . you know . . . her?"

Cole finally exploded. "Cabot, I've got work to do. You figure out what the hell to tell the press. That's your goddamn job. It isn't mine."

*   *   *

All morning Kommissar Zeunert had been basking in glory. His superiors in Stasi as well as a number of respectful subordinates, Party comrades, and other government officials had been calling with congratulations on his spy exposé. Two colleagues from down the hall were paying their respects when Zeunert's secretary burst in to announce that the Secretary-General of the SED himself was on the line. The Secretary-General was a feared and reclusive leader;

Zeunert had never spoken to him before. A hush came over the room as Zeunert took the call, standing, and looking out the window with his back to his two co-workers.

"*Guten Tag, Kamerad General Sekretär,*" Zeunert intoned in what he hoped was an appropriately formal voice. "What an honor to receive your call! . . . Yes, yes, that's right . . . So you approved of the press articles? I am very pleased . . . It will serve the higher purposes of the State? I'm very glad you think so . . . Yes, I agree the Americans must be feeling foolish . . . Serves them right, I agree *Kamerad General Sekretär* . . . Thank you very much for your call."

Zeunert turned back toward his awe-struck colleagues with a smile and calmly replaced the receiver as if talking with the *General Sekretär* was nothing particularly out of the ordinary. He sat down behind his desk, took up some papers, and pleasantly commented: "Comrades, there is a mountain of work left to do."

While his two visitors filed out with renewed words of praise and encouragement, Zeunert sat back, savoring the sudden rise in his prestige. A direct call from the *General Sekretär*! He was now a man to be reckoned with. To maintain that standing, he would have to keep this story—and his part in it—alive.

One of the next calls came from Lieutenant Ossipov. "We are pleased with the press articles," he said. "Exactly what we wanted to throw the Allied Intelligence Services off balance. They were becoming too arrogant. This should cut them down to size."

"Thank you, Lieutenant."

"I particularly liked the photo of the bridge," Ossipov went on. "That was a nice touch."

"Did you notice, Lieutenant," Zeunert asked, "that we smudged that picture a bit so as not to give too clear a view of the bridge?"

"Yes, of course we noticed," Ossipov said sharply. The fact that Zeunert had put one over on the Americans should not lead him to think he was also a step ahead of the Russians. Then Ossipov softened his tone and, speaking in low confidential tones, said, "I am now in a position to give you some information on the work being done near the Frankfurt/Oder bridge."

"Yes, what is it?" Zeunert asked eagerly.

"The excavation is for a new customs house and related living quarters."

"What?" Zeunert exclaimed incredulously.

"That is correct," Ossipov said, laughing. "Just a customs house, some living quarters, and a parking lot."

"I don't understand," Zeunert stammered. "What made anyone think that this was going to be a missile site?"

"Some steel platforms being used in the Frankfurt/Oder construction are similar to— no, in fact they are the same as—those used to buttress missile installations. Not as part of the weapons system, of course."

"But why use those platforms?"

"It appears that a steel plant in Rostock had rods and platforms left over from a job they had completed for our military some years ago. The proportions and weight of these materials were not adapted for more general use, and for some time it was impossible for the plant to find someone to take these heavy components off its hands. At last, they managed to persuade a Polish builder, who was acting as a subcontractor for the border post project, to make use of the girders and platforms. Apparently, some money passed under the table to clinch the deal, which may be one reason it has taken some time to get at all the facts."

Zeunert was puzzled. "Lieutenant, what in the devil's name are they going to do with heavy steel rods and platforms in building a guard house?"

"No doubt it will be a very imposing border crossing," Ossipov said and laughed. "But all joking aside, the report states that broad steel underpinnings will be used to shore up the parking lot, which is on a sandy dune, to prevent it from sliding down into the river."

Zeunert burst out laughing, and Ossipov let himself go a bit to join in the merriment. "This is too good to be true," Zeunert said, wiping tears of laughter from his eyes. "A missile site turns out to be a customs house." A sudden thought struck him. Anxiously, Zeunert asked, "Lieutenant, can this information be released to the public?"

Ossipov could see no reason to prohibit such a release. He said he would check and advise Zeunert promptly.

*   *   *

After the morning conference, Liebman and Pritzer walked back together down Clayallee to the Interrogation Center. Neither of them spoke; they were both deep in thought. Liebman was engaging in some soul-searching about his own ambivalent reaction to the East German press stories. Why was he not outraged by the reports? Was this, he wondered, a lack of patriotism?

Pritzer was unabashedly buoyed by the entire episode. For him it represented an upgrade in his status, recognition as a spy master, a member of the postwar Berlin elite. Of course, he might have to lie low for a while until his sudden prominence subsided. His current assignment to overt work could easily be explained as such a cooling-off period. Moreover, he began to calculate that this publicity—as unwelcome as it might appear—could prove to be the solution to his personal problems.

"I remember Weber," Liebman said. "He seemed like a decent enough chap."

"He was all right," Pritzer agreed. "A little too greedy, though. Couldn't stop himself from always going back one more time."

"I'm sure you did your best to hold him back," Liebman said. Pritzer ignored the remark as well as the sarcasm. "Any chance that he might also have been doing it to help our side, or perhaps just for the excitement of it?" Liebman asked.

"You are naive," Pritzer replied. "He kept going back for one thing only: money."

"A lot of good it'll do him now, the poor bastard. What do you think will happen to him?"

"They'll probably send him to a forced-labor camp," Pritzer

declared. "In the GDR if he's lucky; the Gulag if he's not. They don't kid around, you know."

"No," Liebman said somberly, "they don't think of it as a game."

"That's because they have no sense of humor," Pritzer commented. "Everything is so deadly dull over there."

"Why?" Liebman wondered. "Do you think spying is light-hearted fun and games?"

"I suppose so," Pritzer said, looking sideways at the trim, smaller man walking beside him. "I think of it as a sport, like hunting."

Hunting human beings—some sport, Liebman thought to himself. "Speaking of which," he said, "I'd watch out if I were you, Pritzer. Your face is all over the papers; it'll probably be picked up by the West Berlin newspapers this afternoon. Be careful. Someone may try to take a potshot at you."

Pritzer was startled; that thought had not occurred to him. "Nooo, I don't think so," he drawled. "They wouldn't dare. I'm an American, after all."

"You're the one," Liebman reminded him, "who said that they don't kid around."

As they entered the Interrogation Center, Brigitte Halder rushed up to them with a copy of that morning's *Neues Deutschland.* "Thank you, Brigitte," Liebman said. "We've seen it."

"It's just terrible," Brigitte said. "The news is all over Marienfelde, and the people here in the waiting room are all terrified. I keep telling them that no one here would send them back, but they don't believe me."

"I'm not surprised," Liebman remarked. "This is going to be a difficult day," he said to Pritzer as they climbed the narrow stairs to their office.

Liebman's first refugee to be interviewed was all that he had feared.

"I don't know anything that would interest you. There's nothing I can tell you, and I won't go back and be a spy," cried the frantic elderly woman who had been referred to the Center because she lived six kilometers from the Soviet military airfield in Eberswalde.

"No one is going to force you to do anything, Madam," Liebman said, trying to reassure her. "Let's just talk a little about your home town, Eberswalde."

"There is nothing to talk about," she shrieked. "I'm afraid of being here, of talking to you. I don't know anything. Please let me go back to Marienfelde."

And so it went much of the day: uncommunicative and apprehensive refugees. "Well, those articles sure scared the shit out of them," Pritzer said in mid-afternoon. "There's one motive for those press reports we didn't think of—frightening refugees to keep them from giving us any information."

"Whether that was their intent or not, it sure has worked out that way," Liebman agreed. "Let's hope the effect will wear off in a day or two." They each saw a number of additional refugees with the same meager results.

*   *   *

Anna Weber was in a very fragile state. She no longer blamed Weber for their predicament, her overwhelming emotion being one of terror at the thought of their being separated again. She did not trust Zeunert's smiling promises of forgiveness and rehabilitation. The Webers and their baby had been held together in a dank cell at Stasi Headquarters since their picture-taking session and press interview two days before. Except for food on tin trays passed three times a day through a panel in their cell door, there had been no other human contact in the last forty-eight hours.

Weber had whispered that the cell was surely bugged and that they must be careful of what they said. Looking around furtively, Anna had whispered in his ear that she had sewn the Deutsche Marks in the baby's teddy bear. The cache had not been discovered in the two searches to which Anna and the baby had been subjected. This was not entirely welcome news for Weber since currency smuggling was a serious crime in the GDR. On the other hand, that hard-earned cash might in the end prove to be a life-saver.

There was a loud rattling of a key being turned in the iron lock, and the cell door swung open. A guard stood in the corridor and ordered Weber to follow him. Anna protested that she did not want to be left alone. The guard paid no attention to her and brutally swung the door shut after Weber had emerged, eyes blinking, into the sunlit corridor.

Zeunert was waiting for him in his office. "You're a celebrity, Herr Weber," he exclaimed as he handed him a copy of *Neues Deutschland*. Weber looked with astonishment at the front-page picture of his family. He was permitted to sit down to read the press accounts while Zeunert impatiently paced up and down.

"You can take the newspaper with you," Zeunert said abruptly, stopping next to Weber's chair. "There is a little more information that I need from you."

Weber looked up. "I have told you everything I know," he responded.

"Damn it, wait until you hear my question," Zeunert snarled. "You told me you were supposed to look for evidence of missile installations. Is that right?"

"Yes."

"Tell me again why the Americans suspected missile sites."

"Let me see," Weber answered. "They mentioned the shape and contour of the excavation. A hole on the left side of the dig."

"Are you sure they didn't say something about the building materials?"

"I don't think so."

"Think again," Zeunert shouted. "Why the hell would they think we're installing missiles just because we've dug a hole?"

"How do I know why they think what they do?" Weber replied plaintively.

Zeunert went back to his desk and looked at a report. Then,

speaking more softly, he asked, "Did they say anything about steel construction materials?"

"No, I don't remember any talk of steel construction materials."

"Did they mention platforms, steel platforms?"

"No, I don't remember any mention of platforms."

Weber was pig-headed, Zeunert thought, but probably accurate.

"Please, can we go home now?" Weber pleaded. "I have nothing more to tell you, and my wife is getting very nervous. And also, there are some things we need for the baby."

"What?"

"Baby food, diapers, talcum powder, the usual things."

"I'll see that you get what you need," Zeunert assured him. "We may have a few more assignments for you and your wife before we let you go. Always remember how lucky you are and think of the alternative you were facing if we had not decided to be merciful."

Zeunert buzzed for the guard, and Weber was led back to his cell. Zeunert was disappointed not to have obtained Weber's confirmation of the report about steel rods and platforms. He would try to obtain corroboration elsewhere. But whether he succeeded or not, Zeunert had decided in this case to proceed, if necessary, relying solely on what Ossipov had reported. After all, it might prompt another call from the *General Sekretär*.

Weber thought it best not to tell Anna that they would be kept locked up for some additional time. That would only increase her level of anxiety. He also decided that he must find a better hiding place for their Deutsche Marks.

*　　*　　*

The West Berlin press had been quick to pick up the *Neues Deutschland* story. Inquiries at the Allied Kommandatura in Schöneberg and at U.S. Berlin Command at Clayallee were met with a curt "No Comment." As he had informed Cole earlier, Pearson was being flooded with requests for a statement and unlike the military, which could keep the press at bay, Amerika Haus was overrun by reporters clamoring for additional information.

Pearson had asked Jutta to work in a back room and had given strict instructions to his staff not to reveal her identity. To no avail. Whether the motive was money or enmity toward Jutta—in no short supply—or merely a desire for self-promotion, one book-stacker had alerted a reporter to Jutta's presence. From that point on, Pearson was truly besieged.

"We have nothing to do with intelligence-gathering here," he shouted above the din. "We're here only to hand out informa-tion." His words were lost in the general hubbub.

"Let us speak to the spy master's wife," someone yelled.

"She's not here," Pearson lied.

"Where is she?" someone else called out.

"At home."

"Where does she live?"

"I'm not at liberty to disclose that information," Pearson an-swered, mustering his battered dignity.

The book-stacker could be of no further help. Pearson had taken the precaution earlier that morning to lock Jutta's personnel folder in his top desk drawer. When the reporters finally left, Pearson advised Jutta to slip out unobtrusively and stay at home until he called her.

*　　*　　*

Pritzer was in fine fettle on returning home late that afternoon, a stack of the evening's papers under his arm. He greeted Frau Engelhart with a friendly smile and went upstairs to the bedroom to get something. The telephone rang, and Pritzer answered. A wrong number, the caller apologized.

"The phone has been ringing all afternoon," Frau Engelhart said as he came back downstairs. "Always the same excuse, a wrong number." Someone must be trying to keep track of me, Pritzer thought uneasily, ignoring the possibility that the calls might be for Jutta. He decided he would have the number changed.

Pritzer settled in the living room and began to scrutinize the press reports on Weber's various allegations. The West Berlin newspapers played the story with their respective political spins. The right-wing papers expressed satisfaction that any threatening Soviet military build-up was under close scrutiny. The centrist publications suggested that instead of engaging in propaganda grandstanding, the leaders of the GDR should ask themselves why so many of their citizens were eager not only to flee, but to work against their regime's interests. The leftist press, while giving tepid lip service to the need for gathering military intelligence, bemoaned the fact that German refugees were used as pawns in this big-power struggle.

The stories were very similar, in essence reprints of that morning's *Neues Deutschland* article. Pritzer's role as Steiner, as well as the assignments regarding the Frankfurt/Oder bridge that Weber had been given, were reprinted in detail. Yes, Pritzer said to himself, it's all there, nothing has been left out.

Jutta came into the house, slamming the door behind her. She had spent the afternoon aimlessly walking, window-shopping, stopping at cafés, trying to gauge her next move. She was conscious of being shadowed and had no doubt that she would be stopped if she tried once again to flee to the East. She felt she had no choice except to try and act normally and await further instructions. In the meantime much depended on Pritzer's reactions to the news articles. The evening was going to be *delikat*—one of Jutta's favorite words.

"Hello, Mutiger, how does it feel to be front-page news?"

"Where have you been?"

"Shopping," she said lightly, pretending not to have a care in the world. "You should have seen the mob of reporters looking for me at Amerika Haus!"

"I can imagine," Pritzer said, going over to the bar to pour himself a Scotch.

"Fix me a drink, Mutiger," Jutta said, kicking off her shoes and stretching out on the sofa.

"Fix it yourself," he said gruffly, putting some ice cubes in a tall glass and filling it with a liberal amount of Scotch, topped off with a splash of soda water. Jutta looked up in surprise at his change of demeanor.

Frau Engelhart came into the living room. "Dinner is ready," she announced.

"We'll eat in about fifteen minutes," Pritzer said, and Frau Engelhart returned to the kitchen, mumbling that once again her dinner was going to be spoiled if it had to be kept on the stove any longer.

Pritzer sat in an armchair and, ignoring Jutta, began to sip his drink while perusing one of the number of evening papers he had brought home. Jutta gave him a sarcastic smile. She got up, poured herself a glass of Rhein wine, and picked up one of the newspapers lying on the coffee table.

"This picture in the *Abendpost* makes you look more of a man than you really are," she taunted. Pritzer remained silent but confident. This time, he knew, he had the upper hand.

The delay had not spoiled Frau Engelhart's dinner, and Pritzer made a show of enjoying his meal, praising Frau Engelhart's cooking, asking for second helpings, refilling his own wine glass, and eating and drinking with gusto. Jutta eyed him suspiciously.

When dinner was over and Frau Engelhart had departed, Pritzer and Jutta returned to the living room. "Well, my dear," he said unctuously, "it's time we had a little family discussion."

"What are you talking about?" Jutta asked nervously.

"I'd like to hear more about poor Uncle Friedrich."

"Why?"

"Perhaps I can do something to help him," Pritzer said. "He sounds like he's in real trouble."

"What is this nonsense you're talking, Mutiger?" she said uneasily. "I've done all that needs to be done."

"What a good niece you are, Jutta. I've always known that you have a soft heart. By the way, what is Uncle Friedrich's last name?"

Jutta hesitated. "Don't you know?" Pritzer asked in feigned surprise.

"Of course I do," Jutta answered quickly.

"What is it?"

"Zumegen."

"I see. That was your mother's maiden name, was it?"

"Yes.

"So he's your mother's brother."

"Yes. Now please stop all these questions."

"No, dear Jutta," Pritzer declared with a fixed and determined smile. "The interrogation is just beginning." He stood up and walked over to her chair. Jutta looked up at Pritzer towering over her and decided that she had better humor him.

"Now tell me more about Uncle Friedrich. Where does he live?"

"In Dresden."

"Do you have his address?"

"No."

"Don't worry," Pritzer said reassuringly. "That shouldn't be hard to find. There can't be that many Friedrich Zumegens in Dresden, can there?" Pritzer was enjoying himself, while Jutta was becoming anxious.

Pritzer sat down in an easy chair facing Jutta and continued his questioning. "Where does dear Uncle Friedrich work?" he asked.

"He's a clerk at the Social Welfare Office," Jutta said hastily.

"Really?" Pritzer remarked. "That's very interesting, Jutta. At CIC Headquarters, you told me that he had been fired from an assembly-line job. Now, which is it?"

They glared at each other, Jutta with hatred. "What do you want?" she hissed at last.

"Just the truth, my dear. I know that's a difficult concept for you, just the plain, unvarnished truth."

"The truth, you bastard, is what I told you before. I work for the Stasi."

"And Uncle Friedrich?"

"Just a cover for my handler."

"Not a very deep cover, is it? You see how easily it's blown."

"It's worked well enough so far," she said sullenly.

Pritzer walked over to the bar and poured himself another Scotch and soda, fortification for the end-game. "I think, Jutta dear," he said slowly, "that it's time for us to settle our accounts. You were sent over to trap me, and, I must admit, you almost succeeded."

"I have succeeded, Mutiger," she replied venomously.

"And you never cared for me? Never any affection, let alone love?"

Jutta mistook the question as an ultimate attempt to elicit a speck of human compassion. "None whatsoever," she jeered.

Pritzer felt the blood rush to his head but forced himself to remain reasonably calm. "And the love-making?" he asked. "Was that, like a whore, just part of your profession?"

"Like a well-trained spy," Jutta corrected him. She was beginning to recover her composure. Pritzer seemed less threatening. Perhaps the storm had passed. "I was doing the job I had been prepared for."

"What do you think is going to happen now?" Pritzer asked.

"I don't know. I have to wait for my orders."

"From Uncle Friedrich?

"That's right, dear old Uncle Friedrich," she said. "As far as I'm concerned, we'll continue our lives here. After all, it could be worse. A comfortable house, a cook, enough spending money— what more could a beautiful spy want? And who knows, if you're a good boy, I may even tie you up again once in a while." She smiled at Pritzer, who stood and walked over to the telephone.

"Well, Jutta," he said steadily, "for once you've overplayed your hand." He picked up the phone, dialed a number, and said, "This is Pritzer of the 575th Air Supply Squadron. Send a car over to my house immediately with two MPs. I have an East German spy here for you to arrest."

Jutta was stunned. "You're bluffing," she stammered. "You wouldn't dare turn me in." She tried to get up, but Pritzer pushed her back down roughly. He pulled the Beretta out of the pocket of his jacket and pointed it at her. "Don't move out of that chair," he snarled, "until the MPs get here."

"Have you gone crazy, Mutiger?" she shrieked. "Have you forgotten that I can ruin you? And you know I will."

"There is nothing you can say now, Jutta, that can do me the least bit of harm."

"What are you talking about? I know about Weber, and your cover name Steiner and that you sent him to take pictures of the bridge . . ." She stopped suddenly as her eyes fell on the newspapers spread out on the coffee table.

"Yes, Jutta, you know all that . . . and so does the rest of Berlin," Pritzer declared. "Everything that you wormed out of me can be purchased for a few pfennige at every newspaper kiosk."

"I'll tell them that I learned it all many days ago," Jutta said frantically. "You revealed classified information to me. You can go to jail for that."

"That may be true," Pritzer said unperturbed. "But who is going to believe you? No, Jutta, you've got nothing on me. I have reviewed the press reports carefully, and they contain absolutely everything I've ever told you. You'd better get ready to spend a few of your youthful years in jail."

She looked at the Beretta and tried to gauge whether Pritzer was bluffing. She leaned forward as if to get up, and Pritzer, his hand steady, pointed the pistol right between her eyes. She decided not to take the chance and leaned back again. Even if he didn't shoot, she figured, the thought of wrestling with Pritzer holding a loaded pistol was not a welcome prospect.

"This time, *Liebchen,*" Pritzer said, "you are the one who has been trapped." She spat at him. He took out a handkerchief and wiped the spittle from his face.

"A wildcat to the end, eh?" he remarked. "Well, a jail cell should calm you down. Like in a zoo, except I won't come to watch you being fed." It was his turn to laugh.

All at once, Jutta softened her tone. "Let me go, please, Mutiger," she pleaded. "I'll get out of your life, and you'll never see or hear from me again. Please, I can't bear going to jail. I need my freedom."

"You should have thought of that a little earlier."

Jutta tried to clutch Pritzer's arm, but he moved back, still holding her in the Beretta's sights. She managed to squeeze out some tears to underscore her entreaties. "I was forced to be a spy," she moaned. "They threatened to harm my parents if I didn't co-operate. Like Weber, I was caught. I just had to do it."

"I don't believe a word of it," Pritzer said.

"But it's the truth; all the rest was just bravado I was taught to use on you. To keep you under my thumb. Oh, please let me go. I'll never hurt you again."

"That's right, Jutta, you never will."

The doorbell rang. Pritzer pulled Jutta up out of her chair, and twisting her arm behind her, led her screaming to the front door. He turned her over to two burly MPs, who quickly handcuffed her and pushed her, still yelling, into the back of their patrol car. Before the car pulled away, Pritzer asked the MPs to notify Captain Loring of Jutta's arrest. "Tell him that I'll speak to him in the morning."

*　　*　　*

Schumpeter, Jutta's East German handler, had tried all afternoon without success to contact Jutta. His call to Amerika Haus had been one of hundreds trying to reach her, and he had received the standard answer that she was unavailable. He had tried her at home, but repeatedly it was Frau Engelhart who answered. The last time, at quarter to five, Schumpeter had hung up the phone when Pritzer himself had taken the call.

Schumpeter had been ordered to inquire whether Pritzer had been aware that steel platforms were being used at the Frankfurt/

Oder construction site. The deadline for obtaining that information was five in the afternoon. Schumpeter called Zeunert at five minutes after five to report that he had been unable to carry out his mission.

Day 15 Friday

Carlton Herter awoke to a radio report of another *Neues Deutschland* front-page story of American espionage skullduggery. He again rushed to the Bahnhof Zoo and bought all the newsstand's copies. The man running the kiosk, with typical deadpan Berlin humor, asked whether he should double his daily allotment of the paper.

The articles this time had more of a human-interest slant. The left-hand column, entitled "The Destruction of a Young GDR Family," was illustrated by a photograph of Anna and the baby, holding his teddy bear. The Webers' tragic descent to their present predicament, all due to the pitiless machinations of a warmongering capitalist society, was recounted with wrenching sentimentality. In contrast, their future redemption was heralded as justice tempered by the mercy of a compassionate Socialist society.

In the middle of the front page was a picture of what looked like a metal scaffold. An explanatory article, under the heading "And All for Nothing," trumpeted that this piece of metal was what Weber had been sent to photograph. With heavy irony, the report stated that "misguided American Intelligence (?) Services" had come to the conclusion that steel platforms of this type would be used to support missile batteries. To avoid putting additional lives at risk and with the consent of its Red Army comrades, the newspaper declared that it was publishing a photograph of the platforms for the use of American Intelligence.

It was also pleased to inform the Americans that no missile sites were presently in the process of being installed at the Frankfurt/Oder location. Instead, a customs house was being built on the Polish side of the Oder. The steel platforms would be used to solidify its foundations. The article closed with a mocking admonition to Allied spy services not to count on the paper as a continuing fount of information. "If ever Russian missiles are deemed necessary to defend the People's Republic," it stated, "their formidable strike force will be the first inkling that you will have of their prior installation."

An editorial, this time in its customary second-page slot, once again called for the building of a wall or other protective shield against the influx of spies and saboteurs.

"It is a clever follow-up," Muldane conceded at a second all-hands morning meeting of the 575th Air Supply Squadron in as many days.

"If their purpose is to make us look foolish," Cole admitted grudgingly, "I'd give them an A for both effort and results."

"I don't remember asking Weber about any platforms," Herter said. "Do you, Pritzer?"

"No," Pritzer replied. "I don't."

"When did we first hear about platforms?" Cole asked quickly.

"I'll have to check the files," Herter said, "but to the best of my recollection our first indication was an IAIC from the French."

"And," Muldane added, "there was also that picture of platforms taken in the parking lot of the Bierstube near the bridge. The Potsdam Mission warned us that it had been too easy a shot."

Cole sighed. "Gentlemen," he said, "it's obvious that we—and the French—were set up, and we fell for it. All right," he continued, drawing a deep breath, "let's review our damage control. We've lost one agent . . ."

"And his family," Liebman whispered.

"Another agent sent to look at the bridge is missing . . ."

"But not referred to in the press reports," Muldane commented.

"One handler identified and one target turns out probably to be inoffensive. Not much of a strategic or even tactical setback, I would say," Cole concluded. He looked around the room for reactions to his analysis. No one spoke, but Cole saw many nodding heads and encouraging smiles.

Then Liebman gathered up his courage. "You're right, of course,

Colonel, looking at it from a purely military standpoint," he said. "But from a civilian, or if you prefer from a diplomatic point of view, we've suffered a strategic defeat. At a time when we and our Allies are trying to convince the West Germans to participate in a European Defense Force, there's a lot of sensitivity among Germans about being used as cannon fodder. Therefore, when we're shown to be exposing young people, looking for a decent life, to grave danger by sending them on a laughable errand, the repercussions are going to be severe."

"Goddamn it, Liebman," Muldane exploded. "We're not diplomats nor is this a civilian outfit, even if we're forced to have civilian employees."

"Let's stay calm," Cole said quickly. "We're not going to reach any sensible conclusions if we start shouting at each other. Liebman's right, of course, that we're going to take some heat from the politicians, and Muldane is right that we're a military outfit carrying out orders. I'm afraid we're going to have to let the diplomatic chips fall where they may." He paused, then asked, "Well, gentlemen, what do we do now?"

"Let's call off our observation of the Frankfurt/Oder bridge," Herter suggested.

"OK in principle," Cole retorted, "but remember that for the moment it's still on Wiesbaden's priority list. Let's move it down to priority number 4," Cole decided. "That will give us a chance to look at it every few months." He smiled. "Some day I want to see a picture of that customs house."

Herter was assigned the task of preparing a report to Headquarters in Wiesbaden, including translations of the news articles and suggestions to questions that were likely to arise. As the meeting was about to break up, Pritzer asked to be heard.

"I have another bit of news to announce," he said, somberly. "As some of you know, my wife Jutta has been under suspicion of being an East German agent. Up until last night, I was absolutely convinced that these speculations were groundless. But last night, I discovered that they were true."

There was a gasp around the table; all eyes were focused on Pritzer.

"What did you do?" Cole asked tersely.

"I called CIC immediately," Pritzer replied, "and two MPs came by late in the evening to arrest her. I have an appointment this morning with Captain Loring. I'll give him the details. I just wanted you all to know." He took the many expressions of regret and support in a long-suffering manner.

*   *   *

Jutta had spent the night in a basement CIC cell preparing her story. It seemed senseless to maintain her denial of spying now that Pritzer had turned her in. She had been trained that if caught, with denial no longer possible, she was to do as much harm as possible to the enemy. In this case, she reasoned, that would mean to implicate Pritzer as a spy. All night she had tried to think of some bit of classified information he had revealed to her that had not been reported in the press, but in the end she decided that for once all she had was the truth. Laughable, wasn't it? she realized. With all the false cover stories she had been obliged to memorize, she was ending up with the truth as her best weapon.

Early Friday morning she was led by a matron up to Captain Loring's office. "So we meet once more, Frau Pritzer," Loring said. He had not been surprised to have her in custody again, although the dénouement had occurred more rapidly than he had expected.

"Good morning, Captain," Jutta replied. She was no longer playing the role of a frightened, wronged housewife. Instead, she was composed, as befitted a disciplined East German agent confronting a fellow espionage professional.

"I understand that your husband turned you in. I wonder what made him do that. Just last Tuesday, when he brought you home from jail, he was swearing that you were as innocent as the driven snow."

"He is just trying to save his own skin," Jutta explained.

"Now that's an interesting remark," Loring said, swiveling in his chair to look more directly at Jutta, who was sitting at the side of his desk. "Tell me more about that."

"I can't prove what I say, but it's the truth."

"That's a meaningless statement, Frau Pritzer," Loring remarked. "If you were telling me a lie, you would say the same thing. But go ahead, I'm listening."

In flat, unemotional terms Jutta recounted her mission to seduce and marry Pritzer and then to worm secrets out of him. She described how she had used their sex games to get some initial information, which she had used to blackmail him into keeping quiet about her activities. Her next step would have been to force him to hand over copies of classified documents, but she admitted that she had not gotten that far. The *Neues Deutschland* articles had made public practically everything she had found out. With all the information Pritzer had given her now made public, he felt that he had nothing more to fear. The only thing he lacked, she said, was an excuse for having her arrested. He got that last night by questioning her about her fictitious Uncle Friedrich.

"I'm afraid," she concluded with a smile, "that my cover story was not well enough defined. He caught me in a contradiction and called the police. That's about it."

"You say that 'practically everything' your husband told you has been made public. Is there anything that he said," Loring asked, "anything classified, of course, that has not been published?"

"I don't know if it's classified," Jutta responded. "He told me that he only interviewed people from Frankfurt/Oder and that he sent the agent over to the East without a gun."

Loring sat back and looked at Jutta, calmly sitting near him and perfectly at ease. Her story sounded plausible, yet her revelations—entirely uncorroborated—were too flimsy to sustain a charge against Pritzer. Rather, her accusations appeared to be the last vindictive gesture of a captured spy. "Thank you, Frau Pritzer," he said, buzzing for the guard to return her to her cell. "This has been most informative."

Pritzer arrived at Loring's office an hour later. He had prepared himself to act the part of a saddened man, doubly betrayed—both as a husband and an intelligence professional. Loring heard him out.

"I must admit, Captain," Pritzer confided, "that I've had my suspicions ever since her arrest. It's a professional handicap of ours, isn't it, to always suspect everyone? Well, that story about her Uncle Friedrich just didn't ring true. This gnawed at me and last night I started to ask Jutta some questions about her Uncle Friedrich. Her story soon fell apart." Pritzer shrugged his shoulders. "I was flabbergasted," he said, "but in retrospect I suppose I shouldn't have been surprised. I called the CIC and two MPs came to get her."

Pritzer stopped his recital and looked up. Loring's face was noncommittal; he remained quiet and waited for Pritzer to continue.

"It has been a difficult night for me," Pritzer said, fishing for sympathy. "Imagine me being taken in like that. I suppose it just shows there's no fool like an old fool. Well, I can tell you this is an old fool who's certainly learned his lesson." Pritzer gave Loring what he thought was an ingratiating smile. Loring did not respond.

Here, Loring recognized, was the other side of the story. It was just as plausible as hers, but a little too pat. For the moment he leaned toward Jutta's account, but that would be difficult to prove. It would be the word of an American intelligence officer against the accusation of an admitted East German spy. A tough nut to crack.

"I should tell you, Mr. Pritzer," Loring said quietly, "that your wife has told us a very different story."

"What do you mean?" Pritzer asked anxiously. "What did she say?"

"She claims that you shared classified information with her and that she was using that lapse on your part to blackmail you into covering up for her." Loring looked at Pritzer closely and noted his evident disarray.

"That's absurd," Pritzer cried out, getting up and then sitting down again.

"She went on to say that she was about to force you into some active espionage . . ."

"That's crazy, Captain," Pritzer interrupted loudly. His face was flushed. "You must see that she's lying."

" . . . but she does admit that she never got that far. All she was able to do, she says, was to stop you from denouncing her as a spy."

Pritzer tried to calm down. There was no point in shouting at Loring. That was bound to create the wrong impression. He had to collect his thoughts. Loring asked if he wanted a cigarette. Pritzer refused, saying he didn't smoke, which was a gratuitous lie.

In a shaky voice, he asked Loring: "You can't believe any of that nonsense, can you, Captain? She's just trying to ruin me because I turned her in."

"That's quite likely," Loring conceded.

"Likely?" Pritzer responded, raising his voice again. "It's the truth!"

Loring took a cigarette, crumpled the pack, and threw it into the wastebasket. He lit up, inhaled deeply, and waited for Pritzer to continue.

"What classified information does she say I gave her?" Pritzer asked.

"Basically what's been published in *Neues Deutschland.* According to her, that's why you felt you could turn her in; she no longer had anything on you."

Pritzer managed a mirthless laugh. "That's too easy, isn't it? What a bunch of bullshit!"

"Yes, I agree," Loring replied, paused, and then said meaningfully, "except for one thing."

A tremor shot through Pritzer. "What thing?" he asked anxiously.

"She does seem to have two minor bits of information that were not reported in the press and which, it seems to me, may well be classified."

"What are they?" Pritzer asked with mounting anxiety.

"I'm sorry, Mr. Pritzer," Loring said smoothly, "I'm going to have to keep that to myself for the moment. If the information turns out to be classified, I'll have to see how she might have gotten wind of it—other than from you, of course."

Pritzer became frantic. "Captain, you must believe me," he pleaded. "I never revealed any classified information to her. Maybe her handler gave her some information to use against me. Yes, that must be it. It's all a plot to ruin me." Exhausted, Pritzer leaned forward and buried his face in his hands.

Loring realized that Pritzer was at the end of his rope and for the moment would say nothing more. He came out from behind his desk and, putting his hand on Pritzer's shoulder, said in a kindly tone, "Calm down, Mr. Pritzer. There's no reason to get all excited. If you haven't revealed any secrets, there's nothing for you to worry about. Your wife is a confessed spy and will be dealt with harshly, especially if she is found to be trying to malign an innocent person. But as an intelligence professional, you must understand that I'm obliged to follow up any such accusation, even if, as you say, it is absurd. Thank you for coming in. We'll be in touch."

Pritzer stood, shook Loring's outstretched hand, and walked unsteadily toward the door. Loring watched him leave, scratched his head, and asked his secretary to call Colonel Cole.

"Yes," Cole said when the call had been put through, "I know. Pritzer told us all this morning that he'd turned his wife in. Damn fool ever to have gotten involved with her. It just confirms what I've always thought about him. A lack of judgment."

"It may be more serious than that, Colonel."

"What do you mean?"

"His wife says that she was blackmailing him because she knew about Weber's mission. When it came out in the press, he turned her in. I told him that his wife was aware of some classified information not reported in the press. That was partly, but not entirely, a bluff. He got very excited."

"So would I," Cole replied. "Wouldn't you?"

"I suppose so," Loring admitted.

"What do we do now?" Cole asked.

"I'd put a warning flag in his personnel file to keep him away from any really sensitive stuff."

"That'll be the end of him in this business," Cole remarked.

"You asked for my opinion, Colonel."

"Are you going to pursue the investigation any further?"

"No, I don't think so. I happen to think the wife is giving us the straight scoop, but her word would never stand up against his in court. No matter how much he perspired on the witness stand. And the unpublished information she says he gave her is fairly innocuous and probably not even classified. Anyway," Loring said, signing off, "I've got too much on my plate to worry about some guy's indiscreet pillow talk."

*   *   *

Liebman had always known it would come to this. The picture of the Webers and their baby had been the coup de grâce; it had kept him awake all night. Here was a fact that could not be denied. He had sent Weber to the safe house, the first step on his road to perdition. There was no pretending that he did not know what awaited Weber there. Oh yes, for Weber there had remained an element of free choice. Quite true, a large number of refugees re-fused to return to the East despite the blandishments offered. But if Weber had avoided entrapment, would that, he asked himself, have been any of his doing?

Liebman sat in his office at the Interrogation Center with his pen in hand, staring at a blank sheet of paper. He had asked Brigitte to hold up any referrals to his room while he tried to gather his thoughts. Could anyone, he asked himself, who had lived through the Nazi era dispute the necessity to fight against an evil tyranny? The answer was an unequivocal no. Well then, was someone else supposed to fight these battles, someone else to get their hands dirty? Was it ever dirty to fight tyranny?

Liebman sighed and squirmed in his seat. Rather than liberating, he always found dialectics paralyzing. His difficulty was that he understood abstract concepts such as democracy or freedom best when they were reduced to concrete individual terms. Thus, he had trouble reconciling the struggle for the ideal of freedom with the Webers sitting in an East German jail. Not only sitting there, but having been placed there by his agency. What had Cole called him? A Judas goat.

There was but one thing to do, and having come to that decision, he was anxious to put it in writing. There was so much he wanted to say and so little he dared to put down in a document that would be placed in his permanent personnel file. Therefore, he thought, the shorter and blander, the better. He wrote:

Dear Colonel Cole,

I hereby tender my resignation. To date, I have fulfilled my duties to the best of my ability and trust that you consider that I have carried them out conscientiously and with some measure of success. I am resigning because I feel that I would be better suited for work that is somewhat less operational in nature.

I would appreciate your letting me know when my resignation should take effect. I will of course be at your disposal to acquaint my replacement with the details of my job.

Sincerely yours,
Norman Liebman

Liebman reread the letter only once and then quickly folded it and placed it in an envelope. He would deliver it by hand immediately before his more reserved and nervous nature forced a change of mind. He told Brigitte that he would be gone for the rest of the day and walked with a determined step up Clayallee to the 575th Squadron office. Stopping by the reception desk, he borrowed a pen and wrote "For Colonel Cole's Eyes Only" on the envelope before handing it to the sergeant on duty.

Slightly light-headed, he went home and put on a record of

the Bruch Violin Concerto. The familiar strains were profoundly reassuring. He knew he had done the right thing, even though his future was suddenly completely unsettled. So what? That had occurred a number of times in his life. The important point was that his conscience was at rest. He was at last at peace with himself.

*　　*　　*

The Webers were brought back to Zeunert's office in the late afternoon. "Here they are, my media stars!" Zeunert said mockingly, throwing his arms out wide. "The most famous couple in the GDR! But it is not only here—you can't imagine how many people have been looking at your picture all over the world." With a broad smile he added, "Especially in Washington."

Anna, holding the baby, looked fearful. Eyes cast down, she stood very close to Weber who had his arm around her shoulder. Zeunert motioned them to sit down in the two straight-backed chairs facing his metal desk.

"Have you seen this morning's newspaper?" he inquired cheerfully. "I asked that it be brought down to you."

"Thank you, Herr Kommissar, we have," Weber replied softly.

"Well, what do you think? How does it feel to be celebrities?"

Weber looked at Anna anxiously and then, addressing Zeunert, pleaded, "Please, Herr Kommissar, let us go home. We have done what you asked; now let us go home and take up our lives again. We've learned our lesson. We're just simple folk. We don't want to be celebrities."

"Nonsense," Zeunert responded, still with good humor, "you're too modest. You have become a symbol of the young GDR couple—momentarily betrayed by vicious Western propaganda but now returned to the Socialist fold. We need symbols like you to assure the triumph of Socialism. You want to see Socialism triumph, don't you?" The question distinctly contained a threat.

Weber nodded and mumbled, "Of course."

"And you, Frau Weber?"

"Yes," Anna whispered.

Zeunert looked at the Webers huddled before him and abruptly changed his tone. "Herr und Frau Weber," he barked. "Let me emphasize what I have told you both before. You don't seem to realize the good fortune that has befallen you. You both left the GDR without permission—*Republiksflucht*—that in itself is a crime. Then you, Herr Weber, returned as an enemy spy. The most lenient sentence we have handed out for that offense—and that after the man truly repented and supplied us with valuable information—was ten years at hard labor."

Anna let out a loud sob. "That's right, Frau Weber, ten long years. And that, I repeat, has been the most lenient punishment. And here you both sit and ask to be allowed to return home." Tears of fright and hopelessness ran down Anna's cheeks.

Zeunert stood up and with measured steps walked around his desk. He positioned himself very close to the Webers and, leaning back against his desk for support, delivered a solemn lecture. "Listen to me carefully; your lives will depend on it," he said dramatically. "You are lucky that we have decided to use your experiences for propaganda purposes. The tactic has been a notable success. We intend to exploit this story to the fullest extent possible, and we will need your help in doing that. But we must have your enthusiastic assistance, not those tear-filled eyes and that sorry hangdog look."

"What do you want us to do?" Weber asked with resigned wariness.

"You will both be traveling around the country telling your story about the pitfalls awaiting those who would be foolish enough to be tempted to venture into the West. During the day, you, Herr Weber, will visit offices and factory worksites, while you, Frau Weber, will speak at schools and local women's groups. In the evenings, you will both appear at Party functions and study groups." The Webers listened as if in a trance.

"Your message will always be the same. You will explain that the streets over there are not paved in gold. Your task will be to help unmask the lies of Western propaganda by showing the difference between the corrupt, decadent West and our healthy, moral Socialist ideals. You will repeat how happy you are to be back in your Socialist homeland. You will express tearful gratitude for the understanding shown by the GDR officials in allowing you the freedom to let others learn from your errors, instead of clapping you in jail where you belong."

These last words, spoken harshly, startled the baby, who began to cry. Anna hushed him and began to rock him gently in her arms. Weber asked how long this speaking tour would last.

Zeunert walked over toward the window and, looking out on the street wet with drizzling rain, replied with his back turned, "I don't know. Until you've lost your effectiveness."

"Then," Weber asked, "can I go back to my teaching job?"

"I suppose so," Zeunert said, turning around again to face the Webers. "But it is hard, you know, to predict the future. What I can tell you is that you will both be very busy for the next few months." After that, Zeunert said to himself with grim satisfaction, you traitors will get the full punishment you deserve.

Totally cowed, the Webers sat in their chairs, staring dumbly at Zeunert and waiting for his next orders. Zeunert took pleasure in their docility and decided on a magnanimous gesture. "Cheer up," he told them. "I have some good news for you." They looked at him expectantly. He paused to heighten the suspense, then said, "You can go back home for the weekend."

Anna's face brightened, and Weber hastened to express his thanks to the Herr Kommissar. Zeunert told them that a car would pick them up at their apartment at 7:30 Monday morning. "Don't keep the driver waiting," he said. "And remember, we want a happy, smiling couple."

As the Webers stood up to leave, Zeunert's parting words were, "I need not tell you that a second attempt to leave the GDR would be treated with extreme severity."

*   *   *

Cole, Muldane, and Herter were in the Map Room in the midst of their weekly review of the 575th Squadron's target list. Next they turned their attention to the list of active agents. Two new agents were added to the list that day, with Weber being stricken from the roster. One agent, who had been recruited two years ago and who had suffered a severe heart attack, was also removed. Cole agreed to have a bonus deposited in the man's West German personal bank account into which a monthly stipend was paid.

As he headed back to his own office, Herter informed Cole that he had sent a translation of the day's *Neues Deutschland* article with comments to Wiesbaden that morning.

"Thanks," Cole said. "I hope that'll be the end of it."

"I wouldn't be so sure," Herter answered. "The GDR is going to keep riding that horse until it drops dead."

"Goddamned clever maneuver, I've got to admit," Cole said.

"Yes," Muldane chimed in, "with the wife in that Madonna and Child pose. Effective as hell. Why don't we ever do anything similar? There must be some East German spy we've caught."

"What the hell can we do, Zach?" Cole asked impatiently. "Everyone knows that the Russians and the East Germans send over spies. They never pretend that they're good guys, like we do. That makes an American spy story so much better."

"Particularly when the story is broken by the bad guys."

"Exactly."

An orderly came into the Map Room with word that General Norcross was on the line from Wiesbaden. Cole went back to his office, closed the door behind him and, wearily sinking into his chair, picked up the receiver. "Yes, General," he said.

"Have you seen today's article, Bud?" the General asked.

"Yes, sir," Cole replied. "A translation and comments are on their way to you. You should have them shortly."

"Good. I've just been briefed on some of the highlights. Bud, you know, this is turning mighty serious."

"In what way, General?" Cole asked blandly, keeping his irritation in check.

"I had a call earlier today from the head of Air Force Intelligence at the Pentagon. He's all worked up about this East German propaganda campaign."

"I trust, General, that you were able to put this incident into perspective."

"No, goddamn it, Bud," Norcross replied angrily, "he's the one who put it in perspective. It seems that the story is hurting our image abroad. The USIA has been on his back. Then, some fuckin' Congressman has called saying this will give the CIA a leg up on trying to monopolize all intelligence activities."

Cole was at a loss on how to calm the General down. "I'm afraid, sir," he ventured, "that a flap like this just goes with the territory."

"That's not how the Pentagon sees it. They're royally pissed off. I've been warned, Bud. No repeat performances."

Now Cole was beginning to get hot under the collar. "What the hell do they want us to do, General?" he asked. "Stop sending agents over?"

"No, of course not," the General replied heatedly. "They just don't want them sent on any more harebrained treasure hunts that make us look ridiculous."

Cole was itching to remind the General that it was his office that had made the Frankfurt/Oder bridge a Number One Priority, but he held his tongue. Instead he asked, "How are we supposed to determine in advance, General, whether a target is worth a reconnaissance mission? If you want us to just cover airfields, we'll do that, but I must tell you that's a helluva dumb way to run an intelligence operation. Ignoring leads because they might turn out not to hit the jackpot."

"Now calm down, Colonel," the General replied frostily. "I didn't call to argue with you, but to pass on a warning. The Pentagon doesn't want any more screwups, and neither do I. Just cool, professional intelligence work. Understood?"

Cole understood only too well. In an attempt to cover his own backside, the General was trying to shift the blame onto him. Cole did not take kindly to that type of buck-passing.

"General," he said, his voice steady, "I don't feel there's been any screwup here. I don't see what I would do differently in the future. If you're not satisfied with my performance, may I suggest you send someone else to take over this outfit. I'd be very pleased to go back to flying. And by the way, we've been monitoring the targets according to priorities, many of which have been established by Headquarters in Wiesbaden."

The threat was clear to the General. His people had ordered the surveillance of the bridge; they had made it a priority target. The responsibility for the treasure hunt was his, not Cole's. Consequently, this was not the time, the General thought, to replace Cole. Such a move now would only backfire. He'd settle Cole's hash later for threatening a superior officer. The important point now was to keep the Pentagon in the dark on the origin of this fiasco.

Adopting a calmer tone, the General said, "Look, Bud, let's not get carried away. I know what a fine officer you are. I'm just trying to say that we're both under the gun now and have to be careful to keep our noses clean."

Cole also responded with less heat. "While we're on the subject, General," he said, "one of my civilian employees—an agent handler—has just turned in his wife as an East German spy."

"What?"

"That's right. On top of that, he's the handler identified as Herr Steiner in the *Neues Deutschland* articles."

"I don't believe it," the General said.

"There's more, I'm afraid. His wife accuses him of having passed classified information to her. Of course, he denies it. Wait'll the papers get hold of that juicy story."

"Do you think they will?" the General asked anxiously. His immediate concern was not with the betrayal of secret documents, but rather with the Pentagon's reaction to a new public scandal.

"Hard to tell, General," Cole replied. "There are very few well-kept secrets in this town. Particularly concerning a little East German sexpot married to an American handler. Just thought I'd warn you."

"All right, Bud," the General said resignedly, "I guess you've got your hands full. Sorry if I spoke a little out of turn. It isn't pleasant, you know, to have Washington breathing down your neck. Carry on, and for God's sake try to keep the rest of this stuff out of the papers."

The old blowhard is scared shitless, Cole thought to himself with a smile as he hung up the receiver. He looked with distaste at all the paperwork that filled his desk. God, I'm tired of all this bureaucratic in-fighting. I've got to get back to flying. After all, he reminded himself, that's why I decided to stay in the Air Force, not to play politics and fight turf battles with a bunch of prima donnas.

He looked in his overflowing inbox and picked up an envelope marked for his eyes only. He opened it and read Liebman's letter. Just what I need right now, he said to himself bitterly. They're beginning to jump ship. Why, Cole wondered, would Liebman quit after I let him stay in his job? He knows that I need him. It's a deliberate kick in the balls. Cole stood up and paced angrily around the room. He was too tense, he told himself. He had to calm down. It had been a very stressful day, and he was overreacting. He went back to his desk and reread Liebman's letter.

No, Cole decided, his first reaction had been wrong. Liebman's letter was not intended as an affront. Actually, he should have anticipated his resignation. I rubbed his nose in the fact that there was no rational separation between his job and covert work. That took a few days to sink in and when it did, he followed his conscience. A man of principle, Brigitte would say. I suppose I agree, Cole conceded, even though I don't understand the principle.

Cole rarely smoked, but suddenly he craved a cigarette. There was a stale pack in his middle desk drawer. He found an old book of matches, lit a cigarette, and leaned back in his chair. The smoke burned his throat and he coughed, but the acrid taste was strangely soothing. This isn't my racket, he concluded. It's not a question of principle. I just wasn't cut out for this kind of crap.

*　　　*　　　*

It was early evening, and L. Cabot Pearson was looking down anxiously at the crowd of demonstrators noisily milling about in front of Amerika Haus. The sun was sinking behind some storm clouds, and in the twilight, the West Berlin police, in their gray-blue uniforms and tall black helmets, were slowly moving the protesters back behind barricades they had hastily set up. The picketers were shouting "Ami Go Home" and waving placards with roughly lettered inscriptions, such as "Do your Own Spying" and "Stop Turning Germans Against Each Other." Photographers' bulbs were flashing and curious passersby were looking on from the other side of the street. One of the protesters was being interviewed, and Pearson could well imagine what he was saying.

There was no doubt, Pearson reflected as he turned away from the window, that the Weber affair, cleverly exploited by the East, was turning into a serious PR problem. It was a challenge that Pearson had not yet been able to deflect. Calling attention to Soviet spies would only put the U.S. on the same plane—the very opposite of USIA's claim of American moral superiority. Admitting that errors necessarily occur was not a very positive message, incompetence being in general a very tepid excuse.

Pearson walked over to the wall and straightened the Cézanne painting, which seemed to be a trifle askew. He stepped back, satisfied with his adjustment. If only his other troubles could be put right as easily. Since there was no easy solution to the Weber affair, the only effective response would have to be a diversion. He would not fall into the trap of letting the Communists set the agenda. He picked up the phone and dialed the Amerika Haus Program Director.

"What special films are you holding in reserve, Otto?" he inquired. "Yes, for a special occasion." He waited for the response. *"Gone with the Wind*? Excellent. That always attracts a large crowd. Listen, Otto, I want the film to be shown next week—let's see, Tuesday and Wednesday evenings. Get the posters out today and ask RIAS to make announcements starting tonight. Oh yes, and Otto, be sure that there are some extra guards at the door those nights to keep out any trouble-makers. You'll take care of all that? . . . Fine. Thank you."

Pleased with this tactic, Pearson sat down at his desk to draft a report to Washington. Better to raise the issue, he said to himself, before he got an inquiry. "In order to blunt some adverse publicity," he began his memorandum, "due to a misfired U.S. intelligence operation, I have planned a special showing next week of . . ." That would demonstrate that he was on top of the situation. He explained the picketing as proof that Amerika Haus was a thorn in the East's side and a lightning rod for any Communist protest against American actions. "Indeed," he wrote, "Amerika Haus is in the front line defending American ideas and interests; that is why we get attacked."

He paused for a moment, undecided on how to deal with the case of Jutta—an East German spy on the payroll. His first instinct was not to refer to her at all, but on reflection that seemed unwise, since it was likely that her story would soon become public knowledge. Consequently, Pearson reverted to the universal bureaucratic impulse that the best defense was to find a credible scapegoat.

"Regrettably," he continued to write, "a female employee of Amerika Haus has been revealed to be an East German spy. I hired this woman"—it was always adroit to appear to take personal responsibility— "after she had been thoroughly vetted by our counter-intelligence services. Moreover, she was the wife of an American working for the USAF Intelligence unit in Berlin, which seemed to be an additional safeguard. It is a sad coincidence that her husband now turns out to be the man who has sparked the current uproar."

He reread what he had written and was satisfied. His backside was neatly covered. Yet he could not resist the urge to write more, to differentiate himself further from this unpleasant episode. "There is no doubt," he continued, "that this incident has caused some damage to our image that will take some time to repair. I am not an intelligence specialist, but nonetheless I think it is obvious that some corrective action is called for in at least one of our intelligence-gathering units. There is reason to believe that some amateurism is to blame." Pearson was referring to a conversation the previous evening with the Berlin CIA Mission Chief, who opined that the problem was intrinsic to the "dilettante flyboy" operation.

"To avoid a repetition of this scandal," Pearson concluded his report, "I would hope that in the future all our intelligence activities will be conducted in a more serious and professional manner." That last paragraph, Pearson thought, should deflect any possible criticism away from him and Amerika Haus. Moreover, it should gain him some "brownie points" with the local CIA officials who, he was aware, had close connections to the Washington establishment. And as for Cole, the more he thought about it, Cole really had to accept the blame for approving such a useless mission.

Pearson put on his dark-blue fedora and prepared to leave Amerika Haus at half-past six. The demonstration had broken up half an hour earlier, and there was now a peaceful line in the lobby waiting to check out books for weekend reading. On his way out, Pearson nodded to the new girl at the checkout desk. She was a far cry from Jutta, but was busty and had a pleasant smile. Getting rid of Jutta had been both salutary and necessary; after all, Amerika Haus was no place for an East German spy. And yet her presence had always inspired a *frémissement* that Pearson missed. Not to worry, he comforted himself as he pushed through the revolving door to the street. He would more than make up for that lack in the evening at Fräulein Kitty's.

Day 16 Saturday

The Saturday-morning conference began on time in the 575th Squadron's Map Room. Herter declared without further comment that there were no major changes in target priorities, except that the Frankfurt/Oder bridge had been downgraded to the lowest category. This change was greeted by a nervous chuckle. Muldane reported that a new version of the Mig, code-named the FISHBED, had been reported at the city of Eberswalde so that agents in that area should be alerted to that possibility; also, refugees from Eberswalde should be questioned in that regard.

Referring to recent reports from the Potsdam Mission, Cole advised that anti-aircraft batteries had been installed near ammunition dumps in the outskirts of Leipzig. It would be interesting, he noted, to have some photographs of those batteries to see if they were equipped with the latest radar guidance systems. One of the handlers volunteered that he would give that instruction that afternoon to his agent covering the Leipzig area.

The cartographer reported that new street maps of a number of smaller localities in the GDR were available. Cole told him to be sure that they were forwarded to the Clayallee Interrogation Center and to Marienfelde. The cartographer replied that he had already done so. There followed a review of the past week's operations and a forecast of activities planned for the next seven days. Then some housekeeping matters were dealt with and the latest Berlin Command announcements read.

Before adjourning the meeting, Cole looked around the table and said, "Some of you may already know, but for those who don't, I am very sorry to announce that Norm Liebman will be leaving us." All eyes turned toward Liebman, sitting in a chair against the wall. "As you all know," Cole continued, "Norm has done yeoman service for our outfit these many years, and his departure will leave a void that will be hard to fill. But Norm has decided that it is time for him to seek some new challenges. We'll miss you, Norm, and all of us wish you the best of luck in your new job." Liebman crossed his arms in embarrassment and broke into a shy smile.

"In the interim," Cole announced, "until we find a permanent replacement for Norm, Pritzer will take over his slot at the Clayallee Interrogation Center."

"I hope that the interim will be short," Pritzer said, nervously. "As you know, I prefer covert work."

"Not only do we know it, Pritzer," Muldane broke in, "but the whole world knows it." Everyone, including Pritzer, laughed.

"For the moment, Pritzer," Cole said, "Clayallee is the right spot for you. It's where you can do us the most good." And, Cole thought without saying it, the least possible harm.

*   *   *

Cole had invited Brigitte to go out to dinner that night. How about Richter's, he had suggested. Brigitte said that she would much prefer to prepare dinner for them at his apartment, and Cole was relieved at the prospect of a quiet evening alone with her, away from the turmoil that was now swarming around him.

As he lay stretched out on his living-room sofa with Brigitte puttering about in the adjoining kitchen, Cole thought back fondly to their first meeting in the Grünewald. And now, scarcely three months later, here she was, this lovely girl, in his apartment cooking supper before another night of love-making, so natural and without any of the reticence, taboos, and artifices that he had learned to expect from American women.

"What's the matter, Bud?" Brigitte asked, as she brought in two glasses of Franken wine from the kitchen. "What's that worried frown doing on your face?" Cole sat up, took one of the glasses, and gave her a kiss. She sat down on the couch next to him.

"Don't distract the cook," she said, warding off his hand reaching to cup her breast. "Tell me what's wrong."

"Things are in a bit of a mess," Cole admitted.

"You mean because of those newspaper articles."

"Yes; they started it all," Cole said. "What do you think of all that hullabaloo?"

"Hullabaloo," she laughed. "What a funny word. What does it mean?"

"A big racket. Lots of noise and furor."

"I can tell you what my father thinks."

"Let me guess. He is outraged at the unfair exploitation of poor vanquished Germans."

Brigitte nodded and laughed. "That's it exactly," she said.

Cole put his arms around her shoulders and pulled her to him. "Come here, my favorite vanquished German," he said. He kissed her tenderly.

"What do you think?" he asked.

She sat up and spoke seriously. "I am very sorry for the Webers, and I think that the Communists have scored some propaganda points with their story. But that doesn't fool me. I know that the Communists are the real danger, and therefore, we've got to fight them. And in a fight sometimes people get hurt. This time it was the Webers who got in harm's way. It's unavoidable."

Cole looked at her with admiration. What she had said was so simple, direct and sound. Liebman and General Norcross were full of complicated gyrations. But she had it right. They're the enemy we have to fight, and in combat some people become casualties. That's all. No thought given to not fighting—the Better Red Than Dead gang. No callousness, either; sorry for the Webers as well as, no doubt, for her dead fiancé at Stalingrad.

Cole watched Brigitte return to the kitchen. She was a strong, beautiful, level-headed woman. He suddenly could not bear the thought of being separated from her. He had a premonition that his time in Berlin was coming to an end. Would she, he asked himself, follow him—to live at various air bases around the world— or would their relationship have been for her just a liberating experience until she found a German with whom to spend the rest of her life? The latter was clearly what her father would want. Would she be a dutiful daughter and follow her father's wishes? No, Cole realized, that was the wrong question. The real one was whether or not she loved him as he did her.

"Dinner is served, my lord," Brigitte announced as she brought out a platter from the kitchen and set it on the table in the dining alcove. He put his arms around her and kissed her. She responded with her usual abandon and then disengaged herself. "Not now, Bud," she said, laughing. "I'm hungry and I don't want the delicacies I've prepared for us to get cold. We have the rest of the night for our other hungers."

The rest of the night, yes, Cole thought, but a lifetime?

*   *   *

Hans and Anna Weber were back in their Frankfurt/Oder apartment, which they had left just over two weeks ago. Herr Metzger had been standing at the building's entrance, witnessing their arrival with a sarcastic grin. After all, as he repeated to everyone who would listen, it had been his timely warning that had foiled a dangerous spy plot. He was miffed that there had been no mention of his crucial role in the many news accounts. In fact, it was Weber—the spy—who was now in the limelight.

Anna was in tears. "We're lost," she cried, throwing herself on their bed. "Our lives are over. We might as well be dead."

Weber did his best to comfort her. "Not at all, Anna," he said. "Look, we're back home and together again. If we do what they say, I'll avoid jail, and we'll be able to live here quietly for some time." He handed her a handkerchief, and Anna blew her nose. "Then, one day," he continued, lowering his voice, "they can't watch us forever, and we'll slip back into the West. This time, don't worry, I won't let them send me back. Thanks to you we still have all the Deutsche Marks, which I'll go hide tomorrow. That money will let us start a new life."

Anna sat up and wiped her tears away. Weber kissed her cheek, patted her shoulder, and said, "There, there, stop crying. Things could be so much worse. Go on out and get us something to eat."

Anna left the building furtively and went to the small grocery store in the next street. She avoided people's eyes, convinced they were all staring at her. After returning home, she fed little Manfred, then prepared their own supper, after which she and Weber went to bed and fell into a long, exhausted sleep.

The baby woke up early the next morning and cried for food and attention, but the Webers were dead to the world. When they finally awoke after nine o'clock, Anna went into the baby's room and let out a scream. In his boredom little Manfred had undone the covering of his teddy bear and had amused himself by tearing into little pieces the many slips of colored paper he had found stuffed inside.

®